S...
ANGELS

Praise for these bestselling authors

BRENDA NOVAK

"Brenda Novak's *Snow Baby* should appeal to readers
who like their romances with a sophisticated touch."
—*Library Journal*

"This is an author destined for stardom."
—*RT Book Reviews*

B.J. DANIELS

"B.J. Daniels spins a tight story full of suspects
and danger sure to keep you guessing."
—*RT Book Reviews* on *Hotshot P.I.*

"Interesting twists abound... *Hotshot P.I.* is
extremely satisfying romantic suspense."
—*Gothic Journal*

Brenda Novak is a two-time Golden Heart finalist. Her first book, *Of Noble Birth,* was published in 1999 and she has since sold nine books to the Superromance line. She and her husband, the parents of five children, make their home in Sacramento, California, where Brenda juggles her busy writing career with the demands of field trips and softball games.

A former award-winning journalist, **B.J. Daniels** had thirty-six short stories published before she wrote and sold her first romantic suspense, *Odd Man Out,* which was later nominated for the *RT Book Reviews* Reviewers' Choice Award for Best First Book and Best Harlequin Intrigue. B.J. lives in Bozeman with her husband, Parker, two springer spaniels, Zoey and Scout, and an irascible tomcat named Jeff. She is a member of the Bozeman Writers Group and Romance Writers of America. To contact her, write to P.O. Box 183, Bozeman, MT 59771.

BRENDA NOVAK

B.J. DANIELS

SNOW ANGELS

Harlequin®

TORONTO NEW YORK LONDON
AMSTERDAM PARIS SYDNEY HAMBURG
STOCKHOLM ATHENS TOKYO MILAN MADRID
PRAGUE WARSAW BUDAPEST AUCKLAND

ISBN-13: 978-0-373-68881-4

SNOW ANGELS
Copyright © 2004 by Harlequin Books S.A.

The publisher acknowledges the
copyright holders of the individual works
as follows:

SNOW BABY
Copyright © 2000 by Brenda Novak

UNDERCOVER CHRISTMAS
Copyright © 1997 by Barbara Johnson Smith

Recycling programs
for this product may
not exist in your area.

www.Harlequin.com

Printed in U.S.A.

CONTENTS

SNOW BABY

Brenda Novak

For my sister, Debra Cundick, a beautiful child, a beautiful adult, the inspiration behind this book.

Sometimes in life we meet people who encourage us, who teach us that we are worthy of our dreams, who set an example for us of courage and determination in the face of formidable challenges. I married one of those people—and that is something for which I will always be grateful.

CHAPTER ONE

I'M NEVER GOING to make it.

Chantel Miller hunched forward, trying to see beyond the snow and mud being kicked up onto her windshield by the semi next to her. She could barely make out the taillights of the Toyota Landcruiser she'd been following for miles, and she longed to pull over and give her jangled nerves a rest. But the narrow two-lane highway climbing Donner's Summit was cut into the side of a cliff, and she didn't dare stop. Not in a storm like this.

In the back of her mind she heard her father, who'd been dead for nearly five years now, telling her to slow down, keep calm. He'd taught her to drive and had offered all the usual parental advice—never let your gas tank get below half, keep your doors and windows locked, never pull over in the middle of a storm.

God, she missed him. How could so much have happened in the past ten years? At twenty-nine, she already felt battle-weary, ancient.

She shrugged off the memories to avoid the regret they inspired, and focused on her driving. Her sister, Stacy, was waiting for her in Tahoe, only an hour away. She'd be able to make it that far as long as she could get past the big rig that was churning up the mountain beside her, nearly burying her car with sludge.

She gave her red Jaguar—her only concession to the life she'd left behind—some gas and shot around the semi, then eased down on the brake. The road was covered with black ice. Her stomach clenched as the Jaguar fishtailed, but then its tires grabbed the asphalt and the taillights that had been her beacon appeared in front of her again.

"Hello, Mr. Landcruiser," she breathed in relief, and crept closer, determined to stay in the vehicle's wake. The plows were long overdue. Snow was beginning to blanket the shiny road.

Stretching her neck, Chantel tried to release some of the tension in her shoulders, then cranked up the defrost. A pop station played on the radio, but she barely heard the familiar lyrics as she listened to the wind howl outside. Ice crystals shimmered in the beam of her headlights, then flew at her face, clicking against the windshield.

She shouldn't have left Walnut Creek so late. If it hadn't been her first week at her new job, she would have insisted on heading home when everyone else had, at five o'clock. But she not only had a new job, she had a new profession, back in her home state of California, clear across the country from where she'd lived before.

Changing careers was probably the most difficult thing she'd ever done, but Chantel was determined to overcome her insecurities and be successful at a job that required a brain—if for no other reason than to prove she had one.

Overhead a yellow sign blinked *Chains required over summit*. To the right, several cars waited, engines running, as their owners struggled in the cold and wet to get chains on their tires. A couple of men wearing orange safety vests worked as installers for those willing to pay for help.

Chantel was studying the shoulder, looking for a place to pull over, when brake lights flashed in front of her. She screamed and slammed on her brakes, but the car didn't stop. It slid out of control. With a bone-jarring crunch, her Jag collided with the Landcruiser ahead of her.

Pain exploded in Chantel's head as her face hit the steering wheel. She sat, breathing hard, staring at the black snowy night and the back end of the white Landcruiser, which was now smashed. Then someone knocked on her window.

Dazed, she rolled her head to the side and saw a tall dark-haired man looming above her. "Are you all right? Unlock the doors!" he shouted.

Immediately her father's warnings echoed back: *Always keep your doors and windows locked....*

When she didn't respond, he scowled at her through the glass and tapped again. "Did you hear me? Open the door!"

She let her eye-lids close and put her hand to her aching head as her senses began to return. She'd just been in a car accident. This was probably the other driver. She had to give him her driver's license and insurance information, right? Of course.

With trembling fingers, she sought the automatic door lock and heard it *thunk* just before the man flung her door open and leaned inside.

A freezing wind whipped around him and flooded her car, carrying the smell of his aftershave with it—a clean masculine scent, far different from the trendy fragrances used by the male models she'd worked with not so long ago. Then a firm hand gripped her chin and tilted her face up. "Your lip's bleeding, but not badly. Any other injuries?"

She struggled to rearrange her jumbled thoughts. Stacy, accident, aftershave, blood... "Just a lump on my head, I think."

"Good." He stood and jammed his hands into the pockets of his red ski parka, frowning at the crushed metal in front of them, and it suddenly dawned on Chantel that he was angry. Really angry. The signs were all there—the terse voice, the taut muscles, the furrowed brow. "Is something wrong?" she asked.

He looked at her as if she had two heads. "You mean other than what you just did to my SUV?"

She winced. "I'm sorry. I'm worried about my car, too. I haven't owned it more than a year. But you stopped right in front of me. There was nothing I could—"

"What?" He whirled on her, the furrow in his brow deepening. Ice crystals lodged in the dark stubble of his jaw gave his face a rugged appearance, but the long thick lashes fringing his eyes looked almost feminine. "You're kidding, right?"

"No, I'm not." Chantel's tongue sought the cut in her lip. She reached across the console to the glove box and retrieved a napkin to wipe the blood from her mouth. "How could you expect anyone to stop so fast in this kind of storm?"

He stiffened. "I managed to miss the car ahead of me. And you want to know why? Because I wasn't tailgating him for the past thirty miles!"

"I wasn't tailgating you," she said, but a memory of her struggle to keep up with his taillights raced through her mind and made her wonder if she'd been following too closely, after all. She'd hardly been able to see anything— except his lights.

"Regardless," he said abruptly, "we have to move off to the side. We're stopping traffic. Are you okay to drive?"

She nodded, shivering despite her navy wool coat. "I think so."

"Just pull over there." He indicated a couple of spots other cars had just vacated. It seemed to Chantel that his initial anger had softened to mere irritation.

Feeling jittery, she slowly eased the Jaguar over so the traffic behind them could get through. A couple of motorists paused to see what had happened and a chain installer jogged over and hollered something at the guy she'd hit, but the weather was too bad for anyone to linger. No ambulance, no fire trucks. The accident wasn't nearly as interesting as it could have been.

Thank God!

Chantel watched the man from the Landcruiser stride toward her and wished she was safe in her new condominium in Walnut Creek, curled up in front of the television. She was exhausted and cold and rattled. But she had to make it to Tahoe. After all the years she and her sister hadn't spoken, Stacy was finally ready to give her another chance.

I won't blow it, Stace. I've changed, grown up. You'll see.

She lowered her window as the Landcruiser's owner gave her car a skeptical frown. "You look like you belong on the streets of Beverly Hills," he said. "I bet you've never driven in snow."

"Listen, I come from New York. You've never seen snow until you've spent a winter back East." She didn't add that she hadn't owned a car for most of the ten years she'd lived in the Big Apple. Taxis, public transit or, more often, limousines had always carried her where she'd wanted to go, but she wasn't about to volunteer that information. He didn't need to know how precisely his accusation had hit its target.

"Excuse me," she said to get him to step back. "I want to see the damage." She buttoned up her coat and scrambled out of the car, wincing as her white tennis shoes sank deep in the cold slush. Her vision swam for a moment, but she kept one hand on the door for support and soon the world righted itself.

Like most people, the Landcruiser's owner did a double take when he saw her at her full height. His gaze started at where the snow buried her feet, then climbed her thin frame until it met the withering glare she reserved for gawkers.

She raised a hand before he could make any comment. "I know, I hear it all the time. I'm almost six feet, so you don't have to ask." She gave him a glacial smile to cover the way her body shook with reaction to the blizzard and the accident. "That doesn't make me a freak, but it does intimidate some men."

He grunted. "Short men, maybe."

Chantel had to admit he didn't look like a man who could be easily intimidated. Similar to her in age, he had shoulders twice the width of her own and was taller by at least four inches. But she'd always hated her height, even when she stood next to bigger people. She'd grown up to taunts of "Daddy Long Legs" and "Miller High Life" and couldn't see herself as anything but gangly and awkward, despite a successful modeling career.

She shut her door and leaned into the wind, fighting the weakness of her legs as she trudged over to check out the damage. "Ouch," she said, sheltering her face from the snow so she could view the Jag's crumpled front bumper and broken headlight. The Landcruiser sported a smashed right rear panel. "Well, my car certainly got the worst of it, don't you think?"

He cocked an eyebrow at her, but didn't say anything. He didn't have to; she could guess what he was thinking.

"It was your fault, too," she said, irritated by his smug attitude, which reminded her too much of Wade, even though this stranger looked nothing like her ex-boyfriend. "You slammed on your brakes for no apparent reason."

He gave an incredulous laugh. "The car in front of me stopped. What did you want me to do? Drive off the cliff?"

Is it too late to consider that option? Chantel bit her

tongue, knowing her hostility was spurred by the memory of Wade and not this stranger. Not really.

Glancing at her car's smashed front end a final time, she hurried back into the driver's seat. The accident had caused some expensive damage, but it was still pretty much a fender bender. She wanted to swap information and be on her way, or Stacy would think she wasn't coming.

She hoped this guy wouldn't insist on waiting for the Highway Patrol.

"Why don't you grab your driver's license and insurance card and come get in my truck?" he called after her. "It'll be drier and warmer than trying to do it out here."

Never get in a car with a stranger, her father's voice admonished.

Especially such a powerful-looking stranger, Chantel added on her own.

"I'll just write it all down and bring it to you. You're not planning to wait for the police to arrive, are you? There's really no need. In a collision like this, the rear ender's always on the hook."

He smiled, transforming his expression from a Terminator-style intensity to the guilelessness of an All-American boy. "There's a good reason for that, you know."

"Okay, so I might have been following a little closely, but in a storm like this, calling the cops could hold us up for hours. Can't you just file a report in the morning or something?"

"No problem. I want to get out of here, too."

"Great." She gave him a relieved smile—a semblance of the smile that had made her a living for the past ten years—and hurried back to her car. After scribbling down her policy number, insurance agent's name and phone number, license-plate number and driver's license number, she walked toward his truck.

He rolled down his window and glanced at the slip of paper she handed to him. "What about *your* name and telephone number?"

"My agent will handle everything."

"No way. You're not leaving here until I have your name, your number and your address. Just in case."

Chantel fought the wind that kept blowing her long blond hair across her face. "In case of what?"

"In case I need to contact you."

"I don't think my husband would like me giving out that information," she hedged, blinking the snow out of her eyelashes.

He scowled. "I'm sorry, but you just rear-ended my truck. I want to know I can get hold of you. And I don't care whether your husband likes it or not."

This could be a dangerous world, and she was completely alone in it. But what were the chances she'd just rear-ended another Ted Bundy? With a sigh, Chantel gave him the information he'd requested, hoping he'd fallen for the imaginary-husband routine.

He passed her a card. "I wrote my cell phone number on the back. You can reach me on it anytime."

"Fine." She glanced down and read, "Dillon Broderick, Architect," before shoving the card into the back pocket of her jeans to keep it from getting wet.

"Are you *sure* you're okay to drive?"

She was still a little rattled but determined to fulfill her promise to Stacy, despite the storm, despite the accident, despite everything.

"Yeah. You?"

"I'll have a stiff neck tomorrow, but I'll live. Take it easy," he said, and pulled away before Chantel made it back to her car.

DILLON BRODERICK put his Landcruiser into four-wheel drive and merged into the traffic heading up the hill, cursing under his breath.

As if his week hadn't gone badly enough. Now he had the bother of getting his truck fixed—the estimates from body shops, the insurance claims, the rental car—and beyond all that, the maddening knowledge that his new Landcruiser would never be the same.

"'I wasn't tailgating you,'" he mimicked. She'd dogged him since Auburn, when it had started to snow. He'd flashed his brake lights several times, trying to get her to back off. But she'd come right up again and again, nearly riding on his bumper. If a man had done that, he'd probably have broken his nose for risking both their lives, but what could he do with a tall, beautiful woman?

Grin and bear it, just the way he did with his ex-wife.

He glanced at the paper where Chantel Miller had written her name and address. She lived in Walnut Creek, not far from his own house in Lafayette. At least they were both local. That should make things easier.

He shook his head at the thought of the damage the accident had done to her Jaguar XJ-6. What a sweet car! Her husband wouldn't be pleased when she got home.

If she got home.

The thought of Chantel Miller heading up the mountain with only one headlight caused Dillon a moment of guilt. It was difficult enough to see the road with two working lights. He probably should have waited to make sure she had chains and could get them on. But he was already late. His friends had been expecting him for hours.

He flipped open his time-planner and turned to the page where he'd jotted down the information about their rental cabin. He punched in the number, and a cheerful voice greeted him on the other end. "Hello?"

"This is Dillon. Is—"

"Hey, guy! It's Veronica. We were afraid you'd gotten into an accident or something."

"Actually I did, but no one was hurt."

"Omigosh! What happened?"

"I'll tell you when I get there. I just wanted to let everyone know I'm still a half hour away. Traffic's been moving pretty slow in this mess."

"Don't worry, the drive'll be worth it. The ski resorts are getting something like sixteen inches of snow."

He smiled. He needed a rigorous physical vacation to steal his thoughts away from his ex-wife and all the dirty custody tricks Amanda was playing on him with their two little girls. "That sounds great."

"We'll see you when you get here."

He was just about to hit the "end" button when his call waiting beeped. He looked at the digital readout on his caller ID, wondering who'd be phoning him this late, but didn't recognize the number. He switched over. "Hello?"

"Mr. Broderick?"

"Yes?"

"This is Chantel Miller. You know, the woman who just…well, we were in an accident a little while ago."

How could he forget? He pictured her almond-shaped eyes gazing up at him, the high cheekbones, the small cut on one pouty lip, and refused to acknowledge how incredibly beautiful she was. Only, she sounded different now, almost…frightened. "Is everything okay?"

"Well, um, I really hate to bother you. I mean, you don't even know me and I can't have made the best impression—" she gave a weak laugh "—but, well, it looks like I'm lost and—"

"Lost! How could you be lost? I left you not more than fifteen minutes ago. Aren't you on Highway 80?"

What was this woman? Some kind of trouble magnet?

"No. Actually I turned off about ten minutes ago. I've got directions to a cabin where my sister is staying, but it's so difficult to see through the snow. I must have taken a wrong turn somewhere."

"Can't you call your sister and find out?"

"The cabin's just a rental. I don't have the number. I was in such a hurry to get going tonight and the directions seemed so clear. I never dreamed the weather would be this bad. It's been nothing but sunny at home."

It was March. Who would have expected a storm like this when it was nearly spring? He hadn't checked the weather himself, but then, he had a four-wheel drive and probably wouldn't have checked it even in the dead of winter. "Do you have your chains on?"

'Yeah, I paid one of the installers to put them on just after you left, but they're not doing any good."

"What do you mean?"

"My car's stuck."

"It's *what?*"

"Stuck. There hasn't been a plow through here for a long time, and the drifts are pretty deep—"

"And you drove into that?"

Silence. "I'm sorry. I shouldn't have bothered you," she said softly, and with a click she was gone.

"Dammit!" Dillon tossed his phone across the seat. How stupid could this woman be? Anyone who drove a wrecked sports car onto an unfamiliar side street in the middle of a storm like this had to be a few cards short of a deck.

"Let her call the Highway Patrol," he grumbled, and tried to forget her, but another mile down the road, he saw the dim shadow of an exit sign. He'd left Chantel Miller not more than fifteen miles back. She couldn't be far. It might cost him another hour, but he could probably find her more easily than anyone else. More quickly, too.

Veering to the right, he headed down the off-ramp. All roads, except the freeway, were virtually deserted and lay buried beneath several inches of snow.

He stopped and flipped on his dome light to study the sheet of paper with Chantel's personal information.

She hadn't included a cell-phone number. He tried her home, hoping he could at least get hold of her husband. Someone should know she was in trouble, just in case she didn't have sense enough to call the Highway Patrol or tried to walk back to the freeway or something. A person could easily freeze to death in this weather.

After five rings, a recorder picked up, and Dillon recognized Chantel's voice telling him to leave his name and number. He hung on, waiting to leave a message for her husband, and was surprised to hear her continue, "Or, if you'd rather try me on my car phone, just call—"

Bingo! He scrounged for a piece of paper and a pencil and jotted down the number, then dialed it.

Chantel answered, a measure of relief in her voice. "Hello?"

"It's me, Dillon Broderick. I'm coming back for you. Tell me where you are."

She paused. "It's all right, Mr. Broderick—"

"Dillon."

"Dillon. Maybe I need a tow truck. I'm thinking about calling the police."

He thought of her sitting in her wrecked Jag, the cold seeping into the car, the storm howling around her, and for some reason, remembered her smile. This woman had just smashed the back end of his truck, but for a moment that didn't matter. She was alone and probably frightened.

"Well, maybe you should do that, but I'm coming back, anyway, just to see that you're okay."

"Are you sure? I feel really bad. I mean, for all I know, your wife and kids are waiting for you, worried..."

"No wife and kids, at least not worried ones." Just the rest and relaxation he'd been craving. He thought of his friends sitting around the fireplace, drinking wine, laughing and talking, listening to Janis Joplin or Patsy Cline, and turned around, anyway.

"Now," he said, "how did you get where you are?"

CHAPTER TWO

"FORTY-FIVE BOTTLES of beer on the wall, forty-five bottles of beer, take one down, pass it around, forty-four bottles of beer on the wall."

Chantel gave up trying to distract herself with the repetitive chant and glanced impatiently at her watch—again.

She'd talked to Dillon Broderick more than a half hour ago. Where was he? Her hands and feet were frozen, but she dared not run the car's engine any longer for fear she'd use all her gas. Fueling up was one of those things she hadn't had time for when she'd dashed out of the house four hours earlier. Now she could only stare, disheartened, at the gas gauge, which read less than a quarter of a tank.

Closing her eyes, Chantel rubbed her temples and willed back the tears that threatened. She'd been so stressed with the move and her new job, and so focused on reaching Stacy at a decent hour, that she hadn't done *anything* right. Now her new car was wrecked, and she was stranded on some nameless street in the middle of a snowstorm.

She let her head fall forward to rest on the steering wheel, hearing Wade's voice, despite her best efforts to banish it from her mind. *That's what you get when you don't use your head. You never think, Chantel. Never. What would you do without me?*

Well, she was finding that out, wasn't she? She'd left him six months ago, and despite all his calls and letters, she wouldn't take him back. She was fighting for the person she used to be, before Wade and modeling had nearly destroyed her—the girl her father had raised.

But it all seemed so hopeless sometimes. Or at least it did right now.

She glared miserably at her car phone. She didn't even have anyone to call. The only friends she'd had when she and Wade were living together in New York were *his* friends. The only hobbies, his hobbies. He'd made sure her whole world revolved around him, and she'd been as stupid as he always told her she was, because, to save their relationship, she'd let him. *You're just another pretty face, Chantel. Good thing God gave you that.*

The phone chirped and Chantel grabbed it.

"Hello?"

"I can't find you. Are you sure you turned right and not left at the second stop sign?"

It was Dillon Broderick. He was still coming.

She said a silent prayer of thanks and tried to retrace in her mind the route she'd taken. When she hadn't been able to find the street her sister had written down, she'd taken several turns, always expecting the cabin to appear around the next corner. Now it was hard to remember exactly what she'd done.

"I turned right," she insisted with a sigh of defeat. She was tired, so tired she could barely force herself to stay awake. After six months she still wasn't completely recovered, she realized. "I don't know why you can't find me."

He didn't say anything for a moment, and Chantel pictured his face, with its strong jaw, chiseled cheekbones and light eyes, which had been filled with anger about the accident. Would he get frustrated and decide not to continue searching? Her stomach clenched at the thought.

"Did you call the police?" he asked.

"Yes, they said they'd send a car."

"And you gave them the same directions you gave me?"

Chantel felt another pang of despair. "You're saying the police won't be able to find me either, right?"

He cleared his throat. "Let's not jump to any conclusions. They certainly know the area better than I do and might have some idea where to look. I'll go back the way I came and try another route from the freeway."

Chantel knew that courtesy demanded she tell him to return to his original route and not to trouble himself further. The police were coming—eventually. But the snow piling ever higher on the hood of her car would soon block out everything else. And she already felt so alone.

"Dillon?"

"Yeah?"

She wanted to ask him to keep talking to her, not to hang up, but her more practical side admonished her against running up his car-phone bill, to say nothing of her own. She wasn't in any real trouble, not with the police on their way. She didn't need anyone to hold her hand. "Nothing. Thanks for trying."

"That sounds like you think I'm giving up. I can't let anything happen to you. How do I know your insurance will take care of my truck?"

He was teasing her. Chantel heard it in his voice and smiled. Fleetingly, she wondered about his wife and kids—the ones he'd said weren't worried about him.

"Where were you headed before you came back for me?" she asked.

"Tahoe. I'm going skiing for a week. What about you?"

"Same here. Just for the weekend, though."

"So you know how to ski?"

She got the impression he was just being nice to her, trying to calm her down, but she didn't care, not as long as his voice hummed in her ear. "Yeah. My dad used to take us when we were kids."

"You ever been to Squaw Valley?"

"Not yet. I grew up in Utah and used to go to Snowbird or Alta."

"That's some great snow there. My buddies and I took a trip to Utah when we were in college."

"I'll bet college was fun." Chantel fought the chattering of her teeth, not wanting to let him know how terribly cold she was.

"You didn't go to university?"

"No."

"Hey, you got your headlights on?"

"You mean headlight, don't you?"

He laughed. "Yeah. Otherwise, with this snow piling up, I won't be able to tell you from any other car sitting by the side of the road."

"It's on."

"Good. What about the heater? It's pretty cold outside."

"No heater. Not enough gas." This time, the chill that ran through her echoed in her voice. "And it *is* cold."

"How much gas have you got?"

"Just enough to make it to Tahoe once you pull me out of here."

"Listen, this is what I want you to do. Dig through your luggage and put on all the layers of clothing you can. I don't want to find an ice cube when I get there, understand?"

"I've already done that."

"What about gloves and boots?"

Chantel curled her toes and frowned when she could no longer feel them move in her wet tennis shoes. "No such luck. I was going to buy all that once I reached Tahoe."

"Damn. This just keeps getting better, doesn't it?"

Pinching the bridge of her nose, Chantel swallowed back a sigh. "I guess I wasn't very prepared."

"I can't believe you had chains."

"I did only because I bought them shortly after I got the car and stuffed them in the trunk."

He chuckled. "Too bad. Otherwise you'd have been forced to turn back."

"I couldn't turn back," she said, thinking of her promise to Stacy.

"Why not?"

"There's something I have to do in Tahoe."

"What's that?"

Penance.

DILLON SQUINTED as he tried to see beyond the pale arc of his headlights. White. Everything was white—and stationary. He called Chantel again and told her to honk her horn, then rolled down his window, hoping he'd hear something, but the wind carried no sound other than its own vehemence.

What now? Dropping his head into his hands, he rubbed his eyes. He'd been searching for two hours. He would have given up long ago, except that the police hadn't found Chantel, either, and he could tell from the sound of her voice that her initial uneasiness was turning to panic.

He called her cell phone again. "I'm going to return to the freeway and start over."

"No!" She sounded resolute. "You're crazy to keep looking for me, Dillon. I never should have called you. I thought it would take you a few minutes to come and pull me out, nothing more. I never expected anything like this."

"I know, but you can't be far away. If I could just spot you, we could both be on our way to our respective vacations—"

"Or you could get stuck, too. The police called to say

they can't look for me anymore, not until morning. The storm's too bad.''

"What? Why not?" She could freeze to death before morning!

"They don't want to risk anyone's life, and I don't want you to risk yours."

What about *her* life? Dillon wondered.

She took an audible breath. "You're going to have to head back, before the roads get any worse."

Dillon maneuvered around a parked car that looked like a small snow hill. His tires spun, then finally propelled him a little farther down a road that was quickly becoming impassable. The slick ice and heavy snow were making him nervous, but he'd canvassed the area so completely, he could only believe he'd find her in the next few minutes.

"You can't be far," he muttered.

"It doesn't matter. The police know what they're doing. Anyway, they told me not to use my car phone. I'll need the battery when they resume the search."

Conserving her battery made sense, but cutting off a frightened woman did little to help her. "I'd better let you go, then."

Two hours ago Dillon had cared only about making it to the cabin in time to enjoy the party. Now he could think of nothing but Chantel Miller, a beautiful young woman stranded alone in the middle of a snowstorm. He sighed. "It's hard for me to give up after all this."

"Just think about what I did to your truck. That should make it easier." She attempted to laugh, and Dillon had to admire her for the effort.

"You'll probably be on the news in the morning, talking about how some brave fireman saved you," he said.

"Yeah. I'll be the tall one."

"The tall one with the knockout smile and the sexy

voice," he added, "but I probably shouldn't say that to a married woman."

"Dillon?"

"Uh-huh?"

"There's no husband. I just…you know, a woman can't be too careful."

"Are you telling me I look like an ax murderer?"

"Actually I think you look like Tom Selleck."

He laughed. "It's the dimples. I hated them when I was a kid, thought they made me look like a sissy. When I was five or so, my mom dressed me up as a girl for Halloween, and I never lived it down—or at least I didn't until I passed six feet and could grow a full beard."

"I'll bet no one teases you anymore."

He could hear the smile in her voice, and it made him feel slightly better. "No, they don't." He paused, wondering what to do next. "Damn, Chantel. I'm sorry about this mess. You must be—"

"Anxious for morning. That's all."

"Sure." He continued to steer his truck through the fresh powder and felt his tires give more than they grabbed. He knew that if he stayed out any longer, he'd get stuck, too. "Well, I won't use up any more of your battery."

"Okay."

The edge that crept into her voice reminded him of the way his little girl sounded whenever she didn't want him to leave her, and that made it hard as hell to hang up. He and Chantel Miller might have been complete strangers three hours ago, but now they seemed like the only two people in the world."

"I'll call you tomorrow."

"Right."

"Goodbye, Chantel."

"Hurry back to the freeway, Dillon…and thank you. I'm

sorry about your truck. I've got your card. I'll send you a thank-you note.''

Yeah, you can say, "Thanks for nothing."

THIS IS WHAT HAPPENS, Chantel, when you try to do something without me, Wade sneered.

Chantel covered her ears with her hands, even though she knew the sound came from inside her own head. "Shut up," she whispered. "You're gone and I'm glad."

His laugh echoed through her mind, and she almost turned on the radio to block it out. She hadn't seen Wade in six months, but they'd spent ten years together before that—ten years that weren't easy to erase.

She blew on her hands, then hugged herself again. She'd taken off her wet shoes and pulled up her knees so she could warm her toes with her piled-on sweaters, not that it made any difference. She was freezing. If it got any colder....

She pictured Stacy at the cabin and wished she could reach her sister. Her car phone lay in her lap, cradled against the cold and darkness, but the number for the cabin was at home, on the easy-wipe board next to the refrigerator. Why hadn't she transferred it to the sheet of directions Stacy had given her? Why hadn't she gone back when she realized she'd left it?

She'd been in too much of a hurry, that was why—but it was useless to berate herself now. Except that it kept her from succumbing to the exhaustion that tugged at her body. The police had warned her not to go to sleep. If she did, she might never wake up.

She thought about Wade and the choices he'd encouraged her to make and all she had suffered because of them—the low self-esteem, the anorexia, the past six months of constant effort to become healthy again. If she was going to die, why couldn't she have done it in the hospital, before the long haul back?

Because that would have been too easy. She needed those experiences. The past six months had made her a stronger person than she'd ever been before.

That truth blew into her mind with all the force of the raging storm, then settled like a softly falling snowflake. Yes, she was stronger. When the nurses told her she'd probably die from her disease, she'd decided it wouldn't beat her. She'd given up modeling. She'd left Wade. She smiled, knowing, in the end, that she'd surprised them all.

But the past had left its scars. Her illness had cost her the one thing she wanted more than anything....

She winced and shied away from the longing. She wasn't ready to deal with it yet. A new career, a new life. That was enough for now. Then, perhaps someday—

Suddenly Chantel sat bolt upright and tried to see through the snow on her windshield. Her headlight had gone out, hadn't it? The police had told her to turn it off, to conserve the car battery, as well as the telephone battery, but she couldn't bring herself to relinquish the one thing that might actually get someone's attention. Without it, the Jaguar would look just like every other car, every *empty* car.

Gripping the steering wheel with numb hands, she shifted to her knees to see above the mounded snow, then squinted down at her instrument panel. The lights were dimming. She could barely make out the fuel gauge. The white needle pointing to ''E'' wasn't the most comforting sight, but without it, she'd be sitting in complete darkness, alone, as the storm continued to bury her alive.

She should start the car and recharge the battery. She needed the heat, anyway. What good was saving gas now? Either she made it until morning when the police would come for her. Or she didn't.

Turning the key in the ignition, she heard the Jag's starter give a weak whine, then fall silent. She was too late. The battery was already dead.

Should she get out? Look for help on foot? She fingered the phone, wishing Dillon would call—he was the only one who might—but she knew he'd never risk using up the rest of her battery. By now he was probably sleeping beneath heavy quilts in a cabin that smelled of pine and wood smoke.

She imagined him bare-chested, the blankets coming to just above his hips, a well-muscled arm flung out. Would there be a woman beside him? A woman who'd been waiting for "Dillon Broderick, Architect" in Tahoe?

Chantel shook her head. It didn't matter. Only sleep mattered. Her body begged her to close her eyes and simply drift away.

Soon her lids grew so heavy she could barely lift them. She couldn't feel her nose anymore, could no longer see her breath fogging the air. She tried to sing the *Titanic* theme song, but even that was too much effort. Instead, she heard the melody in her head and told herself her heart would go on. And her father would be there to greet her. Her father...

Why hadn't she left Wade sooner?

I'm free, Daddy. And I'm finally coming home...to you.

With a strange sense of eagerness, she closed her eyes, but a persistent thump on the outside of the car pulled her out of sleep's greedy clutches.

"CHANTEL! IT'S ME, Dillon!"

Dillon wiped all the snow off the window and flashed his light inside. It *had* to be her car. How many smashed Jags could there be with one dim headlight still reflecting off the white flakes falling from the sky?

"Dillon?" He heard her voice through the glass and

breathed a sigh of relief. He'd found her! He couldn't believe it. He'd turned around and tried to drive back to the freeway, but he hadn't been able to leave her behind. And now he was elated to think he'd beaten the odds.

She fumbled with the lock and opened the door, and he pulled her out and into his arms.

Pressing her cold face against the warmth of his neck, she held him tightly.

"You all right?" he asked.

She didn't answer, just clung to him, and he realized she was crying.

"Hey, what kind of a welcome is this?"

"I'm sorry," she mumbled, drawing back to swipe at her eyes. "I just, I just…" She began to shake from the cold, and he knew he had to get her warm and dry—as quickly as possible.

"Let's go. You got anything else in there we can use to keep you warm?"

She shook her head. "I'm wearing everything I've g-got."

He chuckled at her mismatched and odd-fitting layers. "Good girl. We're out of here, then."

He took off his ski hat and settled it on her blond head, carefully covering her ears. Then he shoved her hands in the leather gloves he'd been using.

"My hands b-b-burn," she complained.

"That's good. At least you can feel them." Then he saw her feet. "Where the hell are your shoes?"

She blinked down at her toes. "They were w-wet. I had to t-take them off."

"You have to put them back on, at least until we make it to my Landcruiser." He reached inside the car for her tennis shoes.

When he finished tying her shoelaces, she glanced around and frowned. "Where's your truck?"

He raised his brows, wondering how to tell her the truth of the situation. "You're not still worried that I'm an ax murderer, are you?"

"Why?"

"Because I've got some good news and some bad news. The bad news is that my Landcruiser's stuck. We're not going to get out of here tonight." He grabbed her cell phone from the car, took her hand, and started to pull her over to where he'd left his vehicle. "But the good news is, you're no longer alone."

"That's not such g-good news for you," she said.

He grinned and looked back at her, admiring the unique shape of her amber-colored eyes. "It's not as bad as you might think."

CHANTEL LET DILLON lead her up the side of a sharp incline through waist-deep snow. Pine trees stood all around them, tops bending and limbs swaying as they fought the same wind that flung ice crystals into her face. Her clothes and shoes were soaked through, and even with gloves on her hands, she didn't have enough body heat to warm her fingers. Never had she been so cold, not in ten years of New York winters.

She slipped and fell, and Dillon hauled her back to her feet. "Come on, we've got to hurry. I don't want you to get frostbite," he said, pulling her more forcefully behind him.

Chantel angled her face up to see through the trees in front of them. Other than the small circle from Dillon's flashlight, everything was completely dark. The falling snow obliterated even the moon's light, but the night wasn't silent. The wind alternately whined and howled, and tree limbs scratched and clawed at each other.

"Are you sure you know wh-where we're going?" she called. It felt as though they were scaling a mountain, heading deeper into the forest, instead of toward civilization.

"I'm taking a more direct route, but we'll get there."

"I d-don't think I can walk any farther." The air smelled like cold steel, not the pine she'd been anticipating, and suddenly Chantel wondered why she'd ever wanted to go to Tahoe in the first place. She had enough to take care of in the valley. She wasn't ready to deal with the issues between her and Stacy yet.

"We gotta keep moving. It's not much farther." Dillon sheltered her with his large body and tugged persistently at her arm.

"I'm freezing!"

"So am I. Come on, Chantel, we need to keep walking. Talk to me. That'll keep our minds off the cold."

She looked at the man who'd risked his life to save her. Hadn't she wrecked his car earlier? Yet here he was, trudging through the snow, pulling her along, telling her to talk to him. Without him...

Chantel didn't want to think about what might have happened without him. "You're c-crazy, Dillon. Why didn't you leave me?"

"Freud would probably say I'm trying to prove my masculinity."

She thought he was smiling but couldn't see his face in the darkness. "There are easier ways to do that."

He laughed. "I've always had to do things the hard way. My poor mother used to shake her head in exasperation and tell me how wonderful my sisters were to raise."

"F-F-Freud would probably have something to say about that, t-t-too."

"No doubt. Only I don't think being a troublemaker has anything to do with my sexuality."

"I think it's the t-testosterone. My c-cousin once kicked a hole in the wall when I put him down for a nap."

Dillon paused. "How old was he?"

"Three. It was my f-fault, really. I forgot to take off his cowboy boots."

Dillon put his arms around her waist and half carried her over a fallen log. "Your cousin's my kind of kid. But girls can be hellions, too. My littlest is a spitfire."

"How many—" Chantel could barely form the words "—children do you have?"

"Two girls, nine and seven."

She pictured him with a couple of dark-haired, blue-eyed daughters. If they looked anything like their father, they would be beautiful. "So you're m-married?"

"Divorced."

"I'm s-sorry."

"So am I."

Chantel fell silent again. She had no strength left.

"Tell me about you," Dillon suggested. "Is there a man in your life?"

"No." Wade was too long a story, and she was far too weary to expand on her answer. "I can't g-go any f-farther," she said, sinking to her knees in the snow. Somehow she wasn't cold anymore. She just didn't care. There wasn't anything left inside her with which to fight. "You g-go on…"

"I'm not leaving you." A strong arm swept her to her feet, but she pulled away again, shaking her head. *I can't,* rang through her thoughts, but she could no longer speak. Her mind seemed clouded, her senses dulled. Her body simply slowed and stopped moving, like a cheap windup toy.

"Chantel!" The command cut through her lazy thoughts, but she refused it. *Let this be over.*

The second time Chantel heard her name, she knew Dillon would not be denied. Weakly she tried to move toward to his voice, then felt the world tip and sway as he lifted her in his arms.

"So you're going to make me carry you, huh?" he breathed, his chest heaving as he bore her weight through the wind and snow.

Silence fell for what seemed a long time. Then, from somewhere far above her, Chantel heard Dillon again. "Stay with me, baby," he whispered urgently. "Don't go to sleep! Fight the darkness, Chantel."

Chantel wasn't sure she wanted to stay, let alone fight, but something about his voice enticed her toward his strength. *Don't let me go…I won't let go.*

"I see it now."

His words made no sense, caused no reaction in Chantel. She only knew that he'd left her. But he was close. She could hear him talking to himself, moving a few feet away. A car door slammed, twice, then she felt herself being jostled about as he pulled and tugged at her arms, her legs, her…

What was it? What did he want from her?

Then it all came clear. He was stripping off her clothes.

CHAPTER THREE

CHANTEL'S BODY burned as it warmed by degrees, slowly turning from what felt like dead wood to living flesh again. She didn't know how much time had passed, only that she was in some sort of sleeping bag, crushed against something strong and hard—an expansive chest? Two sinewy arms circled her as large hands chafed her back. A rough stubbled chin grazed her cheek as thickly muscled legs became entwined with her own, moving constantly, trying to warm her lower extremities.

She was being held by a naked man. And he was warming a great deal more than her extremities.

She stiffened.

"Chantel? Are you back with me?"

The voice identified Dillon immediately, but still she raised her head to make out his face in the darkness. "Wh-What happened?"

Closing his eyes, he shamelessly hugged her to him, belly to belly. It was then that Chantel realized how fast his heart was beating.

"What's wrong?" she asked, still disoriented.

"Are you kidding? I thought I was going to lose you. It was nip and tuck there for a while."

Slowly the memory of being stranded in her car came back to her. She remembered how Dillon had rescued her, remembered trudging behind him through the snow. Then there was nothing but blackness until the burning and tingling started and grew painful in its severity.

"How do you feel?" he asked.

"Like I'm on fire."

"That's good."

"Where are my clothes?"

"I don't know. Outside somewhere. I wasn't concerned with what happened to them. I just knew I had to get them off you—fast."

"Because…"

"Because you were soaking wet and freezing to death. And that's what you're supposed to do with someone in that situation." His voice sounded slightly defensive, as though she'd accused him of being some kind of pervert.

Realizing he'd just saved her life, Chantel tried to act nonchalant. She wasn't sure he'd needed to remove *every* stitch of their clothing, but he'd obviously acted in what he thought was her best interests. "I've seen it before on television," she admitted.

"How's the burning in your arms and legs? Getting any better?"

"A little."

Chantel shifted to remove her lower body from contact with Dillon's, which was nearly impossible in the snug bag. While modeling, she'd seen a score of naked men, changing from one outfit to another, and lots of men had seen her doing the same thing. But somehow she couldn't treat being with Dillon as indifferently as she'd handled working around those fellow models, photographers, costumers and artistic directors. Especially since his body felt good enough to melt her bones.

"Relax."

Though nervous and vulnerable, she tried to do as he suggested, but ended up simply keeping as still as she could.

It had been almost a year since she'd been with a man. She'd gotten so skinny in her final months with Wade that he hadn't wanted her, at least sexually. And the memory of it made her even more self-conscious than she would normally have felt in this particular dilemma.

"I'm sorry I got you into this mess," she said to break the awkward silence.

His chuckle rumbled in her ear. "Don't be. From my perspective, there are worse things than having a beautiful woman in my arms."

Chantel smiled. So he was generous, as well as kind. "What do we do when we're warm?"

"Wait for morning."

The thought of spending the entire night in Dillon's arms sent a shiver up Chantel's spine. He hugged her closer and began to rub her back again, as though he assumed her reaction had something to do with the cold. But Chantel knew it had much more to do with the man holding her, stroking her.

"That feels good," she whispered.

Dillon's shallow breathing—and more obvious proof lower down—told her he agreed. "I guess this might get a little awkward," he said, knowing, of course, that she couldn't possibly miss his arousal. "But don't worry. I won't, you know, try anything."

She smiled at his attempt to reassure her. "We just have to relax, like you said."

"Unfortunately, even that won't change some things."

"I know," she whispered. "It's okay."

Chantel had felt exhausted only moments earlier, but now her blood zipped through her veins and wouldn't let her lie still. "We're not going to be able to rest," she said, "if we feel we can't move."

"We can move."

"I know, but I'm hesitant to put my arm here or my leg there…"

"Do whatever makes you comfortable."

Sighing, she snuggled closer, laying her head on his chest and slipping one cold foot between his. The burning in her arms and legs had eased, but her fingers and toes still felt like ice. "Thanks," she said. "I guess we should probably get some sleep. I'm a lot warmer now, aren't you?"

"I'm plenty warm," he told her, but to Chantel his body didn't feel as though he was ready for sleep. His muscles were taut, his chest rising and falling too fast.

Dillon's breath stirred her hair, but he said no more. Chantel listened to the storm outside until sleep began to woo her. Then, when she was finally warm, she drifted slowly toward it. As her brain lost its override on her body, she relaxed even more and pressed closer to the muscled chest beneath her hands, the powerful limbs entwined with her own. The steady beat of Dillon's heart lulled her that final step, and she fell into peaceful oblivion.

DILLON STARED into the darkness, willing his body to forget the soft flesh pressed against his, to block out the smell of woman that filled his nostrils. He and Chantel Miller were merely two strangers surviving the storm together. Morning would come and everything would be the way it was before.

Still, he had to admit that the person he held in his arms was no everyday woman. She was slender and elegant, but it was her smile and her eyes that appealed to him most. Unique, exquisite, haunting.

Beautiful. She was simply beautiful. And, of course, her body did nothing to change that overall impression. Long legs, smooth and shapely, slid against his own; her small perfect breasts were crushed against his chest. He'd longed to touch them from the moment he'd taken off her shirt, to feel them in his palms…

She smashed my truck. She smashed my truck. She smashed my truck. And she made me miss the party at the cabin.

He repeated Chantel's shortcomings over and over to himself, but nothing quelled the hot desire that smoked through his veins. To make matters worse, he'd begun to feel a little proprietary toward her. He had found her. He had saved her. It was that old *finders keepers, losers weepers* thing, and he knew it. But no matter how many times he told himself no, his groin tightened, insisting on a different answer.

If it hadn't been so long, he wouldn't be like this, he told himself. He and Amanda had divorced two years ago, and he hadn't slept with a woman since. He'd come close a few times, but the commitment that went with sex had always pulled him up short—because he didn't want to give his daughters any competition. He owed Brittney and Sydney his wholehearted loyalty. Divorce was hard enough. He knew firsthand how difficult it could be to get along with a stepparent. Why would he do the same thing to his kids that his parents had done to him?

Chantel stirred. One of her hands climbed across his ribs, and he had to stop himself from cupping the roundness of her derriere and pressing her more firmly against him. It was simply the most natural of responses. But she was sleeping peacefully and had no idea she was driving him mad.

And he'd promised he'd be good.

A sweet mewling sound came from Chantel, but her eyes remained closed. She was probably dreaming. He gazed through the darkness, finding the curve of her cheek, the silky spray of hair that fanned out over his arm, and caught sight of her lips. They were slightly parted…and wet.

He clenched his jaw. It was going to be a long night.

THE CELL PHONE broke the silence, waking Chantel with a start. Next to her, Dillon stirred and they both fumbled around until Chantel came up with the phone, which turned out to be her own, and answered it.

"Hello?"

"Miss Miller?" a man's voice said.

"Yes?"

"This is the police dispatcher just checking to make sure you're okay. The storm hasn't lifted yet, but I want you to know we'll get there as soon as we can."

"Okay."

"You sound tired, Miss Miller, but I can't stress how important it is that you not fall asleep. With the windchill factor, it's well below zero outside."

"I understand, but I'm not alone anymore."

"What?"

"I, um… A friend of mine came to find me. Only he's stuck now, too."

"The two of you are together?"

Dillon shoved himself up onto one elbow. "Give me the phone so I can tell them where we are."

"We're sheltering in a Toyota Landcruiser," she said into the receiver. "Here, he wants to talk to you."

Chantel listened as Dillon identified himself and gave the dispatcher directions. When he ended the call, she looked at him expectantly. "What did he say?"

"To sit tight. Someone'll be here as soon as the storm lifts." He flicked on a flashlight and looked at his watch.

"What time is it?"

"Three o'clock."

Chantel groaned. "No wonder I'm still tired. Did you get any sleep?"

"I dropped off about five minutes before the phone rang."

Now that she and Dillon were both awake, Chantel felt her earlier self-consciousness return but fought it back. They might as well get used to each other. According to the dispatcher, the police were going to be a while yet. "What kept you up?"

She thought he arched a brow at her, but couldn't see clearly enough in the darkness.

"You don't want to know," he said.

"What—was I snoring?"

He laughed. "You didn't have to."

Catching his meaning, Chantel felt her face flush and tried to sidle away, but he wrapped an arm around her and pulled her down beside him. "Come on. It's too cold for that."

She put a hand on his chest, keeping a slight distance between them. "Tell me about yourself, Dillon."

"What do you want to know?"

"Well…tell me about your daughters."

He opened up easily to that question. His voice warmed as he talked about his girls and their accomplishments. His fourth-grader had just competed against a sixth-grader for student-body treasurer and won. She played the clarinet in band and sang in the school choir. His second-grader was in gymnastics and could already do a back flip.

Chantel felt something tug at her heart and knew she should have steered the conversation away from kids. It was always this way when…

Dillon fell silent right in the middle of describing a family trip they'd taken to Disneyland just before the divorce.

"And then what?" she prompted.

He didn't answer, and Chantel berated herself for not listening more closely. What was it he'd said? Something about promising his girls they'd go back every year. Wasn't that it? "Dillon?"

"What?"

"You didn't finish."

"I know. I don't want to talk about it anymore."

"What's wrong?" She propped herself up to look in his face, but in the darkness, she couldn't decide whether his expression was as stony as his voice suggested.

He shook his head. "I'm just angry. It has nothing to do with you."

"It's that damn Mickey Mouse, right? You hate him."

He gave her a grudging smile. "No."

"Then what?" Chantel studied him again and guessed that what she saw was pain. "Forget it. You don't have to talk about it," she said. "Divorce is a hard thing—for everyone."

"I never thought I'd be divorced," he admitted. "I never wanted to be."

"I don't think anyone ever plans on it."

"It's funny how someone you love can turn into someone you don't even know, isn't it?"

"Oh, I see. You're not over your ex-wife yet." For some reason she wanted to pull away, but there was no room to do so.

He laughed harshly. "Wrong. I'm completely over her. I got over her shortly after her second affair, which, ironically enough, was with the mailman."

"You're kidding."

"No. Well, technically speaking, he wasn't our mailman, but he worked for the post office."

"How did she meet him?"

"At the gym."

"Ouch."

He laughed, but his voice was edged with bitterness. "I used to think that sort of thing could never happen to me."

"Does it hurt to talk about it?"

"Not anymore. At first I thought I'd never recover. I blamed myself. We got married too young. I was gone too much, working, trying to put myself through school. I think she was lonely and bored and found the wrong kind of friend. She and the woman next door, who was already divorced, started going out together in the afternoons, visiting bars. I could see what was happening, but I thought I could stop it. I thought if I was meeting her emotional needs, she wouldn't turn to other men. She admitted she didn't love them."

"Did you ever find out why she did it?"

"She said she liked the thrill of it. I think she was on boyfriend number three then, and she was leaving the girls with baby-sitters to spend the day at the gym or tanning. I cut back on my hours at work, but she resented the hit our budget suffered because of it, and her behavior only got worse. I finally realized she had affairs because it fed her ego that other men found her attractive. And she liked my jealous reaction."

"I take it the two of you aren't friends now."

"Actually I'm just trying not to dislike her too much. Not for the old stuff, her betrayal of me—that's history. It's the problems we're having now that make me mad. It kills me that I'm missing so much of my girls' lives. Their mother changes boyfriends like she changes underwear and insists Brittney and Sydney welcome each new guy with open arms. Sometimes she even makes them call whoever it is 'daddy.'"

Instinctively Chantel reached up to caress his cheek. "You sound like a wonderful father. Can't you gain custody somehow?"

"I've spent thousands of dollars trying to do just that. California is touted as being liberal, but the judge still won't award me custody. I'd have to completely discredit Amanda to get them, and I just can't bring myself to destroy my daughters' mother."

"What about visitation rights?"

"I pick up the girls whenever I legally can, but a lot of the time Amanda takes off so that they're not home when I arrive. Or she leaves them at her mother's, who thinks I've let her daughter down and won't even open the door to me."

"Fighting all of that must get old."

He paused. "I'd rather fight it than not see them. Now Amanda is trying to get permission from the court to move to Iowa."

"Iowa!"

"Yeah." He scrubbed his face with his free hand. "I'm sorry. I don't know why I'm telling you this."

"Because it's the middle of the night, and we're naked and huddled together in your sleeping bag."

"I'm fully aware of the naked part, but how come I'm the only one baring my soul?"

So I don't have to tell you about the skeletons in *my* closet.

"Do you like being an architect?" she countered.

"I love my work, but we're going to talk about you now. What do you do?"

"I work in the district office of my state senator."

"Were you involved in politics in New York?"

"No."

"'No'? That's it? What, were you a stripper or something?"

"I was a model."

"Really? Who'd you model for?"

Chantel bit her lip, reluctant to discuss her modeling experience because she was afraid of where the conversation would lead. "Let's talk about something else."

"Why? You didn't like modeling?"

"I loved it."

"Then tell me about it."

Cocooned against the weather, Chantel breathed in the smell of the aftershave she'd first noticed when Dillon had leaned into her car, and smiled. She could trust him. He'd come for her despite the storm, even after the police had given up.

"I did runway modeling, and some work for high-end catalogs. I was in the *Sports Illustrated* swimsuit issue a couple of years, used to model for Calvin Klein a lot. Oh, and I was on the cover of *Vogue* once."

"Wow, sounds like you were pretty successful. What happened?"

Chantel thought of Wade and his demands, demands that increased with her success. "I had a boyfriend…well, more like a husband, really. We lived together for the ten years I was in New York. He modeled, too, and when he didn't get the breaks I did, he became fanatically jealous. He insisted I cancel contracts I never should have canceled, had me refuse jobs I should have taken. I did it to preserve the relationship, to prove he came first. We'd talked about having a family, and I wanted to get married, but he kept putting me off. He said he didn't see the point of making it official since all that mattered was what we felt, not some piece of paper. The harder I tried to please him, the more difficult he became. And then I got sick and had to quit altogether."

"What kind of sick?"

Chantel sighed. She hated telling people what had happened to her and usually didn't. They didn't understand anorexia, were generally frightened of the self-hate that spurs it on. "It wasn't anything communicable."

"I wasn't thinking that." He smoothed the hair off her forehead, and Chantel closed her eyes, wishing he'd go on caressing her until the devils from her past were forgotten. "Tell me what happened," he whispered.

"I had anorexia."

"How bad?"

"I had to be hospitalized. The doctors didn't think I'd make it. Neither did Wade."

"Wade's the man you were living with?"

She nodded. "Wade Bennett. I believe, deep down, he was hoping against me. Maybe that's what made me decide to prove them all wrong."

Dillon was silent for a long while. "Where's Wade now?"

"In New York, still trying to make it, I guess. I won't open his letters."

Dillon's arms tightened around her. "And you're well now, aren't you? You look… I mean, I've never seen a more beautiful woman."

She'd heard those words before, over the years, from numerous men who'd tried to pick her up. But Dillon sounded sincere. "Anorexia is like alcoholism. You're never really cured. It's a constant battle."

"It's a battle you'll win."

Unable to stop herself from giving him a simple gesture of affection, Chantel played with the hair on his arm, then slid her hand up to his shoulder. "I think your wife must've been crazy."

He laughed and rolled her onto her back. In the process his hand brushed her nipple, which immediately drew up hard and tight.

"Chantel?"

"Mmm?"

"Are you seeing anyone now?"

The huskiness of his voice told her he wanted her, and Chantel felt an answering warmth in the pit of her stomach. "I'm not dating anyone. I only recently moved back to California."

"Good."

"Why?"

"Because I'm going to kiss you."

His head descended and his lips found and molded to hers, tasting her, teasing her, gently prodding. The practical side of Chantel screamed that she'd known this man for mere hours. But her heart felt as though she'd known him for years.

She opened her mouth to welcome his tongue, surprised that the small cut she'd received in the accident didn't bother her, and he deepened the kiss until the warmth blooming in her belly began to spread out to her limbs. He tasted the way his breath smelled, like spearmint gum, she thought lazily, and began exploring his mouth. Circling his neck with her arms, she let her hands delve into the thickness of his dark hair, threading the short silky locks through her fingers, tugging him closer.

When she groaned, he made an identical sound in his throat, and quickened the pace of their kiss until Chantel was so hungry for more she was shaking. She shifted, pressing her body more fully against him, then gasped when his large rough palm clutched her breast.

Two fingers flicked across her nipple as he trailed kisses down her throat, whispering how wonderful she felt and tasted and looked. Chantel arched toward him, wanting him to kiss her breasts.

He read her need quickly and easily, and responded with an eagerness that made her desire spiral even higher. His mouth clamped on to her nipple, and as his tongue darted and teased and suckled, hot jolts of pleasure went through her. "That's good," she murmured.

He moved to the other breast, and she kneaded his powerful shoulders, reveling in the way his body fit perfectly against hers. Dillon's size made her feel small for the first time in her adult life. And what he was doing to her—it was so fulfilling. Dillon had already touched something deep inside her, something Wade had never reached.

"Chantel?" Dillon's raspy breath tickled her ear as he nuzzled her neck. "Do you want me to stop, Chantel? I know I said I wouldn't touch you, but I never dreamed it would be so…"

She wrapped her legs around his so he couldn't put any space between them. "No, don't stop," she whispered.

"What about birth control?"

"We don't have to worry about it." Chantel swallowed hard, willing back sudden tears. "I can't have children."

He paused above her, as though trying to see her face in the darkness. "The anorexia?"

"They told me in the hospital that my reproductive system has shut down and will never work properly again. I haven't had a real period for over a year." She drew a shaky breath, and then realized she was crying.

"I'm sorry," he murmured, kissing her forehead and her cheeks. "That's a tough break, especially if you want kids."

"There's nothing like a baby, right?" She tried to sound flippant, but couldn't stifle the sob that gave her true feelings away.

The sympathetic tone of Dillon's voice caressed her as effectively as the fingers that found and wiped away her tears. "There are other good things in life," he whispered.

Her arms tightened around his neck. "Show me one, Dillon. Show me this one," she said, and pulled him down for another mind-numbing kiss.

CHAPTER FOUR

IT WAS THE SILENCE that woke him.

Dillon blinked and raised his head to listen. The wind had died. What time was it? Difficult to tell. The snow piled on top of the truck kept the inside dark, but he'd bet it was morning.

He shifted slightly, trying not to wake Chantel as he let some of the blood flow back into the arm she was sleeping on. It had been quite a night! He grinned, remembering Chantel's first warm willing response and the times he'd made love to her since. Sometimes she was a little shy and reserved, sometimes she played the temptress. But the crazy thing was that he couldn't get enough of her. Even now, just looking at her face, sweet and passive in sleep, he wanted to wake her and lose himself in her arms again.

"Is the storm over yet?" she asked, her eyelids fluttering open, despite Dillon's decision to let her sleep.

"I think so."

"Darn."

He kissed the tip of her nose. "What does that mean?"

"They'll be coming for us."

"Isn't that what we want?"

Her large eyes gazed up at him, and he caught his breath. Was it possible to fall in love in only one night?

"I don't want reality to intrude," she complained. Then she sighed. "I have to go see my sister. You have your friends waiting for you." Her silky limbs wrapped around him again, and she kissed his neck. "Mmm, I guess we got a little sweaty last night. You taste salty."

He laughed. "We got a lot sweaty, among other things."

"It was incredible, wasn't it?"

"Good enough that you won't forget me before we get home?"

"How could I forget the man who saved my life?"

"Hey, that's right! Doesn't that make you my slave or something?"

"No!" She tried to wriggle away, but he restrained her.

"Come on, slave, I'm getting hungry for more of you…"

She groaned. "You're insatiable! Not again! I'm tired." Running her fingers up and down his spine, she massaged the stiff muscles in his back, then pulled him down for a long searching kiss.

Dillon savored the taste of her, wishing they were at his place so they could get up and take a hot shower together and eat something. "If we were home, I'd make you breakfast in bed," he told her.

"Where's home?"

"Lafayette."

"We live that close to each other?"

He ran a hand through his sleep-tousled hair. "Yep. And then, after breakfast, I'd get you in the tub and lather your hair and massage your scalp and lick water off the tips of your breasts…"

"Hmm…maybe I'm not as tired as I thought," she said, but before Dillon could take her up on the invitation, they heard some kind of heavy machinery moving toward them.

Chantel groaned. "A snowplow. They're here, aren't they?"

Dillon listened to the noise get louder and louder as the plow made its way through the heavy snow. "That's my guess."

She sighed and studied him, looking somber for the first time that morning. "I haven't thanked you for coming back for me, Dillon. Who knows how long I would've had to wait before the police found me? I couldn't even give them good directions. What you did was so brave."

He wiggled his brows to make her laugh again. "And I've been handsomely rewarded."

"Roll over and let me hold you," she said. "Just until they get here."

He obeyed, and she curved her body, spoon-fashion, along the back of his.

"What are we going to do about clothes?" she asked, the noise of the plow nearly drowning out her voice. "I don't like the idea of being caught in such a vulnerable position."

"Don't worry. I'll get out and take care of everything. You can stay modestly covered back here."

"Thanks, Dillon."

"Chantel?"

"Uh-huh?"

"Can I call you when we get home?" he asked, half-afraid she'd refuse him for some reason only she knew.

But a *yes* sounded in his ear, and he smiled and pulled her arms more tightly around him.

CHANTEL DREW a deep breath and stared up at the A-frame log cabin that corresponded to the address on the directions Stacy had given her—and wished she was still with Dillon. After all the highs and lows of the past night, she felt physically and emotionally spent. The last thing she wanted to do right now was face her sister.

If only she hadn't given her word and could simply head back home—

"Omigosh, Chantel, what happened to you?" Stacy appeared in the doorway and frowned at the damaged Jaguar. "Now your car doesn't look any better than my Honda."

Chantel gave her a tired grin, feeling awkward and unsure of how to greet her sister. Should she rush over and hug Stacy as though they hadn't been estranged for ten years? Just smile and wave "hello"?

Remembering her sister's cold response the first time Chantel had contacted her—when she'd just returned from New York and had blubbered her way through a painful apology—she opted for the smile and jammed her hands in her pockets. "Would you believe I got stuck in the storm last night and had to wait for the police to bring a tow and get me out?"

"Are you kidding? Why didn't you call me?"

I've been worried. For a split second, Chantel hoped to hear those words, but Stacy didn't add them. "I drove off without the phone number." She chuckled, feeling her palms start to sweat and wishing, more than ever, that she could climb back in her car and drive away.

"Are you okay?"

I've been worried.

Again the words didn't come. Chantel clenched her fists in the pockets of her baggy jeans. Her sister would never say anything that indicated that she still cared. Why hope? "I think I'll be better after I shower and have something to eat. Tell me this place has hot water."

"It does. Everyone else left to go skiing, so the bathrooms are free."

"Oh! I'm sorry if waiting for me made you miss the fun."

Stacy paused halfway between the door and the Jaguar. "No, actually I'm expecting someone else. He'll be here anytime."

Chantel felt a blush heat her cheeks. What had she been thinking? She forced a smile. "So you've met a guy, huh?"

"Yeah."

"You never mentioned him on the phone."

"There wasn't any reason to go into it. I told you I was inviting a few friends, and I did."

"Well, tell me about him," Chantel said, trying to act like any normal sister would. Besides Stacy's father, who lived a hermit's life somewhere in New Mexico, they had no family left. Whether either of them wanted to admit it or not, they needed each other.

Stacy shrugged. "What do you want to know?"

"Where did you meet?"

"At the hospital. We've known each other for a couple of years."

"He's a doctor?"

"No, he was there for a meeting with one of the doctors. He was handling the majority of the tenant improvements for the medical building next door."

"And you really like him?"

For a moment Stacy's hard shell cracked and she gave Chantel a genuine smile. "Like him! You should see him! I've never been so head over heels in love. I'm going to marry this one or die trying."

Chantel laughed. "Wow. He must be something. I can't wait to meet him."

The shadow of old pain fell across Stacy's face, making Chantel regret the simple offhand remark. "Stacy—"

"I know. You'd better have that shower," she said briskly. "Let's take your stuff inside."

Trying to remember the warmth and approval she'd felt with Dillon, Chantel focused on his parting kiss and his promise to call her as soon as she arrived home.

She could do this. She was only staying in Tahoe till

Sunday, and thinking of Dillon would get her through the weekend.

Thinking of Dillon could get her through anything.

HAD STACY'S BOYFRIEND arrived? Chantel stepped out of the shower and listened for voices in the living room as she pulled on the jeans and long-sleeved T-shirt she'd had her sister toss in the dryer, but heard nothing beyond the distant drone of the television.

"Stace?" she called out.

A light step sounded in the hall, and her sister poked her head into the bedroom just as Chantel began to work the snarls out of her long hair. "You done?"

"Yeah. It felt great. Is your friend here?"

"Not yet. He called to say he stopped off for a late breakfast. He'll be here any minute."

Chantel smiled at her sister's barely concealed excitement. "You still want to get married, Stace?"

"If I want kids, I don't have a lot of time to waste. I'm already thirty-two." She fingered Chantel's expensive leather luggage.

"That's only three years older than me." *Only, I don't have to worry about getting married…or having kids.* Instinctively Chantel pressed a hand to her stomach. The ultimate price. She wondered if Stacy would more easily forgive her if she knew, then rejected the idea. She wouldn't play on her sister's sympathy. That was cowardly. She'd gotten what she deserved. Wasn't that what Wade had said the last time she'd seen him?

For once in his life he'd been right.

"After age thirty, three years counts for a lot," Stacy said, plopping down on the bed while Chantel applied lotion to her face.

"While the rest of us were dreaming of having careers,

you always wanted to marry and settle down," Chantel murmured.

"Ever since I graduated from high school, but all too often I made the mistake of bringing them home. Then they'd see you."

And what had stopped her from finding a husband during the past ten years, while Chantel was in New York?

Chantel stifled the defensive retort. She didn't want to start a fight. She was here to rebuild her relationship with Stacy, not destroy it. "I'm sorry, Stace. I can't understand why anyone would rather be with me than you."

Her sister sighed. "Look in the mirror, Chantel. That explains everything."

Chantel gazed into the mirror that contrasted her tall lean form with her sister's short slightly stocky build, her light eyes with her sister's chocolate-colored irises.

"We're as opposite as night and day, aren't we?" Stacy said.

"My father was tall and blond, yours short and dark. Mother loved them both. We didn't get to place an order. I certainly never asked to be six feet tall."

"And I never asked for saddlebags. Them's the breaks, I guess."

Chantel glanced at her sister's curvy figure. "You don't have saddlebags. I've always wanted to be petite, like you."

A knock from the front of the cabin interrupted them, and Stacy jumped to her feet. "He's here!"

Waving her out of the room, Chantel said, "You go enjoy him. I'm pretty tired after last night. I think I'll lie down for a while. Which bunk is mine?"

There were two unmade beds and two that hadn't been touched. "Take your pick of those," Stacy said, already on her way out. At the door she turned back. "On second thought, why don't you meet him before your nap? We may as well get it over with.''

Chantel cringed at the tone of Stacy's voice. She sounded as if she'd rather have root-canal work than introduce her sister to her boyfriend, but Chantel threw her shoulders back and took a deep breath.

Stacy was in love. It was time to meet her sister's Mr. Right—and to let him know he'd better not so much as throw a friendly smile in her direction.

Following her sister, she headed into the small cluttered living room, filled with a half-dozen pieces of mismatched furniture surrounding a black fireplace insert. Through the front window overlooking the drive, she caught a glimpse of a white sports utility vehicle. But the sight struck no chord in her until Stacy opened the door, and she saw Dillon Broderick standing on the front porch.

CHAPTER FIVE

"CHANTEL! WHAT ARE YOU doing here?" Dillon looked from Stacy to Chantel and back again. There were hundreds of cabins in the Tahoe area, and thousands of people came up on any given weekend to ski. What were the chances of running into her again? Not that he was unhappy about it. He'd been thinking about the new woman in his life ever since they'd parted, missing her, already looking forward to calling her. It just wasn't a pleasant surprise to find Chantel in company with the woman he'd been dating for the past few weeks.

Stacy's brows knitted together. "You two know each other?"

Dillon smiled uncomfortably. "Actually we—"

"Got in a car accident coming up here," Chantel cut in, her voice brisk. "We don't really know each other, just met briefly out in the storm to exchange insurance information." She shrugged. "I'm sorry about our little fender bender, by the way."

Just met briefly out in the storm? After what happened last night? Dillon wasn't sure how to react. The time he'd spent with Chantel meant something to him. *She* meant something to him. At the same time, he'd been dating Stacy for the past few weeks, and while they hadn't become serious or exclusive or anything, he wasn't sure exactly what she expected of him.

"I'm sure the insurance will take care of the Landcruiser,'' he said shortly. ''How do you two know each other?''

''Chantel's my sister,'' Stacy replied.

Dillon wished he could step back into his truck until his head stopped reeling and he could catch his breath. Stacy's sister? He'd just slept with Stacy's *sister?* His gaze flew from Chantel's elegant fine-boned face, now devoid of color, to Stacy's pixie cuteness, and he wondered where the family resemblance was. He and Stacy had been friends for two years, but he couldn't remember her ever having mentioned a sister.

''It's cold outside. Come on in and tell me about last night,'' Stacy said with a quick welcoming hug.

Dillon glanced helplessly over Stacy's head to Chantel, but she wouldn't meet his eyes. Jamming her hands in the pockets of her jeans, she stared at the carpet.

Stacy hooked an arm through his and pulled him inside. ''When Veronica said you'd called and weren't going to make it, I thought you'd turned back. What's this accident all about?''

Normally Dillon didn't mind Stacy's demonstrative nature, but today it grated on his nerves. Her touch seemed more familiar, more *possessive* than he'd noticed before. ''It wasn't a bad one,'' he said simply, setting down his large duffel bag. ''Is everyone else already on the slopes?''

''It took them a while to dig out from under the snow, but they're at Squaw Valley now. I told them we'd meet them after lunch.''

''Great.'' His eyes darted to Chantel again. Her hands were still in her pockets, and she was sidling toward the hallway.

''I'm going to go blow-dry my hair,'' she said before ducking out of the room.

Dillon tried to keep his gaze from following her, but it

was virtually impossible. He was too taken with her after last night. He was too concerned about the revelations of the morning.

"I gather the accident was my sister's fault," Stacy said, studying him.

Dillon rubbed his neck. "Not really. It was the storm more than anything. Where should I put my stuff?"

"You can room with Bill and Tony, if that's okay. There're four bunks in the back."

"Fine." Dillon let Stacy lead him down the hall. The high-pitched whir of a blow-dryer came from behind one of the doors they passed, tempting him to barge in and try to explain his relationship with Stacy to Chantel. But he told himself there'd be a better time and kept moving until they came to a small square room with two sets of bunk beds pushed against the walls. Cheap comic-strip curtains hung over one window, and a few well-worn rugs covered the wooden floor—standard furnishings for a rental cabin.

"How come you never mentioned having a sister?" he asked Stacy as he dropped his duffel on a wrinkle-free bed.

"Because, for a long time, I didn't," she replied.

WAS SHE IMAGINING IT or had Dillon's eyes really lit up the moment he saw Chantel? Stacy stood in the hall outside Dillon's room, chewing her upper lip. He was just surprised, she told herself. Not every man she met was going to throw her over for her sister. Still, she couldn't shake the feeling of foreboding that had shot through her veins when she'd introduced the two of them a few minutes ago.

Maybe she shouldn't have invited Chantel to join her this weekend. She simply wasn't up to living in her sister's shadow again.

Closing her eyes, Stacy took a deep breath, remembering Chantel's apology when she'd returned to California. The way she'd offered it, humbly and without hope, had melted Stacy's heart, reminding her how much Chantel had meant to her while they were growing up. Life was okay back then, better than okay, until one incredible year—when the tall gangly Chantel had suddenly become a stunningly beautiful woman.

Then things began to change. Stacy and her sister couldn't go to the mall anymore without boys falling all over themselves in their eagerness to get close to Chantel. They couldn't go dancing together without Stacy playing the wallflower while Chantel was swept onto the floor by one boy after another.

And now Chantel was back, and Stacy feared she'd find herself right where she used to be, playing second fiddle to the golden girl of the family. Life was almost easier when she and Chantel weren't speaking. If not for seeing Chantel's face plastered on the front of countless magazines, Stacy could almost convince herself that she didn't have a sister. And after what Chantel had done, she felt perfectly justified in doing so.

And yet…sometimes Stacy longed for the old days. The Christmas Eves they'd whispered together in one big bed, too excited to sleep. The Halloweens they'd poured all their candy into one common pot. The summers they'd spent together—the trees they'd climbed, the lemonade stands they'd run, the games they'd played.

They'd lost so much since then. Where had it gone?

Pushing away from the wall, Stacy crossed to her sister's door. The blow-dryer was quiet now, but she could hear Chantel moving around the room. She knocked softly. "It's me."

At her sister's invitation, Stacy slipped inside and sank onto the bed. "So what do you think?" she asked.

Chantel stood in front of the dresser, brushing her hair. "About Dillon?"

"No, about the price of eggs in China. Of course about Dillon."

Her sister smiled at her in the mirror. "He seems pretty special. I think you've chosen a great guy this time."

Stacy waited, sensing something more in her sister's voice, but Chantel didn't elaborate. "Are you going to tell me what happened last night? About the accident?"

"Oh, that." Chantel set the brush down and turned to face her. "Unfortunately I rear-ended him. It was so snowy and slick, I just couldn't stop in time."

"And then?"

Chantel cleared her throat. "And then I gave him my insurance information."

"But you said you got stuck."

"That was after the accident."

"What happened to Dillon?"

"I don't know."

Chantel had spoken so quietly, Stacy could barely hear her. "What?"

"I said I don't know. Maybe the Highway Patrol closed the freeway. I've heard they do that sometimes."

"Yeah, they do." Stacy toyed with the fringe on one of the throw pillows that decorated the bed. "So, do you want to go skiing with us today?"

"Actually I think I'll stay here and read, or just take it easy. Last night was pretty traumatic."

"Okay." Stacy tossed the pillow aside and stood to go, feeling instantly relieved—and hating herself for it.

CHANTEL COULDN'T STOP shaking. Long after Dillon and Stacy had left, she sat in the living room, staring out the window at the crumpled fender of her car and wondering how much more could go wrong before something finally went right. She'd almost died last night. If not for Dillon, she would have fallen asleep and never awoken. But he'd come for her, risked his own life to save hers, and his sacrifice and all they'd shared afterward had forged a bond so quick and sure Chantel wasn't sure how to sever it. She only knew that she had to. For Stacy.

How ironic that it would come to this, she thought. Or maybe it was simply justice.

The telephone rang, and Chantel glanced at the Formica counter where it sat on top of a narrow phone book. She had no desire to talk to anyone. She had even less energy. But the ringing wouldn't stop.

After several minutes she climbed to her feet and walked slowly across the room to answer it. "Hello?"

"Chantel?"

It was Dillon. Chantel's breath caught at the sound of his voice, and the memories of last night crowded closer. Memories of a rough jaw against her temple, words of passion in her ear. "I thought you were skiing."

"I'm in the lodge. I wanted to talk to you."

"Where's Stacy?"

"She took the lift up with the others."

There was an awkward pause.

"Listen, Chantel, I just want to say that I was sincere last night, that it was real. I didn't mention Stacy because she and I have only dated a few times. And nothing's ever happened. I mean, we haven't had sex or anything, in case you're worried about that."

Part of Chantel was relieved to think he hadn't slept with Stacy. A bigger part of her cringed to imagine what her sister would do if she found out about the two of them. "She cares about you, Dillon."

"I care about her, too. We've been friends for almost two years."

"So you wouldn't want to hurt her."

"Of course not."

Chantel took a deep breath. "Then you understand why this—whatever it is that sprang up between us—can't go on."

Silence. Then, "I'm not sure I understand at all."

"Stacy's my sister, Dillon."

"A fact I'm not likely to forget and one I wasn't very happy to discover. But I'm not sure I'm willing to give up a relationship that could work for one that wasn't going anywhere to begin with."

Chantel blinked against the tears welling in her eyes. She thought they'd shared something special; it was gratifying that Dillon felt the same way. But it made no difference in the end. Because nothing mattered except regaining Stacy's trust and proving herself a true friend and sister at last. She needed to do that for herself as much as her sister. "I just…can't "

"Why? I'm not saying we have to do anything right now. We can give it some time, let things cool off—"

"No. I don't want to be responsible for you backing away from Stacy. Last night was a mistake. I'm sorry, Dillon."

Chantel hung up while she still had the mental fortitude to do so. She didn't want him aware of the turmoil inside her. If he sensed her doubt, he'd push, and she couldn't afford that. Couldn't afford to be tempted into forgetting all her new goals and desires. Especially her desire to be the type of sister she should have been in the first place.

The phone rang again, but Chantel refused to answer it. She wouldn't open the door between her and Dillon, not even a crack. She was going to be bigger than she'd been before. Stronger and better. Safer.

"It's too complicated, Dillon," she whispered, even though she knew he couldn't hear her.

The phone kept ringing, on and on. Finally she covered her ears and wept.

HOW SHE MADE IT through the weekend, Chantel didn't know. They were some of the hardest days she'd ever spent, and she'd had her share of hard days in the past year. But she'd managed to keep Dillon at arm's length. He'd tried to talk to her several times and had watched her closely, his confusion and desire showing clearly in his eyes.

She'd turned a cold shoulder to him, refusing to entertain memories of their time together or to consider any contact in the future. He was Stacy's. Off-limits. Period. There was no margin for error in that.

Kicking off her shoes in the middle of her own living room on Monday evening, Chantel turned on the television before going into the kitchen to root through the refrigerator. At least work was getting easier. Today she'd forwarded several letters to Congressman Brown from constituents who needed help on federal issues. There wasn't much a state senator could do to assist someone with the IRS, except to pass on the request. She'd responded to myriad letters on child-support reform, somehow managing to figure out how to do a mail merge on her computer. And she'd learned how to handle the scheduling for the congressman so she could fill in if Nan, in the capitol office, was ever away.

She was beginning to think there was life after modeling. But she still regretted that she had no education. Stacy was a nurse, with a good job in the maternity ward at the hospital. Chantel envied her the pay but knew she could never work so closely with newborns. Always seeing someone else go home with what she wanted most would cause her constant pain.

A knock at the door interrupted her consideration of a frozen burrito. "Who is it?"

No answer.

Frowning, Chantel shut the freezer door and went to peek through the peephole. Whoever it was was standing too far to the right. She could make out nothing more than part of one denim-clad leg. Another solicitor for some worthy cause? They always seemed to come at dinnertime.

Chantel opened the door as far as the chain would allow. "Who is it?"

Wade shifted so she could see him. "It's me. Can I come in?"

Chantel's stomach dropped. *Oh, no. Not now.* It had only been six months since she'd left him in New York, but already he looked different. His hair was bleached blond, an earring dangled from his left ear, and he'd obviously been hitting the weights again. "No. How'd you find me?"

He gave her the grin that had won her heart when she was only nineteen. "We're both from this town. Where else would you be?"

"So what do you want?" she asked warily.

"Just to see you. We didn't part on the best of terms, and…" He ran a hand through his short thickly gelled hair. "I owe you an apology for not being there for you when you were in the hospital."

"I didn't want you with me in the hospital. I told you that."

"I know. You said it was something you had to do for yourself, but that's crazy. For all intents and purposes, you're still my wife, Chantel."

"I was never your wife, Wade."

He jammed one hand into the pocket of his Tommy Hilfiger jeans. "My folks would like to see you."

"I'll try and stop by," she replied, but she said it only

to placate him. Visiting the people she'd once considered her in-laws would prove too awkward. She liked them, but they'd never spent much time together, and she needed her break with Wade to be as clean as possible.

"Steve wants to know if you're coming back. He says he could put you to work right away."

Steve Morgan had been her agent, was still Wade's, evidently, and one of the few people Chantel actually missed. "Tell him I appreciate the thought, but I don't want to model anymore. You both know that."

"Well, I've gotten a few covers. Have you seen them?"

Chantel shook her head. She purposely stayed well away from the magazine racks at the grocery store. The allure of New York was strong enough without reminding herself of the life she'd led there. The easy money. The glamour and the parties. The attention. In those respects, the Big Apple had more than its share of appeal, but that kind of life was lethal to her. She couldn't keep herself well when everything depended on her looks. And when she was there, she couldn't stay away from Wade. He was an addiction as dangerous as any drug, because he thrived on her destruction.

"Are you going to keep me standing outside all day?" he asked. "Can't we at least be civil about this?"

A voice in Chantel's head urged her to refuse him. She supposed that was the voice of wisdom. Instead, she listened to her heart, which told her they'd been together for ten years and should be able to speak kindly to each other now. Closing the door just long enough to slide back the chain, she opened it again, and Wade stepped in.

"I thought you liked contemporary decor," he said, studying her living room, which could have been featured in the magazine *Country Living*.

"*You* like contemporary," she said simply, which pretty

much summed up their problems. Wade had to have everything his way. No one else mattered.

"Well, what you've done here is nice. You look great, by the way."

Chantel had no intention of returning the compliment, even though he did look good. He'd always looked good. And he smelled even better. The Givenchy that was his favorite cologne invaded her senses, bringing back memories she would rather forget.

"Where are you working now?" he asked.

She perched on the edge of a plaid wing-back chair, wishing he'd say whatever he'd come to say and then just go. "I work for a state senator."

"Wow. How'd you get that?"

He thought she wasn't smart enough to do a real job. That hurt her, as always, but she kept her shoulders straight and her head high. "I applied."

"Good for you."

"Are you going to tell me why you're here?"

"You don't know?"

"If it's to talk me into coming back, you can save your breath." Chantel knew she sounded much tougher than she felt and hoped he couldn't see through her.

"How come you never answered any of my letters?"

"Because I never even opened them." She didn't add that she'd saved them, though. They were all lurking in a drawer in her bedroom.

"Why?"

"You know why."

"You think this whole thing is my fault, don't you?" He propped his hands on his narrow hips. "What did I ever do but love you and take care of you?"

And criticize and punish me. "I don't want to go into it anymore."

A fleeting look of fear crossed his face, but he quickly masked it. He'd probably thought she'd come crawling back to him eventually, unable to function without him. Well, she *was* functioning, perhaps not well but adequately, and she was going to continue to stand on her own two feet if it killed her. Even though, after what had happened with Dillon, she felt weaker now than ever. More alone...

"It's Stacy, isn't it?"

"It's you. It's me. It's us. We just don't work. I wish I'd seen it years ago."

A knock at the door interrupted them. Grateful for the reprieve, Chantel ducked around Wade to answer it.

"Hi." Dillon stood on her front stoop, wearing a pair of faded jeans and a chambray shirt, the wind ruffling his hair. The sight of him made Chantel's heart skip a beat and then go into triple time, even though her head warned her he was as dangerous to her peace of mind as Wade.

"Dillon."

He slanted her a crooked smile. "Can we talk?"

Chantel threw a glance over her shoulder, wondering what to do. Wade, always the jealous type, might say something to embarrass her, even though private punishment was more his style. When they were a couple, he'd withhold his affection and pout if he thought she'd paid too much attention to another man. Or, more times than not, he'd just get back at her by being obvious about the petite dark-haired groupies he sometimes slept with.

But none of that mattered anymore, she reminded herself. Opening the door, she let Dillon in.

"Dillon, this is...an old friend, Wade Bennett. He just got here from New York and stopped by to say hello."

Dillon's face grew shuttered, speculative, telling her he recognized Wade's name, but he nodded.

"Wade, this is Dillon Broderick."

Wade didn't bother to smile. Instead, he eyed Dillon from the top of his dark head down to his leather Top-Siders. Just over six feet, Wade wasn't exactly a small man, but Dillon had a few inches on him, broader shoulders and a more powerful build. He also looked far less groomed. While Wade had no doubt checked the mirror only moments before to make sure every hair was in place, Dillon had probably come after a long day at work without bothering to fuss about his appearance. His hair was unruly, as though he'd been running his fingers through it, and a five-o'clock shadow covered his jaw. His "take me as I am" air made him all the more appealing, in Chantel's opinion.

"What's he doing here?" Wade demanded.

"Wade, don't," Chantel said, placing a hand on the doorknob. "You were on your way out. Don't let Dillon stop you."

"I just want to know what's going on. Is this guy trying to move in on my turf?"

"You have no turf, at least not here," she responded.

"So what? You think he just wants to be friends?" Wade chuckled. "Then you don't know guys. He's just trying to get in your pants." Wade spoke to Chantel, but his stare was a challenge, directed at Dillon. And Dillon seemed more than ready to answer it. His jaw tightened and his right hand curled into a fist.

Chantel stepped between them. The crudeness of Wade's words brought a heated blush to her cheeks, but she wasn't about to let the two of them start fighting. "That kind of talk's not going to help anything," she said. "And you have no right. Now, please go."

Wade looked from her to Dillon and back again.

Dillon put one hand on the door, opening it wider. "You heard her, buddy. Out."

"Who the hell do you think you—"

Without even waiting for him to finish, Dillon grabbed Wade by the shoulders and tossed him outside. Chantel gasped, expecting her ex-boyfriend to come up swinging, but Wade merely scrambled to his feet, called them both a few choice names once he was out of range, and took off.

CHAPTER SIX

DILLON TOOK a deep breath, waiting for the adrenaline pumping through his body to subside. "Are you okay?" he asked, watching Chantel make her way over to the sofa and sink into it.

"I'm fine. I just thought... I didn't think he'd go without a fight."

"Guys like him never fight. They talk tough, but when someone calls their bluff, they run."

"Not Wade, at least not if he thinks he can win."

Dillon tried a smile, hoping to calm Chantel down. She'd lived with Wade for something like ten years, if he remembered correctly. "A man who's that concerned about what he sees in the mirror is going to be pretty careful," he said. "Gives whole new meaning to saving face."

Chantel blinked up at him, then laughed. "Can you always tell so much about someone you've just met?"

"Not everyone's that transparent. Take you, for instance. I've only known you four days, but I'm already confused." He took the seat next to her. "I was hoping you could explain a few things."

A certain wariness entered Chantel's eyes, but she nodded.

"I want to know how you could cut things off between us so quickly and easily. I thought you felt something that night. If I wasn't dreaming, you *told* me you did."

"That was before I knew about you and Stacy."

"There is no me and Stacy."

"Dillon, you were dating my sister. I hope, for her sake, that you still are."

"You want me to pretend to feel something I don't?"

"No…yes." Her fingertips flew to her temples as though she had a headache. "I don't know. I just want you to do whatever you would've done if you'd never met me. Stacy's a wonderful person. She'd make someone—you—a great wife."

The alarm that had gone off in his head when he'd first realized who Chantel was rang louder. All weekend he'd been telling himself that they just needed some time to talk, time alone. He'd been sure he could convince her that they should tell Stacy what had happened, explain that it was beyond their control and gain her blessing to keep seeing each other. Now he doubted he could reach Chantel, after all, and wondered if she'd ever open up to him again. "You can say that, after Friday night?" he asked.

She stared at the carpet, and her voice was soft when she answered. "I can't say anything else."

Dillon stood and began to pace. "Chantel, I've already made love to you." He whirled to face her. "I want to do it again, here, now, tomorrow, the day after that and the day after that. I can't forget how it felt to hold you, our bodies joined, and hear you cry out my name. I lost myself in that moment—"

"Stop!" She covered her ears, and when she looked up at him, he saw the tortured expression in her eyes. "It was a mistake, Dillon. We didn't even know each other. I nearly died that night. You saved me. It was an unusual situation. Things happened that otherwise wouldn't have."

"That's bullshit and you know it! It wasn't a passing attraction kindled by the heat of the moment. The spark is still there."

"What? What do you want from me?" Tears started down Chantel's face, and Dillon wanted to kiss them away as he had the night they'd been stranded in the storm. He remembered the silky feel of her cheek beneath his lips, the salty taste of her tears. She'd closed her eyes and given herself up to his comfort. He wished she'd do the same now.

"I want what we had."

"It was an illusion! *I'm* an illusion! Don't you know that? If not, ask the guy you just threw out of here."

"I don't give a damn what he thinks." Dillon knelt before her and tried to pull her into his arms, but she resisted. "Look at me, Chantel."

"You don't know me," she insisted. ' If you did, you wouldn't want me. Men like you are a dime a dozen. They like the idea of having a fashion model to hang on their arm. Big man bags model. That's all."

The insult stung, bringing Dillon's anger back full force. He shoved away and got to his feet. "I didn't know you were a model when I went back for you. How can you say that?"

"Because if you cared about me, you wouldn't ask me to hurt my sister!"

Dillon let the words hang in the air. Was he being selfish to fight for what they had, what he thought they could have? "Stacy can't care that much for me. We've only dated a few times."

"She thinks she's in love with you."

"But that's crazy!" He turned away to stare at the Thomas Kincaid painting above the fireplace. "How?"

Chantel gazed up at him. "Easily," she murmured.

"What about you? Don't your feelings count for anything? Or are you trying to tell me you don't have any feelings for me?"

Dillon held his breath, waiting, hoping she'd give him a crumb of encouragement. But she spoke only of Stacy.

"I almost lost her once, Dillon, my only sister, my only living family. Our mother died of breast cancer when we were in junior high. Stacy's father took off when she was only three. Then my father—the father who raised her—died of a heart attack five years ago. I'm all she has left. And family is family. I'm going to be the type of family she can count on, through thick and thin. I'm going to be there for her, even though she doesn't think I have it in me. Because I love her. And because it's my duty. And because I owe it to her for the past."

He ran an impatient hand through his hair. "What do you mean? What happened in the past?"

"I told you. I nearly lost her."

"How can you *lose* a sister?"

"By stealing her fiancé and running away with him to New York!"

Dillon stared at Chantel's bent head. She was openly crying now. "Wade?" he asked numbly.

She nodded.

DILLON STARED at the ceiling of his bedroom, trying to figure out what he should do. He cared about Stacy, but he didn't love her. He thought he could love Chantel, but she wouldn't let him. And regardless of all the other confusing emotions swirling around in his head and his heart, he wanted Chantel physically, and more powerfully, than he'd ever wanted any woman.

With a groan he rolled over and faced the wall, seeing the crest of an early-morning sun through the branches of the crepe myrtle outside his window. He'd told himself over and over that he wouldn't get emotionally involved, not with anyone. Considering the way Amanda was acting, his two daughters needed him, not more competition for his time and attention. In the two years since his divorce, he'd dated and had fun, but no woman had come close to unlocking his heart. Until now.

Ironically enough, Chantel held the key and didn't want it.

Damn, life could be difficult.

He pictured Stacy's bright smile, the dimple that dented her cheek. He didn't want to hurt her any more than Chantel did, didn't want to ruin their friendship. He liked her, maybe even loved her in a brotherly sort of way, but after meeting Chantel, he knew he had to distance himself. Just in case there was ever a chance—

The telephone on his nightstand rang, and he picked up the receiver, hoping it was Chantel. He'd scribbled his home number on a slip of paper and placed it on her counter when he'd left. But deep down he knew she wouldn't use it. She'd already made up her mind, and her past experience with Wade, along with her drive for self-respect, wouldn't let her change it.

"Hello?"

"I can't believe I finally caught you home."

Dave, his uncle. Dillon smiled. "I went out for dinner last night. Have you been trying to reach me?"

"I've called half a dozen times, just never bothered to leave a message."

"Why not?"

"I hate answering machines."

Dillon released an exaggerated groan. Some of the older generation resisted change more than others. Dave, with his hulking build and gray crew cut, looked like some kind of tough guy. And he was. He was a childless retired marine with a history of promotions and a heap of awards. But Dillon knew him to be a gentle and compassionate man.

The type who talked little but meant every word he said. Dave had made a world of difference in Dillon's life. Though he'd never told Dillon he loved him—he wasn't vocal enough for that—Dillon had never doubted it. Despite all the stepfathers who'd sworn Dillon was worthless, Dave had believed differently. And Dillon had finally decided to prove him right. "I guess e-mail's out of the question, too, huh?"

Dave chuckled. "Damn computers. It's not enough people got 'em in every room in the house. Now they're packing 'em along everywhere they go."

"How's Reva?"

"Still badgering the hell out of me. Won't let me eat my steak and eggs without fussin' about the cholesterol. Weighs all the damn food. I swear, the farm looks as good as it does because work is my only refuge."

Dillon didn't believe that for a minute. Dave loved his Vermont farm, his retirement haven. And he loved Reva as much as any man could love a woman. Dillon knew that if anything happened to her…well, he didn't want to think about what would become of Dave.

"She still make you that chicken-and-broccoli casserole I like?"

"Yeah. I guess she has her moments."

Dillon could hear Reva saying something in the background and knew Dave was catching hell for what he'd said. He smiled to himself. "Tell her I appreciate that she's trying to take good care of you, even if you don't."

"If you call naggin' takin' care of a man…"

"She's the only one who could put up with you."

"That may be true."

Dillon could hear the smile in Dave's voice. They went on to talk about sports and the weather. His uncle never approached subjects any deeper than that, but beneath the surface of everything they said, Dillon felt the strong bond between them.

"When you comin' back this way?" Dave asked.

Dillon had visited the farm twice since the divorce, had taken the girls both times, and knew he'd go back again this summer. Brittney and Sydney loved running around with the dogs, climbing on the tractors and pulling carrots out of the garden. And he loved being with Dave and Reva. "I'll come for a week sometime in July or August."

"Good. Reva will make that casserole you like."

Of course she would. And she'd also make pies and bread, salads with the vegetables in the garden and, despite the cholesterol, they'd grill steaks. They'd drink lemonade on the porch after dinner. Dillon would try to pretend that Dave wasn't getting on in years. And he'd know they were some of the best days of his life.

"Gotta go. Reva says it's time for breakfast."

Dillon smiled again as he hung up and decided he might as well get out of bed. But the telephone rang again before he could so much as move.

"Hello?"

"Dillon, this is Helen."

Helen? His mother-in-law Helen? She hadn't called him once since the divorce. He sat up and propped himself against the headboard. "It's six o'clock in the morning. What's wrong, Helen?"

"It's Amanda." She coughed, then continued in her throaty smoker's voice. "She went to Las Vegas for the weekend with a…friend."

The way she said "friend" let Dillon know it was a man. With Amanda, of course, it would be. "And?"

"And she was supposed to be back last night, but I haven't heard from her."

"Where are the girls?"

"Here. With me."

"Did she leave you a number, tell you where she was staying?"

"No. She called on Saturday morning, but that was it. I'm worried. Brittney and Sydney missed school yesterday, and I missed work. I thought she'd be home anytime, but now…I don't know what to think. I can't miss another day of work or I'll lose my job."

"I'm coming to get the girls," Dillon said, dressing as he spoke. "Do you know the name of the man she went with? Maybe we can call the hotels to see if—"

"She said his name's John Heath, but I've already called all the hotels I can think of. None have a John Heath registered."

"Are the girls upset? Do they know what's going on?"

"They're still asleep. They know we've been waiting for their mother to come back, but they don't seem too worried. They're used to being here with me…a lot."

Dillon clamped down on the anger he felt at that statement. They didn't have to be at Helen's—ever. He wanted all the time he could get with his daughters, but Amanda kept them from him out of sheer spite. That her mother went along with it only added to his frustration and fury. He often wondered what Amanda had told Helen to poison her so completely. "Have you called the police?"

"They said I could file a report tomorrow, but they didn't sound like they were going to do anything about it. I filed one last year when Amanda disappeared for a few days, but it turned out to be nothing, so they think this is just the same kind of…situation."

"I never heard about that. Where was she?"

"Palm Springs."

"With a man?"

"What do you think?"

His poor girls. Their mother had degenerated into a complete mess. What had happened to the woman who used to read to them and play with them and rock them to sleep? "Are you going to let me in this morning, Helen? In the past I haven't caused a scene, for the girls' sake. But this time I won't go away. I'm taking my girls home and—"

"I called you, didn't I?"

"Yes." He sighed. "And that's exactly what frightens me."

Because you wouldn't have done it unless you felt you had no other choice.

"STACY? IS THAT YOU?" Chantel called from the bedroom when she heard the front door open and close. She hadn't expected her sister to drop by the condo this morning, but Stacy lived only fifteen minutes away and she had her own key. Chantel had asked her to keep it in case she ever needed a spare. Stacy had never used it before, but who else could this be?

"Yeah, it's me. Aren't you going to be late for work?"

Chantel glanced at the digital clock on her nightstand as she slipped on her shoes. It was almost eight o'clock already. She'd been up most of the night, unable to sleep because of Wade's sudden appearance and Dillon's disappointment when she'd sent him away. She'd finally drifted off in the wee hours of the morning and then had difficulty waking up when her alarm clock went off at six.

"Darn."

"What?"

Chantel heard Stacy walking down the hall toward the bedroom. "I *am* going to be late. And it's only my second week."

"What happened?"

"I took a sleeping pill."

"Why?"

"Why do most people take sleeping pills?" Chantel said as she brushed past her sister on the way to the kitchen. "Don't you have to work today?"

"No. I only work Thursday through Sunday this week."

"Must be nice."

"Do you want me to come by at lunch? We could go out."

Chantel's breath caught at the casual, offhand invitation, simply because it sounded so natural. Finally Stacy was beginning to trust her again, or at least to like her a little. She turned and threw both arms around her sister in a quick, impulsive hug, the first in more than ten years.

Stacy stiffened, but after a moment, she patted Chantel's back. It wasn't the warmth Chantel was hoping for. But it was a start.

"What's up with you?" she asked as Chantel broke away and grabbed her car keys.

Everything. Nothing. "I'm just glad to see you."

"You're not going to embarrass me today at lunch, are you?" Stacy teased.

Chantel laughed. In her current frame of mind, there was no telling what she might do. "I can't give you any guarantees."

"I brought you a bagel."

Food? Chantel grimaced to herself. She hated food. She waged a constant war with herself—trying to eat when normal people ate, forcing herself to consume amounts that resembled normal portions. She wasn't going to bother this morning. "Thanks, but I'm not hungry. Is that why you came over? To make sure I ate?"

"No, I came over because someone called me last night, and I wanted to talk to you about it."

Chantel paused at the door. "Who was it?" she asked without turning around.

"It's too late now. We'll talk about it at lunch."

DILLON SAT in his newly remodeled kitchen and watched his daughter Brittney frown at her oatmeal. She'd scoop up a bite, stare at it for a moment, then let it drop off the end of her spoon.

"That will do you more good if you eat it," he said, setting the morning paper aside.

"I hate oatmeal."

"It's healthy. Doesn't your mother ever make you hot cereal?"

"No."

"What do you normally eat for breakfast? Eggs?"

"Fruity Pebbles."

"Your mother gives you sugared cereal every morning?"

"No. She tells me to get it myself so she can sleep."

Dillon rubbed his forehead. "Who feeds Sydney?"

"She gets her own, like me."

"I see. Do you get yourselves to school, too?"

"Mom drives us."

Dillon wondered how Amanda managed to get out of bed for that. "Well, I'm going to take you this morning, okay?"

Brittney nodded as the toilet flushed and Sydney came out of the bathroom.

"Did you wash your hands, kiddo?" Dillon asked his youngest daughter.

"Oops." Sydney went back in and emerged with her hands dripping wet. Dillon dried them with a paper towel, then pulled out a chair for her at the table.

She sat down and studied her cereal with the same morbid interest one might view a dead bug on the windshield. "What is it?" she asked at last.

"Oatmeal," her sister replied, the disdain in her voice revealing that it was nothing she was going to like.

"Oh." Sydney glumly considered the prospect of her breakfast. "When's Mom going to be home?"

Dillon wondered which they missed more—their mother or their Fruity Pebbles. "Your grandma and I aren't exactly sure. She's been delayed, but it shouldn't be too much longer." He stood to clear away the dishes, wondering what he was going to do about getting his daughters picked up from school. He had a full day planned at the office, complete with an afternoon of meetings that would be difficult to cancel on such short notice.

"Do you still go home with Mary Beth Hanson after school sometimes?"

Brittney nodded, but Sydney wrinkled her nose. "Mary Beth's mean."

"Only because she doesn't like you always tagging along with us. You should play with Jeremy. He's your age," her sister told her in a condescending voice.

"But he's a boy!"

Dillon gave Sydney a mock wounded look. "Hey, what's wrong with boys?"

"Well, there's nothing wrong with you," she clarified.

"Do you want me to call Mary Beth and see if we can go over there today, Daddy?" Brittney asked.

"Actually, why don't I call so I can talk to her mother."

He dialed the number Brittney recited, but no one answered. "Don't they have an answering machine?" he asked.

"Yeah. Their mom's always on the phone, though. She's probably talking to someone else and just not switching over."

"Great." Dillon took one last look at the list of appointments he had scheduled for the day and sighed. He transferred the Hansons' number to his day-planner, then herded the girls toward the bathroom to get their teeth brushed. They'd come to him with only one change of clothes, which had been dirty, and no toothbrushes. A stop at the drugstore had remedied the toothbrush situation, and a load of laundry at seven this morning had provided clean clothes, but Dillon couldn't help wondering what Amanda was spending all his child support on. Twenty-five hundred a month should stretch far enough to include toothbrushes.

The girls said little on the ride to school. Were they afraid for their mother? Dillon was starting to worry himself. Amanda wasn't the best parent in the world, but he believed she loved the girls. She should have called by now.

He remembered Helen's mentioning that Amanda had disappeared on one previous occasion, and wondered how many things had changed since they'd lived together. Amanda hadn't taken her marriage vows very seriously, but she'd been a responsible mother. Was she still? Or had she become so immersed in a life that wasn't conducive to raising children that she was neglecting the girls? He'd tried to ask Helen this morning, but Amanda's mother was too protective to say any more than she'd already said on the telephone.

"Here we go," he said, pulling over to the curb behind a station wagon and a string of minivans.

The girls piled out, toting their backpacks.

"Do you have your lunches?" he asked.

Brittney waved two brown paper bags at Dillon, then handed one to Sydney. "Dad made them."

"Is there a treat inside?"

Dillon chuckled. "There's a turkey sandwich, carrot sticks, pretzels and apple slices. Plus a juice box." Another item from the drugstore.

Sydney groaned. "No cookies or potato chips?"

"Not today." Dillon looked at his daughters' freshly scrubbed faces. In their own ways they both resembled Amanda, but Brittney, with her dark hair, piercing blue eyes and long limbs, looked a great deal like him, too. Sydney, on the other hand, was petite and blond, with dark brown eyes and a small turned-up nose.

For a minute the doubt that had festered like a sliver beneath his skin prickled Dillon again. Was she his? Short of doing a blood test, there was no way of knowing, and he refused to go that far. Amanda would certainly never admit that there was any question, not while she had him on the hook for so much child support. But every once in a while he wondered—and was tempted to find out for sure.

Until he thought through all the ramifications. What if Sydney *wasn't* his? Would he love her any less? Would he see to Brittney's needs and not Sydney's?

No. Regardless of the genetic reality, he'd committed himself to be her guardian, her protector, her *father*. He wouldn't back out on her now. Which meant he would never seek the truth. And if they were both lucky, she'd never notice the physical dissimilarities between them.

"We'll go out for ice cream tonight, okay?" he told them.

This proposition met with squeals of approval, just as Dillon had expected. At the sound of the bell, they gave him a hug and a kiss and hurried off.

As Dillon sat and watched them cross the schoolyard, concern for their well-being flooded his heart. He'd never wanted to be a part-time father. He'd always imagined himself as the kind of parent his own dad hadn't been—kind, loving, a source of unlimited strength, and an equal partner with his children's mother.

But Amanda hadn't made the kind of commitment marriage entailed. She'd turned to other men, and his marriage had fallen apart. During and after the divorce, he'd refused to let the children be used as pawns, which meant he'd given in to most of Amanda's demands. Only now he wasn't so sure he'd done what was best for the girls. Amanda was getting too wrapped up in her own life and wasn't taking proper care of them.

Maybe it was time he took the gloves off.

Except, if Sydney wasn't his and Amanda knew it, he could never win. He'd lose one daughter trying to save the other. And he wasn't sure he was willing to take that chance.

CHAPTER SEVEN

"So what does an aide to a state senator do, anyway?" Stacy asked, standing just inside the lobby of the office where Chantel worked.

Chantel slung her purse over her shoulder and slid her chair under her desk. "A little bit of everything, really. I'm not a true aide, in that I don't represent the senator at district functions. The field representatives do that. I just open all the mail and schedule their appearances and—"

"Do you do the scheduling for the senator, too?"

"No. Nan at the capitol office in Sacramento does that."

"Is the senator ever here?"

Chantel nodded. "He works in the district office on Fridays and whenever the legislature isn't in session."

"This is a nice place." Stacy surveyed the burgundy-and-gold wallpaper, the molding along the ceiling and the expensive drapes that made the office look more like someone's personal library.

Maureen smiled up at them from her desk across the room. "California senators are treated like princes, although an office this nice is a bit unusual. We got this on a sublease from some attorneys. Our capitol office certainly looks more standard."

Chantel introduced Maureen Ross, the office manager, to Stacy.

"Chantel's doing a great job," Maureen volunteered. "She's particularly good at helping constituents."

Stacy raised her brows. "I should probably know what that is, but I don't."

"A constituent is anyone who lives in the senator's district," Chantel answered. "The people he represents can call or write us when they're having a problem with one of the state agencies, and we sort of act as a liaison to see that the problem gets worked out fairly."

"Like what kind of problem?"

"Oh, for instance, this morning Chantel helped a guy who needed to get his real-estate license right away," Maureen said. "He didn't have time to wait until the Department of Real Estate got around to scheduling the test, so he called us."

"If he didn't get his license quickly, he was going to lose his job," Chantel added. "He works for a mortgage company."

"And did you fix everything up?" Stacy asked.

Maureen motioned to the flowers sitting on Chantel's desk. "She sure did. He takes his test next week. Sent those to thank her."

Chantel smiled, feeling a genuine pride in her job. She certainly wasn't making the kind of money she'd made in New York, but she was doing good things for people and learning a lot about the political process. She even planned to participate in the senator's election campaign next year. "Are you ready for lunch?" she asked Stacy.

"Where do you want to go? Riley's?"

"Sounds good."

They both said goodbye to Maureen, then headed out the front door to Stacy's Honda.

"Do you think I should call and ask Dillon to join us?" Stacy asked, settling herself behind the wheel.

Chantel focused on getting in and snapping her seat belt. While she hoped Stacy would be happy—to the point of allowing her sister the relationship with Dillon she desired herself—Chantel didn't particularly want to spend much time in their company. She didn't know if she could watch the two of them get closer and wonder if she and Dillon might have had a chance if he hadn't met Stacy first.

"If you want to," she said, trying to sound neutral.

Stacy started the car and shifted into Reverse. "Well, I was just thinking it might not seem like I'm asking him out that way, since there's two of us. I don't want to come on too strong, you know. He's met you already, and it could be like three friends getting together for lunch. No big deal."

"Sure. That's great." Chantel couldn't help the lack of enthusiasm in her voice. Fortunately Stacy seemed too busy concentrating on merging into traffic to notice.

"Will you dial the number for me?" She pulled into the street, then handed Chantel her cell phone and recited the number from memory.

Her heart sinking, Chantel dialed. "Ready?"

Stacy sent her a nervous smile and took the phone. "Here goes."

Propping her elbow on the door, Chantel leaned her head on her hand as she listened to Stacy give her name to what must have been a receptionist. After a minute Dillon came on the line.

"Hi, this is Stacy. Chantel and I were just heading out to lunch and thought it might be nice if you joined us. Any interest?"

Please, no, please, no, please no… Chantel chanted to herself. *Come on, Dillon, don't do this to me.*

"…right now…we're going to Riley's Pub… Yeah, it's by the mall… Okay, great! We'll see you there in fifteen minutes or so."

Chantel choked back a groan. Dammit! He'd accepted, just as she'd known he would.

"He's coming," Stacy announced, beaming with excitement. "Do I look okay?"

Stacy's cream sweater and slacks set off her dark hair and eyes and shaped her figure nicely. "You look beautiful. He'll be dazzled." *And I'll be sick.*

"He's *so* handsome, don't you think?"

Damn, was Chantel going to have to sing Dillon's praises every time she saw her sister? Weren't things hard enough? "He's very handsome," she repeated. *And fantastic in bed and courageous in an emergency, and strong in all the right ways, and soft when it really counts...*

"I mean, he's not like Wade," her sister went on, telling her with a fleeting glance that after ten years she was finally able to talk about him. "Wade was probably the most *perfect* looking man I've ever met. Until Dillon, I thought he'd always be the standard by which I measured other men. But for me, he was almost too fussy, you know? I mean, you were with him for ten years. Don't you think he could be too picky, too compulsive about looking good?"

"Definitely." Wade's weaknesses extended far beyond his vanity, but Chantel still carried too much pain and doubt inside her to really open up and discuss him. Reaching across the console, she squeezed Stacy's arm. "I'm sorry, you know. For what I did. Truly."

Stacy kept her eyes on the road. "You've already apologized. And that's not why I brought him up."

"He called you, didn't he? He's the person you were talking about this morning."

She nodded.

"What did he say?"

"That he's still in love with you." She shot Chantel a sideways glance and took a deep breath. "That he wants you back. That you belong together. He thinks your guilt over me drove the two of you apart. He wants me to convince you that it's okay for you to be with him. That I'm over it and I've forgiven you.''

"And?" Chantel fidgeted with the pleat on her slacks.

"And he's right. If you still love him, I want you to go back to him. I don't want you to break up because of me.''

A whirlwind of conflicting emotions assaulted Chantel. She felt guilty for not having made the sacrifice Wade and Stacy credited her with. She felt inadequate because she'd tried to make her relationship with Wade work—after all, she'd certainly paid a high enough price for it—and had failed in spite of her tremendous effort. And she felt angry that Wade would involve Stacy after what they'd both done to her.

"Was it difficult to talk to him?" she asked.

Stacy pulled into the pub's lot and angled the car into a parking place. "It felt weird at first.''

Chantel could imagine. Probably the last time he and Stacy had talked, Stacy had been wearing his engagement ring.

"So? What do you say?" Stacy dropped the keys into her purse and leaned back without making any move to get out of the car.

Chantel glanced longingly at the restaurant. She didn't want to talk about Wade. She didn't want to analyze the many reasons she couldn't go back to him. She wasn't even sure she could explain all of them if she tried. "I can't," she said simply.

"He said your agent has more work for you. You could be on the cover of *Vogue* again. Doesn't that appeal to you anymore? It was all you talked about once you turned sixteen or so.''

Chantel stared out her window, picturing their agent,

Steve, and the photo shoots and the limousines and Wade waiting for her at their artsy apartment.

"Why would you want to give that up to work in a state senator's office?" Stacy asked. "Think of the money."

Finally Chantel met her sister's eyes. "I can't go back, Stace. For a while there...I was sick."

"What does that mean? You don't have AIDS, do you?" She sounded panicky.

"No. Wade's the only man I've ever slept with, not that I couldn't have gotten it from him." She laughed weakly, but Stacy didn't even crack a smile.

"What kind of sick, Chantel?"

Chantel grabbed her purse and opened the door. "It doesn't matter. I'm better now," she lied.

DILLON PAUSED at the entrance to Riley's to allow his eyes to adjust to the dark interior. He liked this place, with its Tiffany lamps, hardwood floors, brass railings and noisy crowds. The food was good here, the company was usually better. Today he didn't really have time for lunch, especially if he had to pick up his girls at three, but the prospect of seeing Chantel again had motivated him to massage his schedule enough to squeeze another hour out of it. She'd asked him not to call her or come to her house again, and he planned to respect her wishes. Which meant he wasn't about to miss an opportunity like this one, even though seeing her in Stacy's presence promised to be awkward, the way it had been at the cabin.

"Dillon!"

Stacy waved at him just as the hostess approached.

"It looks like I've found my party," he said, and weaved through the room to the table where Stacy and Chantel sat. Stacy smiled broadly at him as he sat down, then handed him a menu. Chantel barely acknowledged him before beginning an avid study of the restaurant's offerings.

"How's work going?" Stacy asked.

"Busy," Dillon admitted.

"Well, we're flattered you took the time to have lunch with us, aren't we, Chantel?"

Chantel mumbled something unintelligible, then excused herself to go to the rest room. As she left, Dillon couldn't help but admire how good she looked in her classy suit. And he wasn't alone. She turned a number of heads, both male and female.

Knowing Chantel hated the stares her height inspired, Dillon forced his attention back to Stacy. "What's the occasion?" he asked.

"No occasion. I thought it would be nice to have lunch with my sister."

"Thanks for letting me join you."

She smiled, a little too brightly, and Dillon remembered Chantel's saying that Stacy thought she was in love with him. He hoped she'd wake up one day soon and realize it was just a crush. It had to be. They'd kissed once, but there'd been no real sparks, at least not on his side. Which made it hard to imagine that she'd felt something different.

He studied the colorful ten-page menu, wondering what the chances were of Stacy's meeting someone else. Regardless of the fact that Chantel insisted he not back away from Stacy because of her, things had changed. Rescuing Chantel, making love to her, had made a huge difference in his life. There was no going back now.

"Are you guys ready?" A young waitress, wearing a red-striped golf shirt covered with pins and buttons, a short black skirt and running shoes, stood at his elbow, pad in hand.

"I'm ready," Chantel said, answering his questioning look as she returned to her seat.

Stacy pulled absently on one of her curls. "I'll have the chicken enchiladas."

Chantel ordered the oriental chicken salad. Dillon asked for the Cajun pasta, then passed the waitress their menus.

"You don't have to work today?" he asked Stacy.

"Not until Thursday."

"Must be nice to work only four days a week, huh?"

"Chantel wouldn't have to work even that many if she went back to New York," Stacy said. "Her boyfriend's a model, too, and he's in town right now, trying to talk her into going back with him. He insists she'll be on the cover of next September's *Vogue* if she does."

Dillon felt a prickle of alarm. There might not be any hope for them right now, but he didn't want to see Chantel go anywhere, especially to New York with that jerk he threw out of her house. Especially when she was still fighting the anorexia that had nearly killed her. Even for the cover of *Vogue*. "Is that a possibility?" he asked.

Chantel shook her head. "Not right now."

Stacy drank some of her water. "Personally I think she's crazy if she doesn't go."

"Maybe there's something here she cares more about than fame," Dillon suggested mildly.

"I doubt it. Wade's the love of her life. And fame and fortune are pretty alluring to Chantel. Or at least they used to be."

"Fame and fortune are pretty alluring to everyone," Dillon said.

"Wade's not my boyfriend anymore," Chantel pointed out, although she said nothing in her own defense. She tried to act indifferent, but Dillon knew Stacy's barb had hit its target, and he hurt for her. If only Stacy knew how hard he and Chantel were working to avoid a repeat performance of what had happened with Wade. He wanted to give Chantel's knee a squeeze to reassure her, but he kept his hands to himself.

"Wade still thinks you belong to him," Stacy said.

"Wade has a hard time understanding the word *no,*" Chantel replied.

"Well, Wade's not the only man in New York, you know. Giving up your boyfriend doesn't mean you have to walk away from your career."

Chantel anchored a lock of hair behind her ear. "We talked about this outside, Stacy. I don't want to go back, okay?"

Stacy shrugged. "Suit yourself."

The waitress brought their food, and they fell silent as they started their meals. Stacy moved quickly through her enchiladas, but Chantel mostly picked at her salad, doing more stirring and rearranging than she did chewing and swallowing. Eating was probably hard enough for her when she *wasn't* upset, Dillon thought.

"How are your girls?" Stacy asked.

He swallowed and wiped his mouth with his linen napkin. "They could be better. I had to pick them up from their grandmother's early this morning. On Friday, their mother went to Las Vegas with one of her boyfriends, and she hasn't come back. We're trying to locate her, but until we do, I'm pinch-hitting."

"But you're not used to having them during the school week, are you?"

Dillon barely heard Stacy's question. Chantel had looked up at him with those incredible eyes, turning her full attention on him for the first time since he'd sat down. He managed a crooked smile. "Not really. But I'm improvising."

"Who picks them up after school?" Stacy asked.

"Actually I'm going to have to do it today." He checked his watch. "In just a couple of hours, as a matter of fact. Sometimes they go home with a friend, but I've called and called and haven't been able to reach anyone at Mary Beth's house."

"That means you'll have to leave work early."

He nodded.

"There's no need to do that. I can pick them up for you."

Dillon took a drink of his Coke, just to stall for time. What should he say? He could certainly use the help, but he didn't want to accept anything from Stacy that she might later resent. "That's okay. I'm going to take some work home with me."

Finished, Stacy shoved her plate away. "But there's no need. They know me, so they should feel comfortable about it, and I have the entire afternoon yawning before me with absolutely nothing to do. You know I'm not working today. Let me pick up the girls and help them get their schoolwork done. Then you can come by on your way home." She grinned. "If I'm super-industrious, I might even be able to manage a hot supper for the three of you."

Which sounded entirely too domestic to Dillon. He cleared his throat to refuse, when Chantel lent her support to Stacy.

"Stacy's great with kids," she said. "And she makes a mean lasagna."

"Really, it's no problem for me to—"

"Dillon, stop," Stacy said firmly. "I think your girls are great. I *want* to do this. Now if you'll excuse me, I need to use the ladies' room."

As soon as Stacy was out of sight, Dillon shot an accusing glare at Chantel. "I don't want her to pick up Brittney and Sydney," he said. "That could mislead her into thinking that…I don't know, that there's something more between us than friendship.''

''She's already too far down that road.''

''But what about this dinner thing?''

''You're making a big deal out of nothing. She's an attractive woman with plenty of prospects—''

''Which is exactly what I keep trying to tell you. She certainly doesn't need me.''

''—so it's not like she's going to attack you.''

''I'm not afraid she's going to attack me! Attacks I can handle. I'm afraid she's going to accuse me of using her when she realizes I don't reciprocate her feelings.''

''Then maybe tonight would be a good time to talk about how you both feel.''

''You say that like you have no personal stake in it.''

Chantel played with the condensation on her glass. ''I don't.''

STACY STUDIED HERSELF in the bathroom mirror and groaned. How could she be so stupid? She'd wanted to counteract Chantel's incredible beauty by making her appear shallow.

Instead, she'd made herself look bad and caused Dillon to become defensive of Chantel. She had to get a grip on herself. One minute she felt sorry that she and Chantel weren't closer and wanted to forgive her for everything. The next she did her best to drive a bigger wedge between them.

Love…hate. Love…hate. How did she really feel about her sister? And how badly was she willing to treat her to keep her away from Dillon?

If she kept going on like this, she'd probably chase the two of them right into each other's arms. Somehow she had to calm down and try to develop some confidence. How could Dillon fall in love with her when *she* couldn't think of one reason why he should?

Leaning closer to her reflection, she stared at the small wrinkles that were forming around her eyes and mouth. Laugh lines, she told herself. But they spoke more of age than laughter. She wasn't getting any younger. If she wanted marriage and a family, she needed to coax a proposal out of Dillon—sooner rather than later.

He loved children. Over the past two years, she'd seen him with his daughters lots of times, heard the loving way he spoke of them and to them. They were the center of his life.

Right where she wanted to be.

Stacy pulled her lipstick out of her purse and applied it. She needed some sort of advantage. Something to reassure her that he wasn't going anywhere. Something to make him realize what she already knew: that they'd be perfect together.

She put her lipstick back in her purse and quickly brushed her hair.

Maybe that something should be a baby.

Stacy started to walk out of the rest room, then slumped back against the door, unable to believe her own thoughts. Was she really that desperate? She'd never tried to trap a man before, and she wouldn't stoop to that level now. But if it happened naturally...

She forced a smile to her lips and headed back to the table. If it happened naturally, well, she wouldn't do anything to stop it.

CHAPTER EIGHT

"I HOPE THAT'S a frown of concentration."

Chantel glanced up to see Maureen standing over her desk. She'd been thinking about how Stacy had treated her at lunch. She knew she deserved anything her sister decided to dish out, but that didn't lessen the melancholy that had settled over her in the two hours since then. On top of everything, it had been more difficult than Chantel had ever imagined to see Stacy touch Dillon's arm when he said something funny, or brush against him as they left the restaurant, or smile as though they shared an inside joke. At the cabin they'd had a bunch of friends around and had behaved just like part of the group, but Stacy had treated Dillon differently at lunch.

What if he did as she'd told him to and pursued a relationship with Stacy? What if they got married?

Chantel would have to stay well away. She doubted her attraction to Dillon was something that would ebb with time, but she hoped it would. Especially because she couldn't get close to Stacy if she was always trying to avoid contact with her sister's boyfriend—or husband.

"Are you stuck?" Maureen asked.

Gazing down at the stack of invitations she'd been trying to sort through, Chantel held up one she'd set aside. "I know I'm supposed to schedule the field reps to attend only the functions in their individual areas, but Layne has a chamber mixer at the same time as this ribbon-cutting ceremony. Should I ask one of the other reps to fill in?"

"That'll work. If no one can go, send our regrets. Or pin on a badge and go yourself if you want." She checked the invitation. "It doesn't look like it's going to be that big an event. They're not asking for anyone to speak or anything."

Chantel had secretly hoped to attend some functions in the district. She needed to get out more, meet people. But she hadn't been working for the senator long enough to feel confident representing him. She wasn't even sure of his stand on some issues, only those she'd heard the others talking about over the past two weeks. "Maybe when I've been around a little longer," she said.

"That's fine." Maureen went back to her desk as Lee, another of the senator's three field reps, came in the door.

"Hi, Chantel. Any messages?"

Chantel handed him a couple of slips of paper. "There's more on your voice mail."

"Got those. Thanks."

She was about to ask him if he wanted to attend the ribbon-cutting ceremony, but the telephone rang just then.

"Senator Johnson's office."

"Chantel? It's Stacy."

"Hi, Stace. Did you find Dillon's kids okay?"

"Yeah. I've got them with me now. They're beautiful girls, really sweet, and we're having fun. But you're never going to believe what's happened."

"What?"

"The hospital called. They need me to come in to work. And I'm not expecting Dillon until six-thirty or so."

"Can't you call him?"

"I've tried a couple of times, but the receptionist says he's in a meeting."

"Tell her it's about his kids. I'm sure she'll interrupt."

"I hate to do that. He was so relieved that I was going to do this for him. He must have thanked me three times."

"So you're calling me because—"

"I was hoping you could take them for a little while."

"Stacy, I don't get off until five, and sometimes I stay much later than that."

"You don't have to stay late. No one at the office expects you to."

But they expect me to know something about current events and how to work a computer, and they've given me a huge stack of letters to read and answer. I have so much to learn to make up for the ten years I spent being oblivious to everything but fashion. "I'm just trying to ensure that I'll be successful here."

"You'll be successful. Don't worry. It's not like I'm asking you to get off early or anything. I just want to drop the girls off as soon as you get home so I can run a quick errand at the mall and make it to the hospital by six."

Chantel sighed. She didn't want to take Dillon's kids, because she didn't want to know them. She didn't want to know them, because she didn't want to care about them, or him. She wanted no more links between them.

But this was the first favor Stacy had asked since they'd started speaking again, and she couldn't refuse. "Okay. Will he pick them up at my place at six-thirty, then?"

"Yeah. I'll leave him a message."

"Another call is coming in. I've got to run. See you after work."

Chantel put the call through to Lee, then tried to concentrate on the scheduling again, but it was nearly impossible. Later today she'd meet Brittney and Sydney, the girls she'd heard Dillon talk about with such tenderness that night in his truck. She already felt an emotional connection with them.

How? She and Dillon had had a one-night stand, nothing more, she told herself sternly. And even if what they'd shared was much more than that, she had to get over it.

STACY SMILED to herself as she hurried through the crowded mall, searching for the lingerie store she knew was somewhere near Macy's at the far end. She'd never planned to seduce a man before, but just the prospect of sleeping with Dillon made her feel reckless and excited and aroused. She'd been wanting him to take their relationship into the physical realm for a long time now, but just as he seemed about to get there, he'd suddenly backed off—ever since the cabin in Tahoe. There, they'd gotten into the jacuzzi together, skied together, stayed up late talking and laughing, but there'd been no privacy and he hadn't made a move to touch her since that one chaste kiss after their last date.

That was all going to change, she promised herself. She just needed to buy something he'd find irresistible, make him a great dinner, serve an excellent wine and hope he'd figure things out from there.

Stepping into Monique's Lingerie and Hosiery, Stacy began to admire the filmy nighties and teddies that surrounded her.

"Can I help you?"

A tall thin blonde, who looked a little like Chantel, came forward. For a moment Stacy felt guilty for using Chantel to get the kids out of the way without telling her sister her real plan. But she knew Chantel would only try to talk her out of it. *He'll make the move when he's ready.* That was her favorite line, but Stacy was sick of hearing it.

And she was tired of waiting.

"I'm looking for something that will show my figure to its best advantage," she said.

"A negligee?"

"Or a teddy or something."

The girl's gaze ran up and down her body, assessing her attributes. "Why don't we try something that slims the hips and enhances the bust line? Like a black corset?"

"Fine." Stacy watched the girl select three possibilities, then held them up in front of her while she gazed into a floor-length mirror. A red see-through baby doll with panties was tempting. The feather trim at the top concealed her small breasts. But she wanted something even more wanton, more wicked. Something in black.

"How about this?" the salesgirl asked, presenting Stacy with a black lace push-up bra and matching garter belt to be worn over a pair of thonglike panties. "There's not much fabric here, but it will accentuate your figure in all the right places. Add a pair of silk stockings and high heels, and you'll look absolutely fabulous."

Stacy smiled. Fabulous. That was how she wanted to look. Just like Chantel.

She pushed the thought away. She was short and stubby, with dark hair and ordinary eyes. She could never look like Chantel.

But no man in his right mind could refuse her in an outfit like this.

DILLON SIGHED as he put his briefcase in the backseat and climbed into his rented Taurus. It had been a busy day. He was glad he hadn't had to reschedule all his appointments to go and pick up Sydney and Brittney, especially since he and Jason had just landed another big job this afternoon— drawing the plans for a set of twin towers in downtown Walnut Creek. But he had no doubt Stacy would have dinner waiting for him, and he wasn't looking forward to accepting more of her hospitality while trying to avoid further romantic entanglement. It made him feel like a jerk—even though he would have helped her, had the shoe been on the other foot. They were friends, after all. He just hoped friendship would be enough for Stacy.

Fortunately the girls were going to be there, he reminded himself, missing them. They would make good chaperons and what with homework, baths and school in the morning, they'd provide the perfect excuse for leaving right after dinner. He also wanted to take them shopping for some new clothes tonight. If they left Stacy's early enough, maybe they could swing by the mall before it closed.

Picking up his cell phone, he dialed Helen's number then started his car and eased into the busy street.

"Hello?"

"It's me, Dillon. Have you heard anything?"

"No. I filed a police report today, but like I said, they don't seem to be too worried. They act like she'll turn up when she's ready."

"What do you think's going on?"

There was a long silence. "I don't know. I'd like to think Amanda's not capable of abandoning her children, but I'm not so sure anymore. She really liked this guy."

"She's liked them all. Why is he any different from the rest?"

"He wasn't interested in the girls. Treated them like excess baggage. Amanda always had me take them when he was going to be around."

Dillon was more than eager to have his kids back, especially without further legal complications, but he couldn't imagine the hurt they'd suffer if they ever learned their mother had walked out on them. "Maybe something's happened to her," he suggested.

"Maybe."

It sounded like Helen was crying, but she was a proud, hard-bitten woman, and he knew she wouldn't like him knowing it. "Do you think I should hire a private investigator?" he asked.

"You'd do that?"

"I'm thinking about it." He hadn't made a decision yet. Maybe he and the girls were better off not knowing. For now. But what about later? Amanda would come back eventually. She didn't stay with one man long enough to give Dillon any confidence that things with this new boyfriend would work out.

Either way, the girls would lose, which gave him one more thing to hold against his ex-wife.

"I'll let you know what I decide. Call me if you hear anything," he said.

"I will. Do you want me to take the girls for you next weekend?" she asked.

"No. I'm glad to have them home. I want to keep them."

"Dillon, don't get any ideas about going to court again...."

For a moment, her old hostility was back, but the emotion seemed to falter, along with Helen's words. "Never mind. We'll deal with the custody issues when Amanda gets back. Just be good to them," she said. "And let me see them once in a while, okay?"

How does it feel to have so little control? he was tempted to ask. Dillon had felt almost powerless for two years, but telling Helen how wrong she and Amanda had been wouldn't help the situation now.

"We'll come by on Sunday."

"Thanks," she said softly, and hung up.

Dillon ran a hand through his hair. He needed to work out a car-pool arrangement and a safe nurturing environment for Sydney and Brittney during the afternoons until he could get home from work. Mentally he went down his list of prospects: Children's World, Kindercare, Aunt's Bee's Day-care. He'd have to take time off tomorrow to visit each place, because even if Amanda came back, he wasn't going to let the situation return to the status quo. He wanted his girls, and for their sake, he was finally ready to do whatever it would take to make it official.

"CAN WE RENT a movie?" Brittney asked, setting down the crayons Chantel had bought to entertain them until Dillon arrived.

"Probably not tonight. Your father should be here any minute."

"Where's Mommy?" the younger girl, Sydney, asked her.

It was the first time either of them had mentioned their mother, but after hearing what Dillon had said about her at lunch, Chantel felt a twinge of pity. "I'm not sure, sweetie. She'll probably be back soon, though. Look, I'm making spaghetti and meatballs. Are you hungry?"

They'd already had a snack. Chantel had stopped on her way home from work and bought some chocolate milk and oatmeal cookies, but it was past six-thirty and time for dinner. She'd made an extra large batch of spaghetti, thinking Dillon would be tired and hungry after a long day at the office, but she didn't want to admit to herself that she was doing exactly what Stacy had wanted to do for him.

"Something smells good," Sydney said. "Is it the spaghetti?"

"I think it's the garlic bread. And I've made a little salad. Why don't you girls help me set the table?"

Pleased by the prospect of helping, the two of them put their crayons and coloring books away and started setting out the silverware. "Are you my daddy's girlfriend?" Brittney asked.

Chantel hid a smile. "No. We're just, ah friends."

"He sure has lots of friends," Sydney said.

"I'll bet he does," Chantel muttered, figuring he classified all his romantic interests as friends. It made sense that he'd downplay his relationships, considering how angry it made him that his wife was doing the exact opposite and having the girls call each new boyfriend "Daddy."

"Should we set a place for Dad?" Brittney asked.

Chantel considered the table, wishing she had some flowers for the center. "Yes. I'm sure he'll be hungry."

"Do we have to wait for him? I'm starving," Sydney announced.

Chantel glanced at the clock. Dillon was already twenty minutes late. "There's no need to wait. He can eat when he gets here." As the children washed their hands, she filled their plates. Then she sat down with them and ate some salad while they dug into their spaghetti.

"This is good!" Brittney declared. "I love the meatballs.'"

"I make them out of sausage. Gives them more spice."

It was a quarter after seven when they finished dinner. Leaving a plate for Dillon, Chantel cleaned up the kitchen while the girls watched television. When she was through with the dishes, she decided to read to them. "Anyone got a good book?" she asked.

"We're reading *Charlotte's Web* in school," Brittney said.

"Do you have a copy?"

"It's in my backpack." While Brittney retrieved her book, Sydney turned off the television and settled herself on the couch. Brittney sat on Chantel's other side and they began to read.

"When's Daddy going to get here?" Sydney asked when Chantel had finished two chapters.

"I'm sure he's on his way." Chantel looked at their sweet

faces. *How lucky Dillon is,* she thought. Being a part-time parent was certainly better than not having any children. Like her. "Why don't you go and take a bath for school tomorrow? Afterward, you can each put on one of my T-shirts and lie in my bed and watch TV until your dad comes."

"Cool!" Brittney shouted.

Sydney stood up and clapped her hands. "Cool!" she echoed.

As the girls headed down the hall, Chantel checked her watch again. Dillon was an hour and a half late. Where was he?

She found the business card he'd given her when she'd rear-ended him and called his cell phone, but got only his voice mail.

"Dillon, this is Chantel. I'm getting a little worried about you. Stacy said you'd be here at six-thirty to pick up the girls. They're fine, just so you know, and I'm okay with having them. It's just that they keep asking about you, and I don't want them to worry. Give me a call when you get this message, okay?"

Twirling her hair around one finger, Chantel hung up. Was he all right? Had he gotten into another accident or something?

Please let him be safe, she prayed, trying to will away the apprehension that knotted her stomach. Then she went in to get the girls settled in her bed.

DILLON SAT on the couch, glancing at the clock every few minutes while Stacy cleared away the dishes after the candlelight dinner she'd just fed him. He'd tried to help her clean up, but she'd pressed another glass of wine in his hand and insisted he relax.

He would rather have helped. He already felt bad enough,

letting her baby-sit and now eating her food. He didn't want to add to the list of favors. Besides, he needed some way to keep himself engaged while he tried to work out how he was going to get through the evening without hurting her feelings.

"Do you know when the movie started?" he called to her.

Stacy's voice came from the kitchen. "Chantel didn't say."

"I still can't understand why she'd whisk the girls off to a movie without asking me if it's okay," he repeated for the third time. "I had other plans tonight, and they have school in the morning."

"I told you—Chantel's like that. She's not very practical. She thought a movie might take their minds off their mother and asked me if they could go. Neither of us thought you'd mind. As a matter of fact, I thought it might be nice for you and me to have a little time alone. The cabin was so crowded, you know?"

"Yeah." *Crowded with memories of Chantel.* "Do you mind if I try Chantel's house once more?"

Stacy appeared at the doorway from the kitchen, drying her hands on a dish towel. "I've already left her three messages. She'll call us as soon as they get home."

He set his empty glass on the coffee table in front of him. Stacy's house was far more utilitarian than Chantel's. Chantel surrounded herself with warm jewel tones, lots of textures and art, and it all said, "Welcome home." Stacy's place had functional furniture—vinyl, instead of leather, polyester, instead of silk—and everything was arranged in very symmetrical configurations.

Dillon itched to remodel the twenty-year-old tract house. It needed more light and a fresh coat of white paint. But he felt that way about many of the buildings he entered. He figured it was natural for an architect. Only Chantel's place had felt just right, at least on the inside, and he wasn't sure if that was because of the design, the decor or simply her presence. He suspected the last.

Stacy disappeared, then came back carrying her own drink and a newly opened bottle of wine. "More?" she asked, filling his glass nearly to the brim without waiting for his answer.

"I've probably had enough," he said. She'd served him a couple of glasses of good scotch before dinner, and he'd had quite a bit of wine since. But Stacy was sliding closer, and he didn't know what to do with his hands. So he picked up his glass and began to drink again.

"Are you always this uptight after work?" she asked.

"Am I uptight?" He took another sip.

"You're acting a little jumpy. I'm sorry you're upset about the movie."

"It's not that. It's been a long day."

"Come sit here on the floor. I'll loosen up your shoulders. A friend of mine is a massage therapist. She's taught me a few tricks."

Dillon polished off his drink, then refilled his glass. "Actually I feel fine," he lied. "The chardonnay's great, by the way."

He looked at the half-empty bottle—their second—and realized he'd drunk most of it. He'd probably have a hangover in the morning, but that became the least of his concerns when Stacy slipped her hand beneath his elbow and threaded her fingers through his.

"What ideas do you have about the buildings you're going to design for downtown?" she asked, referring to the new project he and his partner had landed today.

"Something with a lot of glass. We want twin towers that look modern, open. We may have an atrium in the lobby and on the first three floors of each building, or maybe something in the middle that links them. It would break up the space, bring nature back into the concrete world of the city.''

How much longer could the movie last? he wondered. Had Chantel done this to him on purpose? Had she known about the candlelight dinner?

"How's the baby doing? The one who was born last month with the heart condition?" he asked.

"She's hanging in there, but she needs more surgery. She's got a fifty-fifty chance, at least. Ten years ago, she probably wouldn't have survived this long."

"I hope she pulls through."

"So do I." Stacy laid her head on his shoulder and began to snuggle closer, wrapping one arm around his waist.

Dillon loosened his collar by another button and used the excuse of pouring more wine to pull away. "Want some?"

"I've never seen you drink so much," she said. "If you go on like this, you won't be able to drive home." She gave him a meaningful smile. "But I guess we could ask Chantel to keep the girls overnight."

"They're going through a really hard time right now. I don't think that would be wise." He read disappointment in her eyes and felt worse than he had a few minutes ago. Why had he ever asked Stacy out in the first place?

Because they'd known each other for two years, and things were easy, comfortable. She had a lot of qualities he'd liked—still liked. And he'd had no idea their relationship would become so one-sided.

"I'd better get going," he said, standing. "I'll stop by Chantel's later and pick up the girls. I need to hit the mall while it's still open and buy a few things for them to wear. They came to me with very little."

"Want me to go with you?"

"No, it won't be any fun for you. It's just going to be a quick trip. Thanks for dinner."

Dillon retrieved his suit coat and headed out to his car, but he'd gone only a block before he knew Stacy was right—he shouldn't be driving. He'd had too much to drink, and he didn't want to endanger his life or anyone else's. Pulling over to the curb, he used his cell phone to call a cab.

By the time the cab arrived, the alcohol had hit Dillon's blood stream full force, but he managed to remember Chantel's address. He repeated it to the driver.

The cabby blinked, no doubt hearing the slur in his words. "You sure, buddy?"

He didn't care that she wasn't home yet. He'd wait. "I'm sure. Just take me to her."

CHAPTER NINE

THE TELEPHONE startled Chantel awake. She blinked and looked around, confused. She was on the couch and the television was still on, its sound turned low. How late was it?

The chime of her pendulum clock told her the time before she could get her eyes working well enough to check. Nine-thirty. Jeez, it was still early. She must have nodded off as soon as she put the girls to bed half an hour ago.

Shoving herself into a sitting position, Chantel answered the phone.

"Hello?"

"Chantel, it's Stace."

"Hi. How's work?"

"I'm not at work. They ended up not needing me, after all, so I made dinner for Dillon. He's on his way to get the girls. I'm sorry he's so late."

Chantel absorbed this information, wondering why neither Stacy nor Dillon had called her. Maybe they'd been having too much fun.

The thought wounded something inside her, even though she told herself it shouldn't. "No problem. I enjoyed the girls." Which was the truth. If she couldn't have children of her own, Chantel wished Stacy would get married and provide her with some nieces and nephews to spoil.

Maybe that's exactly what'll happen—with Dillon.

"You were really great to baby-sit. I admit I took advantage of you, but Dillon and I haven't had any time alone for a couple of weeks. You understand, don't you?''

''Of course.''

''Great. I owe you one, Chantel. Oh, and one more thing…''

''What?''

''Would you mind telling him you were planning to take the girls to a movie but changed your mind?''

''What?''

''I know it sounds silly, but I didn't want him to worry about Brittney and Sydney, so I told him you'd taken them to a movie. I'd appreciate it if you'd play along.'' She paused. ''I really like him, Chantel.''

So do I. But giving him up was part of her penance, wasn't it? ''What are sisters for?''

''Thanks.''

Stacy hung up, and Chantel let the receiver dangle in her lap as she rubbed her eyes. Dillon and Stacy had spent the evening together while she'd been watching the clock, worrying about him. Stacy should have called her.

Someone banged on her door. Dillon. Already. Chantel put the phone on its cradle, straightened her T-shirt and cutoff sweats, and went to answer it.

He was standing outside, his suit coat slung over one arm, his tie and shirt collar loosened. He looked like he was coming home to her after a long day, and for the briefest moment she felt the impulse to pull him into her arms and bury her face in his neck.

''It appears you've had quite a night,'' she said, instead.

He nodded. ''How are the girls?'' His voice was just a little too loud.

''They're fine. They're asleep in my bed.'' She moved aside to let him in, smelling alcohol mingled with a hint of cologne as he passed. ''How much have you had to drink?''

"Too much." He dropped his coat on the chair by the closet. "Your sister made me a candlelight dinner—steak and potatoes and cheesecake, soft music playing in the background."

Chantel thought of the spaghetti she'd made him, which was a far cry from steak and potatoes and candlelight. "Did you enjoy yourself?"

He cocked one eyebrow at her. "That's what you wanted me to do, wasn't it? Enjoy myself? Fall in love with your sister? You took the girls to a movie so Stacy could create this romantic evening. Would you have been happy if we'd made love?"

Chantel flinched. "If that's what you wanted."

His gaze grew pointed. "Bullshit. You know what I want. I haven't been keeping any secrets."

Rubbing her arms, Chantel walked across the room and settled back on the couch, covering her legs with the blanket she'd brought out from her room. "Did you guys have a talk about your relationship?"

He sat down in the chair opposite her and stretched his legs in front of him, crossing them at the ankle. "What did you think I should say? You won't let me tell her how I feel about you."

"How you feel about me doesn't matter. It's how you feel about her that counts."

"You want me to tell her I feel like she's in the way?"

Chantel decided to change the subject. "I hope you didn't drive here," she said.

"I took a cab."

"Where's your car?"

"Not far from Stacy's."

"Is the cab waiting?"

He crossed his arms over his chest, an act of belligerence. "I sent it away."

Uh-oh. Chantel swallowed, trying to ignore the fact that they were alone. Yes, his daughters were here, but they were asleep down the hall. So she and Dillon had all night—if they wanted it.

Dillon stood and closed the distance between them, sinking onto the couch next to her. Chantel slid over to allow him more room, but the arm of the couch and his large body boxed her in. "Tell me again why we can't be together," he said. "It's crazy, but sometimes I forget."

Chantel closed her eyes. There were times when she forgot, too, or at least wanted to. She could feel the heat of his arm through their clothes and remembered the way his body had warmed her, the smooth supple feel of his skin with nothing between them. She remembered hearing him groan her name when he was too lost in passion to even know he'd spoken. How many times had they made love that night? A lot. Too many times to ever forget.

"Don't make this harder than it already is, Dillon. You've had too much to drink, and you're not thinking straight. I'll wake the girls and drive everyone back to your place."

"Because of Stacy?"

"Because of Stacy. I wish things could be different, but they're not, and there's nothing we can do about that."

"I don't believe it. There's always something that can be done."

"For a price."

He shoved a hand through his hair. "I think it's more than Stacy that's bugging you. I think you're scared."

Chantel took a deep breath. "I *am* scared. I have to believe I've changed. That I'd never hurt my sister again, disappoint my family the way I did when I was nineteen."

"We all make mistakes, Chantel."

"Not this kind of mistake."

"Were you that much in love with Wade?"

Chantel let her rigid control slip a little, felt the support of Dillon's body next to her. "I'm not sure what I felt at first."

"Then what was the attraction?"

"I was awed by him, I guess. Stacy had brought home other boyfriends who sometimes came on to me. But none of them were like Wade. When he was around, the sun shone a little brighter, you know?" She chuckled bitterly. "He was charismatic and charming…and persistent. Even though I'd been teased as a child and still felt quite insecure, I'd been thinking about modeling, and Wade encouraged me, shared that ambition with me. He was always so certain of everything—who we were, where we were going, what we should do next. I let him lead me, and I shouldn't have."

"What about Stacy?"

"He insisted he was going to call the wedding off, anyway, that it had nothing to do with me. But I shouldn't have let him wear me down."

"Did you ever tell Stacy about the things he was saying to you?"

Chantel remembered trying to approach her sister. She'd hinted at it along the way, hoping Stacy would give her the opportunity to be completely honest. But every time she broached the subject of Wade, her sister clammed up and brushed her off. "A few times," she admitted. "But Stacy didn't want to hear it."

"So deep down she knew."

"Probably. I don't know how she could have missed his interest in me, but she wanted the wedding so badly she ignored it. She seemed to care more about catching someone like him, someone other women found attractive, than in marrying the man he truly was. I knew he was too ambitious and spoiled and even selfish, but I was stupid enough to think I could change him."

Dillon put an arm around her and pulled her head down on his shoulder. Chantel tried to resist, but the quiet ticking of the clock in the background and the low hum of the television had a hypnotic effect. She didn't want to think. She just wanted to enjoy Dillon's presence.

"Did you tell your family what you were going to do?"

Chantel shook her head. "Wade insisted it would be less painful for everyone if we simply left." She closed her eyes against the overwhelming regret. "How could I have done such a thing?" she whispered. "When I finally called home, my father told me I wasn't the person he thought I was. He told me never to contact him again."

Chantel felt Dillon gently rubbing her arm, but she was cold inside. So cold she feared she'd never be warm again. She'd betrayed her sister, her father. And now her father was gone. She could never apologize or make it up to him. She often visited his grave on Sundays to say the things she wished she'd said, but she knew it wouldn't change a thing.

"And when you and Wade started having problems? What did your father say then?" Dillon asked.

"Are you kidding? My family never knew. I'd made my bed—I was determined to lie in it. They didn't want anything to do with me. And I didn't deserve their love and support."

"So what *did* you do?"

"Nothing."

"Except nearly starve yourself to death. A self-inflicted punishment."

She rolled her eyes. "That sounds pathetic."

"My father's a psychiatrist. There was a time I wanted to be one, too."

"What changed your mind?"

"A friend who was interested in architecture. He's my partner now. That, and the fact that my father never seems to practice what he preaches. Once he and Mom split, he paid child support, but that was it. I hardly ever saw him. When I did, it felt uncomfortable. And after all these years we're still strangers. Fortunately he lives in Washington D.C. with his second wife and their grown kids, so I only hear from him at Christmastime.''

''Are you glad you're an architect, instead of a psychiatrist?''

''Yeah.'' He smoothed the hair out of her eyes. ''Have you ever seen anyone for counseling, Chantel?''

She laughed weakly. ''Are you suggesting I'm crazy?''

''No. I just think it might be a good idea to talk to someone who could help you come to terms with all this.''

''I've never wanted to tell anyone. I don't know why I told you now.''

''Could it be that you were hoping I'd decide you were a bad person, someone I couldn't possibly love?''

The way he tilted her chin to look into her eyes made Chantel fear he was going to kiss her. But he didn't. He just stroked her jaw with the pad of his thumb until she wished she could feel his lips on hers again, feel the completeness they'd experienced once.

''Let's get some sleep,'' he said. Standing, he turned off the television and the lights. Then he pulled her down beside him on the couch, her body cradled by his, and covered them both with the blanket.

STACY STOOD in front of the mirror wearing her black lace bra and garter belt. What had gone wrong? The meal had been perfect, the wine superb, the music and lighting soft and relaxing. So why had Dillon rushed off?

Taking another sip of wine, the last of the bottle, she sank to the floor. If she looked as good as Chantel did, he wouldn't have left without so much as a peck on the cheek, she thought dejectedly. It was just that she reminded men of their sister or their mother. As a result, they were always friendly but practical. Uninterested in romance.

The telephone rang, and Stacy gulped the rest of her wine before she crossed to the nightstand to answer it. "Hello?"

"You sound odd. Were you asleep?"

Wade. Stacy glanced at her empty glass and wished for more. "No."

"Good. Then you don't mind talking?"

"For a minute." She knew she should tell him to go to hell, but the sound of his voice still stirred something in her. She hadn't been able to hang up on him when he'd called her yesterday, either.

"Did you speak to Chantel?"

"Yeah. She's not going back to you."

There was a long pause. "Why not? Is it that other guy?"

"What other guy?"

"I don't know. Some guy came to the house while I was there."

Stacy considered that for a minute. Chantel had only been in town for a few weeks. Stacy was pretty sure she wasn't seeing anyone yet. "Must be her neighbor or something. She hasn't been dating that I know of."

"He seemed pretty damn possessive for a neighbor."

She couldn't picture Chantel's neighbors. Had she met any of them? She wasn't sure. She'd have to think about it again in the morning. "I don't know who he is. I'll ask her later."

"You do that."

"How long are you in town?"

She heard him sigh. "As long as it takes."

"I don't think hanging around will do you any good. You're not going to change Chantel's mind."

"She's always come back to me in the past."

"She's left you before?"

"Just for a day or two, here and there. No relationship is perfect."

Something else suddenly occurred to Stacy. "She said she was sick while she was in New York."

"Naw, she had it good in New York. She's a fool to walk away."

"Oh."

Silence fell between them, and Stacy fiddled with the ribbons on her corset, wondering what her life would have been like if she'd married Wade. Had he changed much? Did he still have any feelings for her? "Are you staying with your parents?" she asked.

"Yeah."

"Are you comfortable there?"

Another long pause. "You offering to let me stay at your place?"

"Maybe."

"'Maybe' doesn't tell me whether or not to make the drive."

Stacy wavered for a minute, indecisive. Part of her was thrilled at the thought of being with Wade again, at the prospect of possibly stealing him back. Maybe then she could finally assuage her wounded ego and forgive Chantel.

She moved close to the mirror again and stared at her reflection. Maybe her new lingerie *would* come in handy, after all.

"Do you want me to come over or not?" he persisted.

Stacy sucked in her stomach and turned sideways to see her profile. She looked great, she decided. Maybe he'd be sorry he left her.

His regret would feel wonderful. She knew it would. "If you want to," she said, and hung up.

"IT'S LATE. Where are you going?" Wade's father asked, looking away from the television long enough to frown at him.

"A friend's," Wade answered indifferently, searching the keys dangling from a rack of little brass hooks on the wall.

"Chantel's? She taking you back?"

"That's not where I'm going, but she'll take me back. It's just a matter of time."

Henry mumbled something about Chantel and good sense, but Wade wasn't listening. His parents' disapproval of him and his life-style wasn't anything new. "Can I take the Cadillac?"

"You gonna fill it up?"

"Come on, Henry, you know I don't have any money."

His father shook his head, his face revealing disgust. "I'm not likely to forget, not when it's me who paid the rent on your fancy New York apartment for three months before you lost it. But I'll tell ya, I'm getting mighty sick of helping out. You're thirty-three years old, Wade, too old to be depending on us. You said you wanted to come out here and look for a job, so I bought you a plane ticket, but I haven't seen any job search going on."

"My agent called. He thinks he has something lined up for me, something that'll pay me more for one shoot than you've ever made in a year."

"Great!" his father exclaimed, nearly jumping out of his recliner. "Then make more money than me, get another apartment and pay your own damn bills! That's exactly what I want you to do!"

"Henry." Wade's mother's quiet rebuke came from the kitchen, where she was busy cleaning the refrigerator or dishing out ice cream or doing something domestic, as always. "Let's not have words. Wade's just had a run of hard luck lately. Ever since Chantel left, he's been too upset to work—''

"And when she was around, he was doing too well to bother with us. We heard from him maybe once a year."

"They were busy, dear. You know how it must have been with all those photo shoots. You've seen the covers."

"I've seen Chantel on the covers."

Wade's restraint nearly snapped. Who was his father, Mr. Middle America, to criticize *him?* The sum total of his father's working career had given his parents nothing more than twenty-year-old tract house, a modest pension, a 1988 Cadillac and a 1996 Buick.

"If he'd stayed home and gotten an education like his brothers, he'd have a steady income," his father was saying, but Wade had finally spotted the keys to the Cadillac. Scooping them off the kitchen table, he strode from the house, leaving his parents to argue without him. He'd heard everything he wanted to hear from them. The story was always the same. They didn't understand that he was destined for bigger things, that he'd settle for nothing short of the fast-track life he'd enjoyed for the past ten years. He'd had it all until Chantel left him. Then things had gone downhill. But as soon as he got her back, they'd take New York by storm.

Fortunately for him, Stacy had just provided him with the perfect way to get her attention. And possibly a little revenge.

WHERE WAS HE?

Still wearing the lingerie she'd purchased at the mall, Stacy pulled on a silky robe, belted it and poured herself another glass of scotch. Maybe he wasn't coming. She was probably crazy for even inviting him. After Dillon left, she should have gone straight to bed. Instead, she'd gotten herself drunk.

For a moment she considered calling Wade back and telling him not to come. But it was probably too late. He'd be here any second. Besides, she wasn't sure she *didn't* want to see him. She wasn't sure of anything.

Crossing her legs, she admired the way her high heels accentuated the muscles in her calves, then rested her head back on the couch, feeling the gentle burn of the liquor. At first she'd been nervous, almost panicky, at the thought of seeing Wade again. But the more she drank the less she worried. Ten years ago she'd worn his ring, planned to become his wife, warmed his bed, and he'd run off with her sister. Why hold it against him?

Giggling at that, she took another sip of her drink. No big deal, she told herself. She just wanted to see him again. He hadn't been the most giving lover she'd ever had, but he'd possessed the kind of charisma that made whoever he was with feel special. Unless that had changed, along with everything else.

If it had, maybe she *didn't* want to see him again. She couldn't decide. But even that didn't seem to make much difference, not in her current frame of mind.

The doorbell rang and Stacy got up to answer it. "Knock, knock...who's there?" she chirped, suppressing another giggle.

When she opened the door, she found Wade leaning against the railing, wearing a pair of blue jeans, a short-sleeved shirt and a maroon sweater vest. Except for the bleach in his hair and the short cropped cut, he looked very much the way she remembered him, as handsome as ever. Golden skin, well-defined arm muscles, a knowing grin. The earring he wore in one ear glinted in the porch light. She remembered the night she'd met him at a dance club. He'd dazzled her at first sight, made her feel breathless—and he did the same to her now.

Or maybe that was the liquor.

"Come in," she said, holding the door open and trying not to sway on her feet.

He moved past, smelling like expensive hair products and too much cologne, and surveyed her living room. "You own this place?" he asked.

She nodded. "Can I get you a drink?"

His gaze cut to the bottle of scotch on the coffee table, then to the glass she still held in her hand, and his smile widened. "Sure. Looks like you've got a head start on me, though."

"I've had a few." Stacy had already brought an extra glass from the kitchen. She bent to pour him a liberal amount, but he took the bottle from her unsteady hands and filled the glass himself.

"It's been a long time," he said, watching her. "I like the changes."

"Yeah?" She smiled and struck what she hoped was an appealing pose.

"You look good."

"But not as good as Chantel?"

He cocked an eyebrow at her. "Not many women look as good as Chantel," he said simply.

"Is that why you left me for her?"

Downing his scotch in one gulp, he set the glass on the coffee table. "Did you invite me over so you can bitch and moan about what happened ten years ago?"

Stacy chuckled softly. He had no idea what he'd put her through and he didn't care. Well, neither did she, not right now, anyway. "Don't you think you deserve it?"

"Let's just say that's not why I came here. We could have talked on the phone." Reaching out, he loosened the top of her robe and gazed inside it. "And I doubt you wear that little number to bed on a regular basis. I wouldn't want to waste it."

She laughed, feeling attractive, wanton in her sexy lingerie. "Aren't you even going to ask me how I've been before you start taking off my clothes?"

He shrugged, letting his fingers glide back and forth over the curve of one breast. "Okay, how've you been?"

She watched the movement of his hand. "Busy. I'm a nurse, you know."

"Great," he said, pulling her roughly to him. "Let's play doctor."

"DADDY, I'M HUNGRY."

Dillon opened his eyes, and Sydney's face came slowly into focus. He still held Chantel, could smell the scent of her shampoo and feel her arms over his own, as if she was afraid he might let go. He wanted to nuzzle the soft skin beneath her ear, but he didn't. There was no need to confuse Sydney. Or chase Chantel farther away from him.

"You up already, sweetheart?" he asked his daughter, disentangling himself.

Chantel stirred, and he eased out from behind her. As anticipated, he had a splitting headache, and his mouth felt like cotton.

"Can we have sugar cereal today, Daddy?"

Sydney's words seemed to stomp through his head. He winced at the noise, then wondered where Chantel stored her aspirin. "What time is it?" he asked.

"Time to get up," she replied.

He chuckled, but that hurt his head even more. If ever he'd longed for a box of Fruity Pebbles, it was now. He wanted to pour Sydney a bowl of it, then sink into a chair where he could sit quietly until the pain lessened.

"Dillon?" Chantel was awake now, gazing up at him with her long hair mussed and one side of her face imprinted with the pattern of the couch pillows.

And still she looked beautiful to him.

"Sydney's up and she's hungry. Mind if I look for some cereal?"

"There's some Wheaties and All-Bran above the stove."

Sydney wrinkled her nose. "Yuck."

Dillon didn't bother to chastise his daughter for her poor manners; his head hurt too badly. "I don't suppose you have any Fruity Pebbles, do you?"

"You let your girls eat that stuff?"

He would have chuckled again, but didn't dare. "Oatmeal didn't go over too well yesterday. And today I just want to keep the racket down."

She stretched and smiled. "Oh, yeah. Last night." She eyed Sydney without saying more, and Dillon appreciated her discretion. He hadn't had a hangover in years, not since he'd quit partying with the college crowd—except for that first Christmas without Amanda and the kids.

"What happened last night, Daddy?" Sydney asked.

"I had to work late," he replied. "How 'bout we fix up that All-Bran with some honey?"

"Or strawberries," Chantel suggested. "There's some in the fridge."

"Strawberries?" Brittney stood at the end of the hall. "That sounds good."

"On *bran* cereal," Sydney muttered.

"Oh, I get it now."

This time Dillon gave them a warning look. "Hey, when you're a guest at someone's house—"

"—you eat whatever they put in front of you," Brittney finished.

"With a smile," Dillon added.

"They don't have to act like guests around me," Chantel said, throwing off the blanket and getting up. "Here, you guys sit down. You, too, Dillon, and I'll get something for your headache and see what I can come up with for breakfast."

"Just a little cold cereal will be fine," Dillon insisted. "We don't want to put you out. Or we can call a cab and eat back at our own place."

"You won't be talking about eating at your place when you smell my pancakes," Chantel said.

Dillon admired the long lines of her legs as she moved about the kitchen. He wanted to repeat everything they'd done that night in the storm—wanted to make love to her again and again. Only, she wouldn't let him close, and he knew he'd break the fragile person sheltering inside her if he pushed.

Noticing the clean plate and cup she was clearing from the table, he guessed she'd been planning to feed him dinner last night. But that didn't make sense. "What movie did you guys go see?" he asked, pulling Sydney onto his lap. Even though she was getting a little too big to sit there comfortably, he knew it was still her favorite spot.

"We didn't go to a movie," Brittney said. "Chantel helped us finish our homework and read *Charlotte's Web* to us. Then we had our baths, and she dried our hair while we sang to the radio. It was fun."

"And we ate meatballs," Sydney said.

"With sausage," Brittney added.

He kissed Sydney's cheek, picturing the domesticity of the scene and wishing he'd been with them, instead of guzzling scotch and wine at Stacy's. "I'm sorry I missed it."

"No one makes spaghetti like Chantel."

"I'm not much of a cook," Chantel admitted, "but I can make a good pot of spaghetti."

"If I'd known you weren't at the movies, I would've been here. Why didn't you answer the phone?"

"Because it didn't ring," Sydney said.

Dillon's gaze clashed with Chantel's. "Wait a second. It was a set-up, wasn't it?"

Chantel didn't answer.

"Just tell me one thing," he persisted, the anger he'd felt last night returning. "Was it your idea? Were you in on it?"

She paused, spatula in hand. "Would you believe me if I said no?"

He considered the sincerity in her voice and his anger eased, replaced by a glimmer of hope. "If things had gone the way Stacy planned, would you have been happy about it?"

"Please," she murmured. "Don't ask me that."

But the look on her face was all the answer he needed.

CHAPTER TEN

DILLON UNLOCKED the Taurus, which he'd parked near Stacy's house, and got his girls strapped in, then thanked Chantel for the ride—and for the huge breakfast she'd made. Pancakes, eggs and orange juice. A big improvement on cereal, as far as his daughters were concerned. But now they needed to hurry or Chantel would be late for work and the girls would be late for school. Dillon had already called his receptionist to say he'd be taking the morning off.

"Any chance you'd let me thank you for helping with the girls by making you dinner this weekend?" he asked Chantel, bending to see inside the window of her Jag. "Just as friends?"

She started to shake her head, then seemed to think better of it. "Just as friends?" she repeated.

Dillon smiled. "You can't have too many friends."

"Especially when you're new in town." She glanced quickly toward Brittney and Sydney and waved. "I really like your girls, Dillon."

"They like you, too. They want to see you again."

She sighed. "Okay. When?"

"Friday at six-thirty work for you?"

"As long as you invite Stacy, too."

Dillon scowled. "Are you sure you want all three of us to be together?"

"That's the only way I can see you. I won't go behind her back."

He thought for a moment. It would be awkward, but there was certainly merit to doing things as a threesome. Stacy would probably be less aggressive. Chantel might relax enough that he could get to know her better. And neither of them would have to deal with any guilt.

"Okay, you win. I'll ask her today. You'd better get going."

She flashed him a grin, waved to the girls again and drove off.

He watched until the taillights of her car disappeared around the corner, then blew out a long sigh. What was he going to do? He had a missing ex-wife, a friend who wanted to be his lover and a lover who wanted to be his friend. Would there ever be a time when life became less complicated?

Sliding behind the wheel of the Taurus, he started the engine, then remembered that he'd meant to stop by Stacy's. He'd forgotten his pager at her place last night, and Sydney had left something she'd made at school.

He glanced down at his wrinkled shirt. Would Stacy assume he hadn't been home if she saw him? He had yet to shave, and his hair was uncombed, but it would be so much easier to stop there now, instead of driving all the way back later in the day.

"What's wrong, Daddy? Why are we sitting here?"

Dillon looked over at Brittney. "I was just thinking, honey. Sydney wanted me to pick up the puppet she made in school yesterday, which she left at Stacy's. But I think I'd better get you girls off to school first."

She frowned. "I have band today and my clarinet's at Mom's. What am I going to tell the teacher?"

"What time do you need it?"

"At noon."

"Then I'll rent one and bring it to the school, okay? No

worries." He squeezed her hand, hoping to coax a smile out of her, but her brows drew together.

"Does that mean Mom isn't coming home?"

With a click from behind, Sydney released her seat belt and leaned through the crack in the bucket seats. "She's probably coming back today, right, Dad?"

What did he say? Either their mother was too badly hurt to call or find her way home, or she'd abandoned them.

He didn't want his girls to hear either explanation. He didn't want his girls to live with either possibility. "We don't know yet," he said. "I haven't heard from her. But I'm sure I will."

"Why can't we go look for her?" Sydney asked, and it was while he was gazing into her troubled eyes that he realized he couldn't let the mystery last forever, regardless of the ugly truth that might be uncovered.

"Because we don't know where to look," he told her. "But I know of someone who might be able to help us."

"Who?"

"He's called a private investigator."

BY THE TIME he'd gotten the girls off to school, then showered and shaved, Dillon felt like a new man. He had a long list of errands, but his secretary had managed to clear his schedule, and he was determined to use the morning as productively as possible.

First on his list was retrieving his pager from Stacy's, so his office could get hold of him even if his cell-phone battery gave out. As he turned down the same street where he'd parked his car the night before, he thought of the barbecue he'd mentioned to Chantel and made a mental note to invite Stacy. Repaying her for the dinner she'd made him might even the score a little and make him feel less like a traitor.

An old brown Cadillac sat in the middle of Stacy's driveway. He wondered briefly who could be visiting so early, but Stacy had a lot of friends. He assumed it meant she was up and headed to the front door.

But it wasn't Stacy who answered his knock. Wade stood there staring out at him, wearing nothing but a pair of pants that weren't buttoned all the way up. They blinked at each other, then Wade started to laugh.

"Stacy, you've got a visitor," he said. "Let's hope you don't have him throw me out like Chantel did. This is starting to get pretty repetitive."

"What?" Stacy appeared at Wade's side, wearing a silky robe and carrying a cup of coffee. When she saw him on the stoop, her eyes widened and her jaw dropped. "Dillon! What are you doing here?"

Dillon wished he'd decided to do without his pager or had simply bought a new one. "I'm sorry. I didn't realize—"

Stacy's blush climbed from her neck to the roots of her sleep-tousled hair. "Um, it…it's not what you think," she said. "Wade and I used to be engaged, but…actually, he and Chantel are, um, involved now. Not us."

"He knows who I am," Wade volunteered. "We met at Chantel's, didn't we, buddy?"

Stacy's cheeks retained their flush, but the expression in her eyes altered. "You what?"

"This is the guy I was telling you about last night. The one who showed up at Chantel's while I was there," Wade explained.

Stacy looked dazed. "Is that true?"

Dillon didn't know how to answer. He just knew it was imperative she not find Chantel at fault. "I stopped by, but your sister basically told me to get lost."

Wade splayed his hands on his hips. "Oh, yeah? I guess

that was after I left, because I specifically remember her inviting you in.''

Dillon's hand itched to smash Wade in the face. This pretty boy had carelessly cost Chantel her family ten years ago, and he obviously wasn't about to stop causing trouble now. ''As I remember, you were making quite a nuisance of yourself, and we had to handle first things first,'' he said.

''What were you doing at my sister's?'' Stacy asked him. The color had drained from her face, and Dillon could only imagine what she was going to say to Chantel.

''I asked her if she'd be willing to go out with me,'' he admitted.

''And?'' Stacy's voice was barely a whisper.

''She said no.''

''Because she's still in love with me,'' Wade interjected.

Dillon looked him in the eye, then turned back to Stacy. ''No. Because she loves *you*,'' he told her. Then he walked away, leaving behind his pager, his daughter's puppet and the damage he'd wreaked. But not the memory of the pain in Stacy's eyes or the sickening knowledge that Chantel would pay the price.

And it was his fault.

STACY THOUGHT she might throw up. Waking to find Wade in her bed had been bad enough. She'd hoped, until she actually opened her eyes, that last night had been nothing but a bad dream and simply wanted to forget the whole thing. She'd made a mistake. That was all. A big mistake that left her feeling worthless and dirty and used.

But it was nothing compared to the humiliation of Dillon's catching her with Wade. What must he think? Wade had answered the door only half-dressed! And she was sure that her weak attempt to cover for what had happened between them had done nothing to convince Dillon. The truth had been staring him right in the face.

Except that it didn't matter. Dillon didn't care about her, anyway. He wanted Chantel, just as she'd feared from the beginning. It was all happening again. She'd talked herself out of believing Dillon had any interest in Chantel; she'd told herself to have some self-confidence. But he *had* been interested in her sister. Was probably *still* interested in her.

Wade was looking at her oddly. "Are you going to pass out or something? What's wrong?"

What's wrong? she wanted to shout. *What's always wrong—Chantel, of course. And you. And my own stupidity.*

Without another word she fled to her room. She needed to be alone. She needed to shower and wash every trace of Wade from her body, and wished she could wash away the memories just as easily. The thought of his touch sickened her.

But he followed her down the hall and held her door open so she couldn't shut him out. "What's gotten into you?" he asked. "Who was that guy?"

"I *thought* he was my boyfriend," she muttered, glaring up at him.

"And Chantel's been seeing him?"

Stacy didn't know how to answer that. Dillon had said Chantel turned him down, but how was she to know whether or not that was true?

"Stacy?" She felt Wade touch her arm, remembered his hands elsewhere on her body, and swallowed against a rising bout of nausea. She'd wanted to seduce Dillon last night. She'd served him a candlelight dinner and hinted that she'd serve him more. And instead, she'd taken her one-time fiancé into her bed.

Ugh! It was too awful to bear thinking about!

"So what are you going to do?" Wade asked, his brows knitting as he watched her.

"I'm going to talk to my sister, like I should have when I first noticed you panting around her skirts," she said. "Now let go of me and get out. And don't ever come back."

"WHERE DID I PUT that?" Chantel murmured to herself, searching her desk for the form letter she was supposed to send to any of the senator's constituents who were concerned about attaining a "wild and scenic" designation for the South Fork of the Yuba River.

"Did you say something?" Maureen called from her own desk.

"No, nothing." Chantel ducked behind the divider that separated her from Maureen and dug her nails into her palms. Her mind wasn't on her work today. It was on a pair of strong arms holding her through the night, and the thought of seeing that same man again this weekend. But she couldn't afford to daydream about Dillon. She had to focus; she'd made too many mistakes this morning. Chantel knew she still had to prove herself—especially since the senator had hired her despite the fact that his top aide had recommended someone else.

Slowly releasing her breath, she tried to calm down and remember. Then she laughed when her eyes lighted on the letter she needed. It was sitting, plain as day, on the tray where she kept the employees' messages.

The telephone rang and she picked it up.

"Senator Johnson's office."

"Hi, Chantel. This is Tim."

The senator. Tim Johnson. She'd only seen him once since he'd interviewed her. Chantel felt a nervous flutter in her chest. "Good morning, Senator," she said.

"How are you?"

"Fine, thank you."

"Good. Listen, we're going to be having a staff meeting tomorrow morning, so I want you to remind everyone to come in an hour early. Afterward, I'll be seeing a couple of people in my office. Will you make sure we've got doughnuts or something I can offer them? And some decent coffee?"

"Of course."

"Also, tell all the aides I'll be expecting their reports for last month. No excuses."

"Of course." She jotted it down.

"Thanks."

The other line rang, but Chantel waved for Maureen to answer it.

"I'm doing a fund-raiser with the governor, a barbecue," the senator continued. "Will you check with the campaign-committee chair and make sure the invitations went out? I have a new man running things, and I don't want any screw-ups on this."

"I'll take care of it."

"Great. You're welcome to come to the fund-raiser, too, you know. And feel free to bring a friend."

Chantel thought of Stacy and wondered if her sister would like to meet the governor.

"Line two is for you," Maureen called to her. Chantel nodded, her attention still on the senator, who was thanking her and saying goodbye.

"Could you put me through to Layne?" he asked when he'd finished.

"Of course."

Chantel punched the "hold" button, then panicked when she couldn't remember how to transfer the call.

"Star 89," Maureen reminded her, and Chantel breathed

a sigh of relief when she heard Layne's voice boom out from behind his door, "Hello, Senator."

Seeing the flashing light on line two, Chantel picked up, expecting to hear Stacy's voice. Her sister was the only one who'd ever phoned her at the office.

"Stace?"

"It's Dillon."

"Oh, hi. Did you get the girls off to school okay?"

"I did. Then I rented a clarinet for Brittney and brought it by the school so she wouldn't miss band and I ran some other errands." He cleared his throat. "Listen, Chantel, I'm afraid I have some bad news."

"Did you find your wife?"

"Not yet. It's not that kind of bad news, but I wish it was. Then it would be my bad news and not yours."

Chantel felt a chill climb up her spine. "What is it?"

"I went to Stacy's this morning to get my pager. I accidentally left it there last night."

"And you wanted to get Sydney's puppet. I remember you said something about it at breakfast."

"Well, you'll never guess who answered the door."

Chantel couldn't even imagine. Stacy didn't have a roommate. Another man? But why would that be bad news? "You got me. I don't have a clue."

"Wade."

She chewed on the end of her pencil, trying to imagine Wade at her sister's house. "What was he doing there?"

There was a slight hesitation. "I'm not sure. He wasn't wearing much. I think he might have stayed the night."

Chantel expected the thought of that to bother her. But it didn't. Although she was concerned about Stacy. "I hope she's not stupid enough to get involved with him again, Dillon. He'll chew her up and spit her out without a second thought."

"There's more."

"What?"

"He recognized me. And he told Stacy I'd been to your house."

Chantel squeezed her eyes shut. *Please, God, not when she was trying so hard to do the right thing. Poor Stacy!*

"Chantel?"

"I'm here."

"I just wanted to warn you, in case…"

In case Stacy's upset. And of course she will be.

"Thanks for letting me know," she said at last.

"I told her I went to your place to ask you out, but you refused. At this point, I think the truth is our safest bet."

"But not the whole truth, Dillon. Not about that night in the storm. I'm afraid…I'm afraid that would be the last straw."

Dillon remembered the look on Stacy's face and hoped they hadn't reached that point already.

"I won't say any more."

"Okay."

"I'm sorry, Chantel."

"I know."

She hung up and sat staring at the phone, and all the work piled up on her desk around it.

What was she going to do now?

THE INTERCOM buzzed, interrupting Dillon's efforts to fit ten window offices and a reception area into two thousand square feet of garden-style office space on his computer-assisted design program. He generally liked doing tenant improvements. For the most part, they were quick and easy, the bread and butter of his business, but he was having a hard time concentrating on anything this afternoon. He kept seeing Wade, barely dressed, at Stacy's, and wondering what it could mean, in the end, for all of them. And his secretary had interrupted him several times already.

"What is it, Kim?" he asked, buzzing her back.

"There's a Stacy Miller here to see you."

Stacy. She'd come on to him last night, then slept with her ex-fiancé, but knowing her the way he did, he doubted she was proud of it. "Send her in."

Turning off his computer, Dillon pushed back his chair and stood as Stacy stepped into his office, wearing a pair of black slacks and a crisp white shirt, and looking painfully self-conscious.

"Hi, Dillon," she said.

"Hi, Stace. You want to sit down?" He propped himself on the corner of his desk and motioned to one of the chairs close by.

She moved forward and took a seat, but she couldn't seem to meet his eyes. "I came to apologize for last night."

Dillon studied her face, noting the fresh blush that tinged her cheeks. "You don't owe me any apologies, Stacy. We've never had any commitments between us."

"I know, but it couldn't have looked very good, what you saw this morning."

"Are you telling me Wade didn't spend the night?" For her sake, Dillon hoped so.

She squirmed for a moment, but finally shook her head. "No."

He wondered what he could say to make her feel better. She was obviously miserable. "Are you sure you want to start seeing Wade again?" he asked.

"I don't want anything to do with him. Last night I'd had too much to drink, and he and I still had some unresolved issues, and..." She shook her head again. "I don't know. I was stupid and I did something I sincerely regret."

"We all make mistakes."

"I guess. There's a lot of history behind what happened with Wade last night, but that's no excuse."

Dillon smiled. "My advice is to forget it and move on, and to stay away from him in the future. I don't like that guy."

Stacy's eyes searched his face. "That sounds like you care. But it doesn't sound like you're jealous."

Dillon couldn't miss the bitterness in her voice. "I don't want to lose our friendship," he said.

She blinked rapidly, and Dillon suspected she was on the verge of tears. "That's a line I've heard before. 'Hey, I just want to be friends.'"

"It's not a line. You're a great—"

"Stop." She raised a hand. "I don't want any consolation prizes."

He continued, anyway. "I'm being sincere, Stacy. You're a great person, with a lot to offer a man."

She chuckled sarcastically. "Another man."

He didn't answer.

"Are you doing this because of what I did with Wade last night or because of Chantel?" she asked.

Dillon thought about putting an arm around her and trying to comfort her, but she was too close to tears. He wanted to help her salvage what pride she had left, not throw her over the edge. "What I said this morning is true. I'd like to date Chantel, but she won't see me."

"God!" Stacy squeezed her eyes shut as two tears streaked down her face.

"I'm sorry, Stacy," he said softly.

She waved his words away. "Don't be. I made it easy for you with my behavior last night."

"How I feel has nothing to do with last night. I know you can't be glad about any of it—"

She made a sound of utter disgust.

"—and I'm sure this seems trite, but you'll find the right man someday."

"And what do I do then?" she asked. "Just hope he never meets my sister?" She got quickly to her feet and left.

"YOU WEREN'T GOING to tell me?"

Stacy had let herself into the condo and was waiting for Chantel when she got home from work. Chantel had had five hours to prepare herself for a confrontation, had seen her sister's car in the parking lot, but the knot in her stomach wouldn't go away. Ever since she'd spoken with Dillon, she'd been trying to figure out what she could say. There was just one thing: She wouldn't let a man come between her and her sister again. She wouldn't repeat the mistakes that had cost them both so much.

If Stacy could only understand that, could only believe in her…

But Chantel hardly dared to believe in herself, so it was a thin thread to hang her hopes on. How could Stacy ever trust her after Wade? Especially when Dillon was twice the man and held twice the appeal?

"There wasn't anything to tell you," she said, trying to read the level of her sister's emotion as she set her purse and keys on the counter. "Dillon asked me out. I said no. That's all that happened."

Stacy bowed her head. "Why? Why do they all want you?"

Chantel's heart twisted. She hated to see her sister suffer, to know *she* was the cause. "Wade didn't really want me. He wanted the dream of New York and becoming a super-model. I was his security blanket, his second chance at success should he fail. Except, he didn't anticipate hating me for the attention I received. I've often wondered what would have happened if neither of us had done well, or if he'd climbed to the top, instead of me. Probably the same thing. We would have split eventually.''

"And Dillon?''

Chantel took a deep breath, hating the lies. But some things were too precious to risk. Her sister was one of them. "With Dillon it's just a passing whim. He doesn't really know me,'' she said.

"So it's all about looks? Looks mean everything?''

"You know better than that.''

"Then why does this happen over and over, Chantel? Why can't I feel good about me when I'm around you?''

"Maybe because you compare us too often, and most of the time you use the wrong measuring stick.''

Stacy stared at her. "What do you mean?''

Chantel softened her voice. "That you're a wonderful woman and if whoever you're dating can't see that, then he's not worthy of you.''

Stacy shook her head. "If I'm so wonderful, why do my boyfriends all go after my sister?''

"I don't know. Maybe they just don't take the time to get to know you well enough.''

"Because they only care about what they see.''

Chantel bit her lip. When she was young, she'd been teased because she was so tall and skinny and gawky. Now, she was treated as though she had nothing except her looks. Couldn't her sister understand that her life wasn't ideal, either? "We're different, Stacy. We look different. We have different talents. That's okay. But until we agree to accept our differences, we can never be friends.''

"That's easy for you to say. You're the supermodel. You're the one who has it all, including the only two men I've ever loved!''

Chantel rubbed her temples. Stacy was too upset to be rational. Or maybe she just didn't want to see that their problems went far deeper than Dillon and Wade. "I've never purposely tried to hurt you, Stacy. I made a mistake with Wade. I know I can't fix that, but I've tried to apologize—"

"*I'm sorry?* That should make it better?"

"Maybe not, but some things aren't worth worrying about, not in the long run."

"Like?"

"Like which one of us is prettier or garners more male attention."

"I don't believe this! You're basically telling me to lump it and move on. And I don't think you have the right!" Stacy grabbed her purse and headed to the door.

Chantel's temper threatened to snap, but the memory of ten long years without her sister kept her cautious. "Stacy, forget what I said. If Dillon's all you care about, I'll make you a promise. I'll stay away from him. I won't return his calls if he contacts me, won't open the door to him if he comes by. I'll tell him I never want to see him again. Will that make you happy?"

Stacy didn't answer, but the slamming of the door echoed in Chantel's head for several long minutes after she'd left.

"Will that make him marry you?" she asked the now-silent house. And then the tears came.

CHAPTER ELEVEN

"SO YOU'VE HIRED a private investigator?" Helen asked.

Dillon propped the portable phone on his shoulder and flipped the burgers he was barbecuing for dinner, talking over the loud sizzle of the meat. Chantel had called and canceled, so the night didn't look as promising as it once had, but he was trying to make the most of it. "Signed the contract this morning."

"Does he think he can find her?"

"He holds to the theory that people don't simply disappear."

"I guess he's never watched *America's Most Wanted.*" That was exactly what Dillon had thought as he'd sat in Mr. Curtis Trumbull's office. At the same time, the man's confidence had been reassuring. He'd matched the television stereotype: dogged manner, cheap suit, old desk, messy office. Although Dillon doubted he had a bottle of booze stashed away in his drawer. And there'd been no blond bombshell sitting out front to answer phones and greet visitors. Trumbull was a one-man show. "He thinks he can learn something before the weekend's out."

"It's already Friday night."

"His job isn't nine-to-five, weekdays only."

Helen breathed out, and he pictured her smoking another of her cigarettes. She had one in her hand most of the time. "What about the girls? Are they adjusting okay?"

"Can't you hear them giggling?" Just beyond the back

porch, where Dillon monitored the progress of their dinner, the girls were jumping on the trampoline he'd bought them this week, which sat right next to the swing set he'd designed and built for them a year ago. "They're doing great. A van picks them up after school and takes them to Children's World, where they do arts and crafts or play outside for a couple of hours. On Thursdays I take off early to get Sydney to her gymnastics class and Brittney to karate."

"Oh, good." A hacking cough interrupted her. "I think it's important to keep their lives as normal as possible."

"So far, my biggest problem has been getting them to eat healthy food, but a mother at the school gave me some kid-friendly recipes we're going to try."

"Amanda used to be so careful about what they ate."

Certainly not recently, Dillon wanted to add, but he held his tongue. Her voice sounded more gravelly than normal, and he suspected she was crying again. "Trumbull will find her, Helen. Regardless of the outcome, at least we'll be able to get some closure. I think that's important for the girls, too."

Helen cleared her throat but didn't answer.

"Do you still want us to come over on Sunday?" he asked.

"I'd like to take them for the weekend, like I usually do."

All those weekends I was supposed to have them, and you and Amanda forced me to fight for my legal rights. "No, I want to spend some time with them. It's been a crazy, stressful week for all of us. We need a chance to relax and play and simply feel okay together."

The telephone beeped, letting him know another call was coming in. "I've got to go, Helen. We'll see you on Sunday."

She said goodbye, and he switched to the other line.

"Dillon? It's Mom. What's happened? When Lyle and I got home from our honeymoon, we had three messages from you."

"I didn't realize you'd be gone so long."

"I told you we wouldn't be back until the seventh of April. We're actually a few days early."

She probably had told him, but he hadn't paid any attention. That was his way of blocking out her irresponsible behavior. She was on her fifth marriage, her fourth honeymoon—she claimed his father had never taken her on one—and he didn't like this latest husband. Lyle had no profession or money to speak of, and Dillon suspected he'd married Karen for the free ride. But his mother seemed crazy about him. At least for the time being.

He removed the burgers from the grill, wishing again that Chantel hadn't canceled, and told her about Amanda.

"That girl is no good. I don't know why you married her."

"Because she wasn't always like this. She said she wanted the same things I did, but she grew dissatisfied fast. She didn't want to be a stay-at-home mom. But she didn't want to work, either."

"I'll bet she's run off with this guy," Karen said. "How could a woman do that to her own children?"

In a way Karen had done the same thing to Dillon. She'd stuck around, but she'd been gone in spirit ever since her divorce from his father, getting involved with one man after the other. Dillon wasn't sure anymore why he'd wanted to talk to her, except that she lived only a few miles away and it seemed natural to turn to his family during a crisis that concerned his children. At least his mother was more receptive than his father.

"Did you see Dave while you were in New England?" he asked.

Dillon listened to his mother marvel at the beauty of Dave's farm and how little Reva had changed. Then he heard about the rest of her trip across America in the new motor home she'd bought, including her visit to his other uncle, who lived in Indiana.

"I wish they'd both move back to California," she finished, "so we could live closer as a family."

Dillon was glad that Dave, at least, had lived close by most of the years he was growing up. Otherwise he might never have righted his rebellious ways. "You've got Janet and Monica," he reminded her. His sisters.

"When they have the time."

His mother was retired. He and his sisters had families and careers; none of them had that much time. "Our dinner's getting cold, Mom. I'd better go," he said at last. "I'm glad the two of you had fun."

"Do you need me to take the girls so you can go out tonight?" she asked out of the blue. She'd never been much of a baby-sitter. He wondered what prompted the offer now.

"Go out with whom?"

"What about that nice young woman Stacy?"

"We're not seeing each other anymore."

"You've broken up already?"

"We were just friends."

"Well, now that you've got your daughters back, you should start thinking about settling down again."

Dillon squirted ketchup on the buns he had waiting on the picnic table. "I am settled. I like my home. I'm busy with my job. That'll have to be good enough for now."

"But those girls are going to need a mother."

"They've lived without one for the past few weeks and probably much longer," he muttered. "Listen, I've got to go, Mom, or I'm going to have to reheat these burgers."

"Are they done, Daddy?" Brittney yelled, and he waved her over.

"Just tell me you'll start looking for the right woman," his mother said, persistent as ever.

Dillon thought of Chantel and winced. He'd found someone he wanted to be with, but pursuing her would only cause her pain. "I suppose it'll happen when the time's right."

"I hope so. Marriage is so wonderful."

Some smooching sounds came over the phone, and Dillon realized Lyle and his mother were kissing like a couple of teenagers. The mental picture nauseated him a little. He wanted his mother to be happy. He didn't necessarily want her to return to her youth.

"You can still say that after five?" he asked.

"Sometimes it takes a few tries to get it right."

Tries? Dillon shook his head. Getting married wasn't like trying on a pair of shoes. A divorce hurt like hell. When he got married again, he promised himself it would be forever.

CHANTEL SAT in the back row of the movie theater, holding a soda and a large bucket of popcorn. She knew she probably wouldn't eat more than a few kernels. But the smell was nice.

"Is anyone sitting here?"

A young woman stood in the aisle, holding the hand of a dark-haired young man. They both looked about eighteen. "No, I'm alone."

The couple smiled and sat down, then opened a box of mints and talked and laughed and ate. Their companionship contrasted so sharply with Chantel's solitude she felt it like a physical pain in her chest. Stacy hadn't called her all week. Chantel had considered contacting her and apologizing again, but she doubted Stacy was ready to let go of the past, no matter how many times she said she was sorry.

Words could only do so much.

The lights went down and the movie screen flickered to life. The trailers started, but Chantel wasn't really interested. She'd come hoping to distract herself from the knowledge that Dillon had invited her to a barbecue tonight, that she could be with him right now, having as much fun as the teenagers to her right. But nothing could distract her, not even the action-and-suspense movie she'd purposely chosen.

For a brief moment she considered leaving the theater and driving over to his house. Why deny herself? Stacy had shut her out again and might never come around. Tonight's sacrifice hardly seemed worth it. But there was that little matter of the kind of person she wanted to be. And she *didn't* want to be the kind of person that turning to Dillon would make her.

"AMANDA MARRIED John Heath."

The investigator's scratchy voice came over the phone the following Wednesday evening while Dillon was putting away groceries. "When?" he asked, losing interest in his task.

"The weekend they arrived in Vegas."

Dillon glanced through the open kitchen into the living room and thanked heaven that Brittney and Sidney were still engrossed in a Mary Kate and Ashley Olsen movie. "Where are they now?"

"I traced them to Utah. I have their address if you want it."

"Just a minute." Dillon retrieved his day-planner and jotted down an address in Salt Lake City. "Do you have their phone number?"

"Yeah. It's not listed, but they weren't smart enough to know that it can be found other ways."

"Like?"

"They made it easy for me. They gave it to the neighborhood video store."

Privacy certainly wasn't what it used to be, Dillon mused. Not that he planned to contact the happy couple. He already knew what he'd wanted to know. Amanda wasn't lying dead on the side of the road somewhere. She'd left the girls of her own free will, though why she hadn't simply given them to him, he had no idea. Maybe because she knew he would have demanded she sign a custody agreement. This way, she probably believed she could come back any time she changed her mind.

That thought didn't sit well with him, but it certainly wasn't Curtis Trumbull's problem.

"Do you want me to do anything else?" the investigator asked.

"No, that's it. Do I owe you anything more?"

"There's a small balance on your account. I'll bill you."

"Thanks."

The phone clicked as Trumbull hung up, but Dillon continued to stare at the handset, wondering what he was going to do now. He needed to tell the girls right away, needed to relieve their anxiety. But how did a father face his children with such news? And what about Amanda's mother, who'd always stood by her, defended her, assisted her?

Amanda had betrayed them all. For John Heath, whoever *he* was.

The phone started beeping from being off the hook and Dillon finally hung up. He squeezed the back of his neck, where the muscles were so tight they were giving him a headache. Then he heard Brittney giggle as she turned off the television set, and he knew their movie was over. Shoving his hands in his pockets, he headed into the living room.

"Sydney, Brittney, come sit down on the couch with me. I have something I need to talk to you about."

WADE STALKED into his bedroom, barely resisting the urge to slam the door. His father was at him again. When was he going to get a real job? When was he going to grow up and act like a man? When was he going to take responsibility for himself, be more like his brothers?

Slumping onto his bed, he picked up the phone and dialed his agent in New York.

"How's that job coming?" he asked the moment Steve's voice came over the line.

"Wade? It's two o'clock in the morning here. What the hell are you doing calling me at home this time of night?"

"I haven't heard from you in weeks, man. I need that job. Is it coming through or not?"

There was a deep sigh on the other end. "It's not. I would have called you if it was. I told you when I talked to you that it was a long shot."

"So that's it? You don't have anything for me? What the hell do you expect me to live on?"

"I'm doing what I can, but the competition's stiff right now. There's nothing that really pays, you know what I'm saying? I could probably scrounge up some odd jobs here and there, but they're for amateurs. You're way beyond them, and they don't pay squat. They're nothing you could live on."

Wade ground his teeth. It was the same damn story. He'd always gotten these kinds of answers and nothing but chicken-shit jobs, while Chantel had been vaulted to fame and fortune. And *he* was the professional! He was the one who could withstand the pressure. Look what had happened to her!

"It doesn't have to be the cover of *GQ*, all right, Steve?" he said, getting desperate. Something had to break. Henry's patience wouldn't last much longer. His father would cut him off, and then where would he be?

"I told you," Steve said, "the male market is tough. But I've got some work here for Chantel that could pull you guys through. Some big stuff. You still bringing her back?"

Wade had tried and tried to talk to Chantel, but she screened her calls and wouldn't return his. If he visited her condo, she refused to answer the door. When she'd left him in New York, he'd thought she'd come back to him eventually. He'd never dreamed she could survive without him. Her world had revolved around him since she was nineteen.

But he was beginning to fear he'd been wrong.

"Yeah, she's coming back with me," he said with more confidence than he felt.

"Then call me as soon as you're in town. These people don't wait long, you know what I'm saying? She's already missed several golden opportunities. But her look is in. We can still play with the big boys if you guys don't take forever."

"Tell everyone to hold on to their hats. We won't take forever," Wade promised, and hung up.

What now? He had to reach Chantel. She was blowing it, blowing it for both of them. And he was running out of time. If he didn't do something quick, he'd be shit out of luck and working nine-to-five like every other nobody.

He dialed her number. After the third ring her answering machine kicked in. Dammit! He knew she was home. Where else would she be at eleven o'clock at night?

Stacy. She could tell him what was going on—if he could get her to talk to him. He'd tried to call her several times since their night together, but she always hung up on him.

It took almost six rings for her to finally answer. "Hello?"

"Stacy, don't hang up."

"You woke me," she said. "What do you want?"

"I want to know what's happening with Chantel. I mean, is she seeing that Dillon guy or what?"

A long pause. Wade assumed she wasn't going to answer, but then her voice came back across the line. "Not that I know of. I haven't talked to her for weeks."

"Will you call her? Find out why she won't let me in?"

"You're kidding, right? You expect *me* to help *you?*"

"Why not? We're friends, aren't we?"

"No. As far as I'm concerned, you can go to hell."

Wade felt a muscle in his cheek start to twitch. "So that's the way you want to play it, huh? Then maybe I should mention to Chantel how you invited me over to see your pretty lingerie."

She laughed. "You do that, Wade. I doubt she'll be very impressed with the part you played that night, either." Then the phone clicked and the dial tone hummed in his ear.

"Bitch," he muttered.

WHEN HER ALARM went off, Chantel groaned and pulled the pillow over her head. She was still tired, and she felt nauseated. For some reason, she couldn't seem to shake the flu that had plagued her for almost a week. But she couldn't call in sick again. She'd missed two days already and wasn't about to miss the staff meeting with the senator this morning.

She just hoped she didn't throw up on the conference table.

Dragging herself out of bed, she went to the kitchen where she had a fresh supply of 7-Up and crackers, which seemed to be the only food her body could tolerate. As a result she'd already lost weight.

Just what she needed after fighting so hard to get back to normal, she thought.

Taking her makeshift breakfast with her, she headed into the bathroom to get showered.

Almost an hour later, she was wearing her blue pinstripe suit and gathering her keys. Another wave of nausea hit as she hurried to her car, but she forced it back, through sheer will, and unlocked the Jag. Setting her purse and briefcase inside, she was about to get behind the wheel when a hand on her arm nearly cost her the small amount of breakfast she'd managed to get down.

"Wade! What are you doing here?" she cried. "You nearly scared me to death!"

Letting go, he jammed his hands in the pockets of his cargo pants. "What else was I supposed to do? You screen your calls, you won't let me in at the door. I need to talk to you."

He didn't look good. His clothes were wrinkled, as if he'd slept in them, and he badly needed a haircut and a shave.

"What's wrong with you? You look like I feel," she said.

"I can't eat or sleep anymore. I never dreamed you'd really walk out on me."

Wade had walked out on her almost every time she'd ever really needed him, in one way or another, but she wasn't about to go into all of that again. "What we had died a long time ago," she said simply.

"I don't believe that. You still love me. You'll always love me."

"Whatever. I'm not coming back, Wade. I can't say it any plainer than that."

"But you're nothing without me. Look at you, heading off to your little secretary's job."

"There's nothing wrong with my job. I'm glad I've got it."

"But you could be on the cover of *Vogue!* I just talked to Steve a few days ago. He said it's not too late."

"Wade—"

"What's gotten into you, dammit? Doesn't your career mean anything to you anymore? Don't *I* mean anything?"

Chantel stared at him, dumbfounded. Where was all this emotion coming from? He'd left her in the hospital for months with no more than an occasional visit. "I don't want another cover, Wade. I want a family."

He ran a hand through his already mussed hair. "I'm ready to go that route, Chantel. I've been thinking about it a lot."

She was too sick and weak to hide the pain his words caused her. "It's too late, Wade. You know that." Her voice broke. "I can't have children."

She got into her car and tried to shut the door, but he held it. "Then we'll adopt, okay?"

"I'm going to be late."

"Wait, you know that counseling you were always talking about? We'll go there. We'll get some help and make our relationship work. Why throw away ten years, babe? This is me, the man you love, right?"

Chantel pinched the bridge of her nose. Why now? "This is quite a reversal, Wade, and I really don't have time to deal with it."

"Can I come over tonight, then? Just to talk?"

She pictured the senator and Maureen and all the field reps gathered around the conference table and knew she had to leave now or risk walking in after they'd started. "Okay," she said. "Come at six."

"CHANTEL, DID YOU FINISH that summary of legislation I gave you to type?" Lee asked, stopping at her desk.

Chantel cringed inside. Lee had been asking her the same question every day for a week. She should have finished the summary days ago, but she had a list of other priorities, and she just wasn't running at top speed. It was all she could do to answer the phones and do a little bit of scheduling. "Um, not quite," she admitted. "I've been pretty busy. When do you need it?"

"Last week," he said pointedly, and walked away.

Chantel set the constituent case she'd been working on aside and pulled out the file that held Lee's handwritten notes. She'd get his typing done now, she decided, but the nausea she'd felt all day reasserted itself, and she couldn't do anything but lay her head on her desk.

"What's wrong?" Maureen asked. "Are you ill?"

"No!" Chantel jerked her head up and forced a smile. She couldn't go home sick, not again. They'd be sorry they hired her.

"You look pale."

"I'm a little tired, that's all."

"Do you want to take an early lunch?"

Yes! Please, yes! But Chantel knew she couldn't take *any* lunch. She was running too far behind. "Maybe I'll grab something after I finish this for Lee," she said.

"You're sure?"

Chantel pumped more life into her smile. "I'm sure."

"Okay." Maureen seemed hesitant, but after another searching look, went back to her own desk and Chantel let herself slump. How was she going to succeed here? She wasn't used to the pressure of an office situation, still had a lot to learn. And she felt so sick....

Buck up, she ordered herself. She had to perform or she'd lose her job, and she couldn't afford that. She doubted she could face the failure. Besides, she had very little savings left. She'd spent what money she'd salvaged from Wade's reckless life-style on her condo and had to have a salary to survive.

Unless... She thought of Wade and what he'd said this

morning. Had he been sincere about marriage and children? She'd fought so hard to escape him and New York, but it felt as if they were both waiting for her to admit defeat and come back.

Unlike this job, modeling was easy for her. And the lifestyle in New York was comfortingly familiar. Why fight it anymore? She'd come home to California for Stacy, but Stacy didn't want a relationship with her, not after what had happened with Dillon.

Dillon... Chantel felt a lump rise in her throat. She could have loved him. She knew she could. He was everything a man should be—

Give up, Wade whispered. *Look at you. You can't even hold down a simple job. Why would Dillon want you? You belong with me. We belong together.*

But the anorexia was there, waiting for her, too.

She was slipping, slipping away, and she was too sick to stop it. "Help me," she prayed, breaking into a cold sweat, and finally her father's voice rose above the confusion in her mind.

You're my little girl, Chantel. You can do anything....

SOMEHOW SHE SURVIVED the day. Chantel didn't know how, but she managed to complete at least some of her work. Then she drove home, hurried into the condo and collapsed on the couch. She knew she should try to eat something so she could get her strength back. But she couldn't stand the thought of throwing up. It was easier not to eat. She was good at starving herself.

Sleep came quickly, enveloping her in a dark shroud that eased the nausea. But it felt as if she'd barely closed her eyes when someone started banging on the door.

"Chantel? Are you there? It's Maureen."

She'd been expecting Wade. What was her boss doing here?''

Clambering to her feet, Chantel fumbled with the lock and swung the door open, then leaned on it for support.

"Are you all right?" Maureen asked, concern etched on her face.

Chantel nodded. "I'm fine. It's just the flu. I guess I'm not quite over it yet."

"Why didn't you tell me?"

"I didn't want to go home sick again. I was afraid—" she drew a ragged breath "—I was afraid I'd lose my job. But I don't think I'm going to make it in tomorrow."

"Of course you're not working tomorrow. You need to stay home and get well. I guessed something was wrong. That's why I decided to stop by on my way home from work, but I had trouble finding your address."

"I'm sorry, Maureen." Chantel raised a hand to her aching head. "If I weren't sick, I could do the job. But I can't seem to get well. Maybe you should replace me."

Maureen took her arm and helped her back to the couch. "That's a little premature, I'd say. Anyone can come down with the flu."

"But you need someone you can depend on—"

"Chantel?" Wade stood at the open door, gazing in at them. "What's wrong?" he asked.

Maureen answered him. "We don't know. It might be the flu."

"Or some kind of backlash from the anorexia," he added.

Chantel wished he was close enough to pinch. She didn't want anyone at work to know about her anorexia.

Maureen turned back to her. "Sounds to me like we should call a doctor."

"No!" Chantel protested. "I've had enough of doctors and hospitals. It's the flu. I just need to get into bed." She made a feeble attempt to stand, but Wade had to half lift her.

"I knew this would happen if she didn't have someone to take care of her," Wade said, helping her down the hall.

"I don't need anyone to take care of me," Chantel muttered, but Wade's implications were the least of her problems. The room was spinning, and she was afraid she might faint, until she felt the softness of her mattress beneath her.

"Let me help you out of your suit," he said.

"No. I don't care about the suit." She pulled her goose-down comforter up to her chin, resenting Wade for playing the part of concerned husband. But she didn't have the strength to argue with him. And Maureen was there.

Her manager introduced herself to Wade, then put a hand on Chantel's forehead. "She doesn't have a fever. Aren't you supposed to have a fever with the flu?"

"I don't know, but I know someone who does," Wade said, and a moment later, Chantel heard him talking on the phone. "I think you should take a look at her. She's really sick... Seems she's lost some weight... She might need a doctor."

"Do you have to see a specific doctor for insurance purposes?" he asked her, gently shaking her shoulder.

Chantel didn't answer. She just wanted to sleep so she could shut out the nausea. But Maureen took her hand and persisted until she gave them her doctor's name and insurance information, which Wade repeated into the phone.

"We'll be waiting," he said, and hung up.

And finally it was quiet enough for Chantel to sleep.

CHAPTER TWELVE

STACY DASHED OUTSIDE just as the sun began to set on what had been a breezy May day and started her car, then ran back inside when she realized she'd forgotten her purse. She should have called Chantel as soon as her anger had died away. Instead, pride had prolonged her stupid stubborn silence. If Wade hadn't called just minutes ago, she might have let the weeks turn into months with no contact between them. Who knew how long Chantel would have continued feeling sick before she broke down and asked for help? What if Wade hadn't gone over there?

In the face of real illness, Stacy and Chantel's differences seemed minor. Especially when Stacy considered the possibility of losing the last member of her family for good.

Wade had said it might be the flu, she told herself. Healthy young women didn't die from the flu, right? But the guilt she felt about her part in their estrangement nagged at her. Chantel's genetic makeup wasn't her fault. Maybe Stacy would have done the same thing at nineteen, if their roles had been reversed. Only weeks ago she'd slept with Wade simply to bolster her ego.

With a grimace Stacy wished she could blot out that night. She gunned her Honda, and when she reached the freeway, immediately merged into the fast lane. A voice in the back of her head warned her about getting a ticket, but she pressed the accelerator closer to the floor, anyway.

When she arrived, Wade was sitting in a chair by Chantel's bed, staring at her in the dim light filtering through the window. A heavyset woman Stacy recognized as Chantel's manger from the office, Maureen something, sat on the corner of the bed.

"Is she okay?" Stacy directed her question to the woman. It was the first time she'd seen Wade since their night together, and she would rather have avoided speaking to him again, but it was Wade who answered.

"She fell asleep almost the minute I hung up with you."

Stacy gazed down at her sister's face. Despite the poor lighting, she immediately noticed the dark circles beneath Chantel's eyes and the paleness of her skin. "I called her doctor before I left home. It's after office hours, but he said he'd wait, that we could bring her right in."

"I'll carry her out," Wade volunteered.

Stacy looked at Maureen. "Listen, you can go. I'll take care of her from here."

Maureen nodded, glanced worriedly at Chantel and handed Stacy her card. "Call and let me know how she is, okay?"

Stacy agreed, and Maureen left just as Wade slipped one arm beneath Chantel's knees and one under her shoulders, to lift her from the bed.

Chantel groaned. "Where are we going?" she asked. "I don't feel well."

"Chantel, it's me." Stacy touched her arm, and her sister went completely still. "Everything's going to be okay. We're taking you to see a doctor."

"I can walk."

"There's no need. Wade's here. He may as well carry you."

Chantel sighed, but settled into his arms as though grateful she didn't have to prove her words. "You guys are making too big a deal of this. I just have the flu."

"Then I hope you don't mind letting us get a second opinion," Stacy told her. "You look a bit ravaged for just having the flu."

"Evidently you haven't had the flu for a while," she murmured. "But if we have to go, then let's hurry before I throw up again."

Stacy chuckled. "Hang on to your lunch, it won't be long now."

They got to the doctor's office fifteen minutes later. All the nurses had gone home except one, who was kind enough to show Chantel to a room right away. Stacy sat in the empty waiting area across from Wade, staring blankly at the magazines on the coffee table nearby and marveling at what an unlikely threesome they made. "Thanks for calling me," she said at last.

He looked up from an issue of *Mademoiselle*. Stacy couldn't remember ever seeing another man choose that particular magazine. "She could be on here again, you know," he said. "She was once, about five years ago."

"She doesn't seem to want that anymore." Stacy didn't understand what had chased Chantel away from New York, but she did recognize a flicker of hope in herself. If her sister wasn't going to run after fame and fortune again, if she was actually going to stick around, maybe they could rebuild their relationship, after all.

"Ever since she got sick, over a year ago, she hasn't been the same," he murmured, almost to himself.

Stacy pinned him with a hard gaze. "What are you talking about? You said she never got sick in New York, that she had it good there."

He set the magazine aside, and for the first time, Stacy noticed how bloodshot his eyes were. "She was sick," he admitted, hunching down in his seat.

"How sick?"

"She spent months in the hospital."

"*What?*" Stacy nearly leaped out of her seat. "Why didn't you call us?"

"She said she needed to pay the price for her own dumb decisions." He gave her a twisted smile. "I guess that meant me. I wasn't about to call up and announce to everyone that she regretted coming to New York with me."

Stacy felt a cold unease creep over her heart. "What kind of illness keeps you in the hospital for months?" she asked. "Cancer?"

He shook his head. "Anorexia. When she went in, she weighed only ninety pounds."

"What? She's six feet tall!" Stacy felt the sting of tears and squeezed her eyes shut. She couldn't avoid the mental picture of her sister lying in the sterile atmosphere of a hospital for months, believing her family didn't care about her. Chantel couldn't have believed anything else. Her own father had told her not to contact them again. At the time Stacy had thought it a just punishment. Now she realized just how much her playing the martyr had manipulated him into casting his own daughter aside. "And here I thought she was living the high life," she whispered "Miss Cover Model on the front of every magazine."

"She nearly died."

"But you were there for her, right?" Stacy asked hopefully. "I mean, she didn't have to fight that battle alone."

He grimaced. "Oh, like you would have been there for her, had you known. She tried to reach you several times during our first year together, but you wouldn't accept her calls. You could have contacted her once in a while, you know. You could have forgiven her."

Stacy winced at the memory of hanging up on Chantel the one time she did get through. Her father had died and she'd missed the funeral. Chantel had insisted she'd received Stacy's message too late, that she'd been on location at a shoot, but Stacy had chosen to believe she hadn't cared enough to make the trip. "You were my fiancé, Wade, and she—"

"You knew I didn't really love you, that I let it go as far as I did out of a sense of obligation. I remember trying to tell you how I felt about Chantel, but you shut it out and did nothing."

"I was young and stupid."

He sneered at her. "She was younger than you."

DILLON SAT at the exit to the grocery-store parking lot, letting his engine idle. Helen was at home with Brittney and Sydney. She'd stopped by to visit and had joined them for dinner, then he'd gone to pick up a few things for the girls' lunches. He was finished shopping, and home was to the left, but he wanted to go in the other direction—to Chantel's condo.

Another car came up behind him, so he flipped on his signal and made a right-hand turn. It had been weeks since he'd talked to Chantel. He'd called her once to see how Stacy was treating her, but she'd been distant, and he'd known better than to call again. Pressing her would only chase her further away. He'd hoped she'd get in touch with him, but she hadn't, and he was beginning to think she never would. So he'd told himself to forget her and go on.

But it wasn't that easy. She crept into his thoughts at the most inopportune moments—in the middle of giving a presentation on an industrial park, while making dinner for the girls, even while talking to Dave on the phone. He'd been thinking of Dave and Reva's relationship and wondering if he'd ever find a woman he'd want to spend so many years with, and Chantel had just popped into his mind.

She was driving him crazy. He had to see her. He had to

know, without a doubt, that what they'd shared couldn't grow into anything more lasting.

The night was cool and breezy and smelled like rain. Dillon rolled down his window and let the wind ruffle his hair as he drove, and fifteen minutes later, the redbrick walls of her condominium complex appeared on his left. He turned into the drive, telling himself he'd only stay for a few minutes, just long enough to see how she was doing. But before he could even pull into a parking space, he saw something that made his blood run cold: the same brown Cadillac he'd seen in Stacy's drive.

Wade. Had Chantel gone back to him? The thought turned Dillon's stomach, but he knew how easy it could be to fall back into an old relationship. How many times had he wished he could work things out with Amanda? It had to do with knowing a person so well, remembering what had attracted you in the first place, hoping that whatever hadn't worked could change. And there was always the lure of New York. That was something Dillon couldn't offer her, ever.

Damn. He was a fool to have come. Shoving the car into Reverse, Dillon backed out of the drive and peeled away. He was better off without Chantel, he told himself. Where could it go, anyway? He had his girls to think of now. He had no time to build a relationship with a woman. It was just as well.

But he didn't care how logical it all sounded. The idea of Wade with Chantel made him want to bust Pretty Boy's jaw.

CHANTEL COULDN'T get rid of her unlikely caregivers.

At home in her own bed, she rolled over and covered her ears to block out another of Wade and Stacy's many arguments, wishing they'd leave her in peace—but wishing it only halfheartedly. If she was honest with herself, she had to admit she'd never felt better emotionally. Stacy had been more open and giving over the past three days than Chantel ever remembered her being, and she was thrilled by the prospect of what was starting to grow between them. Wade was another story, but his father had kicked him out, so she was letting him stay until he found some kind of work. And she was doing her best to be patient with him.

Now, if she could only get well enough to lead a normal life again.

What was wrong with her? The doctor hadn't been able to tell her yet. He didn't think it was the flu. He didn't think it was any kind of allergy, to her home or to microscopic particles or whatever. He thought her anorexia might be reasserting itself, but was skeptical even there. And all the tests he'd run had shown nothing. They were waiting for a few more—the results of several blood tests—before they had to start all over again.

"Why leave it on the counter?" Wade asked, his voice rising as it came from the kitchen. "Then the food dries on, and the dishwasher's no good. At least rinse it off!"

"And then leave it in the sink like you? Since I'm the one who's been doing all the housework, anyway, what does it matter?" Stacy yelled back. "You know I'll take care of it."

Were they fighting about the dishes? Last time it was who had what section of the newspaper. They were at each others' throats constantly.

"The question is when. Besides, I did some vacuuming yesterday."

"Ooh, big deal—"

"Stop it!" Chantel cried weakly. "I can't take you guys arguing anymore."

There was a momentary silence. "Now look what you've done. You woke her up," Wade said.

"I'm not the one who started ranting about dishes!"

"I wasn't ranting. You make me sound like a fishwife."

"If the shoe fits…"

Their voices came closer, along with the sound of their footsteps, until they both appeared at Chantel's door and tried to fit through it at the same time. With an irritated look at Wade, Stacy squeezed through first.

"What's wrong?" she demanded.

Chantel let out a long-suffering sigh. "Do you guys think you could go a couple of hours without bickering?"

"We weren't bickering!" Wade said. "Bickering's what women do."

Stacy gave him a jaunty toss of her head. "Like I said, if the shoe fits…"

Chantel covered her ears again. "Stop!"

Her sister pointed an accusing finger at Wade. "It's his fault. I can't believe you're letting him stay here."

"So I'm a bit of a neat freak," he admitted, smiling proudly. "At least I'm not a total slob."

Stacy bristled. "Are you calling me a slob? The one who's been cleaning up after you for the past three days?"

Wade shrugged. "I've done my part. Who do you think took care of Chantel last night while you were at work?"

"And left a sinkful of dishes for me to load when I got back."

"At least they'd all been rinsed off."

"That's enough!" Chantel sent them both a reproving glare and shoved her pillows against the backboard so she could sit up. "Are you trying to drive me out of my own home?"

They exchanged quick hate-filled looks but didn't say anything.

"Anyway, I'm feeling a little better today," Chantel went on.

"Really?" Stacy crossed to sit on the end of her bed, and Wade, not to be outdone, joined her. "No nausea?"

Chantel shook her head. "Not right now."

"You think you could eat something?" Wade asked. They'd been force-feeding her almost every time she woke up, then holding her head over the toilet when what went down came back up.

"I'm not sure I want to go through all that again."

"The doctor said you need to eat, Chantel," Wade reminded her.

"But it doesn't do me any good if I can't keep it down."

That worried expression Stacy had been wearing on and off came on again, and Chantel relented just to see her sister's puckered brow relax. "Okay, I'll try."

Stacy looked at Wade. "Make her some pancakes, Wade. You need to do something to earn your keep around here."

He pulled a face at Stacy but spoke to Chantel. "Do pancakes sound all right?"

Nothing sounded worse. Except perhaps eggs, bacon, oatmeal, doughnuts, any kind of cold cereal, any lunch item... Chantel forced a smile. "Sounds great."

Wade left to start the pancakes, and Stacy edged closer. "You're really giving us a scare here, you know that? Everyone's worried about you. Maureen calls all the time to check on you."

Chantel didn't even want to think about work. She'd just missed another three days. "They're going to have to let me go if I don't get better soon." She fought the lump rising in her throat. "I mean, what else can they do?"

"The senator's being pretty good about it." Stacy waved to the large bouquet of flowers the office had sent, along with a card each of her co-workers had signed.

Chantel knew that sending flowers probably wasn't the senator's idea—more likely Maureen's—but she was pleased, anyway. "It's just that this is my first chance to really prove myself. I can't stand the thought of failing."

"You can't help being sick. Let's handle first things first, then we'll worry about your job, okay? Speaking of work, I have to leave for the hospital in a few minutes, but I'm sure Wade will be here." She sneered. "As long as there's free room and board, I doubt he'll be going anywhere soon."

"Is he still talking about moving back to New York?" Chantel whispered.

"When he first got here, he was talking like he had a string of jobs lined up, but he hasn't mentioned them lately."

"You don't think he's still expecting me to go back with him, do you?"

"I don't see how he could. You're not well enough to go anywhere."

"I can't believe his dad kicked him out," Chantel said. "It's the last thing I need."

"You're too nice. I'd kick him out, too."

Ever since Stacy had spent the night with Wade, she claimed she couldn't stand the sight of him. Chantel guessed it was her poor judgment she couldn't stand. Wade just reminded her of it. To a point, she felt the same way, but they'd been together too long for her not to help him out now. "How did you get the day shift?" she asked, changing the subject. "It's not even noon."

"I think the nurse who does the scheduling is losing her mind," Stacy joked. "She gives me completely different hours every week. But I have to run." She checked her watch. "I'll see you later."

Stacy rushed out, leaving Chantel to contemplate the

change in her sister's attitude these past few days. There were still some things they couldn't talk about—like Dillon—but Stacy was treating her more warmly than she had since they were kids. Chantel suspected her night with Wade had humbled her a little, taught her that people don't always use their best judgment and that she was no exception.

The telephone rang. Wade answered it in the kitchen before Chantel could slide far enough toward the nightstand to grab it herself. A moment later, he called out, "It's the doctor, Chantel."

Chantel picked up the phone and waited for the click that told her Wade had hung up. If the news was bad, she wanted to hear it in privacy. "Hello?"

"Ms. Miller? This is Dr. Campbell. Your blood tests are back, and I wanted to ask you a few questions."

"Okay."

"When was the date of your last period?"

For nearly a year she hadn't menstruated at all. But in the past six months, she'd had a couple of brief periods, if you could call them that. Since the anorexia nothing had been the same. "I'm not sure," she said. "There really wasn't any reason to make a special note of it."

"Just hazard a guess."

"Let's see, it's been…jeez, I don't know, at least three months."

Wade came to stand in the doorway again, but Chantel didn't acknowledge him beyond a quick glance. "What do you think's wrong with me, doctor?"

"I don't think anything is *wrong* with you, Ms. Miller. According to your blood tests and what you've just told me, I think you're pregnant."

Chantel dropped the phone, then scrambled to pick it up. "But that's not possible," she said, feeling her hands, her arms, her whole body start to shake. Because Wade was watching her closely, Chantel tried to control her shock so she wouldn't give anything away, but she felt as if the doctor had landed her a hard blow to the head. *He's made a mistake. That's all there is to it.*

"It wasn't probable," Dr. Campbell corrected her. "But anything is possible. Now, I'm not sure if this comes as good news or bad. Perhaps it's something we should talk about. After all you've been through with the anorexia, your body is ill equipped to support another life. If you choose to keep the baby, you'll be facing a high-risk pregnancy."

If you choose to keep the baby... The words reverberated through her head. A baby was all she'd ever wanted. She'd never do anything to endanger it; she'd go through hell to have it. But she still felt as though this must be someone's idea of a cruel joke. "Are you sure that I'm...you know?"

"I'm fairly certain you're pregnant. I'm not very optimistic that you'll be able to carry the baby to term. I want to be honest with you about that right up front."

Tears streamed down Chantel's face, and she was powerless to stop them. Wade hurried into the room and took her hand, curiosity and concern showing in his expression. "What is it?" he murmured.

Chantel shook her head and tried to absorb all the ramifications of the pregnancy at once. If her body could only manage for another seven or so months, she'd have a baby. Better yet, it would be *Dillon's* baby. He'd been the one to give her this gift, and the knowledge that she carried part of him inside her nearly made her burst with joy. Until she remembered Stacy.

"Oh, no," she said, closing her eyes. What was she going to tell her sister? She and Dillon had already told Stacy that he'd asked her out, nothing more.

"Are you okay, Ms. Miller?"

"Fine," she managed. *One step at a time.* There was no

reason to go rushing into any confessions. She might not even be able to carry the baby. She could lose it tomorrow.

Her mind rebelled against that thought, and she wrapped an arm around her abdomen in a protective gesture.

"I need you to see a gynecologist/obstetrician right away, and I have an excellent one I'd like to recommend. Her name is Dr. Bradley."

"Is it serious?" Wade asked.

Chantel ignored the question. "Find me something to write with," she whispered, instead.

He shuffled through the nightstand and came up with a pen and a magazine. Chantel flipped to the inside cover and jotted down Dr. Bradley's name and number.

"I'm sure she'll want you to come in right away so she can do an ultrasound. I'll call her myself, and tell her to expect to hear from you."

"Thanks Dr. Campbell. I'm so…grateful."

He chuckled. "I'm glad you're pleased with the news, and I wish you the best of luck."

Chantel hung up, then stared at the number for Dr. Bradley's office.

"So?" Wade prompted, and Chantel felt a flicker of unease. If she *was* pregnant, it would be a difficult secret to keep with Wade around. But she couldn't let him know, at least not until she decided what to do.

"The doctor thinks I'm okay." She searched for a lie he might believe and drew a blank. "He, uh, just wants to run one more test."

Wade looked skeptical. "You're obviously not okay. You can't even get off the bed."

"The doctor thinks this…will pass."

"So it is the flu?"

Chantel grasped the lie he unwittingly offered her. "Yeah, just like we thought."

"Then you're going to get better."

She nodded.

"And meanwhile?"

"Meanwhile I'll eat whatever you put in front of me," she said, unable to hold back the dazzling smile that was dying to come out. Amid the hope, the fear, the confusion and the guilt, she felt a ray of pure joy at the thought of having a baby, and she couldn't deny it. Especially Dillon's baby. His gift to her. Something to love of her very own.

Wade raised his brows in surprise. "Wow, you really seem better all of a sudden." He surprised her by bending down and kissing her forehead, as he might have done when they were together in New York, and Chantel realized he still didn't believe things were over between them. Oh, well, she had more important concerns right now. "I'm glad it's nothing serious," he said.

Chantel rubbed her stomach, consciously willing her baby to survive. If Wade only knew how serious it was…

CHAPTER THIRTEEN

STACY STOOD in the glass-walled nursery and cooed to the newborn she held in her arms, trying to get him to take some glucose water. His mother wouldn't have milk for a day or two, so an occasional bottle of water was supposed to tide him over.

"How's he doing?" Leslie, the other nurse working maternity, rolled a silver gurney holding an empty plastic cradle to the side and came over to get a better look at him.

"He's a little fussy, but he likes it when I hold him tight."

"Is his mother sleeping?"

"Probably not yet. I just took him in for a feeding. Unfortunately colostrum isn't very filling." Stacy bent closer to the infant and breathed in his fresh sweet smell. Would she ever hold a child of her own?

First comes love, then comes marriage. Then comes Stacy with a baby carriage.

Love. She couldn't even complete the first step of that silly rhyme. She couldn't make a man she wanted fall in love with her. Dillon had called a couple of times to be sure she was okay after that awkward scene in his office, but she knew he was only being kind. It had been almost a month since she'd last heard from him. The more days that passed, the less likely it was he'd call again. She supposed she could contact him and try to salvage their friendship, at least, but her feelings were still too raw for that.

"What are you doing after work?" Leslie asked, interrupting her thoughts.

She'd been planning to go back to Chantel's, but she hated the idea of seeing Wade. The man made her skin crawl. She couldn't imagine what she'd seen in him all those years ago, what had possessed her that night several weeks ago. He was selfish and shallow and lazy. Nothing like Dillon. She shrugged. "Not much. What do you have in mind?"

"Want to come over to my place and order a pizza tonight? We could rent a couple of movies and kick back," Leslie suggested. Her husband was out of town on a business trip, and she'd already admitted she hated to be alone.

"Sure," Stacy replied with more enthusiasm than she felt. Now that she knew Chantel was going to be okay, there was really no point in putting her life on hold any longer. And she certainly wasn't eager to spend more time with Wade. "I just need to call and check on my sister."

Returning to the nurse's station, Stacy dialed Chantel, then grimaced when Wade answered. *Sponge,* she muttered to herself. "Let me talk to Chantel."

"She's asleep."

Stacy tapped the telephone with one long nail. "Did she hear anything about her tests today?"

Wade's voice wasn't any warmer than hers. But he answered. "They say it's the flu. She has another doctor's appointment in the morning."

"If they know it's the flu, what does she have to go back for?"

"How the hell should I know?"

"Oh, forgive me. I thought you were there with her. You're not likely to stray very far from a free ride, right?"

"What's the matter, Stacy? You jealous?"

"Hardly. I thought you were going back to New York, anyway."

"We will. When Chantel's well."

Stacy almost told him Chantel wasn't going back, but she wasn't completely sure. *Would* her sister leave with Wade in the end? "So what's this doctor's appointment tomorrow?"

"Campbell referred her to a Dr. Bradley for one more test."

"Bradley! Are you sure? Bradley's an obstetrician who delivers here at the hospital."

"That's the name Chantel wrote down."

"But that doesn't make sense. The flu is a virus."

"Who knows? She's always had trouble with that female stuff. Maybe it's all tied in. Or maybe they're checking something to do with the anorexia."

"Did she say what kind of test they plan to run?"

"I didn't ask. It's just some precautionary measure. I'm sure she'll be fine."

Bradley. Stacy twisted the phone cord around her finger, then let go. "Yeah. Well, I'm going out with a friend. Tell Chantel I'll see her tomorrow."

"Breaking out the black nightwear, Stace?" he taunted.

"Screw you."

"You've already done that."

"Oh, yeah? I guess you weren't good enough to remember," she said, and hung up.

CHANTEL GLANCED around her dark room, made darker by the lined chintz curtains she'd asked Wade to close before the sun went down. What had woken her? Slivers of moonlight peaked through a few cracks near the sill, and everything looked normal.

She glanced at the clock on her nightstand. Normal for

one in the morning, anyway. She didn't know what had disturbed her sleep. Possibly a bad dream or simply that she'd spent too many days in bed.

Sitting up, Chantel paused long enough to overcome her dizziness before she scooted to the edge of the mattress and headed to the bathroom. Fortunately she felt a little stronger than she had. The nausea wasn't so bad. She suffered only from a slight headache.

When she finished in the bathroom, she washed her hands and shuffled out to the kitchen for a drink, expecting the door to the guest room, where Stacy slept, to be closed and to find Wade on the couch. But Stacy's door stood open, revealing a perfectly made bed. And Wade wasn't in the living room.

Where were they? Wade hadn't mentioned going anywhere when he'd brought her some chicken from a fast-food outlet for dinner, and the last she'd heard from Stacy was that she'd be back when she got off work at eight.

Maybe, now that they believed she only had the flu, they'd tired of their vigil and gone out for some fun. It certainly wasn't typical of Wade to play nursemaid to anyone. He liked things fast and loose and was probably dying for a little excitement. And for her, Chantel reveled in the thought of some time alone.

"I'm going to have a baby," she whispered, suddenly remembering and trying to absorb, again, what the doctor had told her that afternoon. She'd been saying the same thing to herself over and over every time she woke up, but Wade had been around, and she couldn't say it aloud. Now she wanted to shout her good news to the world. "I'm going to have a baby!" she exclaimed. "Dillon's baby!"

A yearning to tell him, to feel his arms around her, swept over her, and she considered calling him. How would he take the news? She'd asked him not to contact her, and he'd called only once since the big blowup with Stacy. Did that mean he'd moved on? That he didn't care? Stacy hadn't mentioned his name or said what had happened between them, and Chantel had been too afraid to ask. For all she knew, they were still dating.

The thought of Dillon and Stacy seeing each other made Chantel feel weak. Her problems with her sister were bad enough already. How was she going to tell either one of them, or even Wade, about the baby?

The moon glinted off the telephone near the couch, and Chantel sat down next to it. She knew Dillon's number by heart, had memorized it from that scrap of paper he'd left on her counter once, simply because she'd looked at it so often.

He'll be sleeping, and he has his girls now. I shouldn't wake him, she thought, but she had to talk to him, if only for a few minutes. The sound of his voice would make the fact that they were having a baby together seem more real.

She picked up the receiver and dialed, her breath growing shallow with nervousness. It occurred to her to use the pretense of asking if his truck was out of the shop, but she knew that would sound pretty silly at one o'clock in the morning. The accident had happened almost two months ago. Of course his truck was fixed.

"Hello?" His voice was filled with sleep, as she knew it would be.

"Dillon? It's Chantel."

Hearing her name seemed to instantly clear away the cobwebs. "Are you all right?"

"I'm fine."

There was a long pause, and Chantel realized she didn't have anything to say. She just longed for him so much it had become a physical ache.

"Did you, uh, have something you wanted to tell me?" he asked.

I'm going to have your baby. "No, I...I don't know why I called."

She heard some rustling in the background and pictured him sitting up in his bed.

"Listen, I'm sorry I woke you," she said, feeling like an idiot. She hadn't even had the ultrasound yet. She could lose the baby at any time. And until she decided what to do about Stacy, she couldn't tell Dillon, anyway. "I'd better go—"

"Chantel?"

"What?"

"Come and see me."

"I can't. It's one in the morning."

"I don't care what time it is."

"I haven't been feeling very well."

"What's wrong? Don't tell me it's the anorexia—"

"No." She swallowed hard and curled her fingernails into her palms. "I think it's just the flu. You wouldn't want to get it."

"Let me worry about that. Come over so I can take care of you. I'd go to your place, but I've got the girls here."

"I know."

"Can you make it to my house?"

Chantel knew she could. And without Wade and Stacy here to stop her, she felt herself giving in. Was it so wrong to want to be with the father of her baby?

Dillon must have sensed her weakness, because he allowed her no chance to argue. He gave her directions, then said, "I'll be waiting for you," and hung up so she couldn't refuse.

DILLON'S ADDRESS was in a woodsy, hilly neighborhood. The lots were large, with a great deal of natural landscaping between homes that were all different. Some had a Mediterranean appearance. Others were California ranch-style. Dillon's looked as if it belonged on the side of a lake. It was relatively new, with a green steep-pitched roof and a front porch that wrapped almost all the way around. A hammock hung between two large trees off to the side, and the large stretch of front lawn had just been cut. Chantel could smell the grass clippings as she got out of her car, could hear the delicate tinkle of wind chimes.

The porch light was already on, a welcoming beacon, but still she felt a moment's hesitation. She'd promised Stacy she wouldn't see Dillon. She'd left her sister and Wade a note, in case they came home, but it said merely that she couldn't sleep and had gone for a drive—hardly enough to keep them from worrying about her should they return while she was gone. There were a thousand reasons she shouldn't have come. But somehow, as the door opened and Dillon walked out of the house to wait for her on the porch, she couldn't remember any of them. He wore only a baseball cap and a pair of faded jeans.

The muscles in his powerful arms flexed as he leaned on the railing, watching her, his face inscrutable. She remembered running her fingers over his ribs and pressing her palms to his chest as she'd sat on top of him, feeling him deep inside her....

He didn't say anything as she approached, and Chantel wondered what he was thinking. She'd showered and blow-dried her hair, but she hadn't bothered with any makeup. The bulky sweater she'd chosen hung loosely on her and did little to enhance her figure. She'd actually been hoping that it would camouflage the evidence of her recent weight loss.

"Aren't you going to say anything?" she asked, feeling

breathless and weak from the effort it had taken to get ready and drive across town.

"Only whatever's necessary to get you back in my arms," he murmured, but the next moment she was there without his having to say another word. He drew her to him as soon as she was within reach, and she did nothing to stop him. He nuzzled her neck, groaned, then ran his hands all the way down her back as though he longed to consume every inch of her. "I've missed you."

Chantel closed her eyes and clung to him. "I shouldn't be here," she whispered.

"I thought it was over. What made you call me?"

"How did I stop myself until now?"

He chuckled into her hair. "Come in before you get cold. You're shaking."

He scooped her into his arms and carried her in. As he was about to set her down on the couch, she tightened her arms around his neck and shook her head. "No. Take me to your room."

He hesitated, then kissed her forehead, her cheeks, the tip of her nose. "What's going on, Chantel? You've lost weight, you don't look well, and after telling me to forget it more than six weeks ago, you show up at my house and want me to take you straight to bed."

The kitchen light was on. It spilled into the area where they stood, throwing Dillon's face into shadow and making it difficult for Chantel to read his expression. "You don't want to?"

His laugh was hoarse. "That's not the problem."

"Then what?"

"What about Stacy? You'd feel guilty and you'd hate me in the morning."

She sighed and turned her face into the hollow of his shoulder. He was right, and she knew it. Besides, the short burst of energy she'd experienced earlier was gone, and in its place was the old fatigue and nausea.

"Tell me why you've lost weight," he said.

Chantel hated to lie to him again. To avoid that, she said, "I don't want to talk about it."

"I think we should."

He placed her on his leather couch, then switched on a lamp that revealed a whole wall of built-in cabinetry, hardwood floors and a round area rug. Sitting across from her on a chest that served as a coffee table, Dillon turned her hands palms up and began lightly tracing her lifelines with the pads of his thumbs. "You haven't been at work."

"How do you know?"

A sheepish smile curved his lips. "I called a couple of times just to hear your voice. Maureen finally told me you've been out for a week."

"You called?" That felt good, knowing he couldn't walk away from her as easily as he'd made it appear. "Maureen didn't pass on the message."

"I didn't leave one." He suddenly looked vulnerable, almost boyish. "What do we have between us, Chantel? Anything?"

Chantel bit her lip. She couldn't tell him about the pregnancy until after the doctor's appointment. She needed final confirmation before facing all the difficult decisions she would have to make. And she needed time. She also wished she knew, in advance, how he'd react to the news.

Or maybe it would be smarter—safer—not to tell him at all. He had enough to worry about with his missing ex-wife and his two daughters. The last thing he needed was this kind of surprise. She'd gotten her life in order again and would now have a child. Did she really want to risk it all on what Dillon's reaction might be?

"I don't know," she said. "If you hadn't kept searching for me in the snowstorm—"

"What?" Dropping her hands, he stood, a scowl marring his handsome face. "Is that all you feel? Well, I don't want your gratitude."

Chantel shook her head, growing weaker by the moment. She shouldn't have come. She doubted she had the strength to make it back home. "I can't answer your questions right now, Dillon. I can't explain anything or promise anything. I just...I just wanted to see you. But I don't feel so good...."

"What's wrong?" Concern replaced his earlier frustration. "None of this makes sense, Chantel."

"I'm sick," she said, because she didn't have the energy to debate with herself any longer. "It comes and goes. Just give me a minute."

Cupping her chin with his hand, he tilted her face toward the lamp on her left and studied it. "You're scaring me."

She took a deep breath, trying to settle her stomach. "I'm okay."

"Like hell you are." Bending, he slipped one arm beneath her knees and the other around her back and easily gathered her in his arms again. "I should take you to the hospital."

"No. I have a doctor's appointment in the morning. I can make it till then."

"When is it?"

"Nine o'clock."

"Fine. I'll make sure you're there on time."

"Where are you taking me now?"

Dillon carried her to a set of stairs that rose into blackness. "To bed."

DILLON AWOKE to the familiar squawk of his alarm and quickly shut off the noise before it could wake Chantel.

Then he wrapped one arm around her middle and pulled her back into the cradle of his body, wanting to hold her for a few minutes more.

She groaned and began to stir, eventually rolling over to face him. He watched her wake up, noting the dark circles beneath her eyes, the gauntness of her face.

She blinked, her magnificent amber eyes finally opening wide as she offered him a shy smile. "Good morning."

"Good morning," he said, content just to look at her. He was still bare-chested, but before he'd gotten into bed with her last night, he'd traded his blue jeans for pajama bottoms. Chantel wore a pair of his sweats, and even with her blond hair in a tangled mess, she was beautiful. What he liked most was the sweetness that showed in her eyes and in her smile. "How do you feel?"

"A little better."

He watched her glance around the room, taking in the ceiling which was made mostly of glass and now revealed the purplish predawn sky, the large bathroom behind him, and the French doors that opened onto a balcony overlooking the backyard.

"This is incredible, Dillon," she breathed.

He smiled, feeling a sense of pride. "I designed it myself."

"For Sydney and Brittney's mother?"

"No. I bought this place after the divorce, and I've been remodeling it a little at a time. You're the first woman I've brought up here."

She blushed, and Dillon wanted to reach out and trace the curve of her breasts, pull off her sweatshirt and hold them in his palms. But if Chantel was indeed feeling better, it wasn't by much. And there was always Stacy standing between them.

Inhaling deeply he decided it was time for a cold shower. "Don't wake up," he said, allowing himself a chaste kiss on her temple before getting out of bed. "I'll drive the girls to school and then bring you something to eat."

"I have to leave."

"No. You're not well enough to go anywhere by yourself. I'll take you to the doctor's this morning. Do you need to stop by your place first?"

The thought of showing up at the condo with Dillon and finding Wade or Stacy waiting for her made Chantel bolt upright—an action she instantly regretted when her head began to swim. With a groan she fell back. "I should. Stacy and Wade are probably frantic by now," she said weakly.

He paused at the side of the bed, his jaw tightening. "Wade again. He was at your house the other night."

"It's a long story," she said, "but he and Stacy have been taking care of me."

"So are you thinking of going back?"

"To New York?"

"To Wade."

Chantel recalled how good Wade had been to her in the past few weeks, how he'd asked her for another chance and promised they could have a family. She had to admit that sometimes she did think of returning to him. It was difficult to give up on a relationship in which she'd already invested ten years of her life. And Wade had changed. He needed her.

But looking at Dillon, she knew, with startling clarity, that every time Wade took her in his arms, she'd be thinking of someone else—a man with dark hair and blue eyes, an architect whose bedroom ceiling was made entirely of sky-lights. She'd be thinking of Dillon Broderick.

And if she *was* pregnant with his child…

"No," she said. "I'm not going back to him."

He propped his hands on his hips. "Chantel, I don't know what, exactly, there is between us, or where it might be headed. But I have to be honest with you. While I was married to Amanda, I became too well acquainted with jealousy. I'm not interested in experiencing those feelings again."

"I was always faithful to Wade."

"That's partially what I'm worried about. Are you still in love with him?"

"No."

"Does that mean you're going to give us a chance? That you'll talk to Stacy? And get rid of Wade?"

"I can't talk to Stacy. At least not yet."

"When?"

Chantel thought of her impending doctor's appointment. "Give me a few days."

He seemed impatient but relieved. "Okay. Then I think we should both sit down with her."

"And if she cuts me off again?"

The look in his eyes grew haunted. "You'd still have me."

And you'd come with what guarantee? she wanted to ask. She'd tried to console herself with Wade, too, but the self-respect she'd lost was too high a price to pay, even for love. "Dillon, what if we tell Stacy we want to see each other and she refuses to speak to me again? And then—" feeling a surge of illness, Chantel took a moment to catch her breath "—two months down the road, we decide we're not meant for each other, after all?"

He studied her for a moment. "I can't answer that. I've never been much good at fortune-telling."

"Neither have I. All I have is the benefit of past experience."

"What happened in the past doesn't have to repeat itself."

Chantel closed her eyes. "Just give me a few days," she said again. "And let me go to the doctor's by myself."

He frowned. "Why don't you want me to take you?"

"It's not that I don't want you to take me." She flailed around for some excuse that might distract him, send him toward an alternative course of action. "It's just that I'm sure you're probably busy this morning. And there's no need to miss work, especially when I'm actually feeling better." She smiled, despite a rising bout of nausea, and wished at the same time that she could force some color back into her cheeks.

He arched a brow at her. "Let me worry about my schedule, okay?"

She gulped, hoping he understood that gynecologists did more than deliver babies. Otherwise he might guess her condition right away. "But what am I going to wear?"

"Just wear what you wore here last night."

Chantel looked at the sweater and jeans that were draped across the arm of an overstuffed chair. They were still clean. She'd only worn them for an hour or so the night before.

"Do you want to give Stacy a call?" he asked, running a hand through his hair, which only made him look sexier. "Just so she doesn't worry?"

"And tell her what?" Chantel groaned.

"That you have a ride to the doctor."

The only thing she could tell Stacy was that she'd gone out for a drive and was planning on getting herself to the doctor. It was a lame reason for being gone all night, and she knew it, but she certainly wasn't prepared to tell her sister anything about Dillon. Not yet, and not when there would be so much to say later.

Dillon rounded the bed and handed her a cordless phone.

She dialed her own number and waited, but on the fifth ring the answering machine picked up. She left a short message saying she was feeling fine and would soon be on her way to the doctor's, without bothering to explain anything else. Then she dialed Stacy's number.

Again she reached only an answering machine, and she left the same message, then hung up and slumped back onto the pillows.

"Dillon?" she called. The door to the bathroom was now closed, the shower running. He couldn't hear her. "How would you feel about having more children?" she asked.

CHAPTER FOURTEEN

"YOU HAVE TO SEE a gynecologist?" Dillon asked, staring at the gold lettering on Dr. Bradley's door.

Chantel had tried to persuade Dillon to run a few errands or get a cup of coffee at the coffee shop down the street while she visited Dr. Bradley on her own, but he'd insisted on accompanying her. And now she was facing the very thing she'd dreaded, trying to keep him from guessing the truth before she was ready to tell him.

"My doctor referred me here. He thought my er, sickness might have something to do with my reproductive system." At least that wasn't a total lie. Her sickness did have to do with her reproductive system, just not in the way he'd think.

Dillon nodded and opened the door. "What do they suspect the problem is?"

That question was a little more difficult to handle. Chantel chose evasion. "I'm not sure yet. I should learn something today."

The nurse behind the front desk glanced up as they approached, and Chantel gave her name. "It'll be just a minute, Ms. Miller, but first we need you to complete some paperwork."

She accepted a clipboard that held several forms asking about her medical history. Chantel filled them out, then returned them to the front desk. Shortly after, an assistant called her back.

Another nurse weighed her and guided her into a small

examination room, where she took her blood pressure. Handing her a paper lap cover, she told her to strip from the waist down.

"The doctor will be with you shortly."

Chantel mumbled a thank-you, but felt too ill to move at first. Occasionally she felt like her old self, but those times didn't last.

Resting her head on her forearms, she tried to talk herself out of the nervousness that only added to her nausea. Somehow it would all work out. But that seemed a hollow and forlorn hope when she thought of her sister's anger and the possibility of having a baby all on her own. Besides her problems with Stacy, she'd assured Dillon that she couldn't have children. What if her pregnancy made him angry? What if he didn't want anything to do with her or the baby?

Wouldn't it actually be better to pretend the baby was entirely her own?

Coward. Hiding the baby's paternity wouldn't be fair to the child or to Dillon. And who was she trying to kid? The truth would come out eventually. It always did. Wasn't her pregnancy proof of that?

Letting her breath go in a hiss, she raked a hand through her hair and began to undress. She'd just finished when a soft knock sounded at the door.

"Come in."

The doctor entered, wearing a white coat and a warm smile. "Hi, I'm Dr. Bradley." She picked up the chart the nurse had left and studied the information. "I see you've already had a blood test. Dr. Campbell had the results forwarded to me. Are you happy about the baby?"

"I am. I'm just afraid of what might happen. Dr. Campbell had some concerns."

Dr. Bradley nodded. "I can see why, but we're going to

do everything we can to make sure your baby arrives safely, Ms. Miller. I see here that you're not married."

Chantel nodded, feeling a twinge of guilt. She wanted to explain how it was that night in the Landcruiser, when they'd believed they might not get out alive. She sighed. This certainly wasn't how she'd always pictured starting a family. She'd hoped to do things the right way, the way she'd been taught. But nothing in her life had really gone as planned. Her only solace now was that the doctor probably wasn't thinking about the moral implications. She was just doing her job.

"You haven't written down the baby's father's name. Does that mean you don't know who he is?" she asked.

"No, he's with me today. I just…I must have missed that question," Chantel responded, unwilling to explain why she hadn't been free to divulge that information at the time she filled in the form.

"What's his name?"

"Dillon Broderick."

Dr. Bradley's pen made a scratching sound. "Okay, fine. Let's get started. I'd like to check your cervix, make sure it's closed and everything else is fine. Then I'll send you to the lab for the ultrasound."

A few minutes later Chantel was dressed again and carrying a slip of paper to the lab across the hall from Dr. Bradley's office. As she passed Dillon in the reception area, she smiled and said, "They need to do a couple of lab tests. I'll be right back."

"Where's the lab?"

"Just over there." She pointed. "You go ahead and read."

"No, I'll come." He set his magazine aside and followed her.

When they reached the other office, Chantel waited until

Dillon had found a chair before she presented herself at the window.

"Thank you, Ms. Miller. We'll call you as soon as the technician's ready," the woman told her.

Chantel sat next to Dillon and tried to distract herself by watching the exotic-looking fish in a large aquarium against the far wall, but the pending ultrasound—the thought of actually seeing her baby—kept her too anxious to relax. Could this really be happening? To her?

Dillon took her hand, startling her out of her preoccupation. "What's wrong?"

"Nothing." She considered telling him right then and there, and inviting him to come with her to see their baby. But at the moment, she couldn't think straight, and too much hinged on this decision. She had to decide what she was going to do, make a plan. The doctor had told her chances were good she'd be feeling better in a few weeks. She'd probably even be able to go back to work, provided she didn't develop any serious complications, like toxemia.

"You look worried."

"No. I'll just be glad when this is over."

"What are they going to do? Draw blood?"

The nurse called her name, saving her from answering. "I won't be long," she said.

This time Chantel didn't have to strip. She merely had to lie down and raise her baggy sweater so the technician could move a silver instrument lathered with gel across her stomach. Staring up at a small screen overhead, she waited as the woman adjusted a few dials on the machine next to her. Then the sound of static erupted over a speaker and a mostly black picture flickered to life.

"Let's see if we can find that little guy," the technician murmured, moving the wandlike instrument just below her

navel before homing in on something that looked completely unfamiliar to Chantel.

"Ah, there he is."

"He?" Chantel croaked.

The technician laughed. "It could just as easily be a girl.
You're not very far along. It's too early to determine the
sex with any accuracy. I just prefer to say he or she, instead
of it."

Chantel nodded, still trying to make out the shape of a
baby. "What part of him is that?"

"His foot. See?" Reaching up to the monitor, she traced
the white form against the black picture and Chantel finally
recognized it as something that looked human.

"Omigosh. There *is* a baby in there!"

"You bet there is. Here, let's get a heartbeat."

The technician moved the wand some more, showing different parts of the baby, the curve of his head, the spine,
what seemed to be a fist. Then a rapid heartbeat came across
the speakers, and Chantel could see a white flutter keeping
time with the sound.

She was awestruck. Just when she'd finally accepted that
she'd never have a child of her own, here she was seeing
inside her womb, watching her baby, hearing his heartbeat.

Dillon. His name popped into her mind, and she wanted
him at her side. He'd given this to her. *He has to see it,* she
thought, and knew then that she could never keep the fact
of this baby from him. She only hoped he'd be as happy as
she was.

And that someday Stacy would understand.

The technician started to move the sensor away, but
Chantel quickly stopped her. "Just another minute or two,"
she pleaded.

The woman smiled and settled the microphone over the baby again, and Chantel closed her eyes and listened—to a miracle.

WHERE WAS SHE? Wade paced the floor, wondering what could have happened to Chantel. After Stacy's call the night before, he couldn't face another night of watching television. He'd phoned an old friend and they'd gone barhopping, but he'd come home at three to find a note from Chantel saying she'd gone for a drive. Only she hadn't come back. He'd been out searching for her all morning.

He called Stacy's again, wishing he could get hold of her, then cursed when her answering machine came on. Wait! Didn't Chantel have a doctor's appointment this morning? She was supposed to see a Dr. Bradley. A gynecologist, according to Stacy.

Jogging down the hall and into Chantel's bedroom, he rummaged through her nightstand for the magazine she'd written on when Dr. Campbell called, but he couldn't find anything. She must have taken it with her. Picking up the phone, he punched in 411 and asked for Dr. Bradley's number.

"A Woman's Place," the receptionist answered when he'd dialed it.

"This is Wade Bennett. Do you have a patient there by the name of Chantel Miller? I think she had an appointment this morning."

"I'm sorry. We're not allowed to divulge that information, Mr. Bennett."

"But I'm her boyfriend. She hasn't been feeling very well and—"

"I'm sorry. We respect our patients' right to privacy."

Damn! Wade cursed and hung up. He'd have to drive over there.

DILLON BEGAN TO TAP his foot, growing anxious. How long could it take to draw some blood? He'd cleared his morning of any appointments, but he had a lot of drawings to do and several sets of plans that needed to go out by overnight courier. Now that he had the girls living with him, he no longer had the time he used to, and his work was quickly falling behind. Not that he'd change anything. He just needed to make more efficient use of the hours they were in school and day care.

Standing, he crossed to the receptionist's desk. "Do you know how much longer it'll be?"

A petite woman with dark hair pulled severely off her face glanced up from a stack of folders. "You're with Chantel Miller, right?"

He nodded.

"I'll check." She disappeared for several seconds, then returned wearing a much warmer smile. "Your wife is doing fine, Mr. Miller. They're just about finished with the ultrasound now."

Dillon was too stunned to correct her on the husband-wife issue. "The what?"

"The ultrasound. The baby looks fine, by the way. Its heartbeat is coming through loud and strong."

Dillon blinked. Then he cleared his throat. "Are you sure we're talking about the right woman? Chantel just went back to have some blood drawn."

"Oh, no, we take the blood right here." She waved to four chairs arranged in an open area to her left. "And your wife is the only ultrasound we have scheduled this morn—" Evidently the look on his face alerted her to his total surprise, because her words suddenly dropped off and a red flush crept up her cheeks. "You brought her here. This isn't some kind of secret, right?"

Evidently it was. And the thought of how he'd sat stupidly in the waiting room, completely unsuspecting, rankled. What was Chantel trying to prove?

"Aren't you the father?" she finished weakly.

Dillon didn't know. Chantel had told him she couldn't have children. They'd been together only one night. Of course he'd made love to her several times while they were in his truck—he hadn't been able to get enough of her, still longed for more—but Wade had been hanging around a lot since then. What if…

He refused to even think it. Chantel couldn't be pregnant with Wade's baby. She had the flu. That was what she'd told him.

But denial did little to stop the anger that began to course hotly through his blood. Without another word, he stalked out of the lobby and back to Dr. Bradley's office, where he approached the front desk. "Chantel Miller is still across at the lab, but she wanted to ask the doctor what her due date is." He pasted a pleasant smile on his face to hide the clenching of his jaw. "I guess she forgot it already."

The nurse's brows drew together. "But that's exactly why we sent her to get the ultrasound. We can't give her a due date until we see how far along she is."

"Can't you hazard a guess?"

"Just a minute." The nurse disappeared and returned with a manila folder. "Can I get your name, please?"

"Dillon Broderick."

She glanced at some notes inside, then said, "With her history, it's hard to say, Mr. Broderick. But according to the approximate size of her uterus, the doctor is guessing she's somewhere between seven and nine weeks. We'll know more when we get the results of the ultrasound."

Seven to nine weeks. Tahoe fell right in the middle of that range. But Wade's appearance did, too. "Right. I'll tell her,'' he said, but as he turned to leave, the door opened and Chantel stood there.

"Ready?'' she asked, her eyes unreadable.

Dillon nodded curtly and strode past her without waiting. When they reached his truck, he left the passenger door standing open for her and came around to his own side. He stuck the key in the ignition as he slid behind the wheel but didn't start the car.

She didn't get in as he'd expected. "Would you like me to find another ride home?'' she asked, hovering at the door.

He propped his hands on the steering wheel. "You weren't going to tell me?''

"I wasn't even sure, until today.''

Please tell me the baby's not Wade's. He knew he couldn't ask, simply because the answer meant too much to him. He wasn't ready for the truth. Not yet... "When did you first suspect?''

"I never suspected. I thought I had the flu.''

"And?''

She clutched her purse tightly, like a shield against his hostility. "When I didn't get well the way I should have, Wade insisted I see a doctor.''

Wade again. Dammit! Dillon wanted to pound the man. He'd mistreated Chantel and left her alone for months in a hospital while she was suffering with anorexia. He didn't deserve her.

"Dr. Campbell called yesterday to let me know the blood tests were back,'' she went on, "and that there wasn't anything wrong with me—at least nothing that nine months wouldn't cure.'' She gave him a hesitant smile.

He sighed. "I thought you couldn't have children.''

"That's what they told me at the hospital before I was released.''

"But it happened, anyway.''

She nodded.

"Get in."

"I don't want to get in if…if you're angry about this."

He stared at her. "How am I supposed to feel? How do you feel?"

"I've always wanted a baby. I'm scared, but I'm excited, too." She glanced down at her toes. "And I was hoping you'd be happy about it."

Then tell me the baby's mine! The emotional impact of that thought nearly stole Dillon's breath away. What if the baby *was* his? He had two little girls already. He'd promised himself he'd be true to them, never give them any competition for his time and attention, at least until they were considerably older. But a new baby was definitely competition. Chantel was competition. Especially when he couldn't stop thinking about her and felt as though his heart was being torn from his chest at the prospect of losing her to Wade.

"I'm not angry," he said softly, struggling to control his emotions. "Get in."

She complied, but she was blinking rapidly, and obviously fighting tears.

"If you're so happy about this, why are you about to cry?" he asked, feeling some of his anger subside.

"Because what I just saw was so incredible, so perfect. I wanted you to be there with me, but I didn't want you to know yet, not until I decide how to tell Wade and Stacy."

Dillon took a deep breath to prepare himself. "Tell Wade what?"

She stared at him as though he'd lost his mind. "About the baby."

"*His* baby?" he asked, the words finally tumbling out, almost of their own accord.

As Chantel continued to stare at him, he felt more vulnerable than he ever had in his life. Amanda would have exploited it, kept him guessing. But Chantel took his hand and kissed the very center of his palm, then nuzzled it with her cheek "You may not believe this, but I've only slept with two men my whole life. And Wade and I haven't been together for over a year. This baby is yours," she whispered.

CHAPTER FIFTEEN

WADE SAT in the parking lot of the medical complex, wondering which building housed Dr. Bradley's office. The receptionist had given him an address when he'd called back, but he hadn't thought to ask her for specific directions once he found the property. He hadn't expected the complex to be so large and sprawling.

He nicked the paint of the neighboring car getting out of his father's boatlike Cadillac. But it wasn't his fault most of the lot had been built for compact cars. What was he supposed to do? Park on the road just because his dad owned a gas-guzzling hog?

Striding to the marquis placed in the middle of a patch of green grass surrounded by marigolds, petunias and some little pink flowers he didn't know the name of, he glanced up at the five high-rise medical buildings towering over him, then began to search the directory for Dr. Bradley's office.

Second building. Third floor. He turned and squinted against the sun, gazing out over the sea of cars in the lot, looking for Chantel's Jag. But he couldn't see it. Turning again, he made his way down the winding sidewalk to a metal-and-glass structure labeled Building 2.

"Excuse me." A young woman dodged around him as he entered, making him miss the elevator. Cursing her, as well as the parking lot, he pushed the button and waited, glancing through the lobby windows. Suddenly he saw a woman who resembled Chantel sitting in a white Land-cruiser parked close to the building.

He did a double take and realized it had to be her. How many other women sat so tall? But who was she with? He took a few steps in her direction, then his stomach sank and his blood pressure rose. Dillon! She was with Dillon. Was that where she'd spent the night, too?

He slipped through the silent swinging doors and stood in the dark shade of the building, watching them, but he could have been doing cartwheels across the lawn for all they noticed. They were deep in conversation. Dillon was touching Chantel's face. And she was closing her eyes as though he was reaching her very soul.

CHANTEL'S HEART pounded as Dillon ran his fingers down the side of her face. "We're going to have a baby?" he asked reverently.

She nodded. "If I can carry it long enough."

His hand continued its downward course, trailing over one breast before he flattened his palm against her stomach, looking dazed.

"You should've seen the ultrasound, Dillon," she told him. "I saw his tiny foot and his hand, and his little heart beating so fast—"

"His?"

Chantel noted the wonder on his face and smiled. "I don't know the sex yet."

"But I could be having a son."

"Or you could be having another daughter."

He grinned. "Maybe she'll look just like you."

Chantel chuckled. "Only please let her be short."

"What do you mean?" he demanded with a scowl. "I love tall women."

Does that mean you love me? Chantel squelched the hope

that someday he might. She didn't deserve Dillon. She'd come back to California to pay penance for what she'd done to Stacy, not to fall madly in love. And she feared that was exactly what would happen if she let Dillon any closer. "It's not fun to be called names and to be stared at all the time," she reminded him.

"We'll teach her to be proud."

We'll teach her... Chantel felt her heart melt, partly because of his words and partly because of the magic of his touch. Hooking one hand behind her neck, he leaned forward and gently brought his lips to hers, as if savoring the taste and feel of her. Her eyes closed as he deepened the kiss, and she remembered the magical way it had been that night when they'd made their baby. "This Landcruiser must work as some kind of aphrodisiac or something," she joked.

He chuckled and she inhaled the spearmint on his breath. "Best make-out car I ever bought. But this time, I'd rather go home to celebrate. How are you feeling, babe?"

"Better."

"Can I interest you in testing out my new bed?"

"We slept in it last night, remember?"

"Oh, I already know it's comfortable enough. I just want to be sure it doesn't creak too loudly." He kissed her again, his lips moving purposefully over hers, rousing more memories of what it felt like to be loved by Dillon, along with a dose of fresh undiluted desire. She thought of the skylights in his room and imagined lying on her back, his muscular form poised above her, the sun shining all around, and wanted to agree.

But losing herself in Dillon's arms still felt too much like betrayal. She had to talk to Stacy first, tell her the truth. Although Chantel doubted that honesty would eradicate her guilt, at least she wouldn't be doing anything in secret.

"Stacy and Wade are probably waiting for me, wondering what the doctor said."

He sat back and looked at her. "And I think it's time to tell them."

Chantel wasn't so sure. What if she miscarried? She would have hurt her sister for nothing.

For nothing, or for a chance at happiness with Dillon?

Would she never conquer the selfishness that kept her seeking what *she* wanted over her sister's best interests? As soon as Stacy learned Chantel was carrying Dillon's child, she'd feel like sloppy leftovers. Her self-esteem would plummet.

And Chantel couldn't be the cause of that again. Not after all her good intentions. Not after all the promises to herself that if Stacy would only give her another chance, she'd move heaven and earth to prove herself worthy.

"You look miserable," Dillon said, slinging one arm over the steering wheel.

"I'm just trying to decide what to do. How can I tell Stacy I'm pregnant with your child?"

He rested his head on one fist. "It won't be easy. But what's the alternative? In seven months, the baby will be here. That's not something we can hide."

"Unless I tell her the baby belongs to someone else."

Dillon stiffened and the blue of his eyes darkened. "Hell, no! The baby's mine, and I don't want anyone thinking it isn't. Especially Wade."

Chantel had known, even as she said it, that claiming the baby belonged to someone else wasn't really a possibility. She couldn't do that to Dillon or their child. She was just searching for a way, any way, to salvage her sister's feelings. And to save herself from having to break the news.

"I'll need a few days."

His scowl grew fiercer. "I don't want to push you into

saying something until you're ready. But you do realize it's not going to get any easier, don't you?''

A lump swelled in Chantel's throat, and as hard as she tried to swallow it, it wouldn't go away. ''I just need a little more time with her before...before she's gone.''

The look on Dillon's face softened, and he reached across the seat to squeeze her hand. ''Maybe she'll surprise us both. Unlike Wade, I never promised her anything. We weren't engaged. We only dated a few times and kissed once.''

''You kissed her?'' Chantel groaned. Considering how much she hated the thought of that, she could guess how terrible Stacy was going to feel when she learned about their night in Tahoe.

''I kissed her goodnight. I didn't see fireworks. That was it.''

''Evidently she saw fireworks. She told me she was in love with you, Dillon, and you guys have been friends long enough for her to know.''

''It was a crush, nothing more.''

''You'd like to believe that because then it's easier to think Stacy won't be seriously hurt by all this. I wish I had that luxury.''

His brows drew together. ''I'm not sure. Maybe you're right, but I was being honest with you when I said Stacy and I were never that close.''

''It's possible to love someone who doesn't return your feelings.''

''I know,'' he said, and Chantel wondered if he was thinking of his ex-wife. How could Amanda have loved Dillon and still have done the things she did?

Chantel hesitated, then voiced the concern that kept flitting across her mind. ''What if *we* don't become that close,

Dillon? We haven't spent a great deal of time together. Heck, you know Stacy better than you know me.''

''Not in the biblical sense.'' He grinned, probably trying to ease the tension, but she was too wound up to let his humor relax her.

''There's more to a relationship than sex,'' she said.

''Do you think you're talking to a man whose sole purpose is to get a good lay? I have two kids already, remember? I think I know what it takes to make a relationship work, or at least I know what can screw it up beyond repair.''

Chantel sighed, realizing she and Dillon were arguing because she was trying to wheedle something out of him he wasn't willing to give, some sort of commitment that would make the coming confrontation with Stacy a little easier. But it was too early in their relationship for that. And it was a cowardly thing to do, anyway—to let go of one hand only after she was hanging on securely to another.

She had to let go of everyone—Stacy, Dillon and Wade—and stand on her own two feet and be strong for her baby. Her meeting Dillon was an accident, a twist of fate, nothing more. If Stacy wouldn't forgive her, Chantel would have to deal with that. And if Dillon didn't end up loving her, she'd have to forge ahead on her own. That was the only way to garner any self-respect. ''Let's go,'' she said calmly.

He turned the key in the ignition, but before putting the truck into drive, he glanced over at her. ''What have you decided?''

''That I've got to do this my way. And that I'll do it when I'm ready.''

Wariness clouded his eyes. ''That sounds suspiciously like you're shutting me out.''

Chantel chuckled humorlessly. ''No, I'm doing the only

fair thing. I'm giving us room to get to know each other, room to decide where we want to go from here and room to breathe.''

DILLON WASN'T SURE he wanted room to breathe.

Then again, he wasn't sure he didn't.

Since that night in Tahoe, he'd thought a lot about Chantel, had wanted to spend time with her. Her quiet strength, so at odds with her vulnerability, had struck a chord in him. But he hadn't thought beyond that to anything more serious. Commitment, children, marriage—those things typically took care of themselves as a relationship developed. He didn't think about them much in advance.

But he and Chantel were having a baby together, and Dillon wasn't exactly sure what he should or shouldn't do about it.

Pulling out of the medical building's parking lot, he turned left and stopped at the first traffic light. He knew he didn't want anyone to think the baby belonged to someone else. He took care of his own. He also knew he desired Chantel, felt protective of her. To a certain extent, that meant he already claimed her, too.

What about Brittney and Sydney? He'd sworn he'd never force them into a stepparent situation, at least not while they were so young. He hated the thought of another adult coming into their lives and their home with the power to make or break their happiness. *Chantel* hardly fit the image of a wicked stepmother, but he'd never—until now—even considered making an exception.

Signaling, he turned left at the next light and moved into the far right lane before merging onto the interstate. He thought briefly of the work that awaited him at the office, but it no loner seemed so urgent. Because he had bigger things to worry about. He was going to be the father of a new baby.

How had this happened? And how could he ever sort out his feelings about it?

Dillon gunned the accelerator and shot over into the fast lane. It suddenly felt as if he was leading two very different lives—the responsible loving father of two young girls, and the lonely divorced man who'd just gotten a beautiful ex-model pregnant. How the hell did he integrate the two?

Chantel stared out the window, less emotional now, almost serene. Instead of calming Dillon, however, her attitude only increased his own anxiety. Most women in her situation would be demanding to know how he felt about them and whether he was going to support the baby. She acted as though she didn't expect anything from him. As though she'd raise the child on her own as easily as accept his help.

If he'd been a different kind of man, that would have given him freedom, he supposed. But he couldn't walk away, didn't want to, even if she'd let him. He just felt a certain panic at knowing they'd come face-to-face with the life-changing consequences of one reckless night.

He shot her a glance and bristled at her composure. Didn't she care whether or not he was part of her life? Whether or not he took an interest in their baby? She'd seemed to at first. But that was before they'd addressed the issue of Stacy.

"Thanks for the ride," Chantel said as soon as they pulled up to his house.

Knowing he couldn't talk her into coming inside with him, Dillon caught her arm as she started to get out of the truck. "Call me if you need me."

She nodded. "Thanks."

He watched her climb into her own car, which was still sitting in his drive, then let his head rest on the steering wheel.

Ready or not, they were going to have a baby.

CHANTEL BRACED HERSELF before opening the door to her condominium. She hadn't seen either Stacy's car or Wade's in the parking lot, but she had no idea what might be waiting for her inside. It seemed like an eternity since she'd been home, and if, by chance, Wade was there—if his parents had taken back their car or something—she knew he'd barrage her with a million questions she'd find difficult to answer. What could she tell him? Now that the baby was real, now that she'd seen its little heart beating and *believed*, she had to reveal the truth.

But dread weighted her movements. Slowly she let herself into the house, then blinked in surprise when she found everything just as she'd left it the night before. At least, she thought it was the same. She hadn't really paid much attention.

"Stacy? Wade? Is anyone home?"

No answer. Chantel did a quick turn through the rooms, confirming that she was indeed alone, then sank gratefully into one of the wing chairs in her living room. She was physically exhausted, emotionally drained.

Drawing a lap blanket up over her legs, she decided that whoever controlled fate sure had a morbid sense of humor. She'd been struggling with her promise to stay away from Dillon Broderick; adding his baby into the mix made that virtually impossible. Her feelings were confused and contradictory. Joy at the thought of having a child, the secret thrill of knowing she now had an unimpeachable excuse to keep in contact with Dillon—and pain and regret that her happiness about these things came at her sister's expense.

Right now the pain won out. Tears trickled down her cheeks as she stared at the blank television set. Outside, the clouds passed over the sun, darkening the room and making it feel more like evening than noon. She should call Maureen at work and give her an update. She should force herself to eat something for lunch. The baby was going to need much more than the samples of prenatal vitamins the doctor had given her. But she couldn't move. She simply sat there and worried about what she'd say to Stacy, without coming any closer to a decision.

The telephone rang just as Chantel started to drift into an uneasy sleep. Jerking back to full awareness, she stood and rounded the coffee table, hurrying toward the phone.

"Hello?"

"Chantel?"

It was Stacy. Talons of anxiety clawed at Chantel's stomach, and she was glad she hadn't eaten, after all. "Hi, Stace. Where are you?"

"I'm at home, getting ready for work. Wade left several messages on my recorder saying he couldn't find you. Are you okay?"

"I'm fine. I've had a good morning." Which meant she hadn't thrown up, despite the nausea. "Why didn't you come back here last night?"

"A friend of mine from work wanted me to do something with her."

"Good, I'm glad you got out. Was it fun?"

"It was okay. How'd it go at the doctor's? You made it there safely, didn't you?"

Chantel tried to take a deep breath, but her chest was too tight to let in much air. "Yeah. It went fine."

"What did they say?"

That I'm due in about seven months. "They said everything's going to be okay. I should be feeling better in a few weeks."

"Weeks! Gee, Chantel. You caught one ugly flu."

Tell her, Chantel's mind urged. But she couldn't, not yet. She needed a little more time before their relationship reverted to the hostility of just a few weeks ago. Besides, she wanted to sit down alone with her sister and explain what had happened in person; anything else was cowardly.

Stacy filled in the silence when Chantel didn't respond. "What about work?"

"I'm going to do as much as I can from home, then go back in when I feel better. I talked to Maureen yesterday, and she insists they can wait."

"That's nice of her."

"I'm sure she's had to battle several of the field reps on that. They want their stuff and they want it right away, which means she's having to pull more than her own weight. I really owe her."

"Well, she seems really nice."

Chantel chewed on her lower lip. "What time do you get off work, Stace?"

"Eight."

"Do you think you could come by? I need to talk to you."

"Sure. What about?"

"I'll tell you when you get here," she said, her hand gripping the receiver so hard her knuckles turned white.

"Okay. No problem."

Stacy hung up, and Chantel let the breath she'd been holding seep out. But none of her fear went with it.

CHAPTER SIXTEEN

DILLON WATCHED his two girls hurry across the schoolyard toward the Landcruiser and waved at them. He hadn't stopped thinking, even for a minute, about Chantel and their baby. Sydney and Brittney had no idea he'd been seeing the woman who'd baby-sat them that one night. And after all the recent changes and upsets in their lives, he hated the idea of surprising them.

Taking a deep breath, he smiled as they climbed in. "Hey, kiddos. How're my girls?"

"What are you doing here, Daddy?" Sydney asked.

"How come we don't have to go to Children's World?" Brittney chimed in.

A gust of cool wind ruffled his hair before the doors thudded shut.

"I got off a little early today." He didn't add that the couple of hours he'd spent at work had been wasted. Unable to focus on anything except the startling news he'd received that morning, he'd scrapped several sets of plans and started over, again and again.

"I got a hundred on my spelling test today," Brittney announced.

Yesterday afternoon Dillon had invested a good hour in drilling her on the words. "Way to go! I think that calls for ice cream. What do you think, Sydney?"

Both girls excitedly agreed. "Then can Suzie come over?" Brittney asked.

Dillon had started making some inroads with the other parents—mostly mothers—getting to know them so they'd feel comfortable letting their daughters come to play at his house, but he hadn't heard of Suzie before. "Have you made a new friend?"

"She just moved here."

"Well, maybe tomorrow. Today I thought we'd do something else. Remember Chantel? She had you over at her house a while ago."

"Yeah, she was really nice," Brittney said.

Dillon glanced into the backseat to gauge Sydney's reaction.

"And pretty," his younger daughter added, struggling to close her seat belt.

"Maybe we could go visit her if she's home. That okay with you?"

They nodded, and Dillon dialed Chantel's number on his car phone, then pulled away from the curb. He didn't dare drop by in case Stacy was there, but he couldn't help wanting to see Chantel and his girls together, to get a sense of how they'd do if they ever became a family.

Was Chantel really carrying his child? He still couldn't believe it.

"Hello?" She sounded as if she'd been sleeping.

"It's Dillon. Did I wake you?"

"I was just resting, but I have to get up, anyway. I have some stuff to do for Maureen. She's coming by later to pick it up."

Dillon slowed for a speed bump as he drove out of the neat middle-class neighborhood where the school was located. "Have you talked to Stacy?"

"She's coming over tonight after work."

"When's that?"

"She gets off at eight."

"So she's at the hospital now?"

"Yeah."

"Does that mean the girls and I can stop by for a few minutes?"

"I'm not sure. I haven't seen Wade all day. I don't know where he is and—"

"You're not going to tell me no because of *Wade?*"

Silence, then, "That's not the only reason, Dillon. I realize this is more my fault than yours. When we were together that night, I told you I couldn't get pregnant—"

"You didn't know."

"True, but you don't deserve to have any more responsibilities right now. You've got your children to take care of, and I'm perfectly capable of handling this on my own."

She was showing him the door again, letting him know it stood wide open. Dammit! Why was she trying to make it so easy for him to walk away? Didn't she care about him?

Dillon looked over at Brittney. She was digging through her backpack, pulling out completed assignments, apparently looking for her spelling test. "I want to be part of this," he said, and it surprised him how much he meant it. Even with all the risks and pitfalls, he couldn't leave Chantel to go through the pregnancy alone. "I can't..." He let the last of the sentence dangle so Brittney and Sydney wouldn't clue in.

"You can't turn your back on your own child, and that's admirable. I just want you to know we don t come as a package deal. I'll be supportive of your relationship and won't ever try to stop you from seeing the baby or being part of his life. You believe me, don't you?"

"Yeah." *Until you want to move somewhere or marry someone else or...* "But what's best for *you?*"

"What's best for me doesn't matter."

"I don't think my taking a hike is best for any of us, though."

"She wants you to go hiking, Daddy?" Brittney asked.

Dillon shook his head at his daughter and gripped the phone more tightly, waiting for Chantel's response.

"You're not listening. I didn't suggest you take a hike. I want you to be part of the baby's life. What more do you want?"

Marry me. Where had that come from? He'd only known her two months. He couldn't marry her, couldn't put his girls at risk. "I don't know yet. Can't we figure it out as we go along?"

"Okay."

"So can we come by?"

There was a short pause. "Sure."

THE DOORBELL RANG just as Chantel finished applying a little makeup. She was feeling surprisingly well, considering how sick she'd been the past couple of weeks. Maybe she was living on adrenaline. Or maybe, as the doctor had said, there was simply no rhyme or reason to morning sickness. Regardless, she was grateful for the reprieve.

Pulling on a clean cotton-knit top, she went to answer the door. Dillon stood there, flanked by his girls. She tried to picture the four—or rather, five—of them becoming a family someday and couldn't imagine it. Things like that happened to other people, not to an ex-model who'd stolen her sister's fiancé and deserved to live out her life alone.

Chantel stepped back so they could enter. Dillon brushed against her shoulder as he moved past, and she had the urge to run her fingers down his arm and hope his large hand closed over her own.

With an effort she kept her hands to herself. "How was school?" she asked, giving the girls a warm smile.

"Great! Brittney got a hundred on her spelling test," Sydney said.

"We got ice cream to celebrate," her sister added.

"Congratulations, Brittney! I'm glad you decided to visit. Would you guys like to stay for dinner? We could order a pizza."

Dillon caught her eye. "Are you feeling well enough to have us here that long?"

"I'm doing better, actually."

He smiled, drawing her attention to his lips, which were soft yet firm. He could kiss more wickedly than the devil, she thought, remembering—and wanting to press her lips to his.

She turned away quickly because she knew that if her eyes revealed half of what she felt, they'd make a beggar out of her.

"Want to sit down and do your homework, girls? If we get it over with now, we won't have to worry about it later," she suggested.

As Dillon's daughters hauled their backpacks to her kitchen table, Dillon came to stand behind Chantel. When he spoke, his voice hummed in her ear and his breath teased the back of her neck. "Why am I sensing a little extra energy here?" he asked.

Chantel slanted him a glance. Noting his cocky grin, she realized that her eyes—or some other body language—had given her away, after all. "I think your receptors are screwed up."

"Where's my math homework?" Brittney asked, sorting through a stack of notebooks.

"Maybe you forgot it," Sydney told her.

Dillon obviously wasn't listening. The girls were preoccupied and so was he. "I think they're working fine," he

whispered. "I think you're sending me these signals because, considering our present company, you feel safe."

She arched a brow at him. "I am safe."

"Not for long," he said.

THAT NIGHT Dillon whistled as he shepherded his girls out
of Chantel's condominium and toward his truck. Dusk had
fallen and the temperature had dropped into the sixties, but
none of them were eager to leave. They'd had an enjoyable
evening together, the four of them—so enjoyable it had been
all he could do not to stake a very personal claim on Chantel, one his girls could see. Through willpower alone, he'd
managed to escape without touching her, but only by promising himself that what *he* wanted would come later. He
needed to take things slowly, let the girls get used to the
idea that there might be another woman in his life.

For the first time he felt hopeful, excited by the prospect
of a more permanent relationship. The girls liked Chantel.
She was kind and easy to be around. He was beginning to
believe she could actually be an asset in his daughters' lives,
instead of a detriment. And for all of Chantel's talk about
her and their baby not coming as a package, she still wanted
him. He could feel the raw physical power of it whenever
she looked at him.

"It's not over till it's over," he muttered.

"What, Daddy?" Brittney looked up at him, her brow
wrinkling.

"Nothing." He chuckled. "I'm just talking to myself."

"You really like Chantel, don't you?" Sydney asked.

He scowled. Was he that transparent? He had to admit
his attraction was difficult to hide. An invisible magnetic
force seemed to pull him and Chantel together, causing them
to brush against each other every time they passed, to touch

at the smallest opportunity. Unfortunately such brief contact appeased nothing, only made him hunger for more.

If she was his wife, he wouldn't have to leave her now...

"Yeah, I like her," he admitted. "Do you?"

The furrow in Brittney's brow deepened. "She's okay." She fell silent for a moment, then murmured, "What if you fall in love with her?"

He cleared his throat to hide his surprise and nearly asked, "What if I already have?" Instead, he said, "What if I do?"

"Then you'll run away and marry her, like Mom did with that guy, right?"

Sydney reached up for his hand. He gave it a squeeze and placed his other hand reassuringly on Brittney's neck. "I'd never run away from either one of you. Are you kidding? We're together forever now. A team of wild horses couldn't drag us apart. All five Power Rangers couldn't separate us. Even King Kong—"

Sydney giggled and Brittney rolled her eyes, but a dimple dotted her cheek. "Okay, Dad. We get the picture."

"Nothing, *nothing* could keep us apart," he promised. But then his cellular phone chirped and when he heard the caller's voice, he realized he might have spoken too soon. There was one thing that could stand in their way. One person.

Amanda.

THE COOL NIGHT WIND came in short gusts, carrying a spattering of rain. Folding her arms across her uniform, Stacy ducked her head and hurried from beneath the hospital's portico to her car. She hoped to climb inside before the light sprinkle turned into a real shower, but Wade rolled down the window of his brown Cadillac idling in another row and waved to get her attention.

"Stacy!"

''What are you doing here?'' she asked, leaving her own car to approach his window. Just the fact that he was there made her wary, but her unease grew when she saw the look on his face.

''What's wrong?''

''We need to talk.''

''I'm supposed to head over to Chantel's. Why don't you follow me?''

He grimaced. ''I'd rather talk here if you can spare a minute.''

Stacy hesitated. What on earth could he want? He seemed so serious. ''Okay.''

''Get in.''

The power door locks clicked as she rounded the old Cadillac. She got inside to the sweltering blast of the heater, then leaned her back against the door. ''Your hair's a mess. That means something catastrophic has happened. What is it?''

''Cute,'' he said, but her glib remark did nothing to ease the tension of his jaw. Evidently something serious *had* happened.

''Did you get bad news from your agent?'' she asked.

''That bad news came a long time ago,'' he admitted. ''I'm not going back to New York. I no longer have a career there.''

Stacy had suspected as much. ''Is that really so bad? You already knew you couldn't model forever. And New York's a long way from California. Your whole family lives out here—''

''I don't care where my family lives,'' he interrupted. ''We've never been close, and I doubt that's going to change anytime soon.''

''Well, your folks did lend you this car, didn't they? They can't be all bad.''

"I'm not here to talk about my family." He pinned her with an unswerving gaze. "Chantel is seeing Dillon Broderick."

Stacy blinked, then swallowed hard. "I don't want to hear this," she said, and started to open the door, but his hand shot out to stop her.

"You may not want to hear it, but it's true. I saw them together in the parking lot at the doctor's office this morning, acting like lovebirds."

"You're just trying to hurt me. You're vicious and mean, and I don't know what I ever saw in you. I'm going over to Chantel's," she said.

"Then you might want to call first."

Stacy turned back, letting her door gape open despite the rain. "What's that supposed to mean?"

"He's there now. I saw his car. And I'll tell you something else. I don't think she's sick."

"What?"

"I think she's pregnant."

Four words. Only four small words, but they hit Stacy like an ax slamming into a tree. "That can't be true," she whispered. "Chantel can't have kids. The doctors told her—"

"The doctors could be wrong. Why else would Dillon be taking her to an obstetrician? You were puzzled by that yourself, remember? Think about it."

"Then it's your baby," she insisted. "Or someone else's. Dillon and Chantel barely met at the cabin. I introduced them."

"I guess lover boy didn't waste any time, because the baby can't be mine. I haven't had sex with Chantel in almost a year."

Stacy stared at the wet shiny blacktop without seeing anything. "It can't be," she said to herself more than Wade. "She's just sick. It's the anorexia."

"I don't think so, Stacy." Suddenly Wade looked tired, like a two-year-old who's spent himself on a tantrum and had no energy left. "What I saw made certain things apparent."

Stacy shook her head, refusing to believe. Dillon. She'd been trying to forget him, get over him, but the thought that he'd been sleeping with Chantel brought back all her old feelings—along with a few new ones, the most prominent of which were jealousy and rage.

She got out, heedless of the rain that now fell in great fat drops. "I can't believe it. She's my sister!"

"Yeah." Wade laughed. "Well, I guess now we know what kind of sister she is, huh?"

CHAPTER SEVENTEEN

IT WAS GETTING LATE. Chantel frowned at the clock on her living-room wall and picked up the phone to call Stacy again. Her sister should have arrived more than an hour ago. A nurse at the hospital had confirmed that she'd left at eight, and no one answered at Stacy's house, so where was she?

The answering machine came on again, but Chantel didn't leave a message. She'd already left two. Fearing that her sister might have had an accident, she tried the highway patrol. Was her number anywhere in Stacy's purse? Would anyone think to call her?

In a distant professional voice, the police dispatcher informed her that there'd been no accident involving a blue Honda.

Thank God! Chantel released her breath and sank onto the couch. Maureen had stopped by, but it had been difficult to concentrate when her mind whirred with what needed to be said to Stacy. After Maureen had left, she'd vacuumed, just to keep busy. But she'd forced herself to quit after doing the living room. This was the longest she'd been up since getting sick and the first day she'd felt anywhere close to human. She didn't want to end up back in bed tomorrow because she'd done too much too fast.

Outside, the storm worsened. Rain beat a steady rhythm as the wind manipulated the trees like marionettes, making their branches sway, clacking them against the windows.

Except for the pink azaleas blooming profusely along the fence of her side yard, it felt more like December than May.

Dropping her head in her hands, she rubbed her face. Stacy would get here, she promised herself. But she found it strange that she hadn't seen Wade. Had he left for good? She hoped he had, but she couldn't believe that. Not when his stuff was still at her house.

Had he come home to find Dillon's car in the lot, somehow recognized it and gone to tell Stacy?

That was a stretch, but possible. Even if he'd recognized Dillon's car, though, wouldn't he have confronted her?

For the next fifteen minutes she put her faith in the belief that he would have. Then she dialed his parents' number.

Wade's father answered the phone.

"Henry, it's Chantel." This man used to be "Dad" to her. She'd visited his house every year at Christmas and felt a moment's awkwardness at reverting to his given name but didn't know what else to call him now that she and Wade had broken up. "I'm sorry to bother you at bedtime, but I was hoping to catch Wade."

"You can call here anytime, Chantel. You'll always be part of the family, even though Wade was fool enough to lose you. You know, Ronnie still hasn't married. You should go for him."

Chantel chuckled. Ronnie was one of Wade's younger brothers and the apple of his father's eye. "Ron's only twenty-three."

"But he's got his head on straight. No wild ideas about runnin' off to New York. He stayed home like he should and now he's nearly finished school. Going to be an engineer."

"Wade mentioned it. I'm happy for him. But I'm sure he has enough women knocking down his door."

"None who can compare with you."

Tears stung Chantel's eyes. She missed Wade's family. They'd never been very close, mostly because Wade and his parents disagreed about everything and argued all the time. But it felt good to know they'd approved of her, if not her decision to become a model. "You were always nice to me."

"As nice as our no-account son would let us be. I tell you, I don't know what's gonna become of him. I wish he was here so the two of you could talk, but I don't know where he is. He took the Caddy a couple weeks ago, and we haven't seen him since."

So they hadn't kicked him out. Wade had lied to her again. She should have known. "I'm sure he'll show up sometime," she said.

"Is everything okay?"

"Fine."

"Well, don't be a stranger. Come see us once in a while now that you're living in the area."

"I will," she promised, then hung up. She tried to picture herself knocking on their door several months pregnant. Somehow she couldn't imagine it.

Tapping her fingernail on the lamp table, Chantel tried to decide what to do next. Should she drive over to Stacy's? What good would that do if Stacy wasn't home? Maybe her sister had simply forgotten their appointment and gone out with a friend.

She picked up the phone and called Dillon, just because she needed to talk.

"Am I interrupting anything?" she asked when his deep voice came on the line.

"Just *The New Adventures of Mary Kate and Ashley Olsen.*"

"Is that a movie?"

"A book."

"Sounds like fun."

"Not the third time around. At this point I think I'd prefer to read the labels on vitamin bottles."

Chantel smiled, picturing his girls all snug in their beds with Dillon sitting next to them, reading. "It's one of the girls' favorites, huh?"

"Yeah, they love it. I need to go out and buy them some more books." He lowered his voice. "How'd it go with Stacy?"

"She never came over here."

"Have you tried calling her?"

"Only a dozen times." The telephone beeped, indicating that she had an incoming call. Chantel's stomach tensed. "Someone's trying to get through," she said. "I'd better go."

"Chantel?"

"Yeah?"

"I need to talk to you. Call me later, okay?"

"That sounds ominous."

"It's about Amanda. Just something we should discuss…in addition to everything else."

Chantel bit her lip, wondering if she was ever going to pull out of the emotional tailspin that had started when she realized Dillon was her sister's boyfriend. "Okay," she agreed.

DRIPPING WET, Stacy propped her head against the cool metal of the pay phone and listened to her sister's voice. "Hello? Hello? Wade, is that you?"

The pain that radiated through her heart grew more severe, despite the hour she'd just spent walking in the rain, trying to get some control of her emotions. "What Wade says—is it true?" she finally asked without preamble.

"Stacy, thank heaven it's you. I've been so worried. Please come over so we can talk—"

"Just tell me if you're seeing Dillon."

"I haven't been seeing him."

"Then you're not pregnant."

There was a brief pause, as if Chantel didn't know what to say, then, "Wade had no right to do this to us, Stacy. Don't let him. He's just trying to hurt me."

"Well, he's done a pretty good job of hurting me, too. He came to the hospital tonight to tell me you're pregnant with Dillon's child. I don't want to believe it, but deep down I know even Wade wouldn't lie about something like that."

"Don't underestimate him. I've made that mistake one too many times myself." Chantel sounded tired, defeated.

"That's not an answer."

"Please come over. I hate this, Stacy. I don't want to lose you again."

Stacy could hear the sincerity in her sister's voice, but it did little to combat the vision of Dillon and Chantel meeting secretly while she stupidly trusted her sister's word. Remembering the candlelight dinner she'd made him and the black teddy she'd bought to wear for him—and what had happened afterward—she flinched, feeling utterly humiliated. They'd both probably laughed at her pathetic attempts to interest Dillon, then laughed again at her stupidity for letting Wade come over. "Tell me it's not true."

Silence.

"Chantel, tell me it isn't true!"

"I can't."

Stacy squeezed her eyes shut and rubbed her forehead. "You promised me," she whispered, feeling the warmth of tears on her face. "I cared about him. Why do you have to have them all?"

"It's not like that—" Chantel started, but Stacy had heard

enough excuses ten years ago, when the same thing had happened with Wade. Dashing a hand across her wet cheeks, she hung up the phone, saying a silent goodbye to her sister—forever.

CHANTEL SCOOPED her keys off the counter and hurried outside. The air was damp and chilly, but she didn't care about the wet or the cold and didn't bother to go back for a jacket. She needed to talk to Stacy. She couldn't leave things as they were—not after the way their telephone conversation had gone.

Wade wasn't going to win this round, she vowed.

She got into her car and pulled out of the parking lot. Somehow she had to convince Stacy that what had happened with Dillon was an accident.

The drive to Stacy's house seemed more like forty minutes than the usual fifteen, but according to the digital clock glowing in her car, Chantel made good time. She turned into the driveway shortly before eleven, cut the engine and headed up the walk.

"Stacy, it's me!" The door was locked, but she banged on it, then looked under the mat for the spare key her sister kept there. It was gone. Using one hand to cut the glare of the moon, she peered through the living-room window to see that the entire house was dark. She could make out the shadows of Stacy's furniture, but no sound or movement.

"Stacy? Are you there?" She knocked again before going to the garage, where she stood on tiptoe, trying to see if Stacy's car was parked inside.

No luck. She was tall, but not tall enough. She walked around the side yard and through the gate to check the back door, but it was locked, too. And all the rooms were as dark as those in front, including Stacy's bedroom.

Where was she? Chantel folded her arms against the wind

and rain and made her way back to her car. She figured her sister had to come home sooner or later. And when she did, Chantel would be waiting for her.

Climbing into her car, which still had a crumpled front bumper because she couldn't afford the insurance deductible, she shivered. She was wet to the skin after walking around the house. She could only pray that Stacy would be home soon.

The minutes ticked away, turning into an hour, then almost two. Chantel's teeth chattered as she rubbed her arms for warmth, wishing she'd brought a coat. She should go home, she told herself, and wait until Stacy was ready to talk to her. But somehow she feared that day would never come. She had to see Stacy *tonight*...

If only she wasn't so darn tired. She started the car and cranked up the heater, which quickly dispelled the chill. But the warmth did little to ease the aching of her head and back, and slowly, she became aware of another kind of discomfort—cramps.

DAMMIT, WHERE WAS SHE? Dillon slammed down the phone after his tenth attempt to reach Chantel. She'd told him she'd call. Why hadn't he heard from her? What had happened with Stacy?

He could only guess things hadn't gone well. When his worry escalated as the minutes passed, he risked calling Stacy's house, but there was no answer there, either. He had to drive over to Chantel's and see what was going on.

Running an impatient hand through his hair, he walked down the hall and peeked in at his girls. They were sound asleep, but they were too young to leave alone, and it was after midnight. Who could he call to come sit with them?

He went into the living room and stared at the phone. His mother. Hadn't she just told him he needed to find himself another wife? Well, he wasn't sure he'd found a wife, but he knew he was having another baby. Not that he thought *that* situation would please her.

"Hello?"

Dillon felt a twinge of remorse for waking her this late. He knew she went to bed early. Now that she was older, her life had finally settled into a routine. She and her new husband had dinner, watched *Jeopardy,* played a board game and retired.

"Dillon? What is it? Are the girls okay?"

"They're fine, Mom."

"Are you hurt?"

"No."

"But it's the middle of the night." He could hear her moving in bed, trying to wake up. "Why else would you be calling?"

"I've got a personal emergency. I need you to come over and sit with the girls."

"A personal emergency? What's that supposed to mean? You said you weren't hurt."

"I'm not." Dillon swallowed his pride and braced himself for a response that would be full of irritation, at best, and a flat refusal, at worst. "I'm worried about a friend. I need to check on her."

"A friend?"

"She's been sick and I can't get hold of her."

"She's probably sleeping!"

"I don't think so. Look, Mom, I know this is putting you out and I'm sorry, but it's not like I've ever bothered you in the middle of the night before."

"When you were in high school, I could never get you to come home on time. You woke me up plenty of—"

"Mom, can we discuss my past sins later? I'm dying to get out of here."

She sighed. "Oh, all right. I'll be over in fifteen minutes."

"Thanks." He hung up and dialed Chantel's again, then Stacy's. Still no answer at either place.

DILLON GRABBED his keys from the top of the refrigerator as soon as his mother arrived. "I owe you one, Mom," he said, pausing long enough to kiss her cheek.

To his surprise, she smiled and embraced him, smelling of rain and the perfume she always wore. "You have a good heart, Dillon. I don't know if I've ever told you that."

She hadn't. She'd been too immersed in her own rocky love life, but he didn't hold it against her. He knew she'd be there if he really needed her. She'd grumble, but she'd come through, the way she had tonight. That was more than he could say for his father, who'd always done just the opposite.

He told her he loved her and strode out as she was removing the plastic hood that protected her permed hair from the rain.

The windshield wipers squeaked and the heater hummed as he drove to Chantel's condo. The roads were still wet, and a light fog was starting to replace the rain. He fiddled with the radio, settled for an old rock station, then cursed when he had to stop for yet another traffic light.

Finally he turned into the lot at Chantel's condo, only to find her parking space empty. It was one o'clock and she'd been ill. Where was she?

He thought briefly of Wade and how badly he might have taken the news of the pregnancy. Could he have become violent? God, he hoped not. In Chantel's current condition, she'd be no match for him...

"Don't borrow trouble," he told himself aloud. Odds

were she was with Stacy. He sat idling, wondering whether or not to go to Stacy's when his cell phone rang.

"Chantel?"

"No. It's Stacy." Her voice sounded odd, strained.

"Are you okay?" he asked.

"I am, but I'm not so sure about Chantel—or the baby."

Dillon's stomach knotted painfully, and his throat constricted until he could hardly breathe, let alone speak. Fortunately Stacy needed no prompting.

"I think maybe you should meet us here."

"Where?" he managed.

"At the emergency room."

STACY GREETED Dillon almost as soon as he entered the hospital. Mascara streaked her face, testifying to earlier tears, but her eyes were dry now.

"What happened?" he asked.

"When I got home, I found her backing out of my drive. She looked terrible. She was shaking and crying about the baby."

"Is she going to be okay?"

Stacy took a deep breath and nodded.

"And the baby?"

"She's cramping and spotting. They don't expect the baby to make it."

Dillon felt dazed. He stared down at Stacy without really seeing her, thinking about the baby Chantel wanted so badly.

"If she miscarries, she may never get pregnant again," he said, stating the obvious.

Stacy pushed the hair out of her eyes. "Probably not."

Don't let her lose it, he prayed.

"She's been asking for you." Her expression was unreadable. Had Chantel had a chance to talk to her about what had happened that night in the Landcruiser? Clearly Stacy knew he was the father of Chantel's child or she wouldn't have called him. But from her attitude, he couldn't tell how she'd reacted to the news.

Only two other people waited in the lobby, a man holding a bloody cloth over one arm and an old woman who sat with her purse at her feet, hands folded primly in her lap. Both were staring at the television bolted to the ceiling.

He and Stacy passed through a door across from the street entrance and hurried down a short hall that led into a large examination room, separated into compartments by blue cloth dividers. A baby cried at the far end. Two doctors conferred near a desk up front. He followed Stacy to the second cubicle on the left.

Chantel was lying on a table, curled on her side and facing away from the door. At first he thought she was sleeping, but at the sound of their approach, she turned. Her eyes were rimmed with red, her hair was a damp tangled mess, and she wore nothing but a hospital gown.

"Thanks for coming," she said.

Stacy had stopped at the door. Trying to be sensitive to her feelings, Dillon didn't pull Chantel into his arms. He wanted to hold her and rock her and bathe her face with kisses—anything to reassure her that he wasn't going anywhere even if the baby died. But he merely ran his knuckles over her arm.

"You sure like to scare everybody," he said, trying to ease the tension in the room.

She made an effort to smile. "I'm sorry I upset everyone with news of a baby and then—" A tremor passed through her, and she didn't finish.

Dillon felt a lump rising in his throat and tried to swallow it down. "Have you already lost it?"

"Not yet. The doctors gave me a muscle relaxant to stop the cramps, but they're not going away."

Forgetting about Stacy, he cupped her chin in his hand and tilted her face toward him. "You really want this baby, don't you?"

Fresh tears streamed down her face as she nodded.

"So do I," he said.

A noise at the door told him Stacy left. Part of him wanted to go after her and apologize for what she had to be feeling, but he couldn't leave Chantel standing vigil over their baby alone. He'd talk to Stacy later.

"Did you tell her?" he asked.

Chantel closed her eyes. "I never got the chance."

"Then how—"

"Wade."

A curse hovered on Dillon's lips, but for Chantel's sake he didn't utter it. There was no need to upset her any more, especially when the damage was already done. He promised himself he'd have a little talk with Wade, though, when this was all over. "So did you tell her how it happened?"

She shook her head. "It doesn't matter. She won't believe me, anyway. Not after hearing it the way she did, and not after what happened with Wade ten years ago."

He smoothed the hair off her forehead. "But she brought you to the hospital. She could have left you to make it here on your own."

"She's a nurse. She would have done as much for any-one."

Dillon's heart twisted. Chantel had lost her career because of Wade. Now she was going to lose their baby. And she felt like she'd already lost her sister a second time.

"Are you sorry about that night in the Landcruiser?" he asked, knowing she had to be and wishing he'd somehow been able to keep his hands off her.

A smile curved her lips, but her eyes drooped again, and he realized she was growing sleepy. The relaxant the doctor had given her was finally taking effect. "Are you kidding?" she asked softly. "That was the best night of my life."

He stroked her hair and bent down to kiss her temple. "I'm just sorry it's cost you so much, babe."

Her eyes flicked open, and her hand went to her stomach. "It gave me what I wanted most. If only I can hang on to it…"

"You can hang on to me," he whispered after a few minutes, even though he knew she'd fallen asleep. "If this baby doesn't make it, Chantel, we'll do whatever is necessary to make another one. And we've got my girls." He paused. "I think I'm ready to share them with you."

CHAPTER EIGHTEEN

STACY DROVE OUT of the hospital parking lot without a backward glance. She knew her sister would probably lose the baby, but she wasn't going to hang around long enough to find out. She was too numb to care; too much had happened. And Chantel had Dillon, anyway. What more could she want?

The rain started again, but Stacy didn't bother with the windshield wipers. It was only sprinkling and there wasn't much traffic. She stared beyond the water beading on her window at the wet streets and remembered the concern in Dillon's eyes the moment he arrived at the hospital. Then there was the gentle, almost reverent way he'd touched Chantel when he'd rushed into her room, and the conviction in his voice when he'd said how much he wanted their baby.

All of it told Stacy he was in love—head over heels in love—and the jealousy that stemmed from this realization almost overpowered her. It was one thing to think he and Chantel had had a steamy sordid affair. It was another to think they cared for each other.

Stopping at a traffic light, Stacy smacked the steering wheel. Why couldn't he have returned *her* feelings? She'd mooned over him for two years! And he'd just started asking her out when Chantel came on the scene.

Stacy chuckled bitterly. *Well, let them have each other. I've lived without my sister before, I can do it again. Only this time, there'll be no turning back.*

CHANTEL AWOKE to the sound of Dillon's voice, hushed as he spoke on his cell phone. "Can you get them off to school for me, Mom…? I know, but I don't want to leave the hospital… Tell them I love them and that I'll see them after school… Okay, I appreciate it… No, there's a van from Children's World that picks them up… You bet… Thanks."

He punched the "end" button, then glanced over his shoulder and gave her a welcoming smile when he saw she was awake. "How are you feeling?"

"Better." She expected the cramping to set in again, but it was gone, at least for the moment. Had she lost the baby while she slept? She was too afraid to ask. "What time is it?"

"Just after seven."

She carefully surveyed the room, searching for any evidence that something significant had occurred, but everything looked as it had the night before. Except Dillon. Lines bracketed his mouth and eyes, revealing his exhaustion, and a dark shadow of stubble covered his jaw. He'd stayed with her all night?

"You look tired."

"I dozed a little—" he indicated an orange vinyl chair that hadn't been there when Chantel had fallen asleep "—but they had a drunk-driving accident about four in the morning, and this place turned into a zoo. I didn't get much sleep."

"You shouldn't have stayed."

He raised a hand to caress her cheek. "I wanted to."

A warm feeling began in the pit of Chantel's stomach and radiated out to her limbs, as though he'd just wrapped her in a cozy quilt. But then she remembered her sister, and the warmth disappeared. "Where's Stacy?"

Compassion flickered in his eyes. "She left."

"When?"

He paused, obviously wishing he could soften the truth for her, then said, "Last night, shortly after I arrived."

"She thinks we've been seeing each other behind her back. I tried to explain, but she wouldn't listen. She was too hurt."

"She'll come around," he said, and Chantel tried to act as though she believed him. There was no need for him to share her guilt. He'd done nothing. She was the one who'd betrayed Stacy with Wade. She was the one who couldn't stop herself from wanting Dillon. And she was the one who'd told him she couldn't get pregnant, ensuring they used no form of protection.

"Hello." A doctor who looked wide awake and freshly scrubbed stepped into the cubicle. Evidently there'd been a change of shifts, because Chantel didn't recognize him. "I'm Dr. Wiseman. How are you feeling this morning?"

"My cramps are gone."

"Good. Let's take a look at the bleeding."

Dillon left the room, giving her some privacy.

Dr. Wiseman made a cursory check. "There's some spotting," he said, pushing her gown higher so he could place his stethoscope on her abdomen. She knew he was listening for the baby's heartbeat. She prayed he found one. Otherwise, they'd do a D&C and finish up what the cramping had started.

He frowned in concentration as he moved the stethoscope to a new place.

Please, oh, please, oh, please, Chantel chanted to herself.

Dr. Wiseman shifted the cold metal end of his stethoscope again, and frowned harder.

"Dillon!" Chantel called to him despite her state of undress. She felt vulnerable, exposed, but she couldn't take the news alone. Not when he was standing right around the corner and could be holding her hand…

The doctor raised his head as Dillon entered the room. "I can't get a heartbeat," he said, straightening and letting his stethoscope dangle around his neck.

Chantel clenched her fists and silently stared up at Dillon. She expected him to comfort her in some way, but he looked almost as bereft as she felt. "Are you sure?" he asked.

The doctor seemed slightly offended. "I just examined her."

"Check again, please."

With a sigh Dr. Wiseman bent over Chantel's belly. Again she felt his impersonal fingers and the cool metal of the stethoscope sliding from place to place. Then he froze and listened for several seconds.

"I've found it," he said at last, blinking in surprise. "The baby's still alive."

"WHO IS SHE?" Dillon's mom asked, once he had Chantel situated in his bedroom upstairs.

Dillon smiled and leaned against the kitchen counter, still euphoric from their victory at the hospital and from Chantel's willingness to let him bring her home so he could care for her. "She's going to be my wife," he said.

That made his mother choke on her coffee. *"What?"* she sputtered. "But you've never even mentioned her before."

"I haven't known her very long."

Her browns descended. "And you're planning to *marry* her?"

He smiled devilishly. All his mother's suggestions came out as commands. He wanted her to think he'd actually followed one for once. "I'm just doing what you told me to, Mother. Didn't you say it's time for me to find another wife? Don't tell me you've changed your mind."

"I meant you should start dating. I didn't mean you

should pick up a woman at the hospital and move her in with you."

He laughed. "Well, it's a little late for clarifications now. You should be more specific when you tell me what to do with my life."

"Dillon Broderick, you're a contrary one. You always have been. Why couldn't you be easy to raise—"

"Like my sisters?" He grinned. "I have news, Mom. I am raised. We all are."

"But you're not acting like you have a lick of sense, marrying a complete stranger. Didn't Amanda teach you anything?"

The mention of his ex-wife sobered Dillon, and he turned away to stare out the window. "She called me yesterday."

"Amanda?"

He nodded.

"What did she want?"

"Money. She plans to leave her new husband."

His mother shook her head as if to say Amanda was no good and never would be. "Already? You didn't give it to her, I hope."

"Not yet."

"That sounds like you will."

Dillon didn't have to see her face. He could hear her disapproval. "Probably," he admitted. "She'll come back and fight for custody of the girls if I don't."

"What makes you think she wants them? She abandoned them just a couple of months ago—"

He raked a hand through his hair. "I'm sure that on some level, she wants them. She's just so screwed up right now. Besides, without the girls she gets no child support."

His mother grimaced. "Talk about taking advantage of the system."

"Bottom line is, I care less about the money than I do

about keeping the girls' world stable and positive, especially with my wedding on the horizon." He shrugged. "If Amanda fights me, I'll be spending money on attorneys."

"Then make her sign over custody before you give her a dime."

He took a sip of his coffee, which had been sitting on the counter ever since his mother had poured it. "I hate that everything seems to come down to dollars and cents. It shouldn't be that way when you're talking about children. But I'll admit I'm tempted to use whatever leverage I've got."

His mother stirred another spoonful of sugar into her coffee. "Do the girls miss their mother?"

That was something Dillon had wondered many times. Brittney and Sydney had to feel Amanda's loss, but they rarely talked about her, unless he didn't allow them some treat or indulgence they were used to getting. "I don't know. I think they're hurt, angry, probably confused."

"Still, they're better off without her. I'm glad she ran off."

Dillon was glad the girls were living with him; he just wished it hadn't happened the way it did. "I'm going to take Chantel something to eat. Why don't you come up with me and get to know her a little?"

He rummaged in the refrigerator, retrieving the sliced turkey breast and other sandwich makings.

"She sure is tall," his mother commented. "Even with you carrying her, I could tell that."

"She's beautiful, isn't she?" He heard the wistful adoration in his own voice and nearly chuckled at himself. He sounded like a lovesick boy.

But if his mother found Chantel as beautiful as he did, she was reluctant to admit it. Her lips pursed as she sipped her coffee. "What does she do?"

"She works for a state senator. But that may not last long."

"Why, for heaven's sake?"

Dillon looked up from spreading mayonnaise on two pieces of whole-wheat bread. "I guess I forgot to tell you. She's having my baby."

His mother's cup hit its saucer with so much force Dillon was surprised it didn't shatter. "How did that happen?" she asked.

He showed her his dimples. "In the usual way."

"DILLON TELLS ME you're pregnant."

Caught completely off guard, Chantel put the sandwich Dillon had brought back on her plate and shifted in the bed. Avoiding his mother's stern gaze, she quickly swallowed the food in her mouth and sought Dillon out where he stood leaning against the bedroom wall. But he merely folded his arms across his chest and smiled innocently.

She cleared her throat. "Yes, Mrs. Sutton, that's true."

Sitting on a chair not far from the bed, Karen Sutton clicked her tongue. "You don't think it would've been wiser to wait?"

"It probably would have been, yes. But we didn't, um, well, we didn't exactly plan for this to happen."

Chantel sent Dillon another glance, this one more pointed than the last. After his mother left, she was going to kill him for putting her on the spot like this.

"Dillon says you're nearly thirty."

Old enough to know what causes these things. The words went unspoken but hung in the air all the same. "The doctors told me I couldn't have children," Chantel explained, knowing she couldn't expect anyone, much less his mother, to understand how it had been that night in the snow. She'd nearly died, he'd saved her life, and she'd fallen in love with him—all in the same night. In the real world it hardly seemed plausible.

Mrs. Sutton sat up taller. "My son's more virile than most," she replied. "Lord knows he has enough testosterone for two men."

At that moment Chantel's discomfort fell away, and she could no longer keep a straight face. The harder she bit her cheeks to stop herself from smiling the more tempted she was. "He's quite a man," she murmured.

Dillon waggled his eyebrows at her, making it even more difficult not to laugh.

Judging by the unchanged tone of his mother's voice, however, Karen Sutton missed these undercurrents and thought they accepted her words at face value. "At least he's doing right by you."

Chantel had no idea what Mrs. Sutton meant—probably the fact that Dillon was taking care of her now. But she'd finally caught on to Dillon's tongue-in-cheek manner where his mother was concerned and realized she shouldn't take her too seriously. "Yes."

"So when's the wedding?"

"Wedding?" Chantel echoed weakly.

"When are you getting married, dear?" his mother asked, obviously trying to hide her impatience.

"We haven't decided on that yet," Dillon said smoothly, finally coming to her rescue. "We'll let you know as soon as we set a date."

"Well, you don't want to wait too long. It won't look right."

"No," Dillon agreed. Chantel made no comment.

"I'm exhausted," Mrs. Sutton announced abruptly. "I need to go home to my husband. He's not used to being without me."

"Mom's a newlywed herself," Dillon said.

"That's wonderful," Chantel replied. "You sound very happy, Mrs. Sutton."

"We are, but it took me long enough to find the right man. I hope you and Dillon have better luck." She stood. Only five-three or so, she looked especially small next to her tall strapping son, but the force of her personality gave her an undeniable presence.

"If Chantel's feeling up to it, why don't we have a family get-together this weekend?" she asked Dillon. "I'm sure your sisters will want to meet your fiancée."

Fiancée? Wedding? Chantel wondered if something had been decided at the hospital, something she didn't know about. When had they gotten engaged? When had they even talked about marriage?

Dillon sent her a sheepish look. "I think she has enough to get used to for the time being. Let's not scare her away before the vows are spoken."

Mrs. Sutton didn't blink. "Nonsense. She'll love Janet and Monica. We'll make it a picnic, on Sunday. Brittney and Sydney will enjoy it."

Dillon didn't argue, but neither did he let her commit him. "It depends on how Chantel's feeling."

"We'll see you on Sunday, dear," his mother said, and suddenly Chantel understood where Dillon got his stubborn streak.

Their voices dimmed as Dillon walked his mother out, leaving Chantel to wonder why he'd let Karen Sutton blind-side her like that. She could tell he thought it was funny, but she'd hoped to make a much better impression on his family, if and when they actually met. Blurting out their news about the baby was emphatically not how she would've done it.

"Would you mind explaining that to me?" she asked as soon as Dillon returned.

He shook his head. "My mother's not easy to explain. She's tough as a Sherman tank and twice as direct, but for all that, she has a soft heart. I learned long ago that the only way to handle her is to let her go, and just focus on damage control."

"That smug smile you were wearing while she was grilling me didn't suggest much worry about damage control."

"I knew you could handle her." He sat down on the bed and took her hand to kiss the very center of her palm. His lips felt so good on her skin. Her irritation started to seep away, and she knew then just how terribly hard she'd fallen for this man.

"I didn't want to 'handle' her," she said, her voice calmer now that her attention was on his mouth—and on the possibility that he might kiss her elsewhere. "I want to get to know her. I want her to like me."

"Mother likes anyone she can't bulldoze."

Chantel bristled. "See what I mean? That might have been good information to share *before* you brought her up here."

He chuckled but was quickly becoming absorbed in running his hands through her hair and entwining the strands around his fingers.

"Why did you tell her about the baby? Couldn't we have talked about it first?"

"I wanted to let her know up front that she didn't have a choice about whether to accept you. A mom can behave almost like a jealous lover at times. I didn't want to leave that door open even a crack. Besides, I don't like secrets." He bent to kiss her neck, and Chantel closed her eyes, her body warming in response to the gentle insistence of his touch, the subtle smell of his aftershave.

"Stop it," she said halfheartedly.

"Why?" he murmured, trailing kisses up to her earlobe, which he took in his mouth and tickled with his tongue.

Chantel shivered. "Because you're making me forget that I'm mad at you."

He pulled back, looking wounded. "Why would you be mad at me? I'm the father of your child, remember?"

He slid a possessive hand up her shirt onto the bare skin of her stomach, and Chantel couldn't resist the smile that started in her heart and spread through her whole body. She could be mad at him later.

"God, I love it when you smile at me like that," he said. "It lights up your whole face and makes me feel as if I'm the only man on earth." Finally he kissed her mouth. As his lips moved over hers, Chantel decided he kissed the way he lived the rest of his life—with passion, confidence and complete absorption. At that moment she felt more desirable, more beautiful than ever before.

"Take this off," she murmured, yanking on his shirt. Then she threaded her fingers through the shiny black locks of his hair and kissed his neck, enjoying the salty taste of his skin and the sensation of his heart beating beneath her lips.

He immediately removed his shirt and let her touch what she'd longed to feel again, ever since the night of the snowstorm: the hard sinewy muscles of his arms and stomach, the soft hair that swirled on his chest.

Dillon was nothing like Wade, she thought distantly. To others, he was probably less attractive. But the strength of his character, combined with his raw masculinity, was a potent combination Chantel could not resist. He was capable and confident, but not conceited. He was possessive, but not selfish. He was a leader, but not an autocrat. The biggest difference between the two men, she realized, was in her own response—because she not only loved Dillon, she respected him. He was far more admirable than most men, and old-fashioned enough to marry a woman simply because he'd gotten her pregnant. But she didn't want Dillon to feel obligated to do the "right" thing. She wanted him to love her.

"Why did you tell your mother we're getting married?" she asked.

He propped his head on one fist. His eyes, darkened by desire, caused Chantel's stomach to flutter, tempting her to throw her pride to the wind. She loved him and he was willing to marry her. Did the reason he was doing it really matter?

To Chantel it did. The fact that she'd wound up pregnant was her own fault. She wasn't going to use her baby to force Dillon into something he wouldn't otherwise have done.

"Because we are getting married, aren't we?" he said.

"I don't remember ever talking about it."

He stroked her arm, obviously still distracted by the passion that had flared so quickly between them "Then let's talk about it." He pressed a kiss to her lips. "There're several reasons. One, you might not be able to work through the pregnancy. You need someone to take care of you, and I want that someone to be me."

Chantel cringed to hear that she'd been right.

"Two, I want my baby to carry my name.'

Of course he'd want that. He was too proud and responsible to accept anything less.

"And three?" she asked hopefully.

He nuzzled his face in her hair and breathed in. "Three, my daughters are living here. I can't have you sleeping in my room unless we're married." He flashed her a grin. "And I'd go mad if you slept anywhere else."

Chantel's desire fled, leaving her cold. He'd just given

her three reasons to marry him, and not one of them was the reason she needed to hear. Trying to hide her disappointment, she slid away from him.

"What's wrong?" he asked.

"While that was definitely a most romantic proposal, I'm afraid I must decline." She hoped he couldn't detect the slight wobble in her voice.

His brows knitted together. "I don't understand. We're going to have a baby—"

"There's nothing to understand. I said no. You didn't really ask, but I'm telling you, anyway. I'll share our baby with you, but I won't foist myself on you as your wife."

He sat up, looking angry. "Who said anything about foisting?"

Chantel blinked rapidly, refusing to cry. "You did."

CHAPTER NINETEEN

WITH A HAND on her chin, Dillon forced Chantel to look at him. "What are you talking about?"

"Nothing. I'm just trying to say it's my own fault I'm pregnant."

"Oh, really? Last time I checked, it took two."

"But I'm the one who said we didn't have to worry about birth control, remember?"

He did remember. He also doubted it would have made much difference. Not that night. "We didn't have anything *to* use."

"We might have been more careful—"

He cocked a skeptical eyebrow at her. "If you think that, then you're more optimistic than I am. Or you weren't feeling what I was feeling."

She blushed. "I think we were feeling the same thing. But I'm happy about the baby and willing to take care of him on my own."

"That's what you keep saying, but who's going to take care of you?"

"I'll manage."

He sighed and glanced at his watch. "Unfortunately we're going to have to finish this discussion later. I have an appointment. You rest. I'll go to work, then leave early and pick up the kids. We'll get some take-out dinner—keep things simple. You and I will talk more tonight."

"Let me pick up the girls."

"I don't think you should get out of bed."

"I won't need much energy to drive to the school, and having company will keep me from getting bored. I can do homework with them here on the bed."

Dillon considered this, wondering if he dared let Chantel take the risk. They'd come so close to losing their baby. But it wasn't very realistic to expect her to do absolutely nothing for the next seven months. And a drive over to the school did seem fairly undemanding. "If you're feeling up to it," he said at last, climbing off the bed. "I'll call the school and let them know you'll be getting the girls. But check in with me before you leave here. If you don't feel well enough, I can do it or they can go to Children's World for an hour or two. Do you know my cell-phone number?"

Chantel nodded.

"Good. I'll bring you some catalogs and brochures to look at tonight."

"I have plenty of reading material at my place. We just need to go over and pick it up."

"Do you have *Bride* Magazine?"

Her delicate brows lowered. "No."

"Then the reading material you have isn't the kind we'll need. We have a wedding to plan." He grinned and ducked out of the room before she could argue. She was going to be his wife. He'd eventually convince her. He had to. Regardless of the baby, he couldn't face the thought of losing her.

BRITTNEY AND SYDNEY chattered happily as they sat on Dillon's bed, telling Chantel all about their day at school.

"This boy in my class named Ryan grabbed my ponytail and pulled so hard it almost made me cry," Sydney complained.

"That means he likes you," Chantel replied, glad that

Dillon had let her pick up the girls and that they had this time together.

Sydney's eyes rounded in protest. "Ryan doesn't like anybody. He's just mean. He's always getting into trouble and—"

"I saw him on his way to the principal's office yesterday," Brittney chimed in.

"He has to go there all the time," Sydney added, as if this confirmed how rotten Ryan truly was.

Chantel chuckled. "Well, this boy might not be all bad. I think your dad probably visited the principal a time or two."

"For what?" they asked in unison, sounding shocked.

"Probably for pulling a little girl's ponytail."

Sydney looked skeptical, but it was Brittney who responded. "I don't think so."

The doorbell rang, and both girls scampered off the bed and charged out of the room to answer it. Chantel could hear them talking and giggling all the way down the stairs, but then they fell silent. "Who is it?" she called.

A feminine voice Chantel didn't recognize floated up to. "Where's your father?"

In her haste to get up, Chantel missed the next exchange between the girls and their visitor. But the woman's voice came through loud and clear when she said, "Get your things. You're coming with me."

A shiver of apprehension slithered down Chantel's spine as she hurried to the top of the stairs. Below she could see a woman standing just inside the front door. A woman about her own age with brown shoulder-length hair and dark eyes, wearing slacks, a shirt and sweater vest, and a pair of pumps. She was hugging Sydney, who looked just like her.

Brittney seemed less sure of giving the woman such a

warm welcome, and Chantel didn't need anyone to tell her why. It was Amanda, their mother.

Clearing her throat, she smiled as Brittney and Sydney glanced up at her expectantly, a hint of fear and worry in their eyes. "Do we have company, girls?"

Brittney nodded. "It's our mom."

"Wonderful. I've never had the opportunity to meet her." Trying to remain calm, Chantel descended the stairs and crossed the floor. "I'm Chantel Miller, a friend of Dillon's."

The woman didn't take her outstretched hand. After an awkward moment, Chantel dropped it to her side, but she kept her smile stubbornly in place. "Unfortunately Dillon isn't here right now, but he'll be back shortly. Would you like to leave him a note?"

Amanda chuckled humorlessly. "No. I didn't come to see him or to write him any notes. I came for my girls. I'm back in town now, and I'm ready to have them come home." She gave Sydney a slight push to prompt her into motion. "Hurry up. Grab your stuff, honey. Mommy's got to go."

Chantel swallowed hard. She could not allow Amanda to take the girls. What if Dillon couldn't get them back? "I'm afraid they can't go with you right now."

Amanda's brows rose toward the widow's peak at the center of her forehead. "I'm sorry?"

"I said they can't go."

Her eyes hardened, but Chantel stood her ground. She could see why Dillon would have found this woman attractive, physically. She had a small compact figure, a pretty face and obviously took good care of herself. What her personality offered was yet to be discovered, but Chantel doubted she'd be impressed there. Divorce often turned both people into the worst possible versions of themselves.

"Who are you to say anything?" Amanda demanded.

"I told you. I'm a friend of Dillon's and I'm watching the girls until he gets home from work. I can t let them go anywhere until he's back."

Chantel stood a good six inches taller than this woman, but Amanda didn't seem intimidated. "They're my kids."

"I realize that."

"Then you should also realize you have no right to keep them from me."

Chantel stepped between the girls and their mother. "Go upstairs, Brittney and Sydney, and finish your homework, please. When your daddy comes home, he'll work all this out, okay?"

Craning her head to see around Chantel, Amanda snapped, "Forget your things. Just come on. This lady is nothing to you. You don't have to listen to her."

The girls looked torn. Brittney moved toward the stairs, but Sydney hovered in the middle of the floor and started to cry. Chantel lowered her voice. "See what you're doing to them? Please, just come back when Dillon's here."

"You're the one who won't let them come with me. They want their mother."

Chantel drew a deep breath and lifted her hand to the open door. "I think they wanted their mother a lot more two months ago. Now go, or I'll call the police."

"You think the police will support you over me? I should call the police myself. They'll come and escort the girls out."

A glance behind her told Chantel Brittney and Sydney were standing on the stairs, watching the drama unfold. Concerned that they might hear, she spoke softly. "Not after they learn that you abandoned them," she said.

Amanda's face went red, and she put up a hand to keep Chantel from closing the door. "You think you know the whole story?" She laughed, then dropped her voice. "Did you know Sydney isn't Dillon's? One blood test is all it would take to get her back, regardless of what I've done. And Dillon wouldn't want her separated from her sister, now would he?''

"No, he wouldn't." Both women looked up in surprise as Dillon came around the front walkway and entered the house. They'd been so immersed in their power struggle that they hadn't noticed his car pull up. Jaw clenched, eyes grim, he glared down at his ex-wife. "And I don't ever want to hear you say that again."

She gave a brittle laugh. "It's true. Remember that good-looking trainer at the gym? Phil?"

The muscles stood out along Dillon's shoulders and back, and Chantel could only imagine the powerful emotions he was feeling. Her heart twisted—for him and for the little girl in danger of overhearing and understanding the significance of what her mother was saying. "The girls..." she warned.

They turned to see Brittney and Sydney inching toward their father, but Amanda didn't seem to care if they heard her. "It would only take a blood test to prove—"

"Shut up," Dillon hissed. For a moment Chantel thought Amanda might defy him, but the expression on his face succeeded in quelling her. When she fell silent he beckoned Brittney and Sydney the rest of the way into his arms, hugged them close, then pointed them back toward the stairs. "Mommy and I have to talk for a little bit, okay? You girls go to your room. I'll come up in a minute."

Reluctantly they obeyed. Chantel began to follow them, to give Dillon and his ex-wife the privacy they needed, but Dillon took her hand and guided her outside with them.

"I don't care whether Sydney's blood father is some trainer named Phil or the man on the moon," he said when the girls were safely out of earshot. "She's mine. I'm the only father she's known."

"If you want to continue as her father, I'd suggest you let the girls come home with me. I'm their mother."

"Then start acting like it."

"I will as soon as you start paying your child support." Amanda angled her chin up at him, obviously thinking she'd played the trump card, but Chantel could see from the anger flashing in Dillon's eyes that his ex-wife had pushed him too far.

"I was going to offer you a deal, Amanda. I was going to pay for the divorce and help you get back on your feet if you signed custody of both girls over to me. But you know what? I've changed my mind. You can sink or swim on your own. And if you think you can win and don't mind every sordid detail about your past being dragged out for the world to see, then take me to court."

With that, he turned on his heel and opened the door for Chantel to precede him.

"That'll get expensive," Amanda taunted. "It would be cheaper just to cooperate with me. I'll let you see the girls whenever you want."

He turned back. "Seems I've heard that story before. Only this time I'm not buying. It's over, Amanda. You're not having the girls because you weren't taking good care of them, and I have no reason to believe you'll do any better in the future."

"How dare you criticize me! You have no idea how difficult it is to be a single mother!"

"You're not single very often."

"But I love them!" Bewilderment emerged beneath her anger, and Chantel felt a moment's pity.

"You sure have a funny way of showing it."

"So I messed up, made a mistake. It's not like *you're* perfect."

"Then pull your life together and we'll set up some visitation. I'm not trying to hurt you, only protect them."

"That's not true! You're trying to punish me for the divorce! But it's not going to work. You'll pay through the nose if you try—"

"Cost doesn't matter anymore, Amanda. Only what's right and fair," he said, walking inside.

"You won't be saying that when the blood tests come back!" she flung after them. "I'll get the girls! You wait and see!"

Chantel felt Dillon flinch and wished she could shield him from the pain. "I can only hope you love Sydney half as much as I do," he said softly, and closed the door behind them.

THAT NIGHT Dillon worked late in his study, trying to finish a set of plans that were already two days late. He struggled to put Amanda and her threats out of his mind, but there was no escaping the terrible fear that clutched at his belly. How vengeful would his ex-wife be? Ever since the divorce, he'd pulled his punches, hoping to protect his girls from the worst of the emotional trauma and confusion. But now he realized there was only one way to achieve the peace and consistency he wanted. Which meant the situation was going to get a lot worse before it got better. Was it fair to drag Chantel through a lengthy court battle?

Dillon thought of her upstairs, sleeping in his bed, and wanted to go to her. She'd been so quiet earlier, all through dinner and putting the kids to bed. He'd wanted to hear that she agreed with how he'd handled Amanda, but he hadn't been ready to reveal his own troubled feelings. So he'd let her go to bed alone.

Now he longed to have her arms around him, her voice whispering in his ear. But she wasn't even sure she wanted to marry him; he could hardly ask her to tackle his fight to keep the girls. Maybe that was what frightened him, kept him from going to her. That and the fact that she had enough to worry about just hanging on to their baby.

Another difficult subject. He gave a frustrated sigh. How did he tell the girls about the baby? He'd told his mother already, so the news had to come out soon. But first he and Chantel had some decisions to make.

DILLON SHOWERED as quietly as possible, hoping not to wake Chantel while he got ready for work. But as he stood in front of his dresser, looking for socks to match his suit, he realized she was watching him.

"You didn't come to bed last night," she said.

"I slept on the couch. I didn't want to disturb you."

She didn't say anything for a minute. "I think you should take me back to the condo. I refuse to put you out of your own room."

"You're not putting me out of my room. I was pretty distracted last night and I couldn't sleep until late. Plus, I had some work to finish."

"I'm feeling better today. I can take care of myself."

He crossed the room to sit on the edge of the bed. Yesterday he'd been so certain they should get married. Now he wasn't as convinced. For the first time he realized, as more than just a passing acknowledgment, that a stepparent situation wasn't hard only on the kids. It could be difficult for parents, too. He wondered if that difficulty was what had caused his mother's many divorces and feared that, by marrying again, he'd be asking for the same kind of trouble. "Are you upset about what happened with Amanda?" he asked.

Chantel shook her head. "I'm not upset, just worried. About you and the girls."

He eyed the sack that held the bridal magazines he'd brought home yesterday. He'd had such high hopes when he'd bought them. But after Amanda's appearance, he hadn't even taken them out of the bag.

"Do you think she'll go through with the blood test?" Chantel asked. "Surely she can see that it's not what's best for Sydney."

"I don't know what she'll do anymore. She's not the same person I married."

"And if she does go through with it?"

"I'll have to comply."

"And then what?"

"And then pray she's wrong."

"But you don't think she is."

Dillon let his doubt finally show on his face. He'd carried it inside him for so long, so deeply hidden. But now that Amanda had confirmed his worst fear, he couldn't hide it anymore, at least not from Chantel. Worse, now that his ex-wife had pointed the finger at Phil, he thought he recognized similarities between Sydney and the muscle-bound trainer. He hated that he saw them, wondered if his mind was playing tricks on him, but there it was. "I don't know what to think," he said at last. "But I know I want you here with me."

He held his breath, waiting for her reponse, and finally she nodded. "Okay."

THE NEXT MORNING the girls came up to say goodbye to Chantel before thudding down the stairs again and slamming the door. She heard the engine of the Landcruiser roar to life, the higher whine of reverse, then nothing. Just silence.

Poor Dillon. She remembered Amanda's vindictive threat

and the pain in Dillon's eyes, and felt the same anger she'd felt yesterday. She was glad Dillon planned to fight for his girls. But she feared for what he might have to endure before it was all over. Sydney didn't look much like him. Given Amanda's past, it was easy to believe the child belonged to someone else, and because of that, Chantel didn't hold out much hope that a blood test would prove Dillon's paternity. But in his heart, where it mattered, Sydney belonged to him, and Chantel ached at the thought of his daughter being torn from him.

If the worst happened, maybe their baby would help ease the loss. She knew one child couldn't really compensate for another, but hoped a new life might do something to fill the absence Sydney would leave behind. Dillon wouldn't be the only one hurt—Brittney would be devastated.

The phone rang, and Chantel scooted over to the night-stand to answer it.

"If this is Brittney, you've grown up awfully fast." The voice was raspy and held a hint of surprise.

"This is Chantel."

"Oh, yeah? Seems to me I've heard that name a time or two." There was a pause during which Chantel didn't know what to say, couldn't imagine whom she was talking to—and then the man finally identified himself. "This is Dave, Dillon's uncle."

Dave. Fleetingly Chantel remembered Dillon's mentioning something about his uncle Dave the night they met. He was like a father to him, wasn't he? But he didn't live close by. "It's nice to talk to you, Dave."

"Did I miss Dillon?"

"Yes, he just left to take the girls to school. Then he's heading to the office."

"Well, I don't need anything, really. Just wanted to call and give him a hard time. His mother phoned here yesterday, saying he was getting married. You wouldn't happen to know anything about that, now would you?"

She could hear the teasing in his gruff voice and liked him instantly. "Actually I wouldn't. I haven't agreed to anything of the sort."

"You're making him work for it, huh? Well, nothing wrong with that. Reva made me sweat for two weeks before she gave me an answer."

Chantel heard a woman's voice in the background but couldn't quite hear what she was saying. Dave laughed at it, though.

"I'm not trying to make him sweat," she told him. "I just want to be sure he's doing it for the right reasons."

"He's an honest boy. You ask him. He'll tell you why he's doing it."

"Are you sure he won't just tell me what he thinks I want to hear?"

"Positive."

Yes, Chantel liked this man. He looked at things in their simplest form. He trusted Dillon, and his trust was absolute.

"He's been goin' through a lot with that ex-wife of his," he added. "You hang on, little lady, and I think you'll be glad."

"I'll hang on," she said, realizing that, at least in one sense, Dave was right. She'd wanted Dillon to woo her with words of love, to hear him speak his undying devotion, but he was dealing with a lot at the moment, and had been almost since they'd met. She'd been so caught up in her own concerns over Stacy, perhaps she hadn't given enough consideration to the obstacles he faced. He wanted to be part of their baby's life. He needed someone to help look after the girls and to take care of him, whether he knew it or not. And Chantel had nothing but time. Why not marry him and let him think he was doing the right thing, taking care of *her?* There were certainly worse things than marrying the man she loved! She stifled a giggle.

"When will I get to meet you?" she asked Dave.

"You tell me when the wedding is, and me and Reva, we'll be there."

Chantel laughed. Everyone was so sure there was going to be a wedding. She was beginning to believe it, too. "Dillon and I will call you tonight."

With a smile Chantel hung up and dialed the senator's office. She had to tell Maureen about the pregnancy and see what her options were at work. She wanted to keep her job, but the next few months presented some uncertainty.

"Senator Johnson's office."

"Getting tired of answering the phones?" Chantel asked, recognizing Maureen's voice.

"We've been busy," she admitted. "How are you feeling?"

"Better. I'd like to come back next week."

Maureen hesitated. "The senator's here, Chantel. He wants to talk to you."

The senator? Chantel's stomach tightened. She hadn't talked to him since before she got sick, but she'd often wondered what he must think of her extended absence. Surely his patience was coming to an end. And now she had to tell him about the pregnancy. Yikes!

Chantel took a deep breath as the senator's voice came on the line. "How are you, Chantel?"

"Better, Senator, thanks."

"Are you ready to come back to work? We really need someone here."

"I understand, sir. And I am ready. But before we make any plans, there's something I should tell you."

"What's that?" He sounded leary, and for good reason.

"I just found out a few days ago what's wrong with me.

I'm pregnant.'' Squeezing her eyes shut, she awaited his response.

"That's good news, isn't it?" he said.

"It is for me, sir. But I know you need someone you can depend on, and this is a high-risk pregnancy. The doctors don't know how much of the next six or seven months I'll be able to work.''

There was a pause. "Do you want to keep working?"

"Yes, sir.''

"Then I'm sure we can figure something out. Why don't you start again on Monday and we'll go from there. If it turns out you can't handle full-time, we'll cut back your hours and hire someone to help you.''

"Really? You'd do that for me?" Chantel could hardly believe it.

"I just had a constituent send me a large donation for my campaign because we'd been so responsive to her in her time of need. Turns out you were the one she dealt with here. You're doing a good job. We'd like to keep you.''

Chantel smiled. *You're doing a good job. We'd like to keep you.* Few words of praise had ever sounded better. Chantel just wished her father was around to hear them. *Goodbye New York. Goodbye modeling.* Wade had been wrong all along. She could make it without him. *Goodbye Wade. There's nothing else you can ever do to hurt me.* "Thank you, Senator," she said. "I'll be there on Monday.''

She hung up. Then, just because she felt better than she had in a long time, she dialed Stacy's number—and when the answering machine came on, she actually left a message.

She knew her call wouldn't be returned, but at least she'd reached out—again. Maybe someday Stacy would change her mind.

CHANTEL PICKED UP THE GIRLS from school and helped them with their homework. They didn't talk much and said nothing about Amanda, but seemed to be in good spirits.

Thank goodness children are so resilient, Chantel thought.

By the time Dillon returned from work, she'd already fed Brittney and Sydney and had his dinner warming in the oven. And she was glad she did. He looked exhausted.

"How was your day?" she asked.

"Busy, but I managed to stop by your condo to water your plants and get your mail." He piled the stack of letters, bills and junk mail on the counter.

"Thanks. That was really thoughtful."

"It's not hard to be thoughtful when you're all I think about," he said with a grin.

Chantel glanced up the stairs to make sure the girls were still playing in their room, then sauntered closer and put her arms around his neck. "I think that deserves a reward." She kissed him, long and hard and hungry, and when she pulled away, she caught the gleam of surprise in his eyes.

"That's quite a welcome. I could get used to coming home to this."

"Then it's a good thing I've reconsidered."

"What?" He bent his head to look at her.

"Your proposal. I'm going to marry you. We're going to become a family."

DLLON FELT SOMETHING lurch inside him, a combination, he guessed, of fear and excitement. "Do you think we can make it work?" he asked. "Despite everything?"

She reached up to stroke his cheek. "I'm not a quitter. Are you?"

He gazed into her eyes, knowing he'd never needed to

hear anything so badly. "You'll stick it out with me, then, even if it gets rough?"

"Even if it gets rough. We'll just batten down the hatches and weather the storm."

He drew her to him and hugged her tightly, bending to bury his face in her neck and to breathe in her clean sweet scent. Chantel, his Chantel. It sounded good. It felt right. God, how could something so wonderful happen to him right in the middle of his emotional tug-of-war with Amanda? "I'll always take good care of you," he promised.

Chantel murmured some kind of response, but Dillon missed it. Instead, he heard two distinct giggles and looked up to see his girls staring down at them through the banister.

"I told you they were kissing," Sydney announced with another giggle.

Dillon almost pulled away from Chantel, afraid that what the girls had seen would upset at least one of them. But then he realized they weren't upset at all. They were grinning from ear to ear.

"I knew it," Brittney said.

"Knew what?" Dillon challenged.

"That you liked her."

"And how did you know that?"

"Because you always look at her like this." She gave her sister a lovelorn glance, batting her eyes dramatically, and Dillon laughed. He should've known there'd be no fooling them.

"Come on down, you two," he said. It was time to announce the wedding, but he'd save the baby for later. "Chantel and I have something to tell you."

CHAPTER TWENTY

DILLON PARKED in front of Stacy's house and sat in his car for a few minutes, staring at the light burning in her window. She was home. Her car was in the driveway, and he could hear her television from the street. Taking a deep breath of warm spring air, redolent with the scent of gardenias blooming in the neighbor's yard, he prepared himself for the confrontation to come. Stacy wouldn't want to see him, but he had to talk to her, for Chantel's sake. Each day he stopped by her place to pick up her mail and check her answering machine; without fail, the moment he walked through the door at home, she asked if there'd been any messages from her sister. And each day he had to tell her no.

Getting out of his truck and pocketing his keys, he strode to the door, wondering if Stacy would even let him in. He had a high opinion of Chantel's sister, wasn't sure he wanted to see her worst side, but with all the emotional upheavals of late, he figured one disillusionment more or less wouldn't really matter.

The porch light flicked on almost as soon as he rang the bell, but the door didn't open right away. Dillon got the distinct impression that Stacy was watching him from her peephole, wondering whether or not to admit him.

"Come on, Stace."

Evidently she heard him. The lock clicked and the door opened a crack. "What are you doing here, Dillon?"

"I just want to talk to you for a few minutes. May I come in?"

She looked at him warily. "I don't have anything to say to you."

"Aren't you even going to ask if Chantel lost the baby?"

"I don't want to know," she said, but he guessed she'd already asked at the hospital. She wasn't as indifferent as she made herself out to be.

"Well, there're a few other things you should know."

"Like?"

"Like the little-known fact that Chantel and I created the baby before I found out she was your sister and before she had any idea you and I knew each other, let alone had dated."

Stacy's expression was skeptical. "That can't be true—"

"It is true. If you'll let me in, I'll explain."

She finally stepped back so he could come inside, but she didn't offer him a seat. Dillon took one, anyway.

"She rear-ended your Landcruiser," Stacy said. "Don't tell me you were both suddenly so lust-crazed you immediately ran into the woods. Or are you saying you met before the accident?"

Dillon told her about the events of that night, even though there was no good way to explain what had happened between him and Chantel. It was the kind of thing that had to be experienced to be believed, but when he finished his story, Stacy didn't seem as angry as she had when he'd arrived.

"Why did she lie to me?"

"You know why. She was trying to live down what she did with Wade. I wanted to continue seeing her, but she told me she wouldn't risk her relationship with you. She didn't want to hurt you."

Stacy made an incredulous sound. "For someone who didn't want to hurt me, she's done a pretty good job."

"I can't make any excuses for the situation with Wade. But I can tell you that she tried to handle what happened between us in the best way she could. She was afraid you'd never forgive her if she told you what happened during the storm. She tried to diminish what we felt for each other, walk away from it. And I tried to respect her wishes because I care about both of you. But I won't lie, Stacy. I couldn't forget her."

"So you love her?"

Dillon hated the thought that his answer might hurt Stacy all over again, but he knew it was time for honesty. Only the truth could possibly repair the damage to Chantel and Stacy's relationship. "I want to marry her."

A tear slipped out of the corner of Stacy's eye, and she wouldn't look at him. He stood and tried to comfort her, but she swiped at her wet cheeks and pushed him away. "Don't touch me."

He moved back. "I'm sorry, Stacy. Chantel and I didn't plan this. Our meeting was just an odd twist of fate. And if not for the baby, we'd probably still be talking ourselves out of believing that what we felt that night was real."

"Well, I'm happy for you," she said on a sniffle, her voice laced with sarcasm. "Tell Chantel I know she'll make a beautiful bride."

"It would mean a lot to her, to both of us, if you'd come to our wedding."

She chuckled. "Sorry but I'm not a glutton for punishment."

Dillon shoved his hands into his pockets, wishing there was something else he could say or do to soften her heart. But now it was up to Stacy. She understood that neither of them had meant to hurt her. Maybe, with time...

"Chantel may end up having to spend much of her pregnancy in bed," he said. "It won't be easy, but she really wants this baby."

"Yeah. I'd want it, too," Stacy replied. Then there was nothing left to do but see himself out.

MONDAY MORNING Wade sat in the parking lot waiting for Chantel to show up for work. He wasn't sure she was back at the senator's office, but he'd tried her condo a number of times and knew she wasn't staying there. Was she living with Dillon? The thought filled him with anger, but it was an impotent anger. He'd lost her. Ever since the day he'd seen her and Dillon kissing in the white Landcruiser, he'd known he wasn't going to get her back. He didn't even know why he was here, except that he had to see her one more time.

Chantel's car pulled into the lot, and she parked without noticing the Cadillac. She stepped out, wearing a green silk sheath that fell to midcalf, then paused to collect her purse and briefcase before starting toward the office.

Wade had told himself he'd just watch, see how she looked, but he couldn't resist climbing out of the car and waving to attract her attention.

She frowned when she saw him and hesitated, as though tempted to keep right on walking. With the morning sun sparkling all around her like a halo, she made quite a sight.

"What do you want?" she asked before he even reached her.

"Just to see you."

With a fleeting glance at the office door, she paused, and he took the opportunity to study her carefully. "You look good."

"I'm feeling better."

He shoved his hands in his pockets. "You with Dillon now?"

She nodded.

"You pregnant?"

"That's what you told Stacy, isn't it?" Her gaze was cool, level, but not hate-filled. She had class. Wade had to hand it to her.

"I'm sorry about Stacy," he said. "I was angry, jealous. I wanted to hurt you."

"That's always been our problem, Wade. You feel the need to hurt me. But you can't hurt me anymore. I'm in love with someone else."

"Dillon."

"Yes."

He let his breath out in a whistle, surprised at how much that admission stung. "So it's completely over between us?"

"Wade, it's been over since I left New York. I'd already given our relationship all I had by then."

He chuckled without humor. "Well, you tried to tell me. I guess I just couldn't figure out why things had to change, how you could turn away from me. We had it good in New York—"

"You had it good. I was miserable most of the time. You were unfaithful to me. You refused to marry me, to have a family. You blamed anything that went wrong on me and my career—at the same time you spent the money I made."

He stared down at the cement. "Maybe I didn't deserve you, but I thought you loved me."

"I did, once."

"So now what?"

"I'm going to marry Dillon. And I don't think you should come around anymore."

''Don't worry. I'll be heading back to New York, after all. Try to make it on my own.''

She nodded. ''Then I wish you the best of luck.''

He itched to hug her, to pull her to him just once more, but he knew she'd have none of it. Not after what he'd done to her and Stacy. So he started to walk to his car, then turned back.

''Chantel?''

She paused, the door to the office half-open.

''I'm sorry,'' he said, and for the first time in his life, he meant it.

''SO WHEN'S THE WEDDING?''

Dillon's sister Monica sat at the picnic table across from Chantel. The two of them had been chatting happily almost from the moment they met. Behind them a small lake shimmered like a jewel in a valley created by gently sloping green hills. To their left, Brittney and Sydney squealed on the swing set, playing with their younger cousins and enjoying the warm Sunday afternoon.

Dillon wasn't sure how to answer his sister's question. They'd originally planned to have a small wedding at a church not far from where he lived, but a notice he'd received from Amanda's attorney had changed all that. Now he just wanted to get married, fast so he could deal with the other issues in his life. And Chantel seemed quite willing to revise their plans.

He met her eye before answering Monica. ''Because of the situation, I think we've decided to keep it simple. We thought we might get married in Vegas next weekend.''

''Hogwash.'' Dillon's mother held court at the head of the table, where she'd been passing out large pieces of a delicious-smelling oatmeal cake. Her busy capable hands paused in their task. ''A small ceremony right here would be lovely. It doesn't have to be extravagant, but Chantel deserves something nice, with a photographer and a real wedding dress. You'll pay for it, and we'll all help.''

"Vegas next weekend is fine," Chantel said.

Dillon grinned. "Good, I'm getting tired of sleeping on the couch.''

"You're getting tired of creeping around your own house, more like," his mother put in, "but you can do it for another couple of weeks if it means giving Chantel a nice wedding."

Dillon nearly laughed out loud. He and Chantel hadn't been intimate since she'd come to stay with him. The doctor had warned them it might cause a miscarriage, and he wasn't going to do anything that could cost them their baby. Beyond that, he'd been determined to set a good example for his girls. So he'd done his best to put temptation out of reach by working late every night and relegating himself to the living room.

"Amanda's back in town and giving me problems again," he said, changing the subject.

"More custody battles?" His mother grimaced. "So she's following up on her phone call. Well, let her do what she will. She can't take the girls after abandoning them.''

"Not when you're doing such a good job with them, Dillon," Monica added. "They seem so happy with you."

Jason, Dillon's nephew by his other sister, Janet, started to cry. They all looked over to the slide area where Janet was picking him up and dusting him off. Evidently he'd taken a little tumble. Mark, Janet's husband, joined her, carrying their baby daughter.

"I know a guy at work whose wife did something similar, and she's never been able to regain custody," Monica said, resuming the conversation. "You're not worried, are you?"

He *was* worried, and with good reason. Chantel reached out to take his hand, and he smiled at her. "I guess I may as well tell you,'' he said, knowing the truth would come out soon enough anyway.

"What?" His mother frowned. She must have known she wouldn't like his news, because she abandoned her task of covering the leftover cake and sank onto the bench beside her short wiry husband, who never said a word.

"Amanda's making me take a blood test."

"Why?" Monica scowled, her posture defensive.

"She claims Sydney isn't mine."

Stunned silence met this announcement, and Chantel squeezed his hand. A lump the size of a grapefruit lodged somewhere in his throat. Damn, why had he said it now, in the middle of a family picnic? Because he wished they'd tell him that it couldn't be? That Sydney looked just like him?

He knew better.

His mother was the first to speak. "Dillon, that child is yours. No matter what the blood test says—"

"I know." He cut her off, wishing he could cut his emotions off as easily. He *couldn't* lose Sydney. What would the girls' lives be like, growing up without each other? How many concessions would he be forced to make, being the only one, as usual, who seemed to care about their ultimate welfare? Would he be faced with the decision of letting Brittney go, too?

"When?" Monica asked.

"The beginning of July."

"That's more than a month away. Why so long?"

"I wanted to stall as long as possible, just in case…" He let his words die off and everyone shifted uncomfortably.

"Does Sydney have to go to the doctor's with you?"

He shook his head. "I'm taking her in separately."

"What are you going to tell her the appointment is for?" his mother asked.

"I don't know. Part of me wants to lie and say she's getting a vaccination. The other part is tempted to sit her down and try to explain, so it doesn't come as a worse blow later on. But there just isn't any way to tell her how I feel—" he fought to control his voice "—and how lost I'll be if—"

"I don't think you should tell her anything yet," Chantel interrupted, her voice soft but firm.

"Why?" His mother and sister looked up in surprise.

"I'll admit I've had my doubts. But now…" She shrugged. "Now I don't know. Something's just telling me not to worry. I think she's his."

Skepticism shone in his mother's eyes, but to Dillon, Chantel's words soothed like cool cream on a hot sunburn. If only the blood test proved her right.

"About that wedding," his sister said, obviously trying to move the conversation in a more positive direction. "I think we could pull it together in three weeks. What do you think?"

Chantel's smile remained unchanged, but Dillon caught the sparkle of excitement in her eyes. So, she wanted the wedding, after all. Well, he certainly wouldn't deny her because of his own preoccupations and worries. She deserved a special day, something far nicer than standing in front of an unknown minister in some gaudy Vegas wedding chapel.

"Three weeks from this weekend sounds good," he said, and bent and kissed Chantel on the mouth. He didn't care if they were married in a barn as long as she became his wife. He just wanted her to be happy.

When Dillon drew back, Chantel gazed up at him with those incredible eyes of hers and asked, "Do you think there's any chance my sister will come?"

Dillon remembered his confrontation with Stacy, a meeting he'd never told Chantel about, and knew she wouldn't.

But he didn't have the heart to tell Chantel that. "Maybe," he said hopefully. "We'll certainly send her an invitation."

STACY KNEW it was the invitation to Chantel's wedding before she even opened the envelope. She nearly tossed it in the wastebasket with the rest of her junk mail, but something about the pretty paper made her pause. Was their picture inside?

Bracing herself, Stacy ripped open the envelope to find a black-and-white photograph of Dillon, Chantel and his girls. Separated from it by a thin piece of tissue was a scalloped one-sided invitation.

Holding the picture to the light streaming in through her living-room window, she carefully examined her sister's face, and then Dillon's. Chantel, forever a friend of the camera, looked wholesome and beautiful in a sleeveless dress and straw hat. The girls wore matching chintz dresses, and Dillon was wearing a pair of slacks and a tie. They were standing in the middle of a meadow, the wind rustling through their hair. And they looked happy—like a family.

Stacy sank onto her sofa and read the invitation, which had a pretty piece of ribbon at the top and delicate cutouts along the fancy edges. The wedding was the last Saturday of the month, a little more than a week away. Dillon had told her how much it would mean to Chantel if she came, but the wound was still too raw. She couldn't sit in the audience and watch them promise to love and cherish each other, pledging all their tomorrows.

And yet, despite everything, there was a calmness deep inside her at the realization that Chantel was in good hands at last.

CHANTEL SMILED HAPPILY as she hung up after her conversation with Monica and glanced over the menu they had planned for the wedding. They were going to have a brunch following a midmorning ceremony, instead of a reception at night, and Monica claimed she knew just the caterers to use. Clippings from various magazines lay spread out on the kitchen table, showing different place settings, gourmet foods, flower arrangements and dresses.

She stood and adjusted the blinds to let in more of the midmorning sun, breathing in the scent of the lemon furniture polish she'd just used to dust, then went back to sifting through her clippings. She had to decide on bridesmaid's dresses for Dillon's sisters and Brittney and Sydney. She was running out of time.

Her own dress was draped over the closest chair. With an empire waist, the style was reminiscent of a Regency-era gown; it had a small train and was made of delicate beaded lace over a satin underlining—understated yet elegant. She compared it to an emerald-green dress that could possibly work for the bridesmaids, at least for Dillon's sisters, then hugged herself. She'd been back at work for a whole week, feeling stronger every day, and could hardly believe she was getting married *and* having a baby. How many times had she tried to convince Wade that they should start a family?

Now she was glad he'd never agreed with her. It had been painful at the time, but she knew, deep down, that Wade could never have made her as happy as Dillon. Stacy's stubborn silence was the only thing that spoiled her contentment. That and her worry about Dillon and Sydney.

Chantel heard keys jingling in the lock at the front door and looked up in surprise. It was Saturday, but Dillon had told her he'd be gone all morning, helping his mother trim some of the taller trees in her yard. The girls had been invited over to Mary Beth's for the day. So who was home already?

"Hi." Dillon smiled as he came in, but Chantel detected a certain strain in his face.

"Hi, yourself. Is something wrong?" she asked. "What are you doing home?"

The dimples in his cheeks flashed. "What if I just wanted to be alone with my fiancée?"

"I'd say you weren't having much fun at your mother's."

He chuckled as she met him halfway across the kitchen and pressed her lips to his, but his usual enthusiasm for her kiss wasn't there. He released her almost as soon as he'd hugged her and went to the kitchen sink, where he washed his hands, then gazed out the window.

"What's wrong?" she repeated.

He leaned his hip against the counter and turned toward her. Bits of leaves and twigs still clung to his hair and clothes. "I went to the doctor's and had the blood test yesterday."

"What?" Dread congealed in Chantel's stomach like cold gravy. "But you said you weren't scheduled to go in until the first of July. That's almost two weeks away." *After the wedding,* she added silently.

He sighed. "I couldn't wait any longer. It was driving me crazy worrying about it, wondering whether or not we'd really be the family I want us to become. I didn't want it hanging over us all through our wedding."

Chantel didn't mention that something much worse than not knowing might be hanging over them now. If Sydney didn't belong to Dillon, the truth would be inescapable. How would they deal with all that in the eight days before they got married? "And?" she said quietly.

"The results are right here." He took an envelope out of his back pocket and stared glumly down at it. "I've been carrying it around all morning."

"They didn't tell you?"

"I wanted to talk to you first, make sure you agreed with me that it's best to get this over with and not drag it out any longer." He set the envelope on the counter and they both watched it warily, as though it had suddenly grown fangs.

Chantel knew Dillon had taken Sydney to get her blood test almost a week earlier. They'd told her the doctor wanted to run some routine tests, and she'd complied, if not happily, at least willingly. Evidently Dillon had gone in a few days later, during work hours, so she'd never connect the two appointments.

"Well?" he asked. "What do you think?"

Chantel didn't know how to answer. This was eating him up inside. She wanted it over as much as he did, but she wasn't sure whether it would be better to face the possible bad news now or put it off a little longer. "I think you should do what you need to do, and if that means you open the envelope today, then do it."

He reached out for her, and she went to him, slipping her arms around his waist and tucking her head in the hollow of his shoulder. The smell of perspiration and the outdoors still lingered on his warm skin and clothes. Chantel breathed deeply and the thought that she'd be able to hug him like this every day of their lives made her happy all the way down to her bones.

"How are you feeling?" he asked above her head. "Any cramps?"

"Not since that day in the hospital. I think the baby's going to be fine."

"I hope so." He turned her in his arms so that her back pressed against his chest and his hands were free to cup her belly. He rubbed it gently, his actions telling Chantel that he was affirming the baby's existence. "I like it that you're starting to show."

Chantel enjoyed the feel of his hands and wondered if the baby could somehow understand how badly they wanted him or her. "What should we name the baby if it's a boy?" she asked.

He kissed her neck. "I kind of like Junior."

Chantel chuckled. *Typical male.* "You want to name him after you?"

"Uh-huh. And if it's a girl, we can name her after you."

"No." She covered Dillon's hands with her own and entwined their fingers. "Stacy's middle name is Lauren. I'd like to use that."

He paused for a moment. "I'm sorry about Stacy, babe."

Chantel turned and lifted her chin, giving him her bravest smile. "I haven't given up on her yet."

He frowned. "That's what worries me. I don't want you to be hurt again."

"There are some things you can't protect me from," she told him. "Just like there are some things I can't fix for you." She eyed the envelope again. "Are you going to open it?"

She felt him haul in a deep breath. Then he moved away and tucked the envelope in the cupboard above the refrigerator. "Not today," he said.

CHAPTER TWENTY-ONE

FOR DILLON, the next few days dragged by. The envelope in the cupboard seemed to beckon him every time he passed the kitchen. But then he'd think of Chantel and their upcoming marriage and force himself to move on.

At least the wedding plans were finally set. On Wednesday afternoon, with only two days to go before the big event, he received a call at his office.

"Don't say I've never done anything for you." It was the voice of a heavy smoker—Helen. Dillon recognized his ex-mother-in-law immediately, even though they hadn't talked since Amanda's reappearance.

"I'm afraid I don't understand," he said.

She chuckled, the sound more bitter than sweet. "This is a courtesy call to let you know that Amanda's gone back to her new husband in Salt Lake City."

"What?" Dillon could hardly believe his ears.

"You heard me."

"But what about the girls, the blood test?"

"She wanted to go through with the test, anyway, but I knew it wasn't for the right reasons."

Dillon agreed with this assessment, but he was cautious about jumping to any conclusions. "And that means..."

"It means I won't let her. I told her if she goes through with the test, I'll do everything I can to help you get custody, even if you're not Sydney's real father. And she knows

I'll do it, too.'' Helen gave a hacking cough. ''Anyway, she's agreed to drop the suit.''

Dillon couldn't breathe for a minute. The thought of how many times he'd nearly reached for that white envelope waiting at home terrified him. ''So, no blood test?''

''No blood test. The girls are yours. May you do a better job of raising them.''

A dial tone hummed in Dillon's ear for several seconds before he hung up the receiver. No blood test. No threat to Sydney. They were going to be a complete family, after all.

''Thank you, Helen, thank you.'' He muttered, and wearing the most carefree smile he'd worn in a long time, he picked up the phone to call Chantel.

CHANTEL LEFT the girls at the kitchen table, where they'd been working on their scrapbooks, to answer the phone.

''Hello, beautiful.''

''Hi, Dillon.'' She smiled, loving the sound of his voice.

''I have some good news.''

Chantel waved for Brittney and Sydney to stop fighting over the glue. ''What's that?'' she asked.

''Amanda went back to Utah.''

''To her husband?''

''Yeah.''

She glanced toward the cupboard over the fridge, where she knew the envelope with the results of the blood test still lurked. ''Does that mean what I think it means?''

''We get to keep the girls. Both of them.''

''Dillon, that's wonderful!'' The invisible bands that had been squeezing Chantel's heart ever since Amanda had appeared at the door were instantly released, and she felt lighter than air. ''You must be so relieved.''

''I am.''

''Is that Daddy?'' Sydney asked.

Chantel nodded.

"Is he calling to tell you he loves you?"

No, he's never told me that, Chantel thought, feeling a flicker of doubt. She wanted to believe he loved her. He *acted* as if he loved her. So she was marrying him on faith. But he'd never said it. "He's calling to say he misses his girls," she filled in.

"Why don't you guys come meet me for lunch?" Dillon asked. "I do miss my girls—all three of them."

All three of them. It wasn't *I love you,* but Chantel was part of the family now. She remembered her own father, and missed him all over again. But the pain of his passing and the regret were gone, because she was finally where she belonged. And somewhere along the line she'd managed to forgive that nineteen-year-old girl who'd screwed up so badly. "We'd love to," she said, and the only empty place left in her heart was the spot she would always reserve for Stacy.

AFTER A LONG NIGHT of tossing and turning, Stacy awoke with her heart pounding. Today was Chantel's wedding. As much as she'd tried to ignore the passing days, her internal clock refused to let her forget.

"I'm not going," she groaned. She hadn't heard from Wade since that day in the hospital parking lot, and she was glad. He had no place in her life. She hadn't seen him around town, either, and guessed he'd gone back to New York, after all. Neither had she heard from Dillon, not since the night he'd come to invite her to his wedding. Her love life was amazingly bleak, but she doubted even a hot new romance would have made any difference to the way she felt today: insignificant, left out, nostalgic, guilt-ridden and confused, all wrapped up together.

She got up and scowled at herself in the mirror. Not a

good hair day. She could tell already. But she wasn't interested in how her lack of sleep had affected her looks. She'd saved a message on her answering machine that she wanted to hear again, just to see if her conscience would let her erase it this time.

"Stacy? This is Chantel. I know you don't want to hear from me, but I'm calling to tell you...I don't know...that I miss you. And that I'm sorry. Not for what I've done. You already know that. I'm just sorry you got stuck with such a lousy sister. You deserve better."

A lump formed in Stacy's throat, but for a moment her finger hovered stubbornly over the erase button. Then she played the message again, and again, until tears streamed down her face. Chantel wasn't such a bad person. She'd been sweet and giving when they were growing up. Until Wade, Stacy had definitely been the more selfish of the two of them. And now, with Dillon, Stacy wasn't sure it was entirely Chantel's fault. When they'd first met, Chantel hadn't known she was dating Dillon. What would *she* have done in a similar situation? With a man like Dillon?

The T-shirt and shorts she'd worn to bed didn't match, but she didn't bother to change before she grabbed her keys off the counter and headed out into the warm July morning. She hadn't been back to Chantel's father's grave since Memorial Day, but she felt compelled to go there now. She missed Grant, needed his advice. If only he was still alive...

The cemetery was large and sprawling, with an older section on the far left and a new section with mostly flat headstones on the right. A small stone structure, built to resemble an ancient Greek temple, sat in the middle; it held, Stacy guessed, the remains of those who'd been cremated.

The scent of carnations and damp soil crowded in close as she walked across the neatly trimmed grass. The sun was beating down, promising temperatures in the upper nineties for the afternoon, but somehow it reminded her of another day, this one in spring.

It was May. She was only fourteen, Chantel not quite eleven. They both stood at Grant's side, gazing at the grave of their mother, who'd died just two months before. It was Stacy's first experience with death and never had she felt so bereft. The one person who had sustained her, loved her, was gone, and now she belonged to a man who had fathered her sibling, but not her.

Would he eventually send her to her real father, a drifter who'd never shown much interest in her? She wasn't sure. She only knew she felt apart from the family, alone, until Chantel had come to stand by her. At that age they rarely hugged, but Chantel put her arm around Stacy and simply stood there until they went home, the contact telling her that she did belong, that she would always be part of the family.

Now Grant, too, was gone. Would she and Chantel maintain their relationship? Was it too late to save what was left of their family?

Stacy sank onto the grass, heedless of the wet ground as Chantel and Dillon's engagement picture flashed in her mind. They'd looked so happy, so right together. Could she really begrudge her sister a man like Dillon? When Chantel was ill with what they'd thought was flu, Stacy had sworn she'd never let anything else come between them. And yet here she was, carrying her old grudge.

Closing her eyes, she said a silent prayer, to God, to Grant, to her mother, to whoever was listening. "Please, help me forgive her," she said. "Neither of us is perfect. But nothing should come between sisters."

STANDING IN THE BEDROOM of her condo, where she'd insisted on getting ready for the wedding, Chantel stared down at her engagement ring. It was a large marquise with a double row of smaller diamonds on each side. She'd never seen a more beautiful piece of jewelry, not even in her New York days, when nothing was out of reach. She and Dillon had gone together to choose their rings, and she'd loved this one from the start. But the price had been exorbitant. She'd immediately shied away and chosen something more reasonable, but Dillon had already noticed the gleam in her eye. After her ring had been sized and they'd gone back to pick it up, she'd stood in the store and opened the plush velvet box to quite a surprise.

She smiled at the memory of Dillon watching her, his eyes warm and soft as the tears rolled down her cheeks. He'd gently wiped them away, put the ring on her finger and pulled her into his arms. "I'm a lucky man," he'd said, but he still hadn't told her he loved her.

He did care about her, she told herself. He showed it in every possible way, down to the flowers he brought home at least once a week.

If only he'd say the words...

Taking a deep breath, Chantel stood and surveyed herself in the mirror. She was wearing her wedding dress. The ceremony was in less than an hour. Then she'd be Mrs. Dillon Broderick. She put a hand to her stomach, which bulged slightly beneath the concealing folds of her dress. Her baby would have its father's name and grow up under his protection. Fortunate child.

"It won't be long now," she whispered as the telephone rang. Even before she answered it, she knew it was Dillon.

"How's my beautiful bride?" he asked.

She smiled to herself. "I'm almost ready."

"Can I come get you?"

"No. I'll drive myself. You can't see me until I walk down the aisle, remember?"

He groaned. "I can't wait. For the wedding—or for tonight."

Chantel thought about sleeping with Dillon again, feeling his bare skin against her own. Unity, love, had no better expression. "No more couch."

"Never. But we'll be very careful of the baby. Don't worry."

"I know you'd never do anything to hurt me or our baby."

"I'm glad you know that, because it's true. I'll see you at the church."

She hung up feeling nervous yet happy. She coiled her hair into a fancy style she'd once worn on the cover of *Elle*, situated her veil and collected her keys. But before she could walk out the door, something called her back into the living room. Stacy. She had to try to convince her sister, one more time, to be part of the wedding, to give them her blessing.

Picking up the phone, Chantel dialed Stacy's number, but got the answering machine. She opened her mouth to leave a message, to plead with her sister to come, but ended up saying simply, "Stacy, I love you."

DILLON'S MOTHER and sisters had done an incredible job decorating the church. Sprays of lilies, accentuated by ivy, lined the steps outside and continued down the aisle. They'd hired a photographer and were serving prime rib and roast turkey at the brunch to follow, along with a variety of side dishes, fresh fruit, breads and gourmet desserts. But the flowers had been the single biggest expense, and now Chantel could understand why. They were everywhere, they were real and they were beautiful.

Her stomach fluttered with nervous excitement as she stood in the small vestibule to the side of the front foyer, watching through the crack in the door as a crowd gathered.

Maureen and her husband went inside, and the senator him
self, along with his wife and one of the field representatives
but Chantel didn't recognize anyone else. They were al
Dillon's friends and family. He'd lived in the Bay Area hi.
whole life.

According to Dillon's sister Monica, who had met Chan
tel at the chapel the moment she arrived and whisked he
away to her current hiding place, Dillon was already inside
But Chantel hadn't seen him. She imagined him standing a
the altar, waiting for her, and felt a tingling rush of antici
pation.

"Oh, you look absolutely stunning!" Dillon's mother ex
claimed, bursting into the room. She clasped Chantel in :
tight hug.

"I'm just glad I'm feeling good enough for this. And I'm
grateful you talked us out of going to Vegas."

"Well, if she's lucky, a girl only gets married once."

Chantel smiled, understanding the allusion to Karen':
own past. "At least you got it right this time. You seen
very happy."

She shrugged. "Dillon doesn't think much of Lyle, bu
my husband treats me well—and I don't want to be alone.'

"I'm sure Dillon will eventually come to like him."

Karen nodded. "He's been through too many stepfathers
But look how well he turned out, in spite of my rocky past
I think he'll forgive me someday."

"I'm sure he already has."

The organ music started, and Brittney and Sydney hurriec
into the room, wearing their matching emerald-greer
dresses. "Everyone's here!" they gasped. "Even old Aun
Maude."

"It's going to be a lovely wedding." Dillon's mothe
kissed Chantel's cheek, then squeezed her hand. "I need to
ask you something."

Chantel raised her brows in surprise. What could Dillon's mother want right before the wedding?

"I know we were planning to have Dillon's business partner give you away when Reva got sick and Dave didn't think he could make it. But he flew in this morning and surprised us all. Would you mind if we let him take Simon's place?"

"No. Of course not." Chantel remembered the gruff but warm voice of Dillon's uncle from their telephone conversation. Before her plans to marry Dillon, Chantel had felt so isolated and alone. She'd had only her sister, who wasn't speaking to her. Now Dillon's family would surround her and become her own—an added blessing.

Karen went out and returned with a stocky, ruddy-faced man with salt-and-pepper hair in a buzz cut. "So here's the beautiful bride," he said when his sister introduced them. Instead of taking her hand, he gave her a hug.

"How's Reva?" she asked.

"Her cold turned to bronchitis there for a few days, but she's ornery as ever and on the mend. She sends her love."

Chantel smiled. Somehow, with Dave, it didn't seem strange that a woman she'd never met would send her love.

"I'm glad you're on board for the ride," he admitted. "And I'm glad my favorite nephew has fallen in love again."

"We all love her," Sydney announced, hugging her legs. Brittney stood a few feet away, smiling shyly.

Chantel lifted Sydney's chin so she could see into her eyes. Then she reached out for Brittney. When her small hand slipped inside Chantel's, Chantel squatted down to the girls' level and said, "And I love all of you. We're going to be happy together, aren't we?"

They nodded and hugged her, and Dillon's mother began

to cry. "Everyone's waiting," she said, sounding impatient with her own emotions. "We'd better get started."

Karen disappeared and Dave smiled reassuringly at Chantel as Monica and Janet arrived to take their places. Then the music changed to the wedding march, and Chantel slid her hand through the crook of Dave's arm.

"Here we go," he murmured. "Don't be nervous."

He might as well have told her not to breathe. Chantel braced herself and they set off, with Monica, Janet, Brittney and Sydney following.

Even though Chantel had seen almost all the guests as they came in, she couldn't stop herself from looking for Stacy. She gazed down the rows of pews and searched each face, but mostly strangers gazed back, smiling.

Sadness filled Chantel's heart, but she forced herself to smile, too. She was getting married. She should be thrilled, she told herself, and she was, once she glanced up and saw Dillon waiting at the altar. He looked even better than Chantel had envisioned. His black tux fit perfectly. His hair had been trimmed and combed back from his face but still curled just a bit in back and around the ears. And the dimples Chantel loved so much deepened as he watched her walk toward him. He had to be the handsomest man in the world, she thought. She already knew he was the kindest.

She gave him a tremulous smile, but then the door opened and closed, stealing Dillon's attention away from her.

Something made his eyes sparkle. What was it? Chantel was tempted to see for herself, but everyone was watching her little procession, and she didn't want to trip on her heels and take her bridesmaids down like dominos.

Dave stopped and put Chantel's hand in Dillon's, but Dillon was still looking beyond her.

"What is it?" she whispered.

"A wonderful surprise," he said, turning her around as soon as her bridesmaids had taken their places.

Chantel scanned the pews again, until she saw what Dillon saw. Stacy, sitting in the back row.

Tears burned behind Chantel's eyes and clogged her throat. Even though the minister, Dillon's family and the entire congregation expected her to do something far different, she let go of Dillon's hand and rushed back down the aisle to give her sister a fierce hug.

"Thank you for coming," she whispered.

Stacy pulled back, tears swimming in her own eyes. "You're my sister," she said.

"NO. NO CLOTHES," Dillon protested when Chantel tried to grab her robe off the chair in his bedroom before they headed down to rummage through the kitchen for something to eat. "I love seeing the curve of my baby in your belly." His hand moved protectively over her abdomen, and he pulled her back against his own nakedness, then breathed in deeply, as though he'd absorb her very essence if he could.

Dillon's mother had taken the girls for a week so that Dillon and Chantel could honeymoon in Hawaii. But they were spending their first night at home. In fact, Chantel wondered if she wouldn't be just as happy staying right where she was and never leaving the bedroom. Dillon had massaged every part of her body with his hands, his lips, his tongue. And while he'd been cautious of the baby, he'd proved himself creative enough to give her a spectacular wedding night, in spite of their restrictions. He'd promised her a nice warm bath next, where he'd said he planned to lather her with soap and...

"What are you thinking about? You're smiling like the cat who swallowed the canary," he said.

Chantel laughed. "I was thinking about what an incredible lover you are."

"Oh, yeah?" He nuzzled her neck. "Tell me more. My male ego is eating this up."

She turned in his arms and pressed her breasts against his chest, then kissed the ridge of his jaw. "Your touch makes me crazy, Dillon Broderick, because you're such a good man, and you're so talented with your hands, and because..."

"And because you love me?"

Chantel drew back to look up at him. "You sound as if you're trying to convince yourself of that."

"Maybe I am."

"Why?" It was well past midnight, but Dillon had insisted they leave the light on. He wanted to watch the expressions on his wife's face when he made love to her, he'd said, and Chantel had enjoyed seeing his expressions just as much. But now she could read doubt flickering in his eyes.

"Maybe I'm afraid you married me for the baby's sake," he murmured. "Or maybe I'm just afraid it's too good to last."

Chantel wrapped her arms around his neck and pulled him into a tight embrace. "You think I might do the same thing to you that Amanda did."

He didn't answer for a moment. "We started out happy," he said at last.

"But you were working and going to school. You were under a lot of stress and you were gone a lot. That can take its toll."

"But she seemed to grow bored so quickly."

"I don't think she really understood what marriage is all about. She still wanted to be young and have no responsibility. And you have to remember that she's a different person than I am, Dillon." At that moment Chantel knew it might take him a while before he could express his feelings for her. It was love that had given Amanda the power to hurt and manipulate him. He was fighting against putting himself in the same vulnerable position again. But he did care for her. She knew that much.

"I love you with all my heart," she whispered, "And I'll never purposely do anything to make you jealous or to hurt you in any way."

She felt his arms tighten around her, crushing her to him as he buried his face in her neck. When he finally lifted his head, Chantel could see he was struggling with some deep emotion. Cupping his cheek in her hand, she smiled up at him. "You'll tell me the same thing someday, when you're ready. Now let's go eat!"

She led him from the room, but he didn't say anything until they reached the kitchen. By then he had his emotions in check and insisted she sit down while he cooked.

They lit a candle, turned off the lights and ate omelets in companionable silence. Afterward Chantel took Dillon's hand and brushed a kiss across the knuckles. "I have a gift for you," she said.

He raised his brows. "I don't think you could give me anything better than what I've already got."

"You'll like it." She went to the cupboard and brought back the envelope that held the results of Dillon and Sydney's blood tests. "The other day, I noticed that this was still here."

He tensed. "I've tried to throw it away several times, but...I can't. I want to put an end to the wondering."

"We're a family, Dillon, a real family. What's in this doesn't matter."

"I know. I think it has more to do with hope, hope that Sydney *is* mine and that Amanda has nothing to come back with."

Chantel smiled and started to open the envelope.

"Don't." Dillon stopped her. "I don't think it's wise. I've debated with myself over and over, and while the wondering's driving me crazy, I think it's better not to look. Let's burn it."

"I said this was a gift, remember?" Chantel touched his cheek.

He didn't answer. He just watched nervously as she pulled out a letter and a report and handed them both to him. Slowly he took the documents from her outstretched hand and, after a final scrutiny of her face, began to read.

"How did you know?" he asked a few minutes later, looking stunned.

"I peeked before you took me home last night. I thought it was worth the chance, and better me than you if things turned out...well, differently from what we hoped. In that case, I planned to carry the secret to my grave."

"She's mine," he said as though he couldn't believe it. "Despite her dark eyes and her small build, despite that weight-trainer guy in Amanda's past, she's mine."

Chantel's grin widened at the incredulity and happiness in his voice. "No one can ever take her away from you again."

"From us," he corrected. "And that's the best gift of all."

CHAPTER TWENTY-TWO

Four Months Later
Lake Tahoe

"HAVEN'T YOU DONE enough?" Dillon asked, coming up behind Chantel at the cabin's kitchen table. "You've been stuffing envelopes for two hours." He grinned. "I'm starting to feel neglected."

Chantel smiled, feeling the same warmth she always felt when Dillon was around. "I'm almost done," she assured him. "I had to finish. I promised Senator Johnson I'd get these in the mail today. The election's close and—"

Dillon slipped his arms around Chantel's bulging middle and kissed her neck. "So is the baby. I don't want you to overdo it. We shouldn't even be up here, so far from the hospital."

"But we had to come and celebrate the first snow." She put her hands over his and threaded their fingers together, enjoying his clean woodsy smell.

"It was nice of Stacy to take the girls," he said.

"Are you kidding? She lives for having the kids come."

"I know, but we should've spent the weekend at home. What if you go into labor?"

"I'm not due for nearly three weeks, and I haven't had any pains. Besides, there's a hospital in Truckee. I'd rather have Dr. Bradley deliver the baby, but if it's an emergency—" she shrugged "—we'll go there." Affixing a stamp to the last envelope, she added it to the gigantic pile of letters encouraging the voters of the seventh district to support Johnson on election day. "Phew! That's the last of them."

She leaned her head back against Dillon. "Did you get the generator started? It's cold in here."

"I started the generator and shoveled the walks—"

"So we can go to the post office?"

"No—so we can make a run for it, if we have to. And I built a fire in the living room. Come sit with me. I've got water heating for some herbal tea."

Chantel stood and tried to stretch her aching back. She loved being pregnant and knowing she supported another life inside her, but it was getting harder and harder to work and to move and to sleep. Gaining enough weight had been difficult, too, but Dillon had made sure she'd eaten properly. And he told her she looked great even when she felt like a moose, which led her to believe he loved her as much as she loved him. Not that he'd ever actually said so.

He seated her on the couch, disappeared into the kitchen and returned with two cups. "I like this place," he said, sitting next to her. "It's certainly a lot nicer than the cabin Stacy rented last March."

Chantel smiled. "It's a lot more expensive, too." Accepting the cup he handed her, she took a cautious sip, admiring the leaping flames beneath the stone mantel, the gleaming hardwood floors, the rough-hewn furniture. "Someday maybe we can afford to buy a cabin up here."

Dillon put his arm around her and pulled her closer, and she curled her legs underneath her and relaxed against him. "We'll build one. I'll design it."

"That would be great. We could bring the kids up whenever we wanted." Her head resting in the hollow of his shoulder, she gazed out the window at the softly falling snow. "Even if I live to be a hundred, whenever I see snow I'll remember the night we met, how you risked your life to save me."

He chuckled. "And I'll remember how you wrecked my new Landcruiser."

She elbowed him in the stomach. "Here I am, being romantic, and you have to bring *that* up. Besides, that accident was your fault. If you hadn't slammed on your brakes all of a sudden—"

"You mean, if you hadn't been tailgating me all the way from Auburn—"

"Then we never would've met."

"And I would have missed the love of my life," he finished.

For a moment what he'd said didn't quite register. When it did, Chantel twisted around to see his face. "Are you trying to tell me something?" she asked, holding her breath and hoping he'd finally grown to trust her enough to talk about his feelings.

"Something that's been true since that very first night," he admitted. "I love you, Chantel. I always have. I always will."

And then he gave her a kiss that told her just how much.

EPILOGUE

Six Months Later

STACY STOOD in the hospital nursery, gazing at the five newborns who had entered the world during the past twenty-four hours. They were small and shriveled, not much to look at, really, but they smelled sweet and they were so innocent, so dependent. Her heart ached to think she might never have one of her own.

She'd had a birthday since Chantel's wedding and was now thirty-three. She'd hoped to have several children by now. But it was Chantel who was busy raising a family. Grant David Broderick had arrived two weeks premature, weighing only five pounds, ten ounces, but he'd survived and now, at six months, was thriving. Chantel and Dillon doted on him and their girls almost as much as they doted on each other. And Stacy had to admit that she thought the baby was pretty special, too, although it was Brittney and Sydney she'd grown close to over the past few months. They came to stay with her once a week, or as often as Dillon and Chantel could bear to part with them.

"Incredible, aren't they?" A man stood at the entrance to the nursery, wearing blue jeans, a golf shirt and a baseball cap.

Stacy nodded, wondering which baby belonged to this handsome father. She hadn't seen him during the night when she'd helped two mothers go through labor and delivery.

She figured he must be with one of the three women assigned to the other nurse.

"Which one's the Hansen baby?" he asked.

Stacy navigated through the jumble of rolling cradles to a big boy who weighed almost ten pounds. "Here he is," she said, wheeling the sleeping bundle toward the door. She automatically checked the man's wrist for the band that would identify him as the baby's father, but found none, so she kept her hands on the cradle and stopped several feet away. "Are you a member of the family?"

He was staring at the baby, looking awed. A crooked grin appeared on a face badly in need of a razor. He'd probably been at the hospital most of the night and hadn't gone home yet to shave. "His father's in the military and couldn't be here. I'm just standing in. I'm his uncle."

"Well, he's a big healthy boy. I'm sure his father will be proud."

The man nodded. "Any chance I can take him to my sister? She'd like to feed him."

"I can't let you take him without a wristband. But we can go together, if you like."

"That's fine."

As he led the way to room 305, Stacy couldn't help noticing his straight back, broad shoulders and tight behind. It'd been a long time since she'd met someone who'd started her heart pumping so furiously, but this man was *definitely* attractive. And she loved his attitude toward the baby. Was he married? She caught a glimpse of his ring finger, but didn't see a wedding band.

He waited at the door while she pushed the cradle inside. Then he went to his sister's bed and praised the newborn extravagantly as Stacy helped nestle him in his mother's arms.

"It's no wonder we thought you were having twins," he told his sister. "This guy's half-grown."

Mrs. Hansen was no china doll. Somewhere close to five-ten she had a sturdy frame and looked almost as big as her brother, although he had her beat by a few inches in height. They both had dark hair, hazel eyes and smile lines bracketing their mouths. Stacy imagined they laughed a lot.

"Just hit the call button when you want me to come back for him," she said.

"Oh, wait. Would you mind taking a picture of us?" the woman asked.

"Not at all." Stacy listened to the quick instructions Mrs. Hansen rattled off, then admired the woman's brother through the lens of the camera. What a gorgeous man! She pressed the shutter release, heard a soft click and whir, then asked if they wanted another one.

"Get Rand holding Jeremy this time," Mrs. Hansen suggested.

Suddenly looking ill at ease, her brother picked up the baby, but held him in an awkward position, away from his body.

Stacy chuckled and moved to show him how to cradle the newborn in the crook of one arm. "You must not have any children of your own," she said.

"Not yet."

"Do you and your wife live in the area?"

His sister's lips curved into a smile. "I don't know, Rand, but I think that might be Nurse—" she leaned forward to read Stacy's badge "—Miller's way of asking if you're married."

Stacy felt herself blush at being so easily found out, and stepped away to hide behind the camera again. After she'd taken another picture, Rand said, "Don't mind my sister. She loves to put people on the spot."

Stacy set the camera on the table. "I guess I was being a little obvious," she admitted, then tried to bolt before Mrs. Hansen could embarrass her again. But the other woman's voice followed her out. "Rand's *not* married, by the way."

"Ugh, I'm an idiot!" she groaned, and raced for the nurses' station, where she slumped into the seat behind the desk. "Why didn't I just come right out and ask for his number?"

"That probably wouldn't have been a bad idea."

Stacy stopped pounding her forehead against her palm long enough to look up. Rand had followed her. "Oh, God. It gets worse."

He laughed, the sound deep and rich and appealing. "But just for the sake of tradition, why don't you give me yours?"

UNDERCOVER CHRISTMAS

B.J. Daniels

To my daughter, Danielle Rosanne Smith.
Thanks for all the laughs, the love
and the encouragement.
You're the best.

Prologue

November 3

A biting cold wind stole down Main Street, sending the last of the shoppers scurrying. Chase pulled his coat around him and stepped to the curb in front of the old Bozeman Hotel to check again. It wasn't like his father to be late. But then Jabe Calloway had been doing a lot of unlikely things in the past few weeks.

Lights flickered off as downtown stores closed for the night. The traffic dwindled, exhausts cloudy and white as the vehicles passed. From the dark sky, snow sifted, covering the town in an icy layer of frost.

Worry stole Chase's thoughts the way the cold stole his body heat. He stomped his feet and rubbed his gloved hands together trying to stay warm. No, it wasn't like Jabe Calloway to be late nor to call his oldest son and ask him to meet him on a street corner.

The memory of something Chase thought he'd heard in his father's voice suddenly chilled him more than the weather. He hadn't been able to put a name to it. Probably because it was a word he'd never associated with his father. Fear. Chase glanced at his watch. Almost an hour late. Jabe had been explicit about the time. Nine sharp. Jabe had some papers he needed to sign at the family attorney's office and he wanted Chase to go with him. But at this late hour? No, Jabe Calloway wasn't himself lately. Either something was terribly wrong or—

Chase turned at the sound of hurried footsteps slapping the snow-coated concrete. Jabe Calloway halted beneath the streetlamp across the intersection ten yards away and glanced upward as if waiting for the traffic light to change. He wore a gray Stetson hat on his salt-and-pepper hair, and a dark plaid shirt, jeans and boots beneath the long stockman duster that flapped open in the wind. At sixty-five, Jabe still stood six feet four and looked as solid as the lamppost next to him.

And yet for one ridiculous moment, Chase thought he saw his father stagger. Thought he saw frailty in those broad shoulders. And vulnerability.

The light changed. Jabe seemed to hesitate. Worried, Chase stepped off the curb and headed toward his father. He could feel Jabe's pale blue gaze. Eyes the same color as his own. Eyes always filled with a stubborn determination that brooked no interference.

Jabe nodded once and started across the street, all that usual arrogance and authority in his step. Chase almost laughed. Had he really thought Jabe Calloway might be in trouble? That this immovable rock of a man might need help?

The truck appeared out of nowhere. Headlights sliced through the snowfall as its engine revved and bore down on the tall cowboy in the street. Chase dived, hurling his father to the gutter as the truck's grill connected with Chase's left leg, the pavement with Chase's head. The lights went out. The truck kept going.

Chapter One

Marni pounded on the motel-room door, panicked by the hysterical phone call that had sent her racing across town on icy winter roads just days before Christmas.

"This'd better be good, Elise," she muttered as she waited impatiently for her sister to answer the door. This was so like Elise. After a five-month absence, a frantic phone call from a motel. And what was Elise doing staying at a motel anyway? She always stayed with Marni between adventures. So what had happened this time?

Only one answer presented itself, flashing on like one of the Christmas lights strung along the motel's eaves. It *had* to be man trouble, Marni thought with a groan. That was the only thing that rattled her sister's legendary composure.

Marni pounded on the door again, trying not to think about how many times she'd had to rescue her sister. Elise had a natural ability for getting into trouble but no talent for getting herself out. She also had a knack for the dramatic. Marni rolled her eyes. Of course Elise did. She was in the theater. It didn't matter that she designed sets rather than performed onstage; Elise loved the drama. All Marni could hope was that things weren't half as bad as her sister had made them out to be on the phone.

On the other side of the door, she could hear Elise fumbling with the lock.

The door opened a crack and El's tear-streaked face peeked around the edge. "Hi," she said with an apologetic smile.

Marni looked into the mirror image of her own face and felt instant relief that Elise appeared to be all right. Her twin sister had made it sound like the end of the world, as if this time she was in serious trouble. So serious that Marni had abandoned her employees at the boutique to come charging over here at two in the afternoon on one of the busiest shopping days of the year, to save her twin who appeared not to need saving at all, just a shoulder to cry on.

Elise opened the door a little wider and Marni pushed her way in, feeling a lecture coming as surely as her next breath.

"El, this better not be another one of your—" The word *stunts* never left her lips. Speechless, Marni stared at her twin.

Elise stood, pigeon-toed and timid, wearing a flannel nightgown and a pair of bunny slippers. She gave Marni another apologetic smile, her eyes filling with tears as she looked down at the source of Marni's speechlessness—her swollen belly.

"You're...pregnant?" Marni cried. "You're pregnant?" Frantically she tried to remember the last time she'd seen her twin. Summer. El had stopped by the boutique, slim and excited about the new man in her life. Admittedly, Marni hadn't been paying a lot of attention. A new man in Elise's life wasn't exactly earth-shattering news. Now, if it had been Marni with a new man—any man—*that* would have been news.

"You're pregnant," Marni repeated. She replayed what she could remember of Elise's phone call five months ago. Something about a theater tour in London. Marni had suspected the "tour" was also a romantic rendezvous but it had never crossed her mind that El might be— "Pregnant!"

Elise nodded. Tears began to trickle down her cheeks and Marni could see the dam about to break. She rushed to her sister, hugged her tightly, then took her hands in hers.

No wedding band. At least Elise hadn't eloped and forgotten to tell her. She'd just gotten pregnant and failed to mention it.

"A baby," Marni said brightly as she led Elise over to the bed. They sat on the edge. A zillion questions buzzed around in Marni's head. "How did this happen?"

A stupid question. And obviously the wrong one. Elise burst into a flood of tears. Marni grabbed a box of tissues from the night table—where already used ones were piled high—and handed several to her twin.

The story came out between sobs, sniffles and nose-blowing. Elise had met a man last summer, fallen head over heels in love and found herself pregnant—and him long gone. "His name is Chase Calloway."

Sounded like a made-up name, if Marni had ever heard one. "Where did you meet him?"

"Remember that fender bender I had last June in Bozeman? It was his truck I ran into." El smiled at the memory. "He bought me dinner because I was upset. He was so sweet and thoughtful."

Marni just bet he was.

"He was in town for a few days so we spent them together."

"In town?"

"He travels a lot, just like me."

Marni just bet he did. "How few days?"

"Four. And don't tell me someone can't fall in love in four days."

Heaven forbid Marni would even suggest such a thing.

Elise could fall in love in four seconds. "He knows about the baby?"

Elise nodded. "He'd been out of town for a while and I was worried about him. When he called in August—" she sniffed "—he said he couldn't see me anymore. He couldn't explain. It was complicated, had to do with his father and his family and the way he was raised."

"So you told him about the baby," Marni interjected.

Elise shook her head. The waterworks started again and through the crying Marni pieced together the story as best she could. In August, El, heartbroken and feeling heroic, had decided to have the baby on her own and had taken off to London to live the tragic life of a romantic heroine. But her bravado started to fail when her belly started to grow, the play closed and her job ended. Now she was having complications and had flown back to the States where her doctor had prescribed bed rest until the baby was born.

"So when *did* you tell him about the baby?"

"Yesterday, when I got back. I called his family's ranch in the Horseshoe Hills. When he came to the phone, he sounded…strange." Elise chewed her lower lip for a moment. "He acted like he didn't know me and didn't know what I was talking about."

"So," Marni said, trying to figure out exactly what her sister wanted her to do about all this. "You want me to find you a place to live and someone to come in and stay with you until the baby is born?"

Elise shook her head.

"You want to move in with me?"

Elise shook her head.

Marni let out a silent sigh of relief. As much as she loved her twin, she couldn't imagine the two of them living under the same roof for more than a short visit. They were too… different.

"You want to go live with Mom?"

"Good heavens, no!" Elise cried.

"Maybe you'd better tell me what it is you want me to do."

"Take me to see him."

"Who?" she asked, wishing she didn't know.

"Chase."

"Did your doctor say you could go?" Marni asked and saw from El's expression that he'd said just the opposite.

"I have to talk to Chase," Elise cried. "He loves me. I know he does. He said he's always wanted a baby. Something is wrong or he wouldn't be acting like this now that he knows I'm pregnant. He's avoiding me because of his family. His father, Jabe Calloway."

Marni reminded herself of all the times since grade school her twin had involved her in "sticky situations," but at the same time she and Elise both knew that Marni McCumber was a registered, card-carrying sucker for anyone in trouble. And her twin was in classic trouble.

"Chase said his father rules the family like a dictator," Elise cried. "Chase wouldn't deny his own baby unless he was being forced to. I know if I could just talk to him—"

Marni looked at the lump on El's lap. All the other times, it had just been Elise in some dilemma. Now there was a baby. Marni's niece or nephew.

"I'll call this Chase Calloway and talk to him," she relented. What could that hurt?

Elise hugged her and provided the phone number at the Calloway Ranch. Marni reached for the phone on the night table and punched in the number.

A woman answered on the third ring. Marni asked for Chase.

"May I tell him what this is in regard to?" she inquired.

"Just tell him it's urgent that I speak with him. My name is Elise McCumber."

She could hear a man's voice in the background. "I'm

sorry, Chase Calloway isn't taking calls,'' she said and hung up.

"Well?" Elise asked, eyes wide and hopeful.

"He isn't taking calls."

"See, I told you." Elise started tearing up again. "He's in terrible trouble. I have to go to him."

"You're not going anywhere," Marni reminded her. "You have to do what's best for the baby and the doctor said bed rest, right?"

"What am I going to do? I'm trapped here, and who knows what's happening to Chase."

Marni tried to assure her Chase was fine, but El wouldn't hear of it. "Surely this can wait until after Christmas." Maybe she could talk Elise out of pursuing this man by then. Or maybe Chase would have a change of heart over the holidays. Sure.

"Chase is in trouble," El cried, her hand going to her stomach. "I feel it."

Marni seriously doubted Chase was in any kind of trouble. The baby, however, was another matter. She knew her sister; she'd never been good at waiting for anything, especially a man. Elise couldn't sit still for a few days, let alone two months until the baby was born, before she knew what was going on with this Chase character.

"I'll go talk to him," Marni heard herself say. The thought of telling Chase Calloway what a lowdown louse he was definitely had its appeal. Maybe the boutique could survive for one afternoon without her being there. "Where's his ranch?"

El quit crying. "I'm sure you can find it, but you can't go there like you are."

"What?" Marni knew she wasn't going to like this.

"You have to pretend you're me, like we used to."

"What? Do I have to remind you how much trouble we got into, pretending to be each other?"

"But this time it's different," El cried. "You have to pretend you're pregnant or Jabe Calloway will take one look at you, think you're me and that I lied about being pregnant, and not even let you in the door."

The last thing Marni wanted to be was pregnant, pretend or otherwise. No thanks. "All I have to do is explain that I'm your twin sister," Marni said reasonably. "You did tell Chase you have an identical twin, right?"

El looked chagrined. "It never came up." She gave Marni another apologetic glance through her tear-beaded lashes. "You won't be able to convince Jabe—or Chase—unless they see *you* like this. Once Chase admits his love for me, you can tell him the truth. He'll listen then. Oh, Marni, it will work. We look more alike now than we ever have."

Marni studied her sister. While they were identical twins, Elise had always been the picky eater and the skinnier one; Marni had what she liked to think of as the more well-fed, "rounded" look. Now that Elise was pregnant, grudgingly, Marni had to admit that her sister was right. They did look more alike than ever. Except for El's protruding stomach.

"Chase will break down when he sees the woman he loves that he thinks is me, pregnant, especially seven months along," Elise said with such confidence, Marni found herself almost believing it. Almost. And she couldn't see even an old ogre as awful as this Jabe Calloway sounded turning away a very pregnant woman. Especially right before Christmas.

All Marni needed was a chance to talk to Chase Calloway and decide for herself if he was avoiding Elise on his own—or because of his dictatorial father.

"El, what if I talk to Chase and he doesn't want a relationship with you or the baby?" she asked gingerly.

"If Chase truly doesn't love me and doesn't want me or the baby, I'll accept it," Elise said with a dignity her bunny slippers belied. "But I know how he feels about kids. He said finding a woman to share his life with and having children was all he'd ever dreamed of."

Marni turned away to roll her eyes. Geez, couldn't El tell a come-on when she heard one? "Okay. I'll go up there and talk to him. I'll give him one last chance."

Elise nodded. "You'll see. He loves me." She patted her round belly. "And our baby."

"I'll go on one condition," Marni said. "That you go to Mom's—at least temporarily." She expected an argument.

But El readily agreed. Marni stared at her sister. Until that moment, she'd had no idea how much Chase Calloway meant to her twin. Marni cursed the man's black heart.

MARNI COULDN'T BELIEVE what she'd volunteered for as she took Dry Creek Road out of town headed for the Horseshoe Hills north of Bozeman. She wound through the snowy foothills that lay in the shadows of the Bridger mountain range. Farmhouses became fewer and farther between, and the road narrowed as she left civilization behind.

Occasionally she'd catch her reflection in the rearview mirror, and do a startled double take at the woman who looked back at her. Elise had insisted on putting a russet rinse on Marni's normally dark-blond, curly, shoulder-length hair. Marni had drawn the line at chopping it off to look like El's short wedge.

"He'll just have to think I let my hair grow," she told her twin. "El, are you sure there's no chance that this guy really *doesn't* remember you?"

El laughed. "Not after the four days we spent together." Her eyes sparkled. "It was…magical."

Magical. Marni suspected that wasn't the way Chase Calloway would describe it, especially now that Elise was pregnant.

"Here, let's do something with your makeup," El had

said. "Then we'll call my friend at the costume shop and get you a maternity form."

Elise had filled her in on how she and Chase had met, where they'd gone and what they'd done, just in case she needed those details to get past Jabe Calloway to Chase. Marni only hoped she could keep it all straight. The last thing she wanted was to get caught in this whopper of a lie.

The deejay on the radio cut into Marni's nervous thoughts with more disturbing news. A winter-storm warning. Great, exactly what she needed. "White Christmas" began to play on the radio. How appropriate. Well, it was too late now, she thought, looking at the darkening sky. All she could hope was that she'd get finished with Chase Calloway before the storm hit. And that he'd have some reasonable explanation for his disappearing act, just as El believed.

But common sense told Marni that Chase's father wasn't keeping him away from Elise; he was just using the old man as an excuse. Even if Jabe Calloway had forbidden his son to acknowledge El and the baby, and Chase had conformed to his father's wishes, what kind of man did that make Chase?

No, Marni decided as she headed up the canyon, there was nothing about Chase Calloway she was going to like. She dropped down a hill through the snowy pines into Maudlow, an old railroad town with an abandoned clapboard hotel and gas station-grocery. Signs over the ancient fuel pumps outside listed gasoline at thirty-seven cents a gallon.

Marni hung a left at Maudlow, driving past the old schoolhouse on the hill up Sixteenmile Creek, and felt her first real trepidation.

The canyon narrowed in a thick fringe of snowcapped pine trees, rocky cliffs and creek bottom. She followed the winding frozen waters of the creek farther up the dead-end road and into the darkness of the approaching storm. She could feel the temperature plummeting outside her four-wheel-drive wagon and realized she hadn't seen another vehicle on the road since the Poison Hollow turnoff.

She cranked up the heater and rubbed her cold fingers as she looked anxiously to the snowy road ahead. A Montana native, she knew how quickly the weather could change. Especially in December. But it wasn't the cold or the storm that worried her. It was not knowing what lay ahead in this isolated part of the country.

She'd convinced herself that she'd missed the turnoff, when she saw the sign. Calloway Ranch. She shifted down, amazed at how cumbersome the maternity form was. How did pregnant women drive? She felt like a hippo out of water.

She turned up the road, feeling even more isolation as she crossed the creek on the narrow one-lane bridge and drove into another narrow dark canyon.

To her surprise the canyon opened up and in the middle of the small valley sat a huge, Gothic-looking house. It towered three stories. Nothing about it looked hospitable. No Christmas lights stretched across the eaves. Nor did any blink at the windows. Under the grayness of the approaching storm, the place looked dismal and downright sinister. Not that she'd expected a warm reception.

Marni pulled her car in front of it and cut the engine. She sat for a moment, rehearsing. She was Elise McCumber. She checked herself in the mirror. Nice eye shadow, El. She was seven months pregnant. She patted the maternity form. "How ya doin', 'Sam'?"

Then she shook her head in disbelief that she was doing such a fool thing and opened the car door.

It didn't look as if anyone was home. No dogs ran out to greet or bite her. What few vehicles were parked along the side of the house were snow-covered. What kind of ranch was this? Didn't El say they raised horses?

An uneasiness raised goose bumps on her skin. She looked up. A face peered out at her from a tiny window under the eave above the third floor. Then the face was gone. But the uneasy feeling remained.

"Well, *someone's* home," Marni muttered. "And the family now knows I'm here." She took a deep breath and mounted the steps.

An older woman answered the door with a dish towel in her free hand. "Yes?" she inquired, giving Marni a disdainful once-over.

"I'm Ma—Elise McCumber," Marni said. "I'm here to see Chase Calloway."

"And what may I say this is in regard to?" she asked, even more cool and reserved than before. Unless Marni missed her guess, this was the same woman she'd spoken with on the phone earlier.

"It's personal," Marni said meaningfully as she opened her coat and patted "Sam."

The woman rocked back on her sensible shoes.

"Would you please tell Mr. Calloway I'm here. Elise McCumber." Marni started to step into the foyer but the woman blocked her way.

"Mr. Calloway isn't seeing—"

"I'll take care of this, Hilda," called a male voice from some distance behind the woman.

The moment Hilda moved out of the doorway, Marni stepped in from the cold, breathing a sigh of relief. She'd gotten her foot in the door, so to speak.

Marni wasn't surprised to find the inside of the house as forbidding as the outside. The interior provided little warmth, from the dark hardwood floors and trim to the somber wallpaper and heavy dusky draperies. In the corner sat an artificial Christmas tree, flocked white and decorated with matching gold balls positioned perfectly around its uniform boughs. So different from the McCumber tree at the farm with its wild array of colorful ornaments, each homemade and placed on the tree by the McCumber kids.

At the sound of boots on the wooden floor, Marni turned to see a large older man in western clothing coming down the hall. He filled the hallway with his size alone—he had to be close to six foot six—but also with his imposing manner. Marni took a wild guess. Jabe Calloway.

"Yes?" he asked, assessing her with sharp, pale blue eyes. He seemed surprised by what he saw. "You're inquiring about my son?"

Marni watched the housekeeper scurry toward the back of the house as if the place were in flames.

"I'm Elise McCumber," she said, saying the name over and over in her head like a mantra. Or a curse. "And you're…?"

"Jabe Calloway," he said, plainly irritated. "What is it you want with my son?"

"I want to talk to him. What it's about is between Chase and me." A strange sound made Marni turn. She blinked in surprise as a younger man hobbled into view from down the same hallway Hilda had disappeared. Marni told herself this couldn't be Chase Calloway.

"Chase," his father said, also turning at the sound. "There's no reason to concern yourself with this. Ms. McCumber was just leaving."

"But this *is* my concern," Chase said.

Under normal circumstances, Marni would have reacted poorly to the fact that Jabe Calloway was trying to shuffle her off without even a chance to talk to his son. But what was normal about any of this?

She stared at Chase, too surprised to speak. She'd just assumed he'd be handsome, knowing El. But this man set new standards for the word, from his broad shoulders and slim hips to his long denim-clad legs. He had a thick cap of wild dark hair that fell over his forehead above a pair of blue eyes that put his father's to shame. The resemblance between the two men was remarkable. But while Chase had his father's strong, masterful features, his mouth was wider, his lips more sensual, even turned down as they were now. He was the kind of man women dreamed of. This explained a lot.

Chase's muscular shoulders were draped over a pair of crutches. He limped toward her, his jeans trimmed to allow for the cast on his broken left leg. Eyes downcast, he seemed intent on maneuvering the crutches across the slick floor. Or on avoiding looking at her. On closer inspection, Marni decided it was the latter. The coward.

A few feet from her, he stopped and looked up for the first time, his pale blue eyes welding her feet to the floor.

Marni didn't move an eyelash as his gaze flicked over her. Would he recognize her for the impostor she was?

He frowned, those blue eyes intent on her face. She let out a silent oath. She knew this wouldn't work; any man who'd been intimate with a woman would know whether or not she was his lover when he saw her. One look at this man, and Marni knew she'd never be able to fool him. He made her feel as if he could see beyond the dye job and the eye shadow right into her deceitful soul.

"I wondered when you'd show up here," Chase said.

So much for that theory. "What did you expect?"

His gaze dropped to her swollen abdomen, then insolently moved back up to her face. His eyes iced over. "Not this."

She shot him a look that she hoped would give him frostbite. Had he thought Elise wasn't serious when she'd told him she was pregnant? Or maybe he thought by rejecting her she'd just go away.

"We need to talk about the baby," Marni said, putting a protective hand over "Sam."

Chase clenched his jaw, eyes narrowing. "The baby? I

thought I told you on the phone, this wasn't going to work. What is it you want?''

''For you to own up to what you've done and accept some of the responsibility,'' Marni snapped.

Hushed voices drifted down from the second floor.

''For what *I've* done?'' Chase demanded. He seemed to be fighting to keep his voice down. ''What are you trying to pull here?''

The muffled voices silenced. Marni looked up to see a small crowd gathered at the top of the wide, circular staircase. All eyes stared down at her.

''This is not the place to discuss this,'' Jabe interjected abruptly. ''Let's take it into the library.''

''That won't be necessary,'' Chase said, locking his gaze with hers. ''I don't know who you are or what you want. But I can assure you of one thing, that…baby…isn't mine.''

Chapter Two

After that stunning declaration, Chase turned on his crutches and hobbled off without a backward glance.

Marni started after him, planning to use one of his crutches to help refresh his memory, but Jabe put a firm hand on her arm.

"I'd like a word with you in private," Jabe said. "Come this way."

She had a word for him—*and* his son. "Excuse me, I don't mean to be rude, but you and I have nothing to discuss. Your son, on the other hand, is a whole different matter." She heard a door slam in the direction from which Chase had disappeared. The group at the top of the stairs didn't even bother to pretend they weren't eavesdropping.

Jabe studied her with a look of mild surprise. "I think you're wrong about that, Ms. McCumber, I believe you and I might have a great deal to talk about." He motioned toward an open doorway down the opposite hall. "Please?"

Marni had a feeling the word didn't come easy to him. And although she suspected he planned to read her the riot act once they were behind closed doors, she also saw it as an opportunity to share a few choice words she had for him about his son.

"You might be right," she said to Jabe.

The group at the top of the stairs descended in a scurry

of curiosity before Jabe and Marni could escape. The oldest of the women broke free of the others and approached them.

"Is there a problem?" she inquired, pretending to ignore Marni. She had a diamond the size of Rhode Island on her ring finger and wore her marital status like a badge of honor. This had to be Mrs. Jabe Calloway.

"Nothing to concern yourself with, Vanessa," Jabe assured her. "Go on in to dinner. I'll be along shortly."

Vanessa looked as if she'd been dragged into her late fifties kicking and screaming. From the bleached blond hair of the perfect pageboy to her tightly stretched facial features, she looked like a woman at war with the aging process.

She gave Marni a disdainful look, hesitating on the protruding belly for one wrathful moment before she turned and swept away. Over her shoulder she said, "Don't be late, dear. You know how Hilda hates it when you're late."

Her words sounded hollow, lacking authority. It was obvious who ran this household, just as Elise had told her.

Marni took a calming breath as she followed Jabe Calloway down the hall. She reminded herself why she'd come here. To talk to Chase. To give him a chance to explain, if not rectify, the situation. To give Chase a chance, period. Because Elise loved the man. Although at this moment, good looks aside, Marni could not fathom why.

THE LIBRARY WAS as large and masculine as Jabe himself. He motioned to a chestnut-colored leather couch that spanned one wall. Built-in bookshelves bordered the room. A huge rock fireplace stretched across the only open wall. An oversize brown leather recliner hunkered in front of it. Several other chairs were scattered around. Everything in the room seemed to have been sized to one man—Jabe Calloway.

Marni scanned the bookshelves as she headed for the

couch, curious if the books were for looks only or if someone in this family actually read them.

"Do you like to read?" Jabe asked from behind her.

She nodded as she spotted one of her favorites and pulled it from the shelf, surprised to find the cover worn.

"You're a Jane Austen fan, too?" Jabe asked.

Marni turned, the copy of *Pride and Prejudice* still in her hand. Jabe Calloway didn't seem to be someone who would enjoy Austen.

"She's one of Chase's favorites."

"Really?" Marni said, her surprised gaze momentarily connecting with his before she put the book back and went to the couch. "I didn't know that." She was beginning to realize how little she knew about Chase Calloway; she wondered how much Elise really knew.

"The subject of books probably never came up," Jabe said as he took a seat across from her.

She started to sit on the couch, forgot how awkward sitting was "pregnant" and basically fell into the soft, deep, low sofa.

"Did Chase tell you about this house?" Jabe asked, obviously making small talk, probably thinking he could mollify her once he had her alone. "It was built by a wealthy horse thief turned politician a hundred years ago."

She didn't comment, not half as impressed with the horse thief as he was. Nor was she interested in this house.

He must have realized that. He quit smiling and leaned back in his chair, studying her openly. "Tell me about my son."

Was he serious? "Has he always tried to avoid responsibility?" she asked instead, attempting to get comfortable in the deep couch in her present condition. She ended up resting her arms on Sam.

Jabe seemed to consider her question. "No, as a matter of fact, Chase has always taken his responsibilities very seriously. That's why I'm surprised by his attitude toward you."

"Me, too," Marni said. Although, in truth, she wasn't all that surprised. Furious, yes. Surprised, no.

"I have to be honest with you, Ms. McCumber, you aren't what I expected," Jabe said. "When I heard that a woman was calling here, claiming to be pregnant with Chase's child, well—" He waved a big hand through the air as if it went without saying what he thought. He settled his gaze on her, his look almost kind, but Marni feared he could spot her for the fraud she was.

"Tell me, if you wouldn't mind, how did the two of you meet," Jabe said.

Marni licked her dry lips and related to Jabe the story Elise had told her. But unlike El, Marni began at the beginning. "It started with a little fender bender in Bozeman last June."

"Really?" Jabe said. "In one of the ranch trucks or one of Chase's cars?"

Marni met his eyes. So this was a test. "The ranch's white truck, the three-quarter ton with the stock rack and the words Calloway Ranches printed in dark blue on the doors."

He nodded with an apologetic smile. "Please continue."

Marni told him everything El had told her. Fortunately or unfortunately, depending on how much time and patience a person had, Elise had a way of recounting the smallest, most insignificant details, often overlooking the big picture. It was the thespian in her.

"I felt so awful about running into him that he asked me to dinner. At dinner, something just clicked between us," Marni said, condensing Elise's account. "The rest is history, as they say."

"How long did you date?" Jabe asked.

Date? "We spent four days together."

He lifted an eyebrow at that. Marni couldn't say she blamed him. Only Elise could fall in love over dinner and think four days constituted a lifetime commitment.

"In August I realized I was pregnant."

"I'm surprised Chase wouldn't use protection," Jabe said.

Marni was surprised this conversation had taken such a personal turn, and had it been her who was pregnant she would have told him it was none of his business. But if there was a chance of getting Jabe on Elise's side— "We always did, except for one night in a hot-springs pool near Yellowstone," she said, lowering her gaze, wondering why she felt embarrassed when she hadn't even been there.

When he said nothing, she continued. "Chase called me in August to say he couldn't see me anymore. He said it had to do with his family and was very complicated."

Jabe looked confused. "Why didn't you confront him in person before this?"

Her chin went up defiantly. "I decided to have the baby on my own." Not unlike what Marni herself would have done in the same situation.

"What changed your mind?" Jabe asked.

"I wanted to be sure this was Chase's decision and not yours," she said truthfully. Well, as truthfully as she could, all things considered.

"I see. You think I have that kind of control over my son?"

"I don't know," she replied. After meeting Chase, Marni wondered just how much control anyone could wield over the man. "Do you?"

He shook his head ruefully. "Chase is his own man, I assure you. But I know my son. If you're carrying his child, he'll accept responsibility."

She wished she was as convinced of that as he seemed to be. Could Elise have been wrong about Jabe Calloway?

Could he be an ally rather than the diabolical family patriarch? That would mean, though, that Chase was the louse Marni suspected he was. In her heart of hearts, she'd hoped there would be a good explanation for Chase's denial of Elise and her baby. Marni was a sucker for happy endings.

"When I called yesterday, Chase pretended not to know me and told me not to call again," Marni said. "That doesn't sound like a man who accepts responsibility."

"That doesn't sound like Chase." He frowned as he studied Marni openly. "I'm sure you're aware that Chase has had some...problems since the accident."

Accident? "When he broke his leg," Marni said with a silent groan as she realized her mistake. She should have shown more concern for his injury or at least asked about it. Elise would have. "It looks like he's getting around fine now. Did he break it skiing?"

"You haven't heard then?" Jabe asked, sounding surprised. "I just assumed that you had and that was why you were here."

He made her feel guilty. And that made her mad. "I would have sent a card, but Chase wasn't even taking my calls."

"That was my fault," Jabe said. "I was the one who told Hilda to turn away your calls. I was afraid you were trying to take advantage of my son because of his injury."

"Take advantage of his broken leg?" she asked.

"You don't know about Chase's memory loss?"

Memory loss?

"Chase suffered some temporary memory loss because of the accident."

"I'm sorry, what accident was this?" she asked, wondering if he really believed she was buying the memory loss.

"A hit-and-run driver," Jabe said. "Chase saved my life."

Marni felt a good shot of repentance. Chase had been

injured saving his father's life and she'd thought Jabe was lying about Chase's memory loss.

"Right after the accident, he couldn't even remember his sisters-in-law," Jabe said. "Now it's just gaps in his memory, he says."

Wait a minute. What was he saying? "You think El—I might be a…gap…in his memory?" she asked incredulously. Wasn't that a bit too convenient?

"Fortunately, his memory seems to be coming back. What do you do in Bozeman?" Jabe asked, changing the subject.

Without thinking, she said, "I own a boutique. With my sister."

"Really? Is it profitable?"

Oh, so he thought she'd gotten herself pregnant to get the Calloway money. "Very," she said, then reminded herself she was supposed to be Elise, and added, "My sister runs the shop. I'm a theater stage designer."

"Very enterprising," Jabe said, eyeing her even more closely. "You build sets locally?"

"I just returned from a theater tour in London," she said smugly, proud of her sister's talents and her success, completely forgetting she was suppose to be El. "I'm not after your money, Mr. Calloway. I am more than capable financially of raising this child alone if that becomes necessary. I came here to give your son one last chance to decide whether or not he wants to be part of this baby's life. It would appear, he's already made his decision."

Jabe Calloway seemed to flinch at her candor. His blue eyes took on a remote look. His face contracted in pain. For a moment, she thought he might be ill.

"Are you all right?" Marni asked in concern.

He blinked at her as if he'd forgotten she was there, took a bottle of prescription pills from his pocket, popped two in his mouth and washed them down with a glass of water on the table next to him.

"I'm fine. Just allergies. What did Chase tell you about my relationship with him?"

Another test? Marni met his gaze, wishing he hadn't asked. "I know the two of you have never gotten along."

"Did he tell you why?"

Marni looked at the older man, sensing something far more complex than what Elise had told her about Chase and his father. "He said you were a hard, uncompromising man who cared more about money than people and that you use your money to extract a high price from your sons." She could see that the words hurt him, but also that they must have rung true. "I'm sorry."

Jabe Calloway looked away for a moment and when he turned his gaze back to Marni's, his blue eyes glistened. "Do you love my son, Ms. McCumber?"

"Very much," she said, remembering the look on El's face when she'd talked about Chase. "And I believed he loved me."

Jabe nodded slowly, and with a visible effort pushed himself to his feet. "You will join us for dinner."

"Thank you, but I have to get back—"

"I insist," he said, cutting her off. He must have seen the look in her eye. He quickly softened his tone. "If you would be my guest for dinner, I'll arrange for you to have a chance to speak with my son again without any interruptions."

"I can't see that it would do any good," Marni said, sounding as discouraged as she felt.

"You might be surprised," Jabe said. "My son is a reasonable man. Right now he's extremely frustrated by his immobility and his inability to remember everything. He hates being cooped up. Especially here."

"All right." What could one dinner hurt? She owed it to El to at least give Chase a chance.

Marni worked her body out of the couch's soft cushion and let Jabe usher her to the family dining room.

"Set another place," Jabe ordered as he swept Marni into the room. "Next to me. Elise McCumber will be our dinner guest."

Marni figured the latter part was addressed to the family now seated around the huge slab of an oak table. While they might not have a choice, they didn't pretend to be happy about it. Especially Chase. He met her gaze with an irate scowl. Marni got the impression he would have gotten up and left, but someone had moved his crutches out of his reach, which no doubt added to his irritation.

At the foot of the table, Vanessa's expression was one of shocked disbelief. For a moment, Marni thought the woman would raise an objection.

Instead, she brushed back her perfect pageboy and said, "Cook says the roast is going to be overdone."

"I *like* my roast overdone," Jabe said, pulling out the chair the housekeeper procured for Marni before taking his place at the head of the table.

Vanessa snapped, "Hilda, you may serve dinner now."

The moment Jabe sat down he began the introductions. Starting on Marni's right, he went around the long rectangular table. "Lilly is my youngest son's wife."

Marni recognized the heart-shaped face and large dark eyes from earlier when she'd seen the woman peeking out the window under the third-story eave. A petite, pretty woman, Lilly wore a pale pink dress that hung from her frail frame. Her white-blond hair was pulled severely back into a knot at her slim neck and the only color in her face was her eyes.

She murmured, "Nice to meet you," and drained her wineglass with a trembling hand.

"Lilly, you're hitting the wine a little hard tonight, aren't you, dear?" Vanessa asked too sweetly.

"I'm worried about Hayes," Lilly said as she motioned the housekeeper to refill her glass.

Jabe frowned at the empty chair next to Lilly, then at Vanessa. "Where *is* Hayes?"

"He had to go to Bozeman," Vanessa said.

"What is he doing in Bozeman?" Jabe demanded.

"I certainly wouldn't know. He only told me he planned to be back before dinner. I can't imagine what could have detained him." She looked over at Lilly as if Lilly knew but just wasn't telling out of meanness.

Jabe sighed and continued his introductions. "My wife, Vanessa." He skipped over her quickly. "And this is my middle son, Dayton."

Dayton Calloway had his father's blue eyes and a head of dark hair that he'd had meticulously styled, unlike Chase's more unruly soft locks. A dark mustache curled across Dayton's upper lip like a thin mean caterpillar. While no way near as handsome as Chase, he was good-looking in a petulant, dark sort of way. Marni got the immediate impression that he didn't like her for some reason.

He didn't get to his feet as Marni was introduced. Instead, he just nodded. Out of the corner of her eye, Marni saw Jabe scowl and mutter something directed at his wife about bad manners. Vanessa frowned and glared at Marni as if it were Marni's fault.

"Felicia is Dayton's wife," Jabe continued. A sharp-featured brunette with green eyes, a more than ample chest and a bad disposition sat between Dayton and Chase. Marni knew about Felicia's bad disposition the same way she knew the price of the expensive ethnic-print maternity dress and matching jewelry the woman wore. Marni had sold it to her at her Bozeman boutique—last week.

"You look familiar," Felicia said, eyeing her suspiciously.

The truth seemed the best approach. "I believe you trade at the boutique I'm part owner of in Bozeman." She looked at Chase to see if he registered any shock to hear she owned a boutique. Chase didn't look up; he sat turning the thin stem of his wineglass in his strong fingers, showing no sign that he was paying the least bit of attention to any of this.

Felicia's gaze narrowed. "Yes, I remember now. But when I saw you last week you weren't pregnant."

Marni laughed. It sounded hollow even to her ears. "You probably have me confused with my sister. We look a lot alike." Boy, was that putting it mildly.

Felicia didn't appear convinced, but lost interest as Hilda served dinner: a beef roast the size of Montana, followed by huge bowls of mashed potatoes, brown gravy, fresh green beans, another of hot homemade dinner rolls and butter.

Marni felt famished, having not taken time all day to eat. She ladled gravy over her beef and potatoes, buttered a hot roll and slathered butter on her green beans. Her love of food was one of the reasons she'd never had Elise's slim model-like figure.

Hilda brought Vanessa broiled chicken, cottage cheese and crudités, and Felicia a plate of what looked like Chinese food. Lilly seemed to be the only Calloway woman who didn't ask for a special-order meal. She took a spoonful of everything that was passed to her then hardly touched the food she'd put on her plate. But she polished off the remaining wine at her end of the table, ignoring Vanessa's reprimanding looks. Marni declined wine when Hilda came around to fill her glass, needing all her wits about her. It wasn't until later that she realized pregnant women weren't supposed to drink alcohol and she was a pregnant woman, by all appearances.

Everyone ate in silence, not that Marni minced. She concentrated on the food, rather than the strange family dynamics. The roast was excellent, not in the least overcooked. Halfway through her meal, she glanced up to see Chase staring at her, his expression unreadable. But she noticed he hadn't touched his food any more than Lilly had.

"I enjoy a woman who likes to eat," Jabe said, smiling at Marni.

"This is delicious," she said, a little embarrassed by her appetite.

"You're eating for two," he said. "It's healthy to eat even if you're not expecting."

Vanessa mumbled something under her breath and pushed away her diet plate in what could only be described as disgust. The room grew painfully quiet.

Marni finished her roast beef, thinking about El and the baby. At least she knew her sister wasn't going hungry or not following doctor's orders. By now, Mary Margaret McCumber would have Elise at the family farm. If anyone could get El to do as she was told, it was Mother, Marni thought with a smile.

The door to the dining room swung open and a man in western attire rushed in, apologizing for being late as he took the chair next to Lilly.

"Hayes," Lilly said, lifting her wineglass to him in a less than sober salute. "We were so worried about you." She didn't sound as if she meant it in the least.

Clean-shaven, Hayes Calloway also had his father's blue eyes, a little lighter version of Chase's hair color and a softer, gentler, more handsome face than his brother Dayton.

Hayes seemed to eye his wife warily before brushing a kiss across her pallid cheek. Then he spotted Marni and looked startled to see that they had a guest. Marni got the impression the Calloways didn't have many dinner guests.

"Hayes, this is Elise McCumber," Jabe said. "She's a...friend of Chase's."

Hayes stumbled to his feet, his eyes widening in surprise. "Hello."

"Why are you so late?" Jabe demanded.

He looked past Marni to his father. "The roads are covered in ice and the visibility was so bad I hit a deer on the way home."

"Are you all right?" Vanessa cried, although he obviously was fine.

"What about the damage to the truck?" Jabe asked.

"The truck?" Hayes asked, anger flickering in his gaze as he sat down and began to dish up his plate. "The truck is repairable."

"The truck is the least of our worries," Vanessa cut in, sending a look at Jabe.

He grumbled but returned his attention to his meal.

Marni watched Chase pick at the food he'd put on his plate. He looked as uncomfortable as she felt. She caught both Hayes and Dayton stealing curious glances at her. But then, why wouldn't they be? They had to wonder who she was, what she was doing at their dinner table, seven months pregnant, and why she was sitting next to Jabe as if part of the family.

What *was* she doing here? More and more she felt she was on a fool's errand. What possible good would it do to talk to Chase after he'd already denied even knowing her. And now it sounded as if the roads were probably getting worse by the minute. But she had to give it one last try with Chase. For El's sake.

"I hate to eat and run," Marni said pointedly to Jabe.

He nodded, letting her know he remembered his promise, but then said, "We couldn't possibly let you leave with the storm as bad as Hayes says it is. Not in your fragile state."

Fragile state indeed. "You don't understand, I have to work tomorrow."

Jabe shook his head. "By now the road out of here will be impassable."

"He's right," Hayes said. "It's much too dangerous. Especially in your...condition."

Marni started to argue that she'd driven icy roads all her life, having been born and raised a Montanan, but to her astonishment it was Chase instead of Jabe who cut her off.

"It's settled," Chase said, slamming down his wineglass. "You'll stay the night and leave first thing in the morning after the roads are plowed and sanded."

Marni groaned inwardly, but knew there was no point in arguing. She'd leave in the morning. After she'd finished her business with Chase. What was one night in a haunted house with people who hated her, anyway?

In the deathly silence that followed, Vanessa signaled for Hilda, who hurriedly cleared the dinner dishes and brought in a bottle of champagne on ice and a huge cake with one large pink candle and Congratulations! scripted across the white icing in bright pink.

Marni stared at the cake. She had a strong feeling it wasn't for her and Chase. In fact, she suspected she'd put a damper on a family celebration by showing up when she did.

Vanessa irritably motioned Hilda away the moment the housekeeper had poured the champagne and lit the candle. "We have something to celebrate tonight," Vanessa announced. Her smile looked strained as she glanced almost warily at Jabe.

Jabe appeared surprised. And maybe a little worried.

"Felicia and Dayton have an announcement," she said and took her seat again.

Dayton got to his feet. "Felicia saw her doctor today and it's a girl," he announced without preamble.

If Marni thought the news would be met with cheers,

applause or even halfhearted congratulations from the rest of the family, she was mistaken.

Lilly let out a startled cry, spilling her wine, then rushed from the room. Hayes looked to Marni as if he felt he should say something on behalf of his wife, then hurried out after her. Following their departure, a hush fell over the room. It was Chase who broke it.

"Let me be the first to congratulate you." He raised his glass in a toast. "Dayton. Felicia. To the firstborn grandchild of Jabe T. Calloway. A girl." His gaze shifted to his father. "Jabe finally has what he wanted, a grandchild." A tension Marni couldn't comprehend danced in the air like Saint Elmo's fire.

Jabe got slowly to his feet. He picked up his glass and raised it. Marni started to raise hers, then realized the rest of the family hadn't touched their champagne.

"To my first grandchild," Jabe said, his voice cracking with emotion. Or anger. Marni couldn't tell which.

He looked over at Marni. Her glass seemed filled with lead as she lifted it and he touched the rim of his glass to hers with a tinkling sound that echoed through the room. "To my first grandchild," he repeated.

Marni lifted the glass to her lips. No one else in the room had moved. She took a sip of the champagne, realizing that everyone was staring at her. She quickly put the glass down.

"What's going on here?" Dayton demanded sourly.

Jabe looked at Chase.

Marni thought she could have heard a snowflake drop in the room.

"We may have double reason to celebrate," Jabe said to Dayton. "I may have been blessed with not one grandchild, but two. It seems Elise is also carrying my grandchild. It appears it will be my *first* grandchild." He shifted his gaze to Chase. "Chase's child."

Felicia gasped. Dayton let out an oath. Vanessa looked

across the great expanse of table at Marni, hatred in her eyes.

But it was Chase's reaction that worried Marni the most. He got up, hopped over to his crutches and left the room without a word.

Chapter Three

Jabe excused himself and went after his son, leaving Marni alone in the dining room with what was left of the family and their dagger-throwing glares. The silence in the room was stifling. But it didn't last long. An argument between Chase and his father ensued outside the dining-room door.

"How dare you make such an announcement without even discussing it with me first," Chase bellowed.

"Keep your voice down," Jabe warned him. "You can't just pretend you don't know her."

"I *don't* know her!"

"That's ridiculous," Jabe said. "She told me in no uncertain terms how you feel about me. You must have made her…acquaintance. No one outside the family could paint such an unattractive—or accurate—picture."

"This is all your fault, you and your damned ego," Chase said. "I told you not to change your will. I warned you not to do this. Now look what you've done."

"I offered you a chance to run my business, you turned it down."

"You aren't going to lay this on me! I wouldn't be surprised if you were behind this."

"What are you talking about?" Jabe demanded.

"That woman. I wouldn't be surprised if you put her up to this. You just don't give up, do you?"

"That's ridiculous," Jabe snapped. "You owe it to your-self to find out if she really is carrying your child."

"And I'm telling you I've never seen her before in my life."

"If you talk to her, you'll find she's very convincing," Jabe said.

"Well, she's going to have a damned hard time convincing me. I happen to *remember* the women I sleep with."

"How can you be so sure?" Jabe asked, sounding almost reasonable. "Think of all the other things you haven't been able to remember since the accident."

"Believe me, I'd remember *her*," Chase shot back. It sounded as if he'd started to leave, his crutches clopping across the floor.

"She doesn't seem the type to lie about something like this."

Chase's hobbling stopped. "What type is that, Jabe? A woman like my mother?"

Marni shot a look at Vanessa. She'd paled visibly.

"I won't have my first grandchild be a bastard," Jabe boomed, his voice an iron glove of authority.

"It was good enough for your first *son*," Chase retorted just before a door slammed and silence filled the dining room again.

Marni felt her head swim. Chase was Jabe's firstborn son, wasn't he?

"I'm sorry, dear," Vanessa said to Dayton as he got to his feet again.

"Leave it to Chase to throw cold water on any family celebration, and Father to be…Father." He gave Marni a mocking bow, and snagging a bottle of wine Lilly had missed, headed out through the kitchen with Felicia trailing along behind him.

Chase certainly knew how to empty a room, Marni thought, then noticed with regret that she'd been left alone with Vanessa. And Vanessa looked as if she might start a food fight if given any provocation. What kind of family had El gotten herself involved with? What had Marni gotten herself into?

Jabe returned to the room, looking tired. "I apologize for…" He couldn't seem to find a word for what had happened. Neither could Marni. "But I assure you, I am a man of my word, Elise. You will have a chance to speak with my son before you leave. In the meantime—" He turned to Vanessa. "See that Elise gets a room and anything else she needs for the night." With that he turned and left.

After a long sigh, Vanessa rang for the housekeeper and instructed her to prepare a room for their guest. The way she said "guest" made it sound like "ax murderer."

Marni noticed that the candle had burned down on the untouched cake. It flickered, barely alive, in a pool of wax. Vanessa snuffed it out with the serving knife in one swift swat and stabbed the knife into the heart of the cake with a good deal of what appeared to be pent-up aggression.

Her hostess sat for a moment surveying the empty room before she looked again at Marni. She opened her mouth seemingly to speak and closed it, as though she'd thought better of it. Instead, she cut herself a thick slice of roast beef, stuck it and a half inch of butter into one of the rolls and took a healthy bite. As she chewed, she scrutinized her houseguest as if deciding how best to dispose of her. It seemed Jabe dictated she be nice to Marni. But if looks could kill…

Marni stared down into her empty plate, considered having another slice of roast beef herself, vetoed the idea and sat thinking about the conversation she'd just overheard. She didn't care about any of the particulars except one. Chase was sticking to his story that he didn't know her. He didn't even want to believe it was because of his temporary memory loss. The problem was: No man forgot Elise McCumber.

"You must be tired," Vanessa said after she'd polished off the last bite. "I'll show you to your room." As they go up, she instructed Hilda to save her a piece of cake. A ver large one. Marni got the impression Vanessa had just fallen off her diet.

"I'll leave it in your sitting room," Hilda said conspiratorially.

Vanessa shot Marni a look, daring her to say a word.

Not likely. As they entered the foyer, Vanessa glanced toward the library. "If you'll excuse me for just a moment," she said. Not waiting for a reply, she strode down the hal through the open doorway, closing the door firmly behind her.

Marni grimaced as she imagined the choice words Vanessa must be sharing with her beloved husband at his moment, then turned her thoughts to her own precarious situation.

Snowed in. Miles from everything. Seven months pregnant. Or so it seemed. Forced to spend the night in this huge old—quite possibly haunted—house. With people who definitely hated her. Pretending to be her beguiling sister. Al because of a man who swore he'd never seen her before—nor it seemed—her identical twin. How had she talked herself into this?

She hadn't even had a chance to really speak to Chase And she couldn't for the life of her understand the strange reactions of these people. Why had Vanessa been so happy about Dayton's child but so upset by Chase's? Was it just because this baby was conceived out of wedlock? Or did it have something to do with the argument she'd heard outside the dining-room door about Jabe's firstborn being a bastard?

And why hadn't Elise told her any of this? Maybe Elise hadn't known, Marni realized. She groaned. It seemed clearer and clearer that Elise didn't know much about Chase Calloway. But how much could you learn in only four days?

Marni turned at the soft sound of footsteps directly behind her. Lilly stumbled around the corner, the wine in her glass sloshing onto the floor as she came to a lurching stop at the sight of Marni.

She smiled as she tried to rub the wine into the hardwood floor with her shoe, then staggered over to Marni, leaning toward her confidentially. "It isn't going to work, you know." Her words slurred. "You think I'm a fool? You think I don't know what you're really after? Pretending you're carrying Chase's baby. You don't fool me."

"Lilly, do you want to sit down?" Before you fall down? Marni looked around for a chair. There were none.

Lilly didn't answer. She glanced down the hallway toward the library and dropped her voice. "You don't really want him. It's the money. You're after the baby money."

Baby money? "Lilly, I don't know what you're talking about," Marni said softly, not sure why they were almost whispering, but feeling a little seasick just watching Lilly sway back and forth. She motioned toward the stairs. "Perhaps if we sit down—"

"The first grandchild," Lilly said, following Marni to the stairs. She plopped down hard on the first step, spilling more of her wine onto her dress. It looked like blood against the pale pink of the fabric.

Marni sat down beside her. "What difference does it make if I'm having Jabe's first grandchild or the fifth?" she asked.

"Like you don't know," Lilly said with a smirk. "He told you about the change in Jabe's will. He probably told you everything."

Right, like Chase had told Elise anything. "What does the change in Jabe's will have to do with the first grandchild?" she asked again.

Lilly straightened. "Jabe wants someone he can leave his...empire to. Chase turned it down. So Jabe changed his will to leave a fortune to his first grandchild," she said, bitterness buoying her in a way not even strong, black coffee could have. "The other two sons end up with almost nothing."

"Why would he do that?" Marni exclaimed, realizing now exactly what she'd witnessed at dinner. Jabe Calloway had pitted his sons against one another, a baby race, and Elise had unwittingly become a part of it and was now it appeared, the leading contender. No wonder Dayton and Felicia had been so upset.

"It should be my money," Lilly said. She drained her glass and set it on the step beside her. Her gaze bobbed up to sear Marni with a hateful look. "Not yours."

Marni heard the library door open and the sound of Vanessa's voice drift toward them.

"I assure you I knew nothing about this will," Marni said quietly, but she could tell Lilly wasn't listening, her attention drawn to the library instead.

"I had the first grandchild," Lilly whispered as she stumbled to her feet. "But Vanessa killed it."

"What?" Marni cried, jumping to her feet. Surely Lilly was too drunk to know what she was saying.

But Marni felt a chill as she witnessed the fear she saw in the woman's eyes as Lilly lurched around the side of the staircase at the sound of Vanessa's high heels thumping across the hardwood floor toward them. Marni started to follow Lilly, afraid the woman would hurt herself in the state she was in, but Lilly motioned for her not to. The pleading in her wide-eyed gaze stopped Marni. What was she so afraid of? Vanessa? Or Vanessa catching her this inebriated?

Marni watched in surprise as Lilly touched the wall behind her and a narrow door silently slid open. Lilly slipped into what appeared to be a passageway and disappeared, the door sliding shut behind her with only a whisper.

"Are you ready?" Vanessa demanded.

Marni jumped as she swung around to find Vanessa glaring at her. The conversation in the library must not have gone well.

"Is something wrong?" Vanessa asked, her gaze narrowing as it settled on the empty glass resting on the bottom stair where Lilly had left it.

"You just startled me," Marni said quickly.

Vanessa nodded suspiciously. Then she picked up the empty wineglass with obvious annoyance, and placed it on the marble-topped table to the left of the stairs. "Hilda should have your room ready." Without giving Marni a backward glance, Vanessa started up the stairs.

Marni followed her up the wide circular staircase, realizing that the longer she was in this house, the more questions she had about Chase and his family. She shook her head, confused but too smart to ask Vanessa anything.

As she climbed the stairs, Marni found herself looking over her shoulder. *You're getting a little paranoid. Yeah? Well, who wouldn't be in this house?* She tried to laugh off the feeling that she was being watched. Spied on. That someone definitely didn't want her here. She almost laughed at the thought. *No one* wanted her here and it wasn't as though they'd made a secret of it.

As Vanessa led her toward the third floor, Marni glanced back again, thinking about Chase Calloway. She had so many questions, but only one that really mattered. Could it be possible he was the man Elise thought he was and this was just a misunderstanding because of his memory loss? Then why, her skeptical side questioned, is he so adamant that El couldn't be carrying his child?

Marni had almost reached the top of the stairs when suddenly her right foot slipped. She grasped for the railing but wasn't close enough to reach it. She felt herself teeter and start to fall backward. Two strong hands grabbed her.

"Are you all right?" Hayes cried as he steadied her.

It took Marni a moment to assure herself she wasn't at that moment cartwheeling to the bottom of the long, curved staircase. She looked up, wondering where Hayes had come from so suddenly, and realized he'd been waiting in a small alcove on the stairs. As odd as that seemed, Marni was thankful he'd been there. It also explained that paranoid feeling that someone was watching her. She almost laughed in relief.

"Thank you. I must have slipped." Marni spotted the cause of her near accident—a colorful silk scarf on the stairs—about the same time as Hayes and his mother did.

Vanessa's hand went to her throat, her look one of shock. "Did *I* drop that? I didn't even realize I was wearing it." She stepped back down the stairs to pluck up the scarf. "How careless of me."

"Mother," Hayes said, the reprimand clear in his voice. "She could have been killed and the baby—" He stopped, distress in his expression.

"It mustn't happen again," Hayes said to his mother.

Vanessa looked as if he'd slapped her. "It was an accident." Her voice sounded close to tears.

A chill wrapped its icy fingers around Marni's throat as she watched Vanessa retie the scarf around her neck. *It mustn't happen again?*

"Go find your wife," Vanessa said to Hayes. "She needs you."

Hayes glared for a moment at his mother, a silent accusation in his eyes that even Marni couldn't miss before he turned and left.

Vanessa led the way to what Marni guessed was the guest bedroom. What had Hayes meant by "It mustn't happen again"? Had there been other falls down the stairs? Marni wondered as she stepped through the doorway Vanessa now held open for her. Is that how Lilly had lost her baby? Or had he meant another baby mustn't die in this house? Whatever, it gave Marni a chill not even the fire in the small rock fireplace in the corner could throw off.

The bedroom was spacious and not quite as masculine as the library was, even with the king-size log bed, matching log furniture and antler-based lamps.

The covers had been turned down on the bed and the flannel sheets looked inviting. So did the huge claw-foot tub she glimpsed in the bathroom.

Marni glanced a little apprehensively at the adjoining bedroom door, however.

Vanessa must have noticed. "The room next door is Chase's."

Whose idea was that? Marni asked herself.

"It locks from either side," Vanessa said.

"Thank you," Marni said, still curious about the woman's antagonism toward her. That *had* been an accident on the stairs, hadn't it?

Marni noticed a light blue striped shirt and a black velour robe had been left for her on the bed. Both garments were obviously male. Vanessa frowned when she saw them and Marni wondered whose they were.

"There are candles beside the bed. When it storms, the power often goes out. If there is anything else you need..." Her voice trailed off, then, "Breakfast is at eight."

Marni could see that being forced to be nice was taking its toll on the woman. "I'll be gone first thing in the morning," she said. "Right after I talk to Chase."

If she thought that news would please Vanessa, she was sadly mistaken. The woman gave her an icy stare. "Good night," she said and left, closing the door firmly behind her.

Marni stood in the middle of the room suddenly too tired to move. What a day! She felt worn-out by everything that had happened and even more tired by trying to understand Chase Calloway and his decidedly weird family. That wasn't fair, she told herself. She'd thrown his family into turmoil by showing up in an advanced stage of pregnancy claiming to be carrying Chase's child.

She considered knocking on the adjoining door and trying to talk to him, but it was late and she didn't feel up to it. Morning would be soon enough to have her final say before she left.

Marni walked to the window and looked out into the storm. Outside, a Montana blizzard raged. Snow fell, dense and deep, smothering the mountain landscape with cold white. It was as beautiful as it was confining. A white Christmas. Marni had to remind herself Christmas was just days away. Little in the Calloway house reflected the season. And something told her there wouldn't be much Christmas spirit at the Calloways' this year.

She started to move away from the window, but stopped as she heard a faint sound. It seemed to be coming up through the heat vent. She leaned closer, surprised to hear a baby crying softly. Marni frowned. All that talk about the first grandchild at dinner… Whose baby was this? she wondered.

The sound stopped as abruptly as it had begun. With a shiver, Marni stepped away from the window to lock the hallway door. A hot bath. That's what she needed. Something to get her mind off El, Chase, his family, this house—

As she entered the bathroom, Marni stopped, shocked by what she was doing. Waddling. She was taking this whole pregnancy thing way too seriously.

She started filling the tub, splashed in a generous amount of the vanilla-scented bubble bath she found on a shelf at the foot of the tub and hurriedly undressed, anxious to get the maternity form off and end this ridiculous charade at least for a few hours.

But as she slipped into the tub sans Sam and let the bubbles caress her nakedness, she felt a stab of regret that took her a moment even to recognize. She missed Sam.

With a groan she sank under the water. What was wrong with her? She'd never even thought about children of her own and now she was getting attached to a maternity form? No, not a maternity form, she thought as she surfaced. A pretend child named Sam. Chase Calloway's son. Geez.

She heard a soft knock at her hallway door and started to call that she was in the tub but stopped herself. The last thing she wanted was another confrontation with someone else in this family—especially right now, naked in the tub, with her bubbles dissolving and her body unpregnant.

Whoever it was knocked again. Softly. As if they didn't want the rest of the house to know they'd come to see her? Chase? Surprised, she listened as the person tried the knob. *Please let it be locked.* The knob started to turn. And stopped. Locked. Footfalls retreated down the hall. Marni let out the breath she'd been holding.

Relieved, she leaned back in the tub and closed her eyes, doing her best not even to think about Chase Calloway. But her thoughts went to him as swiftly as an arrow shot from a bow. What was his story? And more to the point, how could Elise have fallen for such a disagreeable man?

The water began to cool and Marni climbed out and quickly dried herself, curious to know who her earlier visitor had been. Would her caller have come in if the door hadn't been locked? It appeared so. She doubted it was Chase. It seemed odd that he'd use the hallway door instead of their adjoining one. It seemed even odder anyone would try the door when she didn't answer the knock.

Whoever it was might return, she thought, realizing she'd have to put the maternity form back on. She didn't relish the idea, but it was better than getting caught unpregnant by Chase Calloway. No amount of explaining would get that man to believe her.

But at least she could get comfortable. After putting the form back on, she wandered into the bedroom, picked up the loaned shirt from the bed and pulled it on over the maternity form. It was large enough that the soft fabric covered her to her knees.

Her earlier tiredness came back suddenly and she couldn't wait to climb between the flannel sheets of the massive bed. That's when she remembered she hadn't locked the door between her room and Chase's. Buttoning the shirt on her way, she waddled to the door and reached for the knob. The door must not have been closed soundly. The moment she touched the knob, the door creaked open and a deep, angry voice bellowed, "What the hell do you want?"

Marni jumped at the sound of Chase's voice. "I—" She grimaced as she heard him limping across the floor toward her, the crutches beating a path to her.

The door banged open and Chase filled the space between their rooms. "Look, woman—" His gaze dropped from her face to her chest. She caught the smell of brandy on his warm breath as he leaned toward her. "Is that one of *my* shirts? What the hell are you doing in my shirt?"

"Someone left it for me," Marni said defensively. "The way your mother acted, I just assumed it was Jabe's." Her chin went up to show him she wasn't afraid, but her traitorous feet stumbled back a step from the fury in his eyes.

"My mother?" His gaze narrowed. "That proves how little you know about me. Vanessa's not my mother."

Marni stared at him. Well, *that* explained a lot. Did Elise know *anything* about this man? "Dayton and Hayes are your…"

"Half brothers." Chase hobbled toward her, forcing her into a corner. "How can you pretend we were lovers and this is my baby, when you know nothing about me?" he demanded.

Marni felt the hellfire of his gaze and wanted to proclaim

her honesty but it was hard to do, all things considered. She lifted her chin again and met his blue eyes, frantically trying to imagine what Elise would say in answer to his very reasonable question. She had no idea, having never met a man like Chase Calloway. All she knew was that he made her nervous. Self-conscious. Unsure of herself.

"I thought I heard a baby crying," Marni said, motioning toward the heat vent, belatedly realizing he'd see right through her clumsy attempt to change the subject.

"A baby? There is no baby in this house." His gaze dropped to her swollen form. "Yet."

No baby? But she'd heard a baby crying. Or had she? Her eyes widened. No, it couldn't be. This pretend pregnancy made her waddle, even vulnerable to emotions she couldn't remember ever having before. But surely it didn't make her imagine crying babies?

She realized Chase was waiting for an answer to his original question. She felt at a loss as to how to reply.

He gave her an impatient look and she knew she'd have to say something. She took a deep breath and, closing her eyes, concentrated. She imagined she was Elise and that this man standing in front of her was her lover. Her eyes flew open; she felt the flushed heat of embarrassment rush to her cheeks as the sudden, crystal-clear image of the two of them unclothed branded itself on her brain.

"Admittedly," Marni said shakily as she sidestepped away from him, "there is a lot I don't know about you and your family." Practically nothing. "All I can tell you is the...truth." She almost choked on the word.

"The truth?" Chase asked, sounding skeptical.

She nodded as she turned to face him, suddenly reminded of the disastrous results the other times she'd pretended to be her twin. "The truth is..." She tried for that slight catch in her throat El had when she talked about Chase. It came out more like a croak. "I'm in...in love with you."

For a moment, she thought he'd laugh in her face. Instead, he let out an animal growl and thumped over to her, slamming any and everything in his path out of the way with his crutches. He stopped, towering over her, his eyes hard as ice chips.

"Don't you see how dangerous this game is you're playing?" he demanded, his voice reverberating through her.

She commanded her feet to stand their ground. He couldn't scare her, she assured herself with only a slight tremble.

"Cut your losses and give up this charade," he said, dropping his voice to a menacing softness as he leaned closer. "You are no more pregnant with my child than you are in love with me."

She couldn't argue that. Not that he gave her a chance.

Before she could move, he took her face in his hands. She felt his calloused hands, warm and strong, on her cheeks. The hands of a man who did an honest day's work. That picture didn't quite fit with the one she'd already painted of him. But she didn't have time to worry about that now. In the depths of his gaze, she saw what he planned to do. Unfortunately, there wasn't time to react before he took her mouth as he'd probably no doubt taken her sister's body, with an intensity that stunned her. And for those few moments, she *was* El. And she knew the power this man had over her twin.

Abruptly he broke off the kiss and shoved himself away from her. "You and I have never kissed before," he said, his voice as rough as his hands. "Believe me, if we had, I would have remembered." He limped a few feet away on his crutches and turned to glare at her.

Marni fought the urge to cry out. In frustration. Her body ached, reminding her how long it had been since a man had kissed her. Had one ever kissed her like that?

Worse yet, he'd been testing her and she'd failed miserably. Failed to pull off her fraud. And failed El. She already felt like a traitor to her sister for just letting the man kiss her.

"Let me give you some advice, Miss McCumber," he said, his voice sending a shiver through her. "You picked the wrong man to fool with. I don't know who you are or what you want, but if you're smart, you'll get away from here as fast as you can. You and your baby aren't safe in this house."

He left, the threat hanging in the air as he slammed the door between their rooms.

Chapter Four

Long after Chase left, Marni lay on the big log bed, her arm protectively around Sam as she stared up at the ceiling and mentally kicked herself. What had she hoped to accomplish by coming here? When was she going to learn that she couldn't solve everyone's problems?

As for the kiss…

She tried to excuse it. It was only a test and a test kiss didn't amount to anything. She shouldn't feel guilty. Really, if she was going to pretend to be Elise, these things were bound to happen. Men kissed El unexpectedly, passionately, soundly.

Not that Marni would let it happen again. One test kiss per sister's boyfriend, thank you. But if it should—

Marni groaned. Why was she agonizing over one silly little kiss? Instead she should be worrying about how El was going to take the bad news. She'd tried to call her sister before climbing into bed but the phone line was dead. Probably the storm.

She stopped a moment to listen, almost sure she'd heard footsteps out in the hallway again. As she drew the covers up around her shoulders, she assured herself the house didn't feel exceptionally imposing or hostile and that all those grunts and groans, creaks and crackings were just from the storm outside. This was Chase's doing. Him and his "you and your baby aren't safe here."

Only silence came from the adjoining room. Chase had no doubt gone to bed and was sound asleep by now. So much for his guilty conscience keeping him awake.

She'd really believed that once she had him alone, she could get him to admit his part in Elise's pregnancy. At least she would have accomplished that much. Not that he planned to do anything about it. But instead, he wouldn't even consider she might be part of his lost memory. If indeed he suffered from such a convenient affliction.

Marni squeezed her eyes closed and searched for sleep, wishing she'd grabbed a book from the library. Nothing could distract her mind faster than a book.

Her stomach growled. How could she be hungry when she'd devoured such a large meal just hours ago?

She tried to ignore the hunger pangs and the mental picture that kept flashing in her brain. Cake. A moist white cake, rich with buttery frosting.

Her stomach rumbled loudly. She opened her eyes. It would be incredibly rude to raid the refrigerator. Not for a woman who was eating for two, she argued, as she slid her legs over the side of the bed.

The embers had burned down in the fireplace and the storm's icy chill settled in along with Chase's warning. He didn't know her very well if he thought he could scare her that easily.

She reminded herself that he didn't know her at *all*. He knew Elise. And the truth was, Elise probably wouldn't have budged from her bed until morning.

Marni opened her bedroom door cautiously and peered out. The hallway was empty. And dark except for a light at the far end beyond the stairs. The house seemed to hunker in silence as if waiting for something. For her, the voice of reason warned. But a piece of cake, rich with frosting, was calling. The cake won. She stepped out and, quietly closing the door behind her, tiptoed down the hall.

A cold draft crawled over her bare feet. She pulled Chase's robe around her. The robe was thick and warm and like the shirt, smelled faintly of its owner, a scent that was both disarming and comforting.

When Marni reached the stairs, she trod down them carefully, her near accident still too fresh in her memory for comfort.

Someone had left a light on and Marni wondered if she was the only one up raiding the fridge. The thought of running into Vanessa almost changed her mind. Marni tiptoed across the foyer, peeked into the dining room, then headed for what she figured would be the kitchen.

The kitchen was spacious like the house. But unlike the house, it had a warm, almost homey feel to it. Marni guessed it was probably because Vanessa never set foot in it. It was the first room that Marni could say she actually liked. And it was blessedly empty.

She found the cake without having to raid the fridge, cut herself a large slice and sat down at the table. The cake was delicious. She licked the frosting from her lips as she eyed another piece. Oh, what would it hurt?

As she was scraping her plate to get the last of the crumbs, she marveled at her increased appetite. Was it just nerves? Or was her body somehow kidding itself into believing she really was eating for two?

Whatever it was, she had to quit or she'd gain a ton.

A short while later, she made her way toward the library. The house groaned and moaned around her. Snow piled up at the windows and cold crept along the bare wooden floors like snow snakes.

Marni had started down the hall when she heard something that made her freeze in midstep.

Crying. At first she thought it was the baby again. Then

realized it wasn't the same sound she'd heard earlier coming up through the heat vent. The heart-wrenching sobs pulled at her and she found herself trailing the sound past the library toward the back of the house.

A faint light shone from a far corner of what appeared to be the living room. The thick, dark curtains along the bank of windows were open to the night. The darkness outside blurred in a thick lattice of falling snow.

Lilly Calloway sat slumped in a large log rocker, in a golden circle of light from a floor lamp beside the chair. She clutched something in her arms and rocked, Marni noticed with a start. Beside the rocker on the floor sat a half-empty wine bottle. The room smelled faintly of gardenias.

Marni reminded herself again that this was none of her business. She should backtrack and go up to bed. But the woman's wail tore at her heart.

"Lilly?" she asked softly, half expecting the woman to rebuff any attempts to console her. After all, Marni was a stranger. And no one in this house had been what she would call friendly.

Neither the crying nor the rocking stopped.

Marni stepped around in front of the woman. "Lilly?"

Lilly slowly raised her head, her rocking motion slowed. The storm outside lit her pale heart-shaped face and Marni saw what the woman clutched in her arms. A rag doll, its face worn and grayed, its yarn hair matted with age. Lilly glanced down at the doll crushed in her arms. For a moment, she made no sound. Then her eyes swam with tears and great, huge sobs racked her body.

Marni knelt and opened her arms to the woman. The rag doll tumbled to the floor as Lilly fell into Marni's embrace. "There, there," Marni whispered, sympathizing with the woman's pain. She couldn't imagine what it would be like losing a child. "It's all right."

As the crying subsided, Marni heard the scrape of a boot

sole on the wooden floor. She looked up with a start, not sure who she expected to see.

Even in shadow and even if he hadn't had the crutches, she would have known Chase Calloway. He filled a doorway. Not only with his body but with his anger.

He stood, watching her, suspicion in every line of his body. She could feel the heat of his gaze on her as surely as she could feel the reproach in that gaze. She glanced down at Lilly, wondering what made Chase so angry with her, that he thought she was pregnant or that he thought she was trying to trap him? When she glanced up again, he was gone.

Marni didn't know how long she held Lilly. The crying had stopped, but the slim arms still held her tightly, as if Marni were Lilly's only anchor in some blizzard far worse than the one outside this room.

After a while, Marni looked down to find Lilly had dropped off to sleep on her shoulder. Carefully, Marni laid her back into the rocker and covered her with a knitted afghan from the couch. Lilly whimpered softly but continued to sleep the sleep of the dead. Or the inebriated.

Marni switched off the lamp and left her in front of the bank of windows and the storm, hoping Lilly slept off the wine before she attempted the stairs.

On the way to her room, Marni stopped at the library and quickly found *Pride and Prejudice*. As she turned out the light and headed for the stairs, she told herself she was ready at last for some sleep of her own.

But back in bed, Marni lay, listening, waiting for Chase to come storming in to admonish her for interfering in family business. After a while, when she heard no sound, she opened the soft, worn volume to chapter one, realizing it had been years since she'd read this book.

The first line jumped off the page at her. Marni groaned as she thought of Chase Calloway. Who was this impossible single man in possession of a good fortune her twin had fallen in love with? Certainly not a man in want of a wife— or a baby, as Elise had been led to believe. That was one truth at least Marni acknowledged.

A few pages into the book, she heard Chase return to his room, heard the clomp of the crutches as he approached the door adjoining their rooms. She held her breath. Then she heard him lock his side of the door. Instead of relief, Marni felt a wave of anger. Did Chase think he had to lock his door to protect himself from her? Did he really think she'd come to his room tonight and throw herself at him? The man couldn't be that big a fool, could he?

Tossing the book on the night table, she threw back the covers and swung her legs over the side of the bed, set on sharing a few choice words with Mr. Chase Calloway, even if it meant through a three-inch-thick door.

The lights flickered, and before her feet could touch the floor, went out. Marni held her breath, waiting for them to come back on. They didn't. And she had a feeling they wouldn't. As Vanessa had reminded her earlier, the electricity often went out during snowstorms in Montana. This far from civilization, it could be out for hours. Even days. Great. And just when she thought things couldn't get any worse.

A thud came from the adjoining room and Chase swore loudly after stumbling into what sounded like a piece of good-size furniture. She smiled, ashamed but no less amused. Served him right for being such a jerk.

Content, she slipped back under the covers. The embers in the fireplace cast a pale patina over the room. If she had been anywhere else, she might have thought it cozy. Outside, the snow fell in a dense suffocating silence. Marni watched it for a few moments, trying not to think about the other people in this house. The night seemed colder, Marni thought, or maybe it was just knowing the electricity had gone off. She felt alone and far from home. At least Elise and the baby were fine, she assured herself. Then she closed her eyes, hoping for the oblivion of sleep.

Chapter Five

Morning came like a blessing. But unfortunately, Marni's nightmares followed her into the daylight. One dream in particular haunted her: Chase standing over her, his blue eyes dark with evil as he told her she would never have the baby. Then something in his hands. An ax? Marni shivered and looked toward the window.

If the remnants of her bad dreams weren't enough, she found herself still trapped by the snowstorm raging outside. Wind plastered snow to the windowpanes and sent icy gusts hammering at the glass.

With a curse, Marni threw off the covers and lumbered from the bed, keenly aware of Sam. She hurriedly dressed, hoping to speak to Chase before he went down to breakfast. But when she tapped softly at their adjoining door, she received no response. She tried the door. It wasn't locked. When had he unlocked it? She thought about him standing over her in the dream. The dying firelight in his eyes. The ax in his large calloused hands.

"Chase?" She stepped into his room. What surprised her was the open suitcase lying in the bottom of the empty closet. Marni frowned as she surveyed her surroundings. The room was exactly like the one she'd spent the night in.

A guest room. Chase didn't live here. She shook her head, continuously amazed at how little her twin knew about the man she'd fallen so desperately in love with. The man who'd fathered her child.

The bed didn't look as if it had been slept in and Marni guessed it probably hadn't, judging from the appearance of the chair pulled up in front of the fire. The cushions were crushed as if he'd battled them in the night searching for comfort and sleep. Marni smiled, taking some pleasure in the thought that Chase might not have slept as soundly as she'd suspected.

As she headed downstairs, she found herself keeping a firm grip on the railing. Her near accident the night before had proved to her just how uncoordinated she'd become thanks to Sam. She couldn't even see her toes.

None of the family appeared to be up yet, although it was nearing time for breakfast. She could hear someone in the kitchen banging pots and pans, and smell the rich scent of coffee. Coffee sounded wonderful, although she wasn't sure a pregnant woman should be drinking caffeine. Marni peeked into the dining room, hoping to sneak a cup anyway.

"Mr. Calloway and his son are in the library," a voice announced behind Marni, making her jump.

She swung around to find Hilda looking harried and flushed. "There's coffee and juice in the library. Mr. Calloway said you'd be joining him."

He did, did he? She wondered which son was with him and hoped it was Chase.

Without a word, Hilda hurried away and Marni headed down the hall toward the library. The sound of angry voices drifted out, making her hesitate long before she reached the library door. She recognized the two male voices at once, confirming what she'd hoped, that Chase was in there with his father. In the cold light of morning, Marni was more determined than ever to get things settled between them—one way or another.

She stepped through the open library door and stopped abruptly at the sound of Chase's angry words.

"You're going to get Elise and her baby killed if you don't do something about this mess."

Chase stood, hunched over his crutches, in front of the blazing fire. His father stood next to him, a hand on the thick-timbered fireplace mantel as if he needed the support. Both had their backs to her.

"Why do you have to be so damned stubborn about this?" Chase demanded. "Isn't it enough that someone tried to kill *you?*"

Marni slipped behind the end of the bookcase, aware she planned to spy on the pair shamelessly. But if Elise and the baby really were in danger— She told herself not even to try to justify her actions. Silent as a mouse, Marni peeked around the edge of the bookcase.

"Ridiculous," Jabe snapped, pushing himself away from the fireplace. "It was just some fool in a pickup going too fast. Didn't see us until it was too late, if he saw us at all." Jabe dropped into a chair in front of the fireplace and reached to pour himself more coffee from the pot on the end table. "Probably some drunk driver."

"Like hell," Chase said, turning on his father. "A drunk driver tried to run you down only minutes before you were threatening to change your will? Not even you can believe that. You just don't want to admit you made a mistake in the first place with this first grandchild foolishness. Or is it that you can't face that it has to be someone in this family or someone closely connected to this family that's trying to kill you now?"

Jabe raised his head to look at his son. "Is that the reason you've been staying here? You think my life is in danger?" He sounded touched that Chase would try to protect him.

Marni was touched as well by this side of Chase Calloway, and surprised.

"You saved my life that night," Jabe said. "I owe you, son, but—"

"You don't owe me anything," Chase snapped. "It was a reflex action, one if I'd given some thought to, I would probably have done differently."

Jabe clearly didn't buy that any more than Marni did. No matter what Chase said, he cared about his father. And it seemed he'd saved Jabe's life in some heroic feat that had left him with a broken leg and memory loss. Marni almost felt guilty for still doubting Chase's memory loss. Almost.

"I just don't want you to concern yourself with my welfare," Jabe said.

"It's not only your fool neck on the line anymore," Chase retorted. "What about this woman and her baby? What about Felicia's baby? Are you willing to jeopardize all their lives, as well?"

"Why would anyone want to harm my grandchildren?" He sounded shocked that Chase should even think such a thing.

Chase dragged a hand through his dark locks in obvious frustration. "Because of that damned will of yours."

"Have either Elise or Felicia been threatened in any way?" Jabe asked reasonably.

Chase let out a curse. "By the time that happens it could be too late."

Jabe shook his head. "I'm not going back on my decision when I don't believe for a moment that my grandchildren or their mothers are in any danger."

Chase sliced a hand through the air between them. "I've never been able to reason with you. I thought you'd finally come to your senses that night in November right before the hit-and-run, I thought you realized how foolish this first grandchild thing was. Why don't you be honest with yourself for once. The only person you care about is yourself and what you want. That's the way it's always been.'' He turned and hobbled toward the door.

Marni ducked back behind the corner of the bookcase and tried to flatten herself to the wall, suddenly aware how ludicrous that notion was. Sam stuck out like the prow of a ship. Marni groaned silently. The last thing she wanted was to get caught in this compromising position by Chase Calloway.

''By the way,'' Chase said, the sound of his crutches halting, ''I saw the face of the person driving that truck right before it hit me.''

A tense silence filled the room.

''I'm going to remember and then I'll know who in this family hates you more than I do.''

Marni held her breath as Chase stormed out, slamming the door behind him. It took her a moment to digest everything she'd overheard and to realize Chase Calloway had trapped her in the library by closing the door and sealing off any surreptitious escape. She was cursing her inquisitive nature when she heard Jabe get up from his chair.

''You can come out now,'' he said wearily.

Marni grimaced as she stepped from behind the bookcase. How long had Jabe known she was there? Shamefaced, she brushed imaginary lint from the front of her maternity top, trying to think of something appropriate to say. Jabe saved her the effort.

''Chase is confused,'' he said as he reached into his pocket and pulled out a bottle of prescription pills. She watched him shake two into his hand and toss them down with the last of his coffee.

''When Chase's memory comes back he'll realize that he was mistaken about a lot of things,'' Jabe said with conviction. His gaze settled on Marni and seemed to soften at the

sight of her pregnant form. "My son is very stubborn. Go
after him. Try to make him see."

Marni stood for a moment, wondering what she could
make Chase Calloway see. "Where—"

"He'll go to the horse barn," Jabe said as he turned back
to the fire.

Dismissed, Marni slipped out of the library, took her coat
from the front closet where Jabe had put it the night before
and trailed Chase out into the snowstorm. Through the
swirling snow, she saw him hobbling toward the largest of
two barns set back in the pines.

Marni came in through the barn door to find herself on
an upper level overlooking an empty arena. The air smelled
of horses and leather. She took the stairs and wound her
way toward the back of the barn, passing tack rooms and
what looked like an office. Both were empty.

She found Chase leaning on his crutches next to a stall
containing the most beautiful horse she'd ever seen. The
name on the stall door read Wind Chaser. Marni remembered Elise telling her that the Calloways had investments
in a little of everything, real estate, all kinds of businesses
and horses. *Not just horses, El.* Wind Chaser had to be one
of the top quarter horses in the country.

Marni shuddered to think what a horse like that would be
worth. She was starting to realize how high the stakes were
in this family intrigue. She wondered how much money Jabe
Calloway had saddled his first grandchild with. Enough that
Chase thought it was dangerous for El and the baby.

Marni stood for a moment, just inside the doorway,
watching Chase. He crooned to Wind Chaser, his voice low
and soft, his manner both gentle and strong as he stroked
the horse's sleek neck. The animal responded with soft nick-
ers, obviously enjoying Chase's touch. And Marni could see
how a woman might respond to this side of Chase, as well.
She imagined that soft gentleness in his touch, the feel of

his fingertips on her cheek, brushing across her lips, trailing down her neck...

He must have sensed her behind him. He turned, the kind look on his face disappearing instantly. "You," he said in disgust.

She stepped closer. The horse in the stall stomped, throwing its head and snorting as if it felt the same way about her.

"I'd keep your distance if I were you," Chase said softly, calming the horse both with his tone and the stroking motion of his hand along its neck. "Wind Chaser can be dangerous when he's upset."

Marni wondered if it was the horse he was worried about or himself. But she didn't go any closer. Nor did she turn and leave. Was it only her imagination or was Chase Calloway still trying to scare her?

When he turned around again, Chase almost seemed surprised to see her still standing there. "What?" he asked with obvious irritation.

She bristled, especially after the argument he'd just made on her behalf with his father. How could he keep contending that he didn't know her, didn't care anything about her or the baby?

"You certainly have a lot of hostility toward a woman you've never laid eyes on before," Marni noted. "Are you angry with me because you think I'm lying or because I'm not?"

"Understand something." He sounded almost patient. "I've never wanted children of my own, never planned to have any and when Jabe—"

"But I thought—" So it had been a line when he told Elise he wanted children. Just as Marni had suspected. She glared at him angrily.

"What?" he demanded, looking defensive.

"You told me that finding a woman to love and having children were all that was missing from your life."

He looked horrified, then burst out laughing. "You couldn't force those words out of me at gunpoint."

The gunpoint part appealed to her. "I guess your usual seduction lines must be one of those holes in your memory."

He growled and moved away from the horse, which snorted and stomped as if their conversation agitated him. Marni knew that feeling as Chase advanced on her and she found herself backstepping away not only from his anger but also the memory of what had happened last night.

"I might have lost some of my memory, but I haven't lost my mind," Chase snapped. "I've never wanted children and I've never made that a secret to *anyone*."

Marni bumped into the solid wall of the stable and realized he'd backed her into a corner. Again. He was so close his warm breath caressed her cheek, she could feel the heat of him, a powerful male energy that hummed in the air between them. A smile played at his lips; he thought he'd trapped her. The only way out would be to go over the top of Chase Calloway. It was an option she was keeping open.

"Last summer when Jabe told me he planned to change his will if I didn't agree to come into the business, I tried to talk him out of it," Chase said quietly as if he was glad to have her undivided attention at last. "When that failed, I distanced myself from the whole mess. Then you come along claiming to be carrying my child. Very suspicious, if you ask me."

She looked down at Sam. "Is that why you can't admit this is your baby, because it will make it look like you're after the money?"

Chase let out a curse. "If you really knew me, you'd know I don't want the money. I don't want anything from my father. I never have." He fixed a look on her that made her squirm "Doesn't it amaze you how little you know about me? It sure amazes me."

"I couldn't help but overhear you and your father in the library," Marni said, quickly changing the subject.

"I'll bet," Chase said. "You always make a habit of eavesdropping?"

She started to inform him that if he didn't want his arguments overheard he should tone them down, but saved her breath. The truth was, she was guilty of far worse than simple eavesdropping.

"You really believe—" She had to catch herself. "My baby is in danger?"

Chase shot her a look. "I told you that last night. Did you think I was joking?"

"I thought you were only trying to scare me."

"You should be scared." He shook his head at her in irritation. "I saw you last night with Lilly. Look, do yourself a favor. Don't get involved with this family. Especially Lilly."

"Lilly needed someone last night. I was just being kind."

He let out a curse. "Kind could get you killed." He raked a hand through his hair. "I'm trying to protect you."

"And why is that? You say you don't know an Elise McCumber and you couldn't be the father of her baby. So what do you care?"

He gritted his teeth. "I don't want to see you get hurt. Or your baby. And if you care about this baby, the best thing you can do is admit that you and I were never lovers and that the baby isn't mine."

"And if I don't?" she asked. Earlier, Marni had almost found something she could like about Chase. A man who would save his father at personal risk to himself. A man who would argue for the safety of pregnant women and their unborn children. That was a man she could like. There was nothing likable about the man standing in front of her now, however.

"How much money do you want?" He tugged his checkbook from the hip pocket of his jeans. "Name your price. I'll pay you double what my father is paying you."

"I don't want your money," she told him. "Nor did your father pay me to say I'm having your baby."

His look said he didn't believe her. "You think you can pass this kid off as the first grandchild and get more?" Chase shook his head. "I'll fight you," he said, anger making his voice crackle. "As soon as that baby is born, I'll prove it isn't mine and you won't get a dime. I can't imagine what my father hopes to gain by this."

She fought to contain her temper. "I don't want your money or your father's. I didn't even know about your father's stupid will until Lilly told me last night."

He glared suspiciously at her. "You probably hadn't heard about my accident either or my memory loss, right?"

"As a matter of fact—"

"How convenient," he said.

"My thought exactly."

He raked a hand through his dark curls. "You don't get it, do you?" he said as he leaned closer.

Reminded of last night and the disastrous test kiss, Marni flattened herself against the wall.

He looked at her, amusement dancing in all that blue, then moved back just enough to give her breathing room. She got the impression that he wasn't going to let her go until he was through with her.

"If someone tried to kill my father to keep him from changing his will," Chase said, biting off each word, "then imagine what that person would do to keep your baby from inheriting all that Calloway money."

Marni thought about Vanessa dropping her scarf on the stairs and wondered if there was any truth in what he said or if this was like everything else, an attempt to frighten her away?

"Let's get back to this memory loss of yours...."

He glared at her a moment, her distrustful tone obviously not lost on him. "I have what they call selective memory loss."

She raised an eyebrow. "*Selective* memory loss?" *Give me a break!*

"My memory's coming back," he assured her quickly. "I remember most everything. There's just a few...holes."

Right. Marni studied him, unable to get past the *selective* part of his memory loss and the *hole* Elise and the baby had supposedly fallen in. "How do you know that...I'm not one of those holes?"

"I know. I don't have to prove it to you or anyone else."

Why did he sound so defensive if he was so positive? Because he isn't sure, Marni thought. Maybe his memory loss was more severe than he wanted to admit. But that still didn't explain why he wouldn't even consider Elise might be part of those lost memories, did it?

"This—" she had trouble even saying the word "—*selective* memory loss of yours, did the doctors say all of your memory will come back?" Marni thought about what she'd heard in the library. If Chase had really gotten a glimpse of the driver of that truck right before the accident, he might have seen the attempted murderer. Even knowing Chase for as short a time as she did, she knew trying to remember that must be driving him crazy. Possibly it explained why he was so angry at her; she'd added to his frustration by being another one of those holes in his memory.

"It's only a matter of time before I remember everything," he said, the threat clear in his voice.

She wanted to say something smart to wipe the smugness from his face. Wouldn't he feel foolish when he remembered Elise? "What about the accident itself?" she asked instead. "Will you be able to remember it?"

"The doctors say I won't but they don't know me."

Jabe was right about Chase's stubbornness, she decided. But while Jabe saw the quality as a flaw in his son's character, Marni saw it as a strength.

But what if he never remembered the face of the truck driver? "If you're right about the driver deliberately trying to run your father down, your life might be in danger, as well. The driver is probably worried you'll remember."

Chase actually smiled. "Are you starting to believe me?"

Was she? "It doesn't matter what I believe," Marni told him. "But I have to wonder, if you're so positive we were never lovers, why are you so worried about me and the safety of my baby? Could you be afraid to remember?"

He narrowed his gaze. "Afraid?"

"Afraid of the feelings you might have for me or this baby." She expected anger. Denial. Recriminations.

She didn't expect him to laugh.

The sound filled the barn as he leaned toward her on his crutches and placed a large palm on either side of the wall beside her head.

Chase was a little too close for comfort. Nor did she like the glint in his eyes. But he had her trapped, and he knew it. He pinned her to the wall with the intensity of his look. She held her breath as he let his gaze travel leisurely over her face, pausing at her lips, as predatory as a wanton kiss.

"Were we passionate lovers?"

"I don't see how that has anything to do with this," she replied primly, feeling her cheeks burn.

"You don't?" He seemed to be fighting back a smile. "As intimate as you say we've been, why look so shocked by my question?"

"Because this has nothing to do with sex."

He lifted one dark eyebrow. "It looks to me like it has a great deal to do with sex." He dropped his gaze to Sam.

She assured herself she could hold her own with him. Even with the memory of last night's kiss still fresh in her mind and on her lips. Even with her limited experience with men. And her total lack of experience with a man like Chase Calloway.

"How long have we known each other?" he asked innocently enough.

"Since June," she said, surprised at how nervous he was making her.

"How did we meet?" he inquired, not moving closer but making her intensely aware of the space he dominated.

"In a fender bender. I ran into you."

"Then there should be a police report, insurance forms, some sort of record."

So proof was what he was looking for. She put a protective hand over Sam; how much more proof did the man need? "We didn't call the police or our insurance companies because there wasn't any real damage."

"If you'd run into a truck I was driving, I would have insisted we call the police, even if there wasn't any visible damage."

"But for some reason you didn't that day," she said.

He seemed to ignore that. "Nor can I remember the last time I drove one of the ranch trucks."

"You can't remember a lot of things," she said. "But you do drive the trucks as part of your job, right?"

He stared at her. "You think I work for my father?" he asked incredulously.

"I just assumed—"

"How could we have been lovers and you not know what I do for a living?" Chase interrupted.

Good question. "You led me to believe you worked for Calloway Ranches."

"You're saying I lied to you?" he demanded, obviously not happy with the prospect of being called a liar.

"Misled me, possibly?" she suggested carefully. How could Elise have gotten things so messed up? "So there isn' any way you could have been driving the ranch's white truck last June?"

He frowned. "I didn't say my father doesn't try to involve me in the family business every chance he gets."

"So that proves nothing," she said, discouraged.

He rummaged a hand through his hair. "How long did we date?"

She was at a loss for words to describe Elise's four-day love affair. Marni couldn't imagine falling that hard in four months, let alone four days. "It was love at first sight."

Chase laughed. "You have to be kidding."

"It was magical," Marni said defensively.

He arched an eyebrow. "Really?"

"Something that only happens once in a lifetime," she added and stopped, having run out of clichés.

"How long?" he demanded.

She swallowed. "Four days."

"Four days!" Disbelief. Shock. Incredulity. He shook his head and laughed. "Four days?"

"It happened very fast."

"I'd say." He reached out and traced his thumb across her lower lip. His thumb pad felt disarmingly rough. "That must have been some four days. I must have kissed these lips often during those magical, fun-filled four days."

It was clear in his eyes what kind of woman he thought her to be. She turned her head and he pulled back his hand, the smile dissolving into a piqued frown. He thought her a liar and a fraud. Among other things. She wanted to knee him, but taking down a man on crutches seemed lower than even the way he was behaving.

"I see that you don't believe two people can fall in love…quickly," she said.

"You're wrong." He speared her with those pale blue eyes. "I believe two people can fall in love instantly. Just not me."

"You're immune to love?" she asked, adopting his disbelieving tone.

"I don't have time for it, and since I never plan to marry—"

"No children *or* marriage?" she interrupted in surprise.

"That's what I've been trying to tell you. I don't get involved."

"But what if you did this time? What if you…" She swallowed. "Couldn't help yourself?" Her cheeks flamed red hot. She wanted desperately to explain to him that she wasn't referring to herself but Elise. Elise had a way with men that caused them to do things they would never do with any other woman.

He leaned back and lazily let his gaze explore the curves beneath her open coat. "I can see where I'd definitely be tempted, I'll give you that." He seemed to be enjoying this a lot more than she was.

"Maybe," he said softly, "it's just a matter of… jogging…my memory."

Marni didn't like the sound of this or the predatory look in his eyes. "I came here to discuss what we were going to do about the baby," she said quickly, realizing Sam was the only thing keeping them apart right now. "Not to—"

"To what?" he asked with wide-eyed innocence.

CHASE MADE a dozen excuses for what he was about to do. All of them were honorable and made perfect sense. Especially in his current state of mind. Was this woman part of some memory loss? Or was she simply taking advantage of the situation? He had a right to prove that she wasn't his

lover, that the baby she carried wasn't his and that she wa
the conniver he suspected she was. She wasn't the firs
woman who'd tried to wrangle the Calloway name with
baby that wasn't his.

Except this woman was different. That he wanted to kis
her again was the least of it. He needed to kiss her to prov
to himself that he was right. He couldn't have forgotten her
memory loss or not. Last night he'd been so sure that onc
he kissed her he'd know the truth. But kissing her had onl
left him more confused. The attraction had been explosive
More than he wanted to admit. Maybe he *did* have a four
day affair with her, his traitorous mind tempted. Or mayb
he just wanted to kiss her again for purely prurient reasons

"I think we should talk about this," she said, her voic
cracking.

"About what?"

She opened her mouth to speak but no words came out
There was something about her mouth... The provocativ
way her lips parted. The soft moan that escaped her throa
last night when he'd pulled her into his kiss. The powerfu
seductive feel of her. It had been so...magical?

He wasn't sure what decided him or if it had been ar
actual decision at all. Suddenly he had a need to feel her
skin as strongly as the need to remember her. He needed to
explore the dark recesses of his mind to find if she wa:
lodged there, the same way he needed to explore her body
Purely to get at the truth, of course. If he felt her skin agains'
his, he would remember, his mind assured him. And oh how
he wanted to feel her naked against him. He couldn't remember ever wanting a woman the way he wanted this one
right now. What was it about her?

His fingers slid down the soft, silken column of her neck
At the hollow of her throat, he could feel the thunder of her
heart beneath his fingertips. What he saw in her golden
brown eyes startled him, but not half as much as the inten-

sity of his body's reaction to her. Desire fired her gaze the
way it blazed in his loins. My God, was it possible? Had
they really been lovers?

"Elise." His voice came out a hoarse whisper. His hand
dropped to the round curve of her breast.

She jumped as if she'd been scalded with boiling water.

Chase frowned at her reaction, all his suspicions coming
back in an instant. Why did she seem as startled as he was
by the strength of the chemistry between them? And as unsure about him as he was about her? "Do I make you nervous?"

"No," she croaked.

"I would think you'd be used to my touch," he said
quietly, watching her face. Who was this woman? Certainly
not one he'd ever spent four amorous days and nights with,
he thought with no small regret. He told himself he'd known
it hadn't been true all along. What was it about her that had
made him doubt that?

Whoever she was, he was now more determined than ever
to find out what she was up to.

MARNI FELT HER BODY begin to vibrate, a fine high vibration
that raced along in her blood. She leaned against the wall,
trying to get her feet back under her. This wasn't going the
way she'd planned. She had to get out of here before she
betrayed her twin. Out of this barn. Away from Chase Calloway. She just didn't know how to do it gracefully. She'd
already stirred up his suspicions again. She could see it in
those pale blue eyes of his.

If she were really his lover— She couldn't keep deluding
herself that another kiss might unlock his lost memories. If
that were true, it would take Elise's kiss—not her own. And
this time, Chase had a lot more than a kiss in mind. It was
put-up or shut-up time and Marni was in over her head.

He looked at her, his gaze challenging her. "What's wrong?"

"We can't do this."

His smile was merciless. "We've already done this. As they say, it's too late to close the barn door after the cow has gotten away."

Her hands went to his chest to push him away. She felt the heat of his skin through his shirt, felt his heart race beneath her palms, and her own instantly match that treacherous beat as his lips descended on hers.

A door banged open. "Chase?" Dayton sounded peeved.

Chase swore softly as his gaze met Marni's, his lips lingered for a moment, hovering over hers, then he smiled, his message clear: This was only a temporary reprieve. "We'll finish this later."

"Chase?" Dayton snapped. Over Chase's shoulder, Marni could see Dayton squinting into the darkness of the stable area, trying to find them. "You're holding up breakfast and you know how Mother hates—" He faltered as his gaze fell on them. Annoyance turned to curiosity. "Everything all right?"

"Everything's just fine," Chase said without turning around. "Isn't it?" he asked Marni softly and then faced his half brother.

Marni leaned against the wall, her heart hammering, her very breath trapped in her throat, her body quaking like an aspen in the wind. She wasn't sure what shocked her more. Chase's behavior. Or her own. She'd wanted to kiss him again!

Worse than that. She actually felt regret that Dayton had rescued her when he did. What was happening to her? This wasn't like her at all.

Inwardly she groaned as a thought struck her. If Chase had this effect on every woman, no wonder Elise had fallen so madly in love with him. But Marni couldn't help wondering how many other women were lost in the man's selective memory loss.

"Vanessa's going to be fit to be tied," Dayton said, sounding as if he looked forward to it since it would be Chase's fault and not his own.

The two brothers exchanged a look. Marni could feel the tension stretch dangerously between them.

Dayton looked away first. "Hey, don't kill the messenger. She just sent me out to get you both into breakfast. Also you have a phone call, Chase."

"Took you long enough to tell me." He shot Marni a look over his shoulder that held both promise and threat, then he turned and hobbled out the side entrance Dayton had come in, the door closing behind him in a gush of cold air and snow.

The spell broken, Marni took a breath to steady herself. Always sensible. Always confident. Always in control. What had happened to *that* Marni McCumber? Chase Calloway. That's what had happened. Chase and this stupid pretense. She wasn't just pretending to be pregnant. She was trying to be another woman, a woman Marni McCumber couldn't even pretend to be.

What was it about Chase Calloway that could be so irritating and at the same time so…tempting? She took a ragged breath and realized Dayton hadn't moved. He leaned against the barn wall, studying her in a way that instantly made her uncomfortable at being alone with him.

She started past him but he stepped in front of her to block her exit.

"So you're having Chase's baby?" he asked, something dark and intimidating in his blue eyes.

"It's really none of your concern," she said, realizing he wasn't going to let her past until he had his say.

"Do you know anything about breeding…horses?"

Marni wanted to wipe that smug, self-satisfied look off

his face. The last thing she'd do was let him see that he frightened her. "No, do you know anything about interior design?"

He looked confused, some of the smugness gone.

"I was just curious who decorated the house," Marni said. "Your mother?"

Dayton looked wary. "Yes, she wanted it to reflect my father and his position."

Marni wondered what position of Jabe's the house reflected. Overbearing, domineering and pompous came to mind. "Then Vanessa was an interior decorator before she married Jabe?"

Dayton's horrified expression confirmed that she'd scored a bull's-eye. "My mother has never...*worked*. She was a Landers of Boston before she became a Calloway."

A Landers of Boston? He made it sound like royalty, the same way he made "work" sound like a dirty word.

She had to bite her tongue not to share her thoughts on the work ethic with him. A job might be just what Vanessa Calloway needed.

"Where are the McCumbers from?" Dayton asked, his nose lifting into the air.

"Montana," she said proudly. "I'm fifth-generation."

"How nice," he said, not even pretending to mean it. "That would make this child you're carrying...?"

"A sixth-generation Montanan," she said.

He gave her a weak smile. "If you knew anything about breeding...horses, you'd know the value of the foal is based on its lineage. That's why you'd never breed a Thorough-bred with a nag."

Marni felt as if she'd been slapped. "I don't know much about breeding horses," she said, surprised at how calm and restrained she sounded, "but I do know a jackass when I see one." She shoved past him but not before she'd seen the look on his face. Pure hate.

She felt a shiver as she hurried toward the house.

Chapter Six

Marni rushed through the back door and nearly collided with Vanessa.

"Breakfast is going to be late," Vanessa announced angrily, then turned on her high heels and stalked back down the hall to the dining room.

Marni mugged a face at her back, wishing the storm would stop and she could get out of this place.

"I wouldn't keep my mother waiting," Dayton warned as he came in the back door and swept past her.

"I'm sure you wouldn't," Marni mumbled as she removed her coat. She wanted to tell Vanessa what she could do with her breakfast and Dayton what he could do with his so-called breeding and Chase what he could do with his—

Come on, Marni, who are you really angry with? She took a deep breath and reluctantly admitted none of those people were really to blame for the way she was feeling.

Dayton, the blizzard, the cold, snowy hike from the barn and even Vanessa couldn't distract her thoughts from her recent encounter with Chase. She made several attempts to downplay her reaction to his touch and finally gave up. The bottom line: She wasn't equipped for this. Pretending to be Elise was too much for her.

"I hope you're hungry," Jabe said, coming out of the dining room to take her coat.

"Not really." Just the thought of another meal with the family—and Chase—

"Wait until you taste Hilda's pancakes," Jabe said as he hung her coat in the closet and closed the door. "You'll change your mind."

"I need to get out of here," she said, sounding as panicky as she felt.

He raised an eyebrow, but didn't ask how things had gone in the barn. "I'm afraid we're snowed in. Until the storm lets up, you have no choice but to stay," he said, patting her hand as he led her toward the dining room. "This is all going to work out. You'll see."

Right, Marni thought. She couldn't imagine things getting any worse.

Most of the family were already seated, overdressed and just as silent and unfriendly as they'd been at dinner last night around the table now laden with plates of pancakes, bacon, ham, eggs, fried potatoes and biscuits and gravy.

As she sat down, Marni noticed two chairs remained empty. Lilly's. And Chase's.

She wondered how they got out of breakfast when she couldn't. Not that anyone really seemed to want her there. Except Jabe. Vanessa didn't even bother to look up from the soft-boiled eggs and dry toast Hilda slid in front of her. Dayton and Felicia gave Marni a brief contemptuous look. She felt Hayes studying her, but when she met his gaze she saw more curiosity than vindictiveness.

"Lilly's not feeling well this morning," Hayes said as if someone had asked. When no one responded, he returned his attention to the large plate of food in front of him, his appetite noticeably improved over last night's.

Marni got the impression that this wasn't the first morning

Lilly hadn't shown for breakfast. She was no doubt sleeping off a major hangover.

Just about the time Marni began to wonder what had happened to Chase, he came in, frowning as he took his chair. She wondered if the frown was due to her or his phone call. It dawned on her that the phone must be working again. She'd call Elise right after breakfast. Elise would be sympathetic to Chase's memory loss; she'd find hope in it. And they'd get through Christmas.

Maybe there'd be a Christmas miracle. And Chase would get his memory back on Christmas Eve and remember his love for Elise and their baby. Marni was so lost in her safe fairy tale that she forgot she wasn't hungry. As Jabe passed her plate after plate of food, he quickly proved he was right about her appetite. She lathered butter and thick homemade peach preserves on a pancake and took a bite, unconsciously closing her eyes to savor it.

At the sound of a soft chuckle, her eyes flew open and instantly she felt the heat of embarrassment wash over her as she saw it was Jabe. She sneaked a glance at Chase, only to find him watching her, looking amused.

"What do you think of Hilda's pancakes?" Jabe asked, still chuckling.

Marni smiled and licked the sweet preserves from her upper lip. "Amazing. I'd love her recipe." She'd make them Christmas morning for the whole family to celebrate Elise and Chase's engagement—

"*You* cook?" Felicia asked.

"My mother insisted we all learn to cook and sew, even my brothers," Marni said, warmed by the pancakes and a subject dear to her heart, her family.

"How many brothers do you have?" Jabe asked.

"Four. They're all older than—" she felt the near slip on her lips "—me and my sister."

Both Hayes and Dayton glanced up. "There's more at

home like *you?*'' Dayton asked, making what could have been a compliment sound just the opposite.

"My sister is nothing like me," Marni said quickly in Elise's defense.

"Your mother sounds like a smart woman," Jabe commented.

"I think I'm going to throw up," Felicia announced, sliding her chair back from the table. She tossed down her napkin and rushed from the room.

Dayton watched her leave with only mild concern.

"Morning sickness," Vanessa said.

"Did you suffer morning sickness?" Jabe asked Marni as he passed her more pancakes.

"I was fortunate," she said, busying herself with the pancakes, eyes averted. "I missed that part."

"Where were you raised?" Jabe asked.

Yesterday his questions had been pointed and part of a test. Today they seemed kindled out of a sincere desire to know more about the woman who was about to give birth to his grandchild. Elise's baby. His first grandchild, Marni reminded herself with growing apprehension.

She told him about growing up in rural Montana, climbing trees, swimming in the creek, playing baseball, camping in the back pasture under the cottonwoods.

She realized with a start that she'd been describing her own childhood—not Elise's. Elise had been more prissy, playing with dolls, holding elaborate tea parties on the front porch and refusing to bait her own hook when she did go along fishing. While Elise didn't have the patience to sit and wait for a fish to bite, she could spend hours planning elaborate skits, which she directed after charming her siblings into participating.

Marni shot a look at Chase, surprised that she seemed to have his full attention, although from the look on his face, he wasn't enjoying her stories. He looked angry and upset.

Had something she said made him remember one of El's childhood stories? Was it possible he would remember everything before Christmas? Remember Elise and give her that happy ending El and the baby so deserved? And let Marni forget all that foolishness she'd felt in the barn?

"Your childhood sounds idyllic," Jabe said.

"It was." Marni said, her hand going to Sam without her realizing what she was doing. "I always thought if I ever had children, that's what I'd want for them."

"You haven't always planned to have children?" Chase asked.

She met his gaze. "No," she answered truthfully. "I always saw myself as a doting aunt." She looked down at Sam again. "Sometimes I still have trouble seeing myself as a mother."

"I'm sure Chase is having the same problem seeing himself as a father," Dayton commented wryly.

"Fatherhood is something a man shouldn't take lightly," Chase said.

Marni couldn't tell whether that was meant for Jabe or Dayton. Both busied themselves with breakfast.

"How was your phone call?" Dayton asked Chase.

"Odd, but it seems the phone lines are still down," Chase answered, not looking up from his plate.

"Huh," Dayton said. "Must have gone down about the time I came out to the barn to look for the two of you."

"Yeah, that's what I thought you'd say." Chase glanced up at Marni, concern in his gaze.

Marni swallowed. Dayton had purposely gotten rid of Chase? What for? Just so he could insult her? Or had he had something else planned for her and changed his mind? She concentrated on her food, telling herself she'd never let Dayton get her alone again.

"Dayton didn't get to tell you last night at dinner," Vanessa said, smiling at her husband. "But Felicia's further along than we all thought. Almost seven months."

That brought everyone's attention up from their breakfasts.

"Seven months?" Jabe demanded, spearing the last piece of ham. "She doesn't look that pregnant."

"She's always watched her figure," Vanessa said, and added pointedly, "Not all women blow up like a balloon when they're pregnant."

Feeling her face burn red hot, Marni chewed her last bite of pancake in the thick, tense-filled silence that followed. When she dared sneak a look at Chase, she found him smiling in obvious amusement, not in the least sympathetic to her predicament.

AFTER BREAKFAST, Jabe announced that he'd picked up the weather report on the mobile radio. Bozeman Pass was closed and some parts of Interstate 90 were open only to emergency traffic because of blowing and drifting snow.

"In other words, we're snowed in," Dayton said, not looking any more pleased by the news than Marni. The road down to Maudlow was impassable and would stay that way until the county plowed it. Or until the Calloways plowed themselves out.

"No reason to start plowing until it quits snowing and blowing," Jabe said. "It would just drift back in behind the plow."

Marni had the unpleasant thought that Jabe might be just trying to keep her here. But as powerful as Jabe Calloway was, he couldn't control the weather, she told herself.

She listened as he barked orders to his two youngest sons and realized that Dayton and Hayes were both involved in the family business with jobs that often took them away from the ranch. Not menial chores such as mucking out the barn since hired hands normally took care of the horses.

But not today. The crew wouldn't be able to get into the ranch to work because of the storm. That meant Dayton and Hayes would have to do all the chores, something that didn't go over well with either of them, judging from the looks on their faces.

But they didn't argue and it became obvious who ran Calloway Ranches, and who took orders. Jabe could be a hard man, she decided. He was used to getting his way. And his sons seemed to dance to his tune. All except one.

"Why don't you stay off that leg and see that Elise doesn't get bored," Jabe ordered Chase irritably after everyone else had left the table.

Chase gave his father a patient smile. "With her active imagination, boredom is the last thing she has to worry about."

Active imagination, huh? If he only knew.

Chase got to his feet and, leaning on his crutches, smiled down at her. "But don't worry, I'll take care of her."

The threat in his voice sent a shiver through her. Just the thought of the two of them alone again together— Everything be damned, she couldn't go on pretending to be Elise. She couldn't let what almost happened in the barn happen again.

"Chase, there's something we need to talk about."

He smiled. "Whatever the lady wants."

Marni didn't like the look in Chase's eyes as Jabe got up from the table. "I'll see that no one interrupts the two of you," he said and closed the door behind him.

Marni didn't like the sound of that. "Look, I'm not the woman you think I am," she said.

"Why don't you let me be the judge of that," Chase said, coming around to her side of the table. "We're completely alone again. That *is* what you wanted, right?"

She got to her feet, backing away from him. "I didn't want to get you alone to—"

"But you did want to get me alone again," he interrupted. "Or did you finally want to tell me that we've never been lovers, never spent four days together, let alone four 'magical' nights and that there is no way you're carrying my child?"

Damn him. That's exactly what she wanted to tell him. And a confession is exactly what he wanted. If she told him the truth now, he wouldn't even listen. All he'd hear was that he'd been right all along: She wasn't pregnant, wasn't his lover and had never been. He'd laugh at the whole twin-sister routine and throw her out into the storm.

"You're going to feel pretty foolish when you remember everything," she said, realizing immediately it wasn't the catchy comeback she'd hoped for.

"When I remember, I fear you're going to regret it."

She didn't doubt that for a moment.

CHASE FOUND HIMSELF backing her into a corner again and looking forward to it. He stopped himself, remembering only too well what had almost happened earlier in the barn. He had to get a grip. After all, he was trying to prove to her that they'd never been lovers. He'd start by trying to reason with the woman. Then if that didn't work...well, there was always making love to her on the dining room table.

He sat down and tried to see past her cute sweet face to the gold digger he knew her to be. Whoever this woman was, she had come here on false pretenses to pass off another man's child as his own, hoping to capitalize on his misfortune and his father's wealth and ego. Well, Chase wasn't about to let that happen.

After sitting through breakfast, listening to tales of her childhood, he was all the more convinced that nothing she could say or do could convince him he'd been her lover. She was the kind of woman he'd avoided since puberty.

There was no way he'd have ever let himself get close to her. Miss McCumber and her perfect childhood were much too dangerous.

"There are a lot of reasons you and I never had a four-day affair," he said, trying to replace the emotions she stirred in him with something safe like good old familiar anger. He'd show up this charlatan for the liar she was. "Number one, you're not my type."

She raised an eyebrow but took a chair a safe distance from him. "And what type is *your* type?"

He didn't want to admit what that had always been. Simple and safe. "Tall, leggy, busty..."

"Shallow?" she offered.

"Noncombative," he said, not liking the way this was going. "Do you have a problem with that?"

She shot him a wide-eyed innocent look. "What man would want a woman who might intellectually challenge him?"

He growled. "Why do women think men want to be challenged? Maybe we just want peace and quiet."

She rolled her eyes.

"Number two," he said through gritted teeth. It amazed him how she could make him doubt himself, make him think against all his arguments that maybe somehow she *had* been part of his memory loss. He'd never thought of pregnant women as beautiful or intriguing or...sensual. But this one— If she had her way, she'd have him thinking he was falling for her. "Why would I ask you to lunch after you'd just run into my truck?"

"I think we both know the answer to that one," she said, giving him a dirty look. "You obviously thought I *was* your type."

He cursed himself for starting this. "Where did I take you for lunch?"

"Guadalupe's."

"That tiny, out-of-the-way Mexican-food place?" he asked in surprise.

"I take it that isn't where you usually wine and dine your...bustier dates?" Her innocent look had a sharp edge to it. "Maybe you didn't want us to be seen."

He frowned, wondering if that was exactly what he'd been thinking, if he had indeed taken her there. Which, of course, he hadn't. "What did I order?"

She gave him a blank look.

"You don't remember," he accused. He always ordered the same thing at Mexican-food restaurants. If she'd said anything but chile rellenos, he would have known she was lying. For just a moment, he thought he had her.

"I don't remember, I was...nervous."

He definitely made her nervous, he knew that. "What did you have?" he asked, studying her.

"Chile rellenos. My favorite."

He groaned inwardly. Her favorite was his favorite. Oh, brother. And on top of that, he liked her appetite as much as his father did. "You're not exactly a light eater, are you?"

She lifted her chin. "Do you have a problem with that?" she asked defiantly.

He had to laugh. It seemed to surprise her. "No. I find it...refreshing." *Just like you find her refreshing?* "Did I kiss you during dinner?"

Marni shook her head and avoided his gaze. He couldn't imagine how any man had impregnated this woman. She seemed so...chaste. He remembered the way she'd reacted to his kiss last night. The way she'd reacted to his touch in the barn. Just the memory stirred something inside him he didn't want stirred.

"We didn't kiss until...later at the...motel," she said.

What? He stared at her. "You're kidding?"

She looked away. "You were...shy."

Right. "I would have kissed you at dinner. Just looking at that face of yours—" He raked a hand through his hair and glared at the ceiling. "If I'd taken you to Guadalupe's, I would have requested a private booth in the back, candlelight even though it was lunch and chile rellenos for both of us. I would have kissed you the moment the waiter walked away."

"How can you be so sure?" she asked, seeming to fight for breath under his gaze.

"Because that's what I'd like to do with you now," he said honestly.

She swallowed. "Take me to Guadalupe's?"

He found himself on his feet, balancing on his good leg. "Kiss you."

She shot up out of her chair. "We already tried that. It didn't jog your memory."

"I don't give a damn about my memory or what happened months ago," he snapped, realizing how true that was. "All I care about is what's happening right now." He was on her before he knew what he was doing.

She looked scared. "You've forgotten about the baby."

"Not likely," he said, looking down at her protruding stomach, the only thing that was keeping them apart—other than the enormous lie she was telling. "That's all I've thought about since yesterday when you walked through the door. You. And the baby." He'd driven himself crazy, knowing she wasn't locked somewhere in his faulty memory, torturing himself with the impossible thought that she was.

"There's only one way to prove that I've never made love to you." He shoved aside the food and plates on the table in one swift noisy movement and lifted Marni up on the table, wondering how far he'd go, how far he'd have to go. He knew how far he wanted to go. "Trust me, I'll be gentle."

Chapter Seven

Oh, no, he plans to take me right here. Right on the dining-room table! "You wouldn't!" Marni cried.

"After those four days we spent together, surely you realize I would do more than make love to you on a dining-room table," Chase said.

No, she told herself. He wouldn't dare.

But she couldn't forget the way he'd made her feel in the barn. She'd wanted to kiss him, wanted him to touch her, wanted him to— *Oh yes, she'd wanted him to make love to her.* Not that she would have let him. Not that she would ever betray her sister. But she wanted him.

And what if the desire she'd thought she'd seen in his eyes had been real? What if he'd wanted her as badly as she'd wanted him? What if he wanted her now—at all costs?

He swung her legs up and spun her around and back, until she lay lengthwise on the table in front of him. Panicked that he might not be bluffing after all, she struggled to get up, but he bent over her face, his breath tickling her cheek as his lips skimmed across her skin in search of her mouth.

She turned her head away from his kiss, and realized that if he was just trying to scare her, he was doing a good job of it. "Chase, let me up. I don't find this in the least bit humorous."

"Humorous?" He laughed softly as he trailed kisses down her throat to the V of her maternity blouse. "Honey, I'm not trying to be humorous."

With a shock, she felt him unbutton the top button on her maternity blouse and realized where his mouth was headed next. *Oh no.* "Chase, pleas—"

His kiss cut her off before she got any further. Last night his lips had taken, demanding nothing in return. This kiss staked claim to her, demanding every ounce of her, warning her of his intentions in a way his words never could have done. This kiss brooked no argument and her traitorous body acquiesced without even a whimper.

She closed her eyes. Tasting him. Savoring him. Letting his lips transmit alien, wonderful, tantalizing sensations to the rest of her body. Amazed to feel her breasts tingle, nipples harden to taut peaks, her aching center long for his touch, for his mouth, for his— Her eyes flew open and she let out a cry of pure agony.

Chase jerked back, his heart a thunder in his ears. He stared at her as he tried to catch his breath. She lay, breathing hard, her eyes wide, her body trembling slightly. He saw that he'd freed the first two buttons on her blouse, laying bare the fair freckled skin above her full breasts.

He stepped back, realizing how close he'd come to taking her right there on the table. The realization frightened him more than he wanted to admit. She filled him with a need so powerful—

She sat up, swinging her legs over the side of the table as she pulled down her skirt and then quickly buttoned her shirt, smoothing it over her swollen belly, tears in her eyes.

He felt like a teenager, as embarrassed by what he'd done as she looked. The words *I'm sorry* came to his lips but he wouldn't let himself say them. The effect this woman had on him scared the hell out of him. He called on the anger, reminding himself that the child she carried was some other man's. He let the wave of jealousy that followed that thought fuel his anger.

"I wondered just how far you would go with this charade of yours," he said, grabbing his crutches as he backed toward the door. "Now I know."

It wasn't until he'd gone out the back door, felt the snow against his face and taken a deep breath of the cold winter air that he let his defenses down. His chest hurt with an ache so foreign to him— He tried not to remember the look of hurt on her face or the way her gaze clutched at his heart. *My God, he was falling for this woman.* It wasn't possible. Not in just twenty-four hours. Then he felt a jolt so strong it made him stumble. *What if she's telling the truth, what if this happened last summer and that baby she's carrying really is yours?*

HE MADE HIS ESCAPE to the barn amazingly fast considering his disability, Marni thought. She stood, leaning against the dining-room table, too shaky to leave the room, too embarrassed. Her pounding heart filled with guilt. Tears of shame stung her eyes.

Chase's first kiss had been unavoidable. The almost kiss in the barn was foolhardy at best. This… She glanced back at the table, the dishes and food pushed aside, and closed her eyes, trying to block out the sensation of his lips, his hands on her skin.

She opened her eyes at the sound of someone entering the room and lifted her head high, ready to put on a strong front for the family members she knew must have been waiting outside the door, listening to each sordid sound.

"What has my son done now?" Jabe demanded.

Obviously seeing how distraught she was, Jabe ordered her hot chocolate with marshmallows and led her into the library, even giving her his chair in front of the fire.

"I wish I could explain Chase to you," he said after

adding more logs to the fire. He took the chair beside her and handed her a large mug of hot chocolate from the tray Hilda had brought in.

She took a sip, still fighting tears. She rarely cried. She'd always seen it as a weakness, one she didn't have the time or energy for. But right now—

"He seems so cold, so distant and unfeeling," she said. "And other times— Has he always been like that?"

"I wouldn't know." Jabe seemed to hesitate. "I never knew my son until he was fourteen. I didn't even know he existed before then."

Marni stared at him in shock.

"I don't know how much my son has told you about his childhood."

As far as Marni knew, Chase hadn't told Else much of anything, especially about his childhood. "Not a lot."

He sighed as if he dreaded what he was about to say. "Chase's mother was the most beautiful woman I've ever known. Her name was Lottie, short for Charlotte. Lottie was my first, my last, my only true love."

Marni frowned to herself. Poor Vanessa. She'd be a fool not to know how Jabe felt and Vanessa was no fool. No wonder she came off as mean-spirited toward Chase.

"Lottie was…to put it bluntly…from the wrong background. Her father worked for mine. So when she came to me and told me she was pregnant with my child—"

"You sent her away."

"My father discharged hers and gave her money to have an abortion, at least that's what he told me." Jabe had the decency to look ashamed. "I was engaged to Vanessa by this time. We'd met at college and her family and mine were…compatible. I thought I would forget Lottie."

"What happened to her and Chase?"

"They had some hard times." He looked away, his face

drawn. "Lottie wasn't well. Chase took care of her the best he could until almost the end."

Chase took care of himself *and* his mother? He was only a child!

Jabe looked into the fire. "Chase finally came to me for help. I realize now how hard that was for him. He was fourteen, proud even then and just as stubborn. He hated me for what he felt I'd done to his mother."

Marni felt sick to her stomach. She thought of Chase and that easy, loving gentleness he had with the horses.

"I might as well tell you the rest, Chase probably will."

His words filled her with dread.

"I wanted something of Lottie so badly that when Chase came to me, I made him a bargain. If he would acknowledge that he was my son, I would help his mother."

"How could you do such a thing?" Marni cried without thinking. Trying to buy his son. How hateful of him. How incredibly selfish. She could see why Chase had told Elise the things he had about Jabe. Chase had to hate his father. And yet he didn't. He was here at the ranch now because he thought Jabe's life was in danger.

"I only wanted what was mine," Jabe said defensively.

And at any price. Just as he had now, changing his will in an attempt to get the grandchild he so desperately wanted.

"Poor Chase," she said, not wanting to think of the childhood he must have had. No wonder he didn't want children of his own or marriage. "He must have needed your help desperately to agree to your terms."

"He's never forgiven me no matter how hard I've tried to make it up to him."

Marni almost felt sorry for Jabe, for the anguish and regret she heard in his voice. Almost. "What happened to his mother?"

"Chase thought my money and influence could save her.

All I could do was to make her last months as painless as possible.''

Marni felt tears rush to her eyes. She turned away. Oh, Chase. She tried to imagine him as a boy, caring for his mother, and finally at fourteen, coming for help to the father who'd abandoned them. How hard it must have been. And then to have his mother die anyway. He must have felt betrayed in so many ways.

''You see why it's important that Chase not make the same mistake I did,'' Jabe said.

Marni saw that Jabe Calloway's motives were anything but selfless. He wanted a grandchild and he didn't seem to care how he accomplished that, even if it meant buying one. Or helping her convince Chase that he was the father of Elise's child.

If only the storm would let up and she could take off this silly maternity form and go back to being Marni McCumber, the sensible, the confident, the woman in control of her life, and more important, the woman in control of her feelings.

''Is there a chance that my baby's in danger because of your will?''

''There is nothing to worry about, I assure you.''

Marni wished she shared his confidence. ''Why is Chase so worried then?''

''Chase is a worrier by nature.''

''I can see that he might not be too trusting,'' Marni said.

''Especially with me?'' Jabe said. ''I'll admit I've made some mistakes in my life. That's why I want to try to right them with a grandchild. Is that so wrong?''

''Yes,'' Chase said from behind them. Neither of them had heard him come in. He stood leaning on his crutches, his face twisted in anger. ''Because you try to buy what you want. You've tried to buy me from the first day I met you. You tried again when you changed your will. If I'd come into the family business, you wouldn't have put a price tag on your first grandchild.''

"So I wanted you to be a part of the family business more than I even wanted a grandchild," Jabe bellowed. "Is that so heinous?"

"Could you leave Jabe and me alone?" he said to Marni without looking at her.

Glad to escape the tension she felt in the room, she left without a word, closing the door behind her. She wanted to be as far away from Jabe Calloway as she could get and wished Elise wasn't carrying Chase's child for more reasons than she wanted to think about.

As she started for the stairs, she realized that she'd lost one of her earrings. The thought of having Hilda find it in the middle of the dining-room table sent her scurrying in to look for it. She found the small silver loop on the floor where it must have fallen and quickly replaced it in her ear. As she was coming out of the dining room, she saw Lilly emerge from under the stairs and heard the soft whisper of the secret passage door closing. Lilly saw her and touched her lips in a mock plea for secrecy and silence, then lifted the glass in her hand in a salute before she headed up the stairs. Marni watched her in concern but she seemed steady enough.

After a few moments, Marni walked over to the spot where the door had opened in the paneling and felt along the wall for a few minutes but no secret doorway opened at her fingertips. If she hadn't seen Lilly appear, she wouldn't have believed the passage existed. Nothing about the wall gave any indication there was a paneled doorway hidden in it.

And where did the passageway go? She remembered Lilly's face peering out of the tiny window below the third-story eave. Is that where she'd come from? Why all the secrecy? Surely Lilly didn't think she was successfully hiding her drinking problem from anyone.

As Marni turned, she collided with Felicia.

"Did you lose something?" Felicia asked, one dark eyebrow shooting up with interest.

She had that same know-it-all look on her face as her husband. Smug. Self-satisfied. What she didn't look was pregnant. The irony of it made Marni smile.

"I was just admiring the beautiful wood," Marni said.

"You like it?" Felicia asked in surprise. She wrinkled her perfect little nose. "It's a little too dark for my tastes."

"It's like the house, it reflects Jabe and his position," Marni said.

"Really?" Felicia's interest in the pretentious house seemed to wane. "When exactly is your baby due?" she asked, her gaze dropping to Marni's protruding stomach.

"Valentine's Day," Marni said.

Felicia looked as if she might want to throw up again. "I heard that you've befriended my sister-in-law."

The change of subject was so abrupt it took Marni a moment to realize Felicia was referring to Lilly. News definitely traveled fast in this house. But Marni did wonder how Felicia had found out. She doubted Chase had mentioned it to Felicia, a woman Marni figured he wished was still in one of those deep, dark holes of forgotten memory.

"Lilly was upset," Marni said. "I just tried to comfort her."

"Lilly is always upset," Felicia said disagreeably. "Upset, drunk and—" She looked up, her eyes darkening. "Dangerous."

"Dangerous?" Marni repeated.

Felicia nodded conspiratorially. "I hate to be the one to tell you this, but Lilly has never been well, and since the baby…died."

"How did it die?" she asked, reminded of Lilly's claim that Vanessa had killed it.

Felicia did a poor job of pretending discomfort. "It says crib death on the poor little thing's death certificate," she whispered. "The baby had somehow suffocated."

When Marni didn't question her about the "somehow," Felicia added, "The truth is, Vanessa found Lilly leaning over the crib with a pillow in her hands and the baby dead. She murdered her own daughter and now she wanders this place crazier than a loon, clinging to that damned stuffed doll and crying."

Marni shuddered at the picture Felicia painted of Lilly.

"That's why I wanted to warn you," she said earnestly. "If you're smart, you'll stay away from her. She could be a threat to you." Felicia let her gaze drop and Marni's hand went protectively to Sam.

Having obviously accomplished what she'd set out to, Felicia turned and strolled away. Marni watched her go, unable to throw off the image of Lilly standing over her daughter's crib, a pillow in her hands. Nor could she forget the sound of the baby crying coming up through the heat vent, when there was no baby in the house.

Chapter Eight

Marni hurried up the stairs to her room, wanting to avoid further contact with Chase's family for a few hours. She tried not to think about what Felicia had told her. It was obvious Lilly needed help, if for nothing more than her drinking problem. So why wasn't someone in this family seeing that she got it?

Marni felt uneasy and almost...afraid as she closed her bedroom door behind her and locked it. Afraid not of Dayton, Felicia or even Lilly, but something less tangible, a feeling of misfortune that seemed to permeate this dark, joyless house.

She checked to make sure the adjoining-room door was locked, as well, feeling silly and strangely paranoid. She couldn't remember ever being afraid before. Not even of the dark.

Part of it is the storm, she told herself as she went to the window to stare out. From the gray of the sky, huge snowflakes continued to fall, spiraling down to form a suffocating blanket of white.

She felt trapped. In this house. In her own dark thoughts. She couldn't stop thinking about Lilly and her infant daughter. Nor about Chase and his mother.

She knew so little about Chase. Elise knew even less. Why hadn't Elise known he had a different mother from

Hayes's and Dayton's? That he'd been a bastard. That he hadn't even known his father until he was fourteen. That he didn't work for Calloway Ranches. What *did* he do for a living? And why hadn't he mentioned any of this to El?

Had he purposely kept things from her or had the two never talked about anything...important? But according to El, they had talked about marriage and children. And El thought he worked for Calloway Ranches. Was it just because he'd been driving one of the ranch trucks? Or had he led her to believe he worked for his father?

Marni couldn't shake the sense that something was desperately wrong here. Or maybe she was just feeling how wrong it was to pretend to be Elise, especially considering her own reaction to Chase.

Unable to call her twin until the phone lines were restored, Marni busied herself building a fire in the fireplace, hoping the physical activity would stop her thoughts of Chase and his family. But when she had the fire going, she couldn't stand still long enough to enjoy its warmth. Instead, she paced the room, worrying about Elise and the baby and what she was going to tell her twin when she could finally call. Marni stopped pacing at a sound in the hallway.

She listened. There it was again. A fumbling, stumbling sound outside her bedroom door. Lilly?

As Marni went to unlock the door, she expected to find Lilly weaving outside.

But when Marni opened the door, the hallway was empty. She stood for a moment, listening, then looked toward the stairs. The thought of Lilly trying to maneuver the steps in an inebriated state sent Marni hurrying to the top of the stairway. She glanced down over the railing.

Silence filled the house. "Not a creature was stirring," Marni whispered.

Wrong. She caught a movement at the base of the stairs, then saw a flash of pale pink.

Marni groaned, remembering Lilly's earlier drinking. She could be much worse by now. Someone needed to see that she was all right. With another groan, Marni hurried after the woman, ignoring that little voice in her head that told her to mind her own business.

As Marni reached the first floor and turned the corner toward the dining room, she saw to her surprise that the secret panel beneath the stairs stood open. She halted for a moment, looking into the narrow darkness. Lilly wasn't her responsibility. Maybe she should heed Felicia's warning about Lilly and go back upstairs.

With a sigh, Marni stepped closer. *When are you going to stop being such a sucker for anyone in trouble?* "Lilly?" she whispered as she stuck her head into the opening. There was just enough room inside for the narrow stairway. She could heard the soft pad of footfalls on the steps disappearing up into the darkness.

Why had Lilly left the door open? Was she so inebriated she forgot to close it? Or had she known Marni would follow her?

Marni felt a chill as she took one tentative step into the passageway. *Don't do this. This is stupid. This is scary. This is crazy.* But she couldn't shake off the feeling that Lilly Calloway was in trouble. That's why Lilly had come to her bedroom door. That's why she'd left the hidden panel open. For some reason, Lilly wanted her to follow.

At least Marni hoped that was the case as she started up the stairs, the steps curling up and up in a tight spiral that seemed unending in the semidarkness. Natural light seemed to filter down from somewhere at the top.

A few steps and Marni heard the secret panel close below her. Her heart thumped wildly. Who'd closed the door? Someone downstairs? Or did it close on its own? What did it matter? That avenue of escape was gone and instantly the stairwell seemed more claustrophobic than before. She felt as if she'd been sealed up in the walls of the old house never to be seen again.

She brushed away such ridiculous thoughts, hoping they were indeed ridiculous, as she climbed more quickly. That's when she heard it. At first she thought it was her imagination. Her hand dropped to Sam as she stopped to listen and catch her breath.

It was faint, but definitely a baby laughing and cooing softly. The sound brought goose bumps to her skin. She shivered, telling herself there was no baby in this house. Someone just wanted her to think there was. But that frightened her all the more. *Why* would anyone want her to think there was a baby here? What possible purpose could they have?

Marni heard a door open overhead. And close again softly. She hurried up the steps only to have them end in a wall. A skylight above her let in what little light there was in the passageway.

Beyond the wall, she could still hear the baby, no longer laughing and cooing, but fussing. She could hear another voice now. A woman's voice, trying to soothe the infant.

Marni examined the wall. She could only assume it also had a secret panel she would have to press. She ran her hand along the dark wood, the memory fresh in her mind how she'd been unable to open the lower door the time she'd tried. Her heart rate skyrocketed as her fingers felt frantically along the wood. A scream rose in her throat.

She felt a narrow vertical notch in the wall and realized with body weakening relief that Lilly hadn't closed the door all the way. Slipping her fingers in the groove, she pushed and the door began to slide open, reinforcing Marni's hope that Lilly had wanted her to come up here.

Marni slid the door aside and stepped into what appeared to be an attic. The air smelled of dust and age, but definitely felt warmer than in the stairwell. Furniture stood like sentinels in front of the doorway. Marni started around a huge antique bureau, remembering Lilly's pale face peering out from the small window on the third floor. Unless she missed her guess, this was the room.

"Lilly?" Marni called, her voice little more than a whisper as she stepped around the bureau. Deeper in the attic, the baby started to cry as a woman's voice tried to hush it.

The rich wood of armoires and chiffoniers, credenzas and tallboys gleamed, the feeling of another, gentler lifetime in the valuable antique pieces. Why didn't Jabe and Vanessa use these wonderful antiques instead of the massive log furniture that looked so out of place in the old Victorian house?

Marni had started to take a tentative step deeper into the room when she heard a rustling sound like taffeta and the scrape of a shoe as someone moved across the floor. She froze behind a massive armoire.

Until that moment, she'd believed it was Lilly who'd maneuvered her up here.

Now she wasn't so sure. The step had sounded sure. Not like that of a woman who'd had too much wine to drink. What if it wasn't Lilly who'd lured her up here? All she'd seen was a glimpse of Lilly's pale pink dress in the shadowed darkness and just the hint of a staggered gait.

The baby quit cooing. The room filled with silence, thick and heavy. Cold fear raced across Marni's skin as quick and frightening as a spider.

"Elise?"

Just that one word, whispered hoarsely in the darkness. Marni's pulse thrummed in her ears. Goose bumps skittered across her flesh. She held her breath, no longer pretending her fear wasn't warranted.

"Poor Elise," came the whisper again.

Marni recoiled at the hatred in the voice, bumping into

the bureau behind her. Instantly she realized her mistake. She'd given away her location. The armoire beside her came toppling over.

CHASE CLOSED the barn door, pleased he'd accomplished what he'd set out to. His arms ached from the hours he'd spent stacking hay and pulling feed sacks down from the storage loft. His good leg ached from standing on it for so long, his casted leg ached from trying not to stand on it. He felt exhausted after all the weeks of inactivity. But he'd been too busy even to think about Miss McCumber. Most of the time.

On top of that he'd had the joy of listening to Dayton and Hayes grumbling and complaining as they shoveled out the horse stalls.

All except for Wind Chaser's stall. The stallion wouldn't allow either of the brothers to get near it. Chase had found no small satisfaction that he was the only Calloway the new horse at the ranch would tolerate. Although he did wonder what had upset the horse to such an extent. Probably the storm, he told himself. Or maybe the horse liked it at Calloway Ranch as much as Chase did and realized they had that in common.

Chase felt good as he came through the back door of the house, assured that his physical exhaustion would keep his mind from wandering to that one particular pregnant woman.

But the moment he closed the door behind him, he felt her presence. And something even worse. A concern for her that he'd promised himself he wasn't going to allow. The house felt too quiet. He started to worry that he shouldn't have left her alone, even with Jabe and others around— maybe especially with them around. He'd been keeping a close eye on Dayton and Hayes, up until about thirty minutes ago when he'd lost track of time and them.

Chase picked up the hall phone and dialed her room. No

answer. He pushed open the kitchen door and stuck his head in. "Have you seen Elise?" he asked Cook.

She looked up from the open door of the woodstove oven. The smell of a large piece of prime rib wafted toward him as she closed the oven door.

She shook her head and went back to her cooking as if she had better things to do than keep track of his women.

Chase swore under his breath as he headed for the service elevator. The stairs were just too dangerous on crutches, although he'd tried them out of stubbornness his first day only because Jabe had insisted he not.

He wondered where everybody was. Probably in their rooms, avoiding each other. If he knew Vanessa, she'd be working out in the exercise room off the master bedroom. Felicia would be doing her nails or something productive like that. Lilly, well, who knew where Lilly might be. He'd seen her sneaking around the house like a drunken ghost in the days he'd been here. No wonder Hayes spent so much time on the road.

And the same could be said of Dayton. He and Felicia seemed to lead separate lives as far as Chase could tell. He doubted a baby would change that. It made him glad he had no intentions of ever getting married, let alone having children.

By the time the elevator groaned to a stop on the third floor, Chase had pretty well convinced himself that Miss McCumber was none of his concern. It wasn't as if he really believed she was carrying his baby. But still he stopped at her door and knocked softly. When she didn't answer, he went to his own room and built a fire, then slumped in the chair in front of it, watching the flames dance along the logs, determined to relax and not think about her. Especially the part where he'd almost taken her on the dining-room table. Whatever had possessed him?

He tried to steer his thoughts to business all the work

he'd have when he finally got out of here. He'd already made up his mind. He was leaving the moment the roads opened. And as for Jabe—well, he was on his own. If Miss McCumber wanted to stay here and continue her charade, that was her problem.

Chase swore again. Wishing she fit his image of a gold digger. If she'd been more like Felicia it would have made things a whole lot easier. But instead, she was so damned wholesome-looking and so…chaste. If he didn't know better, he'd think her a virgin.

Nor could he forget the sight of her kneeling beside Lilly's chair in the garden room, holding the crying, obviously sloshed woman and trying to comfort her. It was that compassion, along with everything else, that threw him. And the feeling that she wasn't the kind of woman who fell in love with just any man, had a four-day tryst and didn't take the proper precautions. She seemed so…nice.

He had to find her. Not to make sure she was all right. No, he had to find her just so he'd know what she was up to.

He knocked at their adjoining door. When she didn't answer, he tried the knob. Locked. He knocked again and listened for even the slightest sound. When none came, he used the key he was sure his father had left for him in the lock and opened the door without even a twinge of guilt.

He'd expected to find her napping or sitting in the chair before the fire, ignoring his knock. He found neither.

Damn. Where had she gone? What was she up to? Trouble. Because trouble dogged women like her who got too involved in other people's lives. As he went to the window, he assured himself she deserved every moment of whatever disaster befell her. He'd half expected her car to be gone.

Of course, it wasn't. She couldn't get out even with four-wheel drive. The snow was too deep. But, to his surprise, he saw that the storm had stopped. Someone was out plowing the ranch yard. It wouldn't be long until the county snowplow would be coming up the road. And Miss Mc-Cumber would be going down the road.

She wouldn't be happy about that, he told himself. She had probably planned to stay here until she got what she wanted. And she seemed to want Chase Calloway. The fool woman.

Turning from the window, Chase decided he'd check downstairs for her again. The best thing he could do for both of them was to get her out of this house. He'd started for the door when he heard what sounded like thunder rumble over his head. He looked up to see dust sifting down from the rafters and realized that a large object had just hit the floor over his head. He stared at the ceiling and frowned. What was someone doing in the attic?

MARNI HAD ONLY an instant before the towering antique closet came crashing down. She fell back into a chest of drawers as the armoire toppled, smashing the credenza behind it as it fell in a loud thunderclap of splintered wood and destruction.

Marni felt the massive wardrobe graze her arm, breeze past her face and hit the maternity form with a force that knocked her breath out. Then it crashed into the credenza, flattening it as if it were built of toothpicks. Marni stood staring down at the pile of splintered wood as she fought to corral her racing heart. She wasn't hurt. No harm was done.

She heard a door open and close on the far side of the room and the sound of footsteps retreat down creaky stairs.

Relief. She leaned back against the chest of drawers, reassuring herself again that it had been a close call but she was all right. She looked down, surprised to see that her borrowed maternity shirt was torn from where the armoire had hit her protruding stomach. She stared at Sam. The form would survive. But would a real baby have? Her blood turned to ice.

All she wanted was out of the attic. She hurriedly stepped over the shattered armoire and around another large wardrobe and stopped. To her left, a child-size door creaked open. From inside, Marni could hear the sound of the baby cooing softly. Her heart thundered in her chest as she slowly knelt to gaze through the crack between the door and the jamb.

Light from a small round window under the eave at the back of the room illuminated the eerie scene. A window much like the one Marni had seen Lilly peering out of yesterday afternoon. Next to the window sat a rocker with a ball of pink yarn on the seat, a pair of knitting needles and two tiny baby booties, the second nearly completed.

The air suddenly filled with the startling cry of a baby. Marni jumped, her heart a sledgehammer inside her chest. An antique crib had been pushed back into a shadowed corner of the room. A mobile of hideous-faced clowns spun slowly above it in an invisible draft. From inside the crib the baby started to cry softly.

Marni had to bend down to see in through the doorway and as she did, she noticed the scrape on the floor where someone had recently moved a large object away from the door.

She stuck her head in tentatively, but the room was empty except for the rocker and the crib. Carefully she slipped in, surprised to find she had room to stand once inside.

As the baby whimpered, Marni moved toward the crib and, calling on all her courage, looked over the side.

Something the size of a baby lay wrapped in a pink baby blanket. With trembling fingers, Marni pulled back the blanket.

A face leaped out at her. She fought back a scream as she realized what was lying in the crib. The blank eyes stared up out of a grayed worn face. Not a baby. But a doll. Lilly's rag doll.

Marni tried to still her thundering heart as she pushed the doll and the blanket aside to reveal a small tape recorder.

"Hush now," a woman said as the baby began to cry again on the tape. With a start, Marni recognized the voice. "Stop that fretting," Vanessa said impatiently.

Marni hit the stop button on the recorder. The baby quit crying. Vanessa fell silent.

Marni felt sick as she stared down at the crib and the doll baby inside it. Who had done this? What was Vanessa's voice doing on the tape? Was this Lilly's way of coping with the loss of her baby? Or someone else's sick way of tormenting Lilly?

Behind her, Marni heard a sound. She spun around. The child-size door shut.

Blindly, Marni flung herself at the closing door.

Chapter Nine

"What the hell?" Chase cried as the door hit him. He dropped the flashlight in his hand. The light spun in an arc, illuminating the source of his pain, then the flashlight hit the floor with a thud at Miss McCumber's feet. "I should have known it would be you."

She looked up at him. "It amazes me that any woman could have ever fallen in love with you." She handed him the flashlight.

"Yeah, well, that makes two of us." He pointed the beam at her.

"Do you mind?" she said, shielding her eyes.

He shifted the circle of light to a spot on the floor between them, but not before he'd noticed two things that surprised him. Her disheveled appearance. And the fear in her eyes. "Want to tell me what's going on?"

Marni glared at him as she drew her shirt together over her swollen stomach. "I was almost killed!"

Leave it to a woman to magnify things.

"I'm the one who got hit with the door," he told her, then recalled the fear in her eyes. Surely just catching her snooping around the house hadn't put that scared look on her face. And it wasn't as though he could frighten her even when he'd tried.

"Why should I expect you to believe me?" she said.

"You're a mess," he said softer than he'd meant to. He reached out to wipe a smudge from her cheek with his thumb. "There's probably a good reason why you're up here."

She looked as if she might cry. But she also looked damned and determined not to. He watched her face, amused and intrigued by her. She wasn't like anyone he'd ever known. And yet, sometimes she reminded him a little of himself.

"So why don't you tell me about this hair-raising experience you had," he said, brushing hers back from her face.

She pulled away and didn't seem all that willing to tell him anything. But he realized something had happened up here that had upset her. Not only was she a dusty mess, it looked as if she'd torn her maternity top. Both filled him with concern, a concern that made him angry. He fought the urge to tell her she had no business in the attic, no business here at all.

"I was worried about Lilly," she began hesitantly.

He bit his tongue to keep his mouth shut. Hadn't he warned her not to get involved with this family? Especially Lilly?

She seemed surprised he hadn't said anything and, obviously encouraged by his silence, charged ahead with her story.

He amazed himself. He kept his mouth shut through the climb up through some secret staircase, as ridiculously stupid as that was, right to where the armoire crashed and she was almost killed, even though he could tell she was purposely leaving out details for whatever reason he could not imagine, probably just exaggerating how close a call it was.

"Didn't I tell you that you were in danger?" he demanded when he couldn't stand it anymore.

"I thought Lilly was in trouble," she cried in high indignation.

"*Lilly* was in trouble?" Chase asked, trying to control his anger, which was matched only by his fear for this woman. It surprised him how relieved he felt that she hadn't been hurt. "It sounds to me like you're the one who's always in trouble." He hobbled toward her. "Do you have any sense at all? Going up hidden stairways to old attics following a woman who at best is an alcoholic and at worst is... unstable?"

"I thought it was a cry for help."

"You're the one who needs help," he retorted. "You just can't seem to stay out of other people's lives, can you?"

"Like yours?"

"Show me this fallen armoire." He handed her the flashlight. "Unless you're afraid to go back there."

Her chin came up, her eyes darkened like clouds before a hailstorm. "Maybe you *should* see it for yourself."

He didn't like the sound of that.

She led him around several large pieces of furniture and he realized he'd had no idea any of this was up here. It surprised him and made him wonder about Jabe Calloway and what else he kept hidden.

She stopped, waiting for him to maneuver the last few steps on his crutches.

He rounded the corner of a huge buffet and came to an abrupt stop. "What the hell?" He took the flashlight from her and flicked the light over the fallen armoire, his gaze widening in horror as he saw the armoire and the splintered credenza beneath it.

"My God, you could have been killed."

"I know, that's what I told you," she said with no small amount of satisfaction.

"Are you sure you're all right? And the baby—"

She gave him a *now*-he-cares look. "I'm fine. The baby's fine. But there's something else you'd better see."

He let her lead him back to the small door she'd nailed

him with earlier. Taking the flashlight from his hand, she shone it inside the room.

Chase bent down to peer in. "A nursery?"

"For a dead baby," she said, giving him a chill. "I *told* you I heard a baby crying." He watched her duck through the doorway. It took him a little more effort to get through the door, even when he left his crutches outside the room.

She went to an antique crib set back against the wall and reached inside.

Instantly, he heard a baby fussing, then start to cry. Something about the sound freeze-dried his blood. Then Vanessa's voice came on the tape.

He limped over and hit the stop button on the tape recorder, a feeling of abhorrence in the pit of his stomach when he saw the worn rag doll lying in the crib.

"See why I'm worried about Lilly?" he demanded.

"She wasn't the only one on that tape. You heard Vanessa's voice."

"That makes Lilly even more perverse," Chase shot back.

"Maybe Lilly wasn't the one who did this. Or pushed over the armoire."

He looked at her. "I thought you said you followed Lilly up here?"

"I thought it was Lilly. At the time."

He raked a hand through his hair. "Based on what?"

"Based on..." She took a deep breath and avoided his gaze. "I saw a flash of pale pink like Lilly wears, and the person seemed to kind of stagger."

He couldn't believe it. "You're not even sure it was a woman?"

She didn't even have to open her mouth. He saw the answer on her face.

"So you have no idea who pushed over the wardrobe. Or if it was even meant for you."

She stepped away from him to finger a hand-knit baby blanket thrown over the back of the rocker, the only other piece of furniture in the small room. "It was meant for me. The person said my name and…"

"And what?" he asked, knowing she and her baby were the targets, but wishing she could give him another explanation.

"It was just a hoarse whisper from the other side of the armoire. The person said, 'Elise? Poor Elise.' Then I bumped against the chest of drawers, and I guess there was no doubt where I was. The armoire toppled over."

He swore under his breath and almost launched into another one of his tirades—not that they seemed to have any effect on this woman. He could tell her that her life and her baby's was in danger until he was blue in the face and she'd still do whatever she damn well pleased, especially if she thought someone else was in trouble.

Why couldn't she be like Felicia, self-centered, mercenary, coldhearted? Just to make his life simpler. He saw her freeze in motion, her fingers on the baby quilt, her gaze directed at the seat of the rocker.

"What is it?" he demanded.

"There were knitting needles and a pair of almost finished pink baby booties on this rocker just minutes ago—" Her gaze leaped up to his; she looked as if she'd seen an apparition. "Do you smell that?"

He caught the scent on a slight breeze that seemed to whisper through the attic. He recognized it immediately. Gardenia. Lilly's cloying perfume.

"Come on, you're getting out of this house." He crawled from the small room, anxious to breathe fresh air, anxious to get out of the attic. He picked up his crutches and took a few steps before he realized she wasn't beside him. He turned to find her standing outside the nursery door, glaring at him.

"We're just going to pretend we didn't find this room?" she demanded. "That the armoire toppled over on its own? That Lilly doesn't have a drinking problem or worse?"

He hobbled back to her. "Don't you get it?" he said through gritted teeth. "Someone tried to kill you and your baby up here today. Forget Lilly. Forget her problems." He gazed into her eyes. She looked frightened and he wondered if he'd gotten through to her. He doubted it. If she was scared, it was for someone else—not herself. The woman was incredible. "Just worry about yourself right now—and this kid of yours."

"What is that, your philosophy of life?" she demanded. "Every man for himself?"

"It works for me."

He could tell she was gearing up for an argument, but he didn't give her a chance. "The storm has stopped. Get packed. You're getting out of here, whether you like it or not." He steered her through a labyrinth of boxes, more furniture and old trunks to a doorway that opened onto the attic stairs. "Give me the keys to your car and I'll get it warmed up," he said when they reached her bedroom door. "Stay here until I get back. Lock your door. And don't argue."

MARNI MCCUMBER had never taken orders well. Especially from men who thought it was their birthright to give them. But most especially from a man like Chase Calloway. The all-out arrogance of the man!

She stood in the middle of her bedroom, indignant and defiant. Pack? She had nothing to pack. She took off the ruined maternity top and threw it in the trash. She'd have to wear Chase's shirt since she had nothing else. Once she'd retrieved her coat from the closet downstairs, she'd be as packed as she could get. So what was she supposed to do until then?

She felt herself begin to tremble. All the anger ran out of her and she stood in the middle of the floor, shaking. Chase was right. She had to think about Elise and the baby. That falling armoire had been for her sister—not Marni Mc-Cumber. But no one knew about Elise, Marni thought, hugging herself to keep out the cold fear. Elise and the baby were safe. For the time being.

She went to the window. It had indeed finally stopped snowing. Bits of blue broke through the grayness, bringing shafts of sunshine that made the snow sparkle like prisms. She could see Dayton behind the wheel of a Calloway Ranch pickup, plowing snow from the ranch yard. She was going home. Home for Christmas. Isn't that what she wanted?

She caught a glimpse of Chase hobbling on his crutches from her car toward the barn. If she could have gotten the window open, she would have thrown something at him. "Whether she wanted to leave or not"? Was he kidding? She'd never even wanted to come here, let alone have to stay two days and pretend to be seven months pregnant and put up with Chase Calloway all that time.

So why was he going to the barn now? Probably to do something with the horses. Chase had a way with horses. And some women, she reminded herself. Maybe all women.

She watched him reach the barn and was surprised to see that Jabe had been waiting for him. Even from this distance, she could tell they were arguing. She figured that's all they did. She wondered what about now. The will? Elise's safety? Or would Chase tell Jabe about Lilly? Would he try to convince Jabe that his daughter-in-law needed help?

Marni couldn't see Jabe Calloway being very sympathetic to Lilly's plight. Actually, there wasn't anyone in this house who seemed to care about Lilly. Except Hayes. Maybe. She promised herself she'd call Hayes once she got to Bozeman and tell him about the nursery in the attic. Surely he'd see that his wife got help. That was the least she could do, no matter what Chase said about not getting involved.

She hugged Sam, remembering the hoarse whisper, "Poor Elise," just before the armoire fell. She was involved as long as there was any chance Elise and the baby were in danger.

Marni glanced toward the barn again. Chase and his father were no longer standing in the doorway. In the distance, she could hear a snowplow coming up the county road. She told herself she was as anxious to get out of here as Chase was to have her go. She already felt she'd betrayed her sister just letting the man kiss her, let alone—

Marni swung around at a sound behind her, remembering belatedly Chase's instructions to lock her door.

The remorseful expression on Lilly's face scared Marni as much as the realization that the woman had just sneaked quietly into Marni's room, closed and locked the door and now stood with her hands behind her back.

"Lilly," Marni said, all her surprise and fear echoed in that one word. "I didn't hear you come in."

She smiled, her lips turning up, her eyes turning hard as stones. "You've been listening to them, haven't you?" She stepped closer, her hands still hidden behind her back.

Marni watched Lilly approach with uneasiness, desperately trying to assure herself that she had nothing to fear.

"The storm's over," Marni said, her nerves taut. What was the woman hiding behind her? "Chase has gone out to start my car for me. He should be back any minute and then I'll be leaving." She hoped.

Lilly didn't seem to hear. Her gaze skittered around the room. "What did they tell you?" she asked, drawing nearer. "Did they tell you I'm crazy? That I've never been well? Did Hayes tell you that I never loved him? That I married him for his money?" She stopped within a few feet of Marni, their gazes locked. Marni smelled alcohol and gardenia, the same scent as in the attic. "Did they tell you I killed my own baby?"

"It wasn't your fault that the baby died," Marni said. "Sudden infant death syndrome is—"

"Is that what Vanessa told you?" She smiled. "They lie to protect the family name. They play tricks on me. They do things to make me think I'm crazy. To even make me think I killed my own baby."

Marni looked into Lilly's eyes, her heart urging her to reach out to this obviously hurting woman. Her brain screaming for her to run.

"I should hate you," Lilly said, her gaze falling to Sam. "But I know it's not your fault." Suddenly Lilly brought her hands out in front of her. Marni stumbled back against the windowsill before she saw what Lilly held.

"I'm sorry they're pink," Lilly said.

Oh my God. Marni stared down at the pair of hand-knit pink baby booties nestled in Lilly's palms. The same ones she'd seen earlier on the rocker in the attic.

"Pink was the only color yarn I had," Lilly said as she closed the distance between them. "I started knitting them for—" She looked up, tears flooded her eyes.

"They're beautiful," Marni said, taking the tiny booties Lilly held out to her. "Thank you." She cradled them in the palm of one hand, her heart a drum pounding in her ears. Lilly had been in the attic. The booties proved it.

But as she looked at the woman, Marni thought of how Lilly had finished the last few stitches of the booties to give them to the baby she thought Marni carried. A baby she thought was stealing everything from her dead one.

Marni felt a surge of emotion at Lilly's generous gift. Her eyes filled with tears as she pulled Lilly into her arms and hugged her, expecting the thin body to be frail. Instead, Lilly felt incredibly strong.

Lilly pulled away first, seemingly embarrassed, then

looked toward the door as if she'd heard someone out in the hallway. Chase? "I have to go."

Marni's heart broke at the fear she saw in the woman's face. "I'm worried about you. What is it you're so frightened of?"

Lilly looked up at her and seemed surprised by Marni's concern. "They wouldn't hurt me. A woman who's too drunk, too crazy, to know what they're planning." Her eyes darkened. "It's you they want—"

She stepped to the door, hesitated for a moment to listen, then was gone in a flash of pale pink, leaving only the hint of her perfume and her imbibed wine wafting through the room like a ghost.

Marni looked down at the tiny pink booties still nestled in her hand.

"You're not going to keep those?" Chase said from the open doorway, making her jump. "For all you know, she tried to kill you in the attic earlier."

Why then did her heart tell her differently?

"You'd be a fool to trust her," he said. "But you're also a fool if you think you and your baby will be safe as long as you continue to claim you're carrying my kid."

He shook his head in disgust as she placed the booties in her purse. "I've started your car to let it warm up. I'm sure you'll want to get going as soon as possible."

"You're so thoughtful," Marni said, not even bothering to hide her sarcasm. Chase turned and thumped down the hallway.

As Marni followed, she couldn't help feeling that she was abandoning Lilly. And that Lilly Calloway was in more serious trouble than Marni McCumber ever imagined.

Chapter Ten

By the time Marni retrieved her coat, Chase was already leaning on his crutches beside her car with a scowl on his handsome face. Exhaust rose thick and white, a spirit curling up into the sunny December day. Everywhere, the snow sparkled, diamond bright.

Marni followed the freshly shoveled path to the car, the knowledge that she'd failed her twin making her steps heavier than when she'd arrived. She'd failed Elise in more ways than she wanted to think about. At least she could put it all behind her once she left here. But Elise—

"I wish I could promise you that once you drive away, you'll be fine," Chase said as he opened the door for her. "It's not too late to straighten things out before you leave."

She climbed in and buckled her seat belt without looking at him. "Jabe has assured me—"

"Have it your way. But don't say I didn't warn you." Chase slammed the door before she could finish. She watched his broad back retreat toward the house and told herself the best thing she could do would be to drive off. Nothing would be accomplished by rolling down her window and yelling something rude at him.

But the thought of letting Chase Calloway have the last word was too unbearable. She rolled down her window. "If you select to remember you have a child—" She was going to say, "Call me." But Elise didn't have a place yet. And Marni McCumber wasn't Marni McCumber. "Call my sister. It's the only McCumber in the Bozeman phone book."

Chase turned, his narrowed gaze a pale blue that perfectly matched the wide-open Montana sky. She thought he'd say something nasty. She wanted him to. She told herself she'd been much too kind to Chase Calloway. He'd tried to frighten her, to intimidate her, to confuse her. She wanted to tell him just what she thought of him. All he had to do was say one word, any word and—

His gaze widened and she blinked in shock as he threw down his crutches and half hopped, half ran back to the car, jerked open the door, unsnapped her seat belt and, to her amazement, pulled her out and carried her toward the house.

For a moment, Marni was too stunned to speak. The moment passed. "Put me down, you—"

He did. But not until he'd kicked open the front door of the house and placed her inside as if putting down a very rare piece of glass. "Stay here," he commanded. Then he turned and hobbled/ran back to the car.

Marni rushed to the window to stare after him, shocked to see that her car appeared to be on fire. Smoke rolled out from under the hood and she could hear flames licking at the metal. She watched in horror as Chase reached in, turned off the engine and popped the hood latch. The flames licked up and out, bright orange; the smoke billowed higher and for a moment, Marni lost sight of Chase. Faster than most men can move without one leg in a cast, he had the hood thrown up and was dousing the engine's fire with shovelsful of fresh snow.

MARNI LET CHASE ease her into a chair in front of the fireplace in the library. The room grew quiet after Jabe had sent the rest of the family away. They hadn't gone easily, still asking questions about the fire and what was going on.

Marni was glad when they were gone. Unable to stop shaking, she watched as Chase rang Hilda for hot chocolate. Neither she nor Chase said anything to the man standing in front of the fire. Jabe looked pale and shrunken. He stood, holding on to the mantel, watching them with a look of total disbelief.

For a long moment, he didn't speak, then, "It was definitely not an accident." It was more a clarification than a question.

"The car was rigged so the engine would catch fire, very amateurish," Chase said and Marni wondered how he knew anything about such things. "This one worked off the heat of the engine. Whoever rigged it planned for the car to catch fire somewhere down the road after the engine got hot. They didn't plan on me starting the car and letting it warm up for such a long time."

Marni listened to Chase's voice but heard only one thing: Someone had tried to kill her because they thought she was Elise McCumber. Again. Because they thought she was carrying Jabe Calloway's first grandchild. This was no possible cry for help from a woman in pain. This was attempted murder. She met Jabe's blue-eyed gaze. "You said I was safe."

Jabe let out a low curse and headed for the liquor cabinet. "You need a little brandy to steady you." His hands shook as he splashed some into a snifter.

"She doesn't need brandy," Chase snapped. "She's pregnant."

Just then Hilda came in carrying Chase's crutches in one hand and a cup of something steaming in the other. Chase tossed the crutches aside and pressed the cup of hot chocolate into Marni's hands. She curled her fingers around it, hoping the warmth would help melt the core of icy fear inside her.

Chase laid a hand on her shoulder. Warm. Reassuring.

She hadn't wanted to believe that he might be right. She thought he was just trying to scare her. Her perception of him kept changing. A kaleidoscope of characteristics. She wondered how many people got to see the real Chase Calloway. Obviously Elise had.

He removed his hand and Marni felt a sense of loss. She took a sip of the hot liquid, forcing the cold to retreat. But nothing could scare off the fear. Someone had really tried to kill her. As crazy as that sounded. This was no toppling armoire. This was so much more deliberate. So much more frightening. If they'd succeeded, they would have only killed Marni McCumber and a maternity form. Of course, after that they'd have realized their mistake. Marni felt a shudder and took another sip of hot chocolate.

"What are you doing?" Jabe demanded.

She looked up to see Chase dialing the phone, knowing he was bluffing because the phones weren't working. Marni had tried again earlier to reach her sister.

"I'm calling the sheriff," Chase said.

"Hang up the phone," Jabe ordered. "This is a family matter."

"Like hell." Chase finished dialing. "Someone in this *family* is an attempted murderer, and has to be stopped."

"I know how to stop this," Jabe said. "And I will, if you hang up that phone. Now."

Chase slowly replaced the receiver. "You'll change your will?" he asked, his voice rough with anger or fear, probably a little of both, Marni suspected. No matter what Chase said, he felt responsible for her and the baby. He'd just risked his life for them.

Jabe looked down at the brandy he'd poured into the glass and drained it in one swallow. "Yes," he said, carefully putting down the glass.

"Get Hilda and Cook to witness it," Chase ordered. "Make sure everyone in this household knows."

Jabe winced, obviously still having trouble accepting that someone in the house had tried to kill Marni. His gaze met hers. He looked as if he wanted to apologize but must have realized the futility of a mere ''sorry.'' With weary steps, he walked to his desk and pulled out a sheet of Calloway Ranch letterhead and a pen. Slowly he lowered himself into the chair.

The door to the library slammed open and Dayton came back into the room. ''Now that Mother isn't here, would one of you like to tell me what the hell is going on?''

''Someone in this house tried to kill Elise,'' Chase said.

''By setting her car on fire?'' Dayton said. ''That's ridiculous.''

''Chase says the car was rigged to catch fire,'' Jabe said wearily.

Dayton laughed. ''What does Chase know about rigging cars to catch fire?''

''You forget the neighborhood where I grew up,'' Chase said.

Dayton closed his mouth and glanced over at his father sitting at the desk, pen in hand.

''He's changing his will,'' Chase said in answer to his brother's unanswered question.

A vein popped out on Dayton's forehead. ''You mean to tell me you're going to change your will because this... woman's car caught on fire?''

''What do you care?'' Chase asked. ''I'd think you'd want the will changed back because right now it appears my child would benefit.''

Dayton threw a mean look at Marni. ''If she's even carrying your child.''

''Stay out of this, Dayton,'' Jabe warned. ''I'm changing my will. It's my decision. Now all of you get out of here so I can finish and put an end to this.''

Dayton stomped out.

"Come on," Chase said to Marni as he took her half-empty cup and placed it on the coffee table, then helped her up from the chair.

"Shouldn't you be using your crutches?" she asked after watching him take a few painful steps beside her.

He swept them up and settled his weight on them. He looked exhausted, his face drained and sooty, and yet he was more handsome than she'd ever seen him, she thought with a stab of guilt.

"Are you leaving the ranch?" Jabe asked his son.

"Not until that codicil is written and witnessed." Chase turned and led Marni out of the room.

They took a service elevator that Marni hadn't known existed up to the third floor. In the cramped confines, the air between them seemed to vibrate with an intimacy that took away the last of the cold she'd felt. Marni stared at the floor, unable to meet Chase's gaze. She felt the need to say something, thank him, tell him she was sorry she hadn't believed him when he'd told her she was in real danger, but she didn't trust her voice. Not standing this close to him.

The elevator door opened and she stepped off, not sure where they were going or why.

"We need to talk," he said and led the way to his room. She took a deep breath and followed.

Chase headed directly to the bathroom but left the door open as he washed up. Marni felt too nervous and upset to sit. She wandered over to the window and looked down at her car, its hood blackened from the fire. It still seemed incomprehensible.

"Once he signs the will, you should be safe," Chase said from the bathroom doorway.

She turned to find him drying his hands gingerly with a towel.

"Your hands," Marni cried, hurrying across the room to

him to take them in her own. Both of his large callused hands were red. ''They're burned.''

''They're fine,'' Chase said, pulling them back. ''My gloves took most of the heat.''

She wanted to argue that he needed to put something on them but bit her tongue. He was right; his hands were fine. She looked up at him, and suddenly she was doing something she never did.

Chase saw what was coming. Her lower lip began to quiver. Her eyes filled, making the golden brown shimmer like rare silk. He watched as one large tear broke free and rolled down her cheek. Damn. He hated it when a woman cried. He hated it because he felt helpless. Downright clumsy. He dropped his crutches and pulled her to him, careful not to smash the baby between them as he took her in his arms. She came reluctantly, but finally surrendered to his awkward hug, bending slightly to press her face into his chest and yet keeping her baby safely away from him.

They stood that way, him balancing precariously on his one good leg while she clung to his shirt and cried. After a moment, she dried her eyes and stepped back, her composure and confidence quickly returning. She was no wimp; he'd give her that.

''Thank you,'' she said with one last sniffle.

He waved her thanks away. A hero he wasn't. And if anyone should know that, it was her. In fact, just being around her made him more aware of what an ass he could be.

He looked at her flushed face and wished— Hell, he wished she *was* part of his memory loss. He wished they *had* been lovers. He wished— He looked at her swollen abdomen. For a moment there, he even almost wished that she really was carrying his baby.

He shook his head at his own foolishness. One moment he was absolute in his knowledge that they could never have been lovers and the next... He limped over to a chair, his casted leg aching, and dropped into it. He hoped to hell he hadn't done so much damage to it that it would have to be reset. He couldn't stand more weeks of immobility, not after being trapped in this cast since the accident back in November.

"I'm sorry things didn't work out for you," he said.

He saw the effect of his words in her expression and mentally kicked himself for being such a jerk. But only moments before, there'd been a soft gentleness to her that made him feel protective. A vulnerability that pulled at some masculine need in him to shelter and care for her.

She raised her chin, all pride and determination again. She reminded him of a porcupine. Prickly enough to make him keep his distance. He and every other man. Last night he'd lain in his bed thinking about the man who'd made love to her. Chase could forgive her for trying to pass off the kid as his to assure her child of a healthy financial future. What he couldn't forgive was her letting some other man past that reserve of hers.

He shook his head, a surge of jealousy that defied comprehension going through him, knowing it made no sense.

"You think your father changing his will is going to make me less pregnant?" she asked. She sounded weary but there was still fight in her.

"No, just not pregnant with my child," he said, feeling like the heel he was. "Once there isn't a price on this baby's head, I'm hoping you'll recant your story. There won't be any reason for you not to." He had no idea for what motive, other than greed, someone had wanted her dead. But who knew what hateful forces were housed in this old mansion. It worried him.

As soon as Jabe finished the will and had it witnessed, Chase intended to contact the police, no matter what his father said, family or no family.

She looked away. "You're that sure I'm not carrying your child?"

He wanted to laugh. He was positive. Because she wasn't his type. Because he was a workaholic who didn't have time to date, let alone take four days off for a wild affair. Because he wasn't a wild affair kind of guy. Because he would never have let a woman like her close enough.

Right. How did he explain what had almost happened on the dining-room table? Or the way she made him feel—in spite of every reason he'd given her for why he couldn't, wouldn't and hadn't felt that way about her last summer.

Chase got to his feet slowly and went to her, forcing himself to meet her gaze, battling feelings so alien to him he wanted to blame them on his injury.

"The only thing I'm sure of is that you and I have never made love," he said softly. "Not yet, anyway."

SHE SHOOK HER HEAD, unable to speak. No, they'd never made love. She felt numb. From her near accidents. From something inside her. A regret she didn't dare put a name to.

For twenty-four hours she'd tried to tell herself that Chase Calloway was the father of Elise's baby. And for twenty-four hours he'd been telling her he wasn't.

All Marni knew was that she wasn't carrying Chase's child. Or any child for that matter. Sometimes she forgot that. Sam seemed so real. Even now, it was hard to let go. He'd been her connection to Chase. Pretend though it was.

Marni felt the warmth of Chase's gaze wash over her.

He reached out to thumb away tears that spilled down her cheeks.

Was she crying again? She never cried.

"My father should be finished with the codicil by now," Chase said softly. "I'll give you a ride to Bozeman."

She met his gaze, surprised that even with him believing

he wasn't the father of her baby, he still felt compassion for her. Now that Jabe had changed his will, there was no reason not to—and every reason to—tell him the truth. "There's something I have to tell you first."

CHASE STOOD looking at her, his heart suddenly heavy. For twenty-four hours he'd been trying to convince her—and himself—that he couldn't have fallen in love with her.

And yet isn't that what had happened? He'd known her less than a day. And somehow she'd gotten to him in a way no other woman ever had. No other woman ever could.

"There's something I have to tell you," she repeated. "Maybe you'd better sit down."

It was almost funny. What could be worse than telling him he'd had a four-day affair with her and she was carrying his child and he couldn't remember even one sensual, sexual moment of it? What could be worse than making him want to be that man?

He looked at her and felt something clamp down on his guts. Stumbling, he limped to the chair and took her advice. He dropped into the rocker and tightened his fingers around the arms.

"You're not pregnant with my baby, are you?" he said, his voice barely audible.

Tears welled in her eyes. She shook her head.

Hadn't he known that all along? So why did it hurt to hear her say it? Because he'd been playing a game with himself, pretending he was the man she described, some fool who'd fallen head over heels and spent four days making love, four days in some magical, once-in-a-lifetime world, throwing caution to the wind. A man Chase Calloway had never been, could never be.

He looked into her guileless face. "You and I have never made love."

She shook her head again.

He tightened his grip on the chair arms. "Let me guess, we never even met before yesterday."

A tear rolled down her cheek and he cursed his stupid, gullible heart. He'd fallen for it. No, he thought, he'd fallen for her.

"I'm not Elise McCumber," she said, taking a swipe at the tears. "I'm Marni McCumber."

"Marni?" Same last name? The only McCumber listed in the Bozeman phone book. The sister, the one he was supposed to call when he remembered his affair with Elise.

"I'm Elise's sister. Her identical twin. I'm not even pregnant." She patted her protruding stomach. "It's a maternity form."

He stared at her. "Why?" It was the only word he could get out.

"Elise is the one who's seven months pregnant with your baby. Not me."

He found his feet somehow. He didn't even feel the pain in his cast. "What?"

"Elise is having complications and has to stay in bed until the baby is born. She talked me into pretending to be her and coming here because you wouldn't take her calls."

"That was Jabe's doing, not mine." Not that any of that mattered. "You're trying to tell me…" What *was* she trying to tell him? He waved a hand through the air, lost his balance without his crutches and sat back down in the chair hard. He didn't even feel it. He felt nothing.

"My twin sister, Elise, is pregnant. With your baby." Marni fished through her purse and pulled out her wallet. She handed him a photograph of two women. Both looked like the woman in front of him.

He stared at the photo, then at her. Identical twins. My God.

She looked up at him. "I never cry." With that she burst into tears again.

Chase stared at her. "You're trying to tell me that you came here pretending to be pregnant on behalf of your twin sister?" He should have been stunned she'd go to such lengths. But knowing her the way he'd come to in such a short time, it made a strange kind of sense. It was the kind of thing this woman, Marni McCumber, would do for someone she cared about. He cursed softly under his breath but found himself wanting to laugh out loud.

"I had to. Elise was so upset I was afraid if I didn't come here she would. And she can't because she has to stay in bed. I did it for the baby."

The baby. "Do you really believe I'm the father of her baby?" he asked, trying to come to terms with the fact that there were two women out there who looked like this one as he got to his feet again.

"Yes, even though you don't remember what my sister is like."

"If she's anything like you—"

"She's nothing like me," Marni cried. "She has a way with men. Don't feel bad. You're not the first to fall for her."

He laughed as he closed the distance between them. Didn't she realize how ridiculous that was? If he'd fallen, he'd fallen for her, Marni McCumber, not her twin. "You're trying to tell me that your sister is irresistible and because of that, it proves I'm the father of her baby?"

"Yes," she repeated.

"Marni." He liked the sound of her name on his lips. He tilted her chin up so he could see her face.

"I look awful when I cry," she said bashfully.

"You look wonderful all the time." Even...pregnant, he thought. "You're the one who's irresistible."

She pulled free. "Please don't say that," she said, looking down at the floor again.

"You felt bad about kissing me because of your loyalty to your sister?" Chase said.

"Of course."

He smiled. He respected loyalty above all else. But his smile faded quickly when he realized things were worse than he could possibly have imagined. Wasn't it bad enough, the way he felt about this woman? And now she was telling him that he'd impregnated her sister? That he was in love with her twin? Impossible.

"Don't you see?" he asked softly. "I couldn't be the man your sister fell in love with." He took her shoulders, refusing to let her go without a fight. "The things you told me that I was supposed to have said, they aren't me. Don't you see? Something isn't right about all this." He looked into her eyes. "You sense it, too, don't you?"

"I want to," she said, wiping her tears.

He smiled at her, cursing his memory loss. If only he could remember enough to prove to her that there was some kind of mistake. Then what? he asked himself.

He looked into her tearful face. Hell if he knew. He was still trying to sort it out.

And right now he had the craziest urge to kiss her. To pull her into his arms, to hold her against him, to kiss away her tears.

He pulled Marni to him, telling himself the last thing he was going to do was kiss her.

But he would have kissed her. He would have held her, maternity form and all, if not for the gunshot that thundered through the house.

Chapter Eleven

Chase rushed out of the room as fast as Marni had seen anyone move on crutches. She stared after him, desperately trying to make sense of the sound she'd just heard. It wasn't until the service-elevator door clanged shut that she found her feet.

She raced down the hall to the top of the stairs. Below she could hear the hammer of hurried feet. The sound of voices raised in panic.

"Was that a gunshot?"

"Where did it come from?"

"Is everyone all right?"

"Oh, my God, no!"

"Where's Lilly?" The last voice was Hayes's; he sounded more afraid than the others.

Then a woman screamed and all hell broke loose.

Hysterical cries and someone trying to calm her. When she reached the main floor, Marni saw that everyone had congregated outside the library door.

No, not everyone, she realized as she headed toward them. The one person conspicuously missing was Lilly. Marni's heart dropped to her feet as she looked into their faces. Whatever had happened, it was bad.

Hilda sobbed into her apron while Felicia yelled at her to shut up. Hayes had his arm around his mother; both looked shocked and all Marni could think of was Lilly. Where *was* Lilly?

"What is it?" Marni asked, apprehension making her nauseated. She heard the elevator door clang open. "What's happened?" she repeated as Chase hobbled toward them, his face strained with worry.

"It's Jabe," Felicia said to Chase as if he'd asked the question. "He's killed himself."

Marni saw her own shock and disbelief mirrored in Chase's face as he pushed his way through to the open library doorway.

"He's dead," she heard Dayton say from inside the room. Marni looked past Chase to see Dayton standing beside his father's desk. Jabe sat where they'd left him. He appeared to be slumped in the chair, his head to one side. Blood ran from his temple down the smooth, soft leather of the chair to pool on the hardwood floor at his feet.

Marni closed her eyes, feeling ill, but the image stayed with her. Jabe sprawled in the chair at his desk. His right arm dangling at his side. His fingertips almost touching the pistol that had fallen from his hand to rest in the blood on the floor.

"Don't do that!" Chase barked.

Marni opened her eyes to see Dayton jerk his hand back. He'd been about to pick up the gun from the floor.

"Don't touch that!" Chase repeated, limping over to his father. Forcing Dayton to step out of the way, he felt for a pulse. After a few moments, he cursed under his breath and looked up at Marni.

She felt a shudder at the anguish she witnessed in his eyes.

"Shouldn't we get him covered up or something?" Dayton said.

"Don't touch anything," Chase ordered.

Dayton's face reddened. "What the hell is wrong with you, Chase? It was suicide not—"

"Who found him?" Chase demanded, cutting off his half brother as he opened the desk drawers with the tip of a pencil and searched inside.

"I did," Dayton said.

"Was the will on the desk?" Chase asked.

"No," Dayton said with a frown. "There wasn't anything on the desk, I don't think. I don't know. I didn't notice. I saw him and I called for Mother."

Chase sighed and raked a hand through his hair. "And you didn't see anyone else in this room or see anyone leave?"

"I was just down the hall when I heard the gunshot. I opened the door and Father was the only one in the room," Dayton said. "No one went in or out." He seemed to realize where that left him. "You don't think I killed him?"

Marni watched Chase finish his search of Jabe's desk, knowing he was looking for the will Jabe had been writing when they left the room. So where was it now?

Lilly suddenly appeared beside Marni, her eyes large and haunted.

"Lilly," Hayes whispered. "Where have you been?" He stepped toward her as if he meant to comfort her.

She sidestepped him and took Marni's hand in her cold clammy one. Marni could smell the booze on the woman's breath and felt Lilly's body tremble as she asked, "It's Jabe, isn't it?"

"Shouldn't we call a doctor?" Vanessa cried, her voice high and brittle.

Chase shook his head. "Call the sheriff."

"The sheriff?" Dayton echoed. "It's obvious Father killed himself. What do you need the sheriff for?"

"Someone call the damned sheriff!" Chase yelled as if he hadn't even heard Dayton. "And close off this room."

No one moved. Hilda cried harder.

Chase looked up, his gaze meeting Marni's again. She stared at him, trying to understand the fury she saw in his eyes.

"Just call the sheriff, dammit. From the barn," Chase snapped when Dayton started to pick up his father's phone. "The phone's still dead. Use the two-way radio in the barn."

Dayton threw his half brother a lethal look, then stormed out of the room, sending the family scattering down the hallway.

All except Marni. She stood alone at the edge of the room, hugging Sam, watching Chase with concern. He had gone deathly still after everyone left. For a long moment, he'd just stood looking down at his father. Then he'd taken one of his crutches and swung it wildly. It came down on the edge of the hearth and broke in a loud crack, but not as loud as the curse that Chase cried out. The sound tore at Marni's heart. She wanted desperately to reach out to him, and even stepped toward him, then stopped, afraid he wouldn't accept comfort from her.

He threw the other crutch across the room and turned to see her still there.

"I wish I'd killed the bastard myself," he said, the cold rage in his voice sending a chill through her.

He picked up his one good crutch and limped toward her. "Let's wait somewhere else until the sheriff comes."

They went into the room where Marni had found Lilly crying last night. Chase sat on the arm of the couch.

"I'm sorry about your father," Marni said quietly.

He closed his eyes for a moment. "You know what this means? Elise McCumber and her baby are in danger until that will turns up." He opened his eyes, his gaze fell on her and softened. "You're in danger."

She hugged Sam. "Why would someone first try to kill

your father to keep him from changing his will and now kill him to keep him from changing it back?''

Chase shook his head. ''Especially when it's my baby who will benefit.'' He eyed her. ''Or so it would seem. The thing is, Elise McCumber isn't carrying my baby any more than you are.'' He gave her a look that said he'd prove it to her.

Marni wished with all her heart that he could.

''Why would a man so hell-bent on having a grandchild kill himself? There is no way my father killed himself. No way.''

Marni had to admit she couldn't see Jabe Calloway committing suicide. Especially now.

''And where is the will he was writing when we left him? Dayton said there was nothing on the desk when he came into the room. There's nothing in the wastebasket or the drawers. I checked. Whoever killed him either took it or destroyed it.''

''But why? The way it stands right now, the money goes to the first grandchild.''

He moved to the window. ''As long—''

''Don't say it, Chase, you're scaring me.''

''You are still in danger,'' he repeated, turning to look at her.

''You mean Elise.''

''Everyone in this house believes you're Elise Mc-Cumber. That's why you have to take off that damned maternity form. Now.''

CHASE WATCHED in frustration as the sheriff and coroner did their thing, knowing each had come to the same conclusion: Jabe Calloway had committed suicide.

''He didn't kill himself,'' Chase said, making Sheriff Tom Danner look up from his notes. Jabe's body had been removed from the library.

"What makes you say that?" Danner asked.

"He was too selfish to kill himself," Chase said, unable to control the anger he heard in his voice. "It would have made too many people happy."

The sheriff shook his head. "I knew your father—"

"Then you knew what an overbearing bastard he was," Chase said. "Do you really think he killed himself?"

Danner rubbed his jaw and eyed Chase warily. "All the evidence certainly makes it appear to be a suicide. He was shot in the side of the head at contact range from the right side with a .38 registered to him." He glanced at Chase. "He was right-handed and the gun is on the right side of his body. There's no evidence of a struggle. The angle of the shot, the fact that only one shot was fired and the location of the gun all would support suicide, and I'd bet we'll find powder burns on his hand. The only thing missing is a suicide note."

"No, the only thing missing is the codicil to the will my father wrote just before he was killed," Chase said.

"He was changing his will?"

"His original will left an equal share to each of his sons," Chase explained. "He changed it recently so the first grandchild would get the lion's share of his estate. When I left him in this room, he was changing it back."

"Who stands to benefit at this point?"

"It would appear I do." He could feel the sheriff's gaze on him, warmer than the fire.

Danner studied him. "Well, unless you killed him, what would be the point?"

"I wish I knew. All I can tell you is that someone in this family didn't want Jabe to change his will back."

"Maybe the autopsy will come up with something," the sheriff said, closing his notebook and putting it into his shirt pocket. "Your father was a complicated man. Who knows what his last thoughts were."

His last thoughts? "If we knew them, we'd know who killed him," Chase said.

"Or we'd know that he left a financial mess for you kids," Danner said. "Knowing your father, that's a possibility."

"Yes," Chase said, not even trying to hide his bitterness. "His first thought was always his children."

THE BIG OLD HOUSE grew unusually quiet after the sheriff and coroner drove away, the lights from the ambulance flashing brightly against the fresh snow. Marni watched from the bedroom window, her hand on the maternity form she still wore. She couldn't take if off. Not yet. Not until she knew that Elise would be safe.

Still in shock Marni watched until the lights died in the distance. The sheriff said he had been planning to head out this way as soon as the roads opened anyway. Someone by the name of Mary Margaret McCumber had called, worried about her daughter.

He promised to call Mrs. McCumber and let her know her daughter Elise was fine and would be calling from Bozeman. Sheriff Danner had offered to give Marni a ride but Chase had insisted he would take her. Where was Chase? He'd promised to come to her as soon as he'd finished with the sheriff. In the meantime, he'd made her promise to stay in the bedroom with both doors locked.

Marni caught a glimpse out of the window of someone hurrying to the barn and recognized Chase's tall, lean figure limping across the snowy yard. What was he doing going to the barn again now?

Marni heard a sound and turned to see that someone had just slipped a note under her door. She rushed over to pick up the piece of paper and, against her better judgement, opened the door to look out. The hallway was empty.

She closed the door quickly and unfolded the piece of paper. "Elise, meet me at the barn. It's urgent, Chase."

Marni looked down at the note, unsure. Who had delivered this? She'd just seen Chase hobbling out to the barn. And she'd never seen Chase's writing. Not only that, she'd promised she'd stay in her room. She remembered how Dayton had tricked Chase into leaving her alone in the barn with him. She didn't want that to happen again.

But the note said it was urgent.

Suddenly more worried about Chase than herself, Marni hurried to the barn. The last of the day's sun made the snow-covered earth glow white. The pines hung heavy and the air smelled fresh and crisp.

Marni pushed open the barn door and stepped in, expecting to find Chase inside. She stood for a moment, waiting for her eyes to adjust to the dim light. The tack room was empty, so was the office. She moved to the edge of the arena and looked down at the soft trampled ground. Empty.

A horse whinnied from the stable area, drawing her in that direction. As she opened the stable door, she could hear one horse in particular. She caught a glimpse of Wind Chaser about the same time she saw Hayes.

Hayes stood back from the stall, a look of concern on his face as he stared at the stallion. Wind Chaser thrashed around, his hooves pounding the ground beneath him, his eyes wild.

"Something's wrong with this horse," Hayes said to himself, frowning. He seemed to sense Marni and turned to smile tentatively.

"I was looking for Chase," Marni said and started to turn.

"I was the one who sent the note," Hayes said. "Not Chase."

"But I just saw him—"

Hayes nodded. "I sent him over to the other barn so I could talk to you alone."

Marni felt a chill wrap its icy fingers around her neck. "What about?"

He moved toward her. "You've been great with Lilly."

"Lilly?" Is that all this was about?

"The thing is, there is so much you don't know. I'm just afraid that Lilly might do something—" He glanced behind him, back at Wind Chaser, and when he turned, stumbled into her, bumping the maternity form. "I'm sorry, I—" He looked from her belly to her face and back again. "My God." He stepped back as if burned. His eyes widened as he stared at her.

Marni felt her heart sink. Hayes knew she wasn't carrying Chase's child! Wasn't carrying *any* child. "I can explain."

But she didn't get the chance. Behind them, Wind Chaser let out a high-pitched whinny followed by the sound of splintering wood. She and Hayes swung around.

Everything happened so fast. The scent of gardenia. The stall door banging open. Wind Chaser, hooves flying as the horse reared, eyes wild.

Marni stumbled back and fell hard, knocking the air out of her. She heard Hayes let out a cry. And the sound of the horse, above them.

She rolled over to find Hayes lying crumpled beside her, silent and bleeding. She crawled over to him

"Elise," he said, his voice barely a whisper. He reached out to her; she took his hand and held it.

"Don't try to talk, Hayes."

"The baby. You have to protect the baby."

"Hayes, it's all right—"

He squeezed her hand and shook his head. "No." His grip loosened. His eyes closed.

"Hayes!" Marni cried. Then she saw the rise and fall of his chest. Thank God, he wasn't dead.

Behind her, she heard Wind Chaser snorting and stomping the dirt. Slowly she turned to look over her shoulder, hoping he'd gone back into his stall, knowing there wasn't much chance of that. The horse stood only a few feet away. He snorted and stomped the dirt, then reared again. She screamed and curled herself protectively around Hayes as the hooves came down.

"EASY, BABY," Chase said, his words soft. Marni opened her eyes, expecting to see Chase leaning over her. Instead, he stood between her and the stallion and his soft words were not for her, she realized, but the horse.

It took a moment to realize exactly what he was doing. Putting distance between her and the horse. "Be careful," she cried as she watched Chase advance on the stallion.

"Hush, and don't move," Chase ordered softly, the softness obviously still for the horse.

He moved slowly toward the stallion, murmuring soothingly as he backed Wind Chaser toward an open stall. "Easy, boy."

The stallion stomped and swung his head. Marni watched in amazement as Chase cajoled the horse into the empty stall and closed and latched the door.

He turned and limped over to her. "Are you hurt?"

She shook her head as she tried to sit up, her muscles like jelly. "Hayes—"

Chase turned to his half brother, checked for a pulse then rushed to the office and the two-way radio. She listened to him call for a medical helicopter. Then call the house on an intercom.

"There's been an injury in the barn."

He reappeared and pulled off his coat to lay it over Hayes. Then he pressed his leather glove to the wound on Hayes's head to stop the bleeding.

"What were you doing out here?" he demanded, not looking at her.

She could hear the controlled anger in his voice. After all, he'd ordered her to stay in her room. She wondered if Chase did anything but order people around "I got a note from you saying to meet you in the barn. That it was urgent."

"I didn't send the note."

"I know that now," she said in exasperation. "Hayes did. He said he'd sent you to the other barn so he could talk to me alone."

"What about?"

"He seemed to want to talk about Lilly." She remembered the smell of Lilly's perfume just after she'd turned to see the stall door standing open. Had she imagined it? Or had Lilly been in the barn?

Chase made a disgusted sound. "You came out here, knowing how dangerous it was?"

"I saw you come out here, then I got the note. I was worried about you."

"About me?" He swore under his breath. "How did the stallion get out?" he asked, obviously changing his tack.

Marni wished she knew. "I found Hayes near Wind Chaser's stall. The horse was agitated." How did she explain what had happened next?

Chase turned to blink at her. "Are you telling me Hayes is the one who left the stall door open?"

Marni looked over at Wind Chaser in confusion. "No, the door was closed. We had turned our backs when I heard the sound of splintering wood. The stall door banged open. Just before that, I think Hayes realized I wasn't really pregnant. And I think Lilly was here," she added.

Chase turned on her, a look of shock on his handsome features. "What?" was all he got out before Vanessa came bursting into the barn, followed by Dayton and Felicia, then finally Lilly.

Vanessa threw herself to the dirt beside Hayes and wept openly, showing much more emotion for her son's injury than she had for the death of her husband.

Lilly stood staring down at her husband, her face the color of snow, her eyes dark and wide. "It's God's will," she whispered, making Marni look up at her in surprise. It was then that Marni noticed that unlike Vanessa, Dayton and Felicia, who had rushed straight from the house, Lilly wore her coat and boots.

Vanessa shooed Chase away, taking over the care of her son. Chase helped Marni to her feet. She still felt woozy as he led her over to Wind Chaser's empty stall. The boards on one side had been splintered by the horse's hooves. The door hung open. Marni watched Chase inspect it. He pulled a piece of broken wood from inside the latch and motioned for Marni not to say anything until they were outside.

"Is that what I think it is?" Marni asked.

"It looks like someone jammed the stick into the latch so it wouldn't lock all the way," Chase said when they were a good distance from the barn.

"That's crazy. Anyone who came into the barn could have been Wind Chaser's victim."

Chase nodded. "Any chance Lilly saw you go to the barn to meet Hayes?"

"I don't know."

He swore and stopped to pull her around to face him. "You have no idea what you've stumbled into. This family—" He waved a hand through the air, then let out a long exasperated breath before he loosened his grip on her. "I know you want to protect Lilly. It's your nature. But Marni, when it comes to Calloway money, Lilly isn't that much different from Felicia."

"What is it you're trying to tell me?" she asked, pulling free of his hold.

"She's already jealous of your baby. If she thought you wanted her husband—"

"Why would she think that?" Marni cried.

Chase shrugged. "It's not like the woman is rational. If she followed you to the barn—"

"Hayes just wanted to talk about her."

"Or warn you about her?"

Marni hugged herself, realizing that was probably more accurate. What had Hayes said? "I'm just worried that Lilly might—" What had he planned to say?

"Get cleaned up," Chase ordered. She bristled and he softened his tone as he reached to pick straw from her hair. "A hot bath will warm you up. You're shivering. I'll find you some clean clothes. Then we're getting out of here before anything else happens."

Until that moment, Marni hadn't realized she was shaking. She didn't kid herself it was from the cold.

MARNI WENT to her room and removed the maternity form with trembling fingers. For the last twenty-four hours, it had been almost her constant companion. Her body now felt slim. Streamlined. That should have made her happy. Instead, she felt so strange without "Sam" and tried to laugh at her own foolishness only to find herself in tears.

Hormones. Wearing that silly maternity form had kicked in more than her hormones. Now she had maternal feelings she'd never known she possessed. There had never been a baby. And yet she was keenly aware of a feeling of loss as she stepped into the large clawfoot tub and sank into the bubbles.

A day ago, she couldn't have imagined how her twin could have fallen in love so quickly, so completely. A day ago, she couldn't have imagined how anyone could have fallen in love with Chase Calloway. Now she knew. Marni's heart ached with that knowledge.

DESIRE. It hit Chase the moment he stepped through the adjoining door of their bedrooms and caught the sweet scent of bath crystals. He'd knocked several times, then, worried, he'd used the key to open the door. That's when he heard the sound of water sloshing against the tub. Instantly he could imagine her, shoulder deep in bubbles. Her skin pink and soft. There would be a sprinkling of freckles across her chest above her breasts. Oh, her breasts. He groaned silently. Full, round, the nipples dark and hardening from the room's chill.

He knocked again on the bedroom door. "Marni?" He took a tentative step, balancing on his one crutch, telling himself all the reasons he should wait until she was out of the tub. But he'd brought her clean clothing. And the gentle lap of the water drew him, along with the sweet scent of the bubbles and the mere thought of Marni neck deep in the large, old tub.

The bathroom door was open. At first all he saw was bubbles. Then her head came up out of the water, her shoulders, the tops of her breasts. A sprite, her body wet and slick, her russet hair trailing down her back.

"Marni." It came out a hoarse plea. Desire almost dropped him to his knees.

She looked up, startled, then slid back into the tub until the bubbles were up to her chin.

He moved toward her, wanting to throw himself into the water with her, the need to feel her against him overwhelming. What had this woman done to him in such a short period of time? All he knew was what she was doing to him right now.

"Chase," she whispered, eyes wide as if she could see how badly he wanted her. It was the pleading he saw there that stopped him. Until he could prove to her that he wasn't her twin's lover—

With his free hand, he pulled a towel from the rack and held it out to her, turning his gaze away. "Get dried off," he said, his voice husky. "Please."

She took the towel.

He could hear her drying herself; the sound of the thick, absorbent towel on her skin skittered across his senses like a live electrical wire. "Get dressed." He hadn't meant it to sound so much like an order. "I borrowed these from Felicia," he said, not knowing what to do with the clothes.

He stood for a moment, a war going on inside him. He wanted to see Marni without the maternity form almost as badly as he wanted to hold her. But he couldn't let himself. Even if Marni would have let him.

He dropped the clothing on the small stool by the tub and stalked out of the room, cursing himself for the feelings tormenting him. He threw what little he'd brought here into the suitcase still open in the bottom of the closet and slammed the case shut with a finality that wasn't lost on him. He couldn't see himself ever coming back. This was his father's house, a place as dark and warped as the man himself had been.

Chase felt sick at heart, less over his father's death than his father's life. Jabe had had three sons, three chances. As far as Chase could tell, he'd blown it with all three. No one would grieve his death. Except Chase's mother, if she'd still been alive. She forgave Jabe everything. Jabe had been his mother's one weakness. A weakness that had slowly killed her.

Chase tried to concentrate on the problem at hand. Once Elise McCumber admitted that she and Chase had never been lovers, then Marni and her sister would be safe. The question was: Whose baby was Elise carrying? Someone who'd been driving the ranch truck that day and had used the name Chase Calloway to impress her, the fool.

It would just be a matter of clearing up this misunderstanding.

"I'm ready," Marni said behind him.

He turned to find her standing in the doorway, looking very pregnant. "What the hell are you doing still wearing that?" He couldn't hide his disappointment. Or his concern that she'd continue this charade knowing how dangerous it was.

"I've decided to stay Elise McCumber," she said, lifting her chin with defiance.

"Have you lost your mind?"

"Elise is in danger. You said so yourself. I have to protect her and the baby. Until we can prove she isn't carrying your child."

He stared at the woman before him, her face flushed from her bath, her damp hair hanging in tendrils on the soft whiteness of her neck, her eyes large as a doe's. "You are without a doubt the most exasperating woman I have ever met."

She smiled. "I'll take that as a compliment."

He shook his head as he reached for his suitcase. "You would."

Chapter Twelve

It was dusk by the time they left the ranch in Chase's pickup, the bare cottonwoods stark against the winter sky. Marni had to drive, to Chase's annoyance, because the truck was a stick shift and he couldn't operate the clutch with his leg in a cast.

They left quietly, none of the family around, it seemed, to say goodbye or good riddance. As they pulled away, Marni looked up at the tiny window under the third-floor eave but couldn't tell if Lilly was there watching them leave.

"Is it too late to go to your mother's farm tonight?" Chase asked.

Marni glanced at her watch. It wasn't quite five but already the sky had turned a dusky deep blue. They could be at the farm in a couple of hours. "Are you sure that's what you want to do?"

"Yes." He shot her a look. "I want this over with."

Was he that sure? Or was it just the opposite? Either way, they were about to find out the truth.

They followed Sixteenmile Creek out of the canyon. Walls of snow banked each side of the narrow road as they drove past Maudlow and on into Bozeman.

They stopped at the hospital emergency room and had a doctor check Chase's leg.

"Since you seem intent on walking on it," the doctor

said, "why don't we just get rid of the cast? It's supposed to come off in a couple of days anyway." The X ray showed that the bone had healed nicely.

While she waited for Chase, Marni called the farm from the hospital pay phone. The sheriff had already let Elise know that her twin had been snowed in and was fine. Her mother quickly agreed it would be best not to tell Elise they were on their way to the farm because she was anxious enough as it was.

Marni's second call was to her boutique. Her manager sounded frantic with all the Christmas shoppers. But, Marni had to admit, her crew seemed to be doing fine without her. Better than fine. Sales were up; everything was going smoothly. She felt a swell of pride in her workers.

When she checked at the desk, the nurse said Hayes had regained consciousness and was sleeping. Marni walked away, relieved, but the memory of Lilly's strange reaction to her husband's accident still bothered her.

"Ready?" Chase asked as he came out of the emergency room, walking a little stiffly.

"How does it feel?" Marni asked.

He smiled. "Great. I can't tell you how glad I am to finally get that damned thing off. I want to look in on Hayes, then let's get going."

She nodded, as ready as she was ever going to be.

They drove over Bozeman Pass, a wonderland of snow and ice, then followed the Yellowstone River east from Livingston. The small western towns they passed looked like Christmas villages all decked out in snowcapped eaves, bright with Christmas lights and decorations.

Chase said little on the drive along the river. Marni wondered if he was worrying about the moment when he would meet her sister. She knew he must be grieving the death of his father, no matter how awful Jabe Calloway had been in life. She also knew Chase wasn't happy about her still pretending to be Elise or the fact that he was still involved in her life as long as she was pretending to carry his child. But that could soon be over. Unless of course he was wrong. Unless Elise was pregnant with his baby.

Marni tried not to think about that as the sky darkened to midnight blue above the whiteness. Stars studded the velvet, each a brilliant sparkling jewel in the night, making Marni think of the three wise men who had followed a star to a manger.

Just as they reached Columbus, the moon rose, a fiery ball of orange over the mountains. Marni looked out into the winter night, unable to appreciate its stark beauty. Too much had happened in the last twenty-four hours and so much was still unresolved.

They turned at Columbus and headed north into wheat country. Once on the snow-covered gravel road, they lost all other traffic. Still Chase kept checking behind them, just as he had since they'd left the ranch.

"You really think someone would try to follow us?" she asked, watching the countryside open up and house lights become few and far between.

He shrugged and kept looking behind them, his mood as dark as the lock of hair that fell onto his forehead.

Marni tried not to think about who might be following them to the farm.

She watched the dark landscape roll by, her thoughts returning to the one thing she couldn't keep from her mind: the moment Elise saw Chase.

CHASE WASN'T SURE what he'd expected as they came over the rise and the pickup's headlights caught on the large old mailbox with McCumber printed on the side.

"Can you stop here?" Marni asked. "I think it would be best if I didn't make an appearance like this." She placed a hand over the maternity form that had become such a part of her in his mind.

He slowed the pickup and came to a stop, the mailbox in his headlights. Someone had tied a big red bow on it. He felt a lump in this throat and looked out at the wheat fields, gold stubble poking up through the snow in the winter moonlight, rather than look at Marni.

"All set," she said.

He glanced at her. She looked small in the dash lights. Small, pretty. And afraid. He wanted to reassure her, but decided nothing he could say would convince either of them right now.

Slowly, he turned the pickup up the long snowy rutted driveway, aiming it between the pine windbreak.

He couldn't help remembering the stories Marni had told about her childhood as he caught sight of the big old three-story farmhouse standing at the end of the lane. The place pulled at him, the same way Marni McCumber had done for the last twenty-four hours.

Marni glanced over at him and must have misread the look on his face. "Having doubts?" she asked.

He wanted to laugh. Doubts? He'd spent thirty-five years growing into the man he was. Now in just one day, this woman had him wondering who he was, what he wanted and just what he was capable of. He doubted everything about himself.

"Let's get this over with," he said.

The farmhouse was everything Calloway Ranch wasn't. Bright, cheerful, inviting. From the moment he stepped onto the porch, he could smell something wonderful cooking inside the house. He passed the worn porch swing and could almost see Marni sitting cross-legged in it against a summer sunset. He started to knock, but Marni opened the door and stuck her head in.

"Anybody home?" she called.

Her question was answered with the frantic patter of feet, shouts and laughter. A half-dozen children, from toddlers to near teens, came flying to the door; several small ones threw themselves into her waiting arms.

"Santa's coming," one of the younger ones proclaimed. "But look at all the presents already under the tree."

Marni smiled back at Chase and pushed her way into the house so he could close the door behind him.

"These are my brothers' children," she said and made the introductions, introducing him as a "friend."

"You're coming for Christmas, aren't you?" one of the older kids said to Marni. "You always come home for Christmas." Home it seemed was this house; each of her brothers had his own house on the family farm but it was the old farmhouse where everyone gathered.

"And it's only four more days," interjected a young excited child.

Marni seemed to hesitate, then smiled broadly. "I wouldn't miss it for the world."

Chase saw Marni blink back tears. He knew how much coming here for Christmas meant to her without ever having to ask. He knew this woman not with his head but his heart. And he wished to hell he didn't. He watched her look around at the Christmas decorations, knowing how much all of this meant to her. Decorations were everywhere, most obviously made by the passel of nieces and nephews now filling the entry hall. Past them, he could see the tree, a large spruce thick with homemade ornaments. Unless he missed his guess, most of them held special memories for Marni.

Chase could imagine Christmas in this house, with this family. He felt those horrible pangs from his childhood when his only wish in life was for this kind of a family, this kind of Christmas. He brushed those thoughts away, trying to keep them where they belonged, with the lonely little boy he'd been. He no longer needed these things, he told himself. His life was just the way he wanted it.

He glanced over at Marni and was shocked by the thought that ricocheted through his head. He missed seeing her pregnant.

MARNI COULD SMELL her mother's famous Christmas cookies baking in the kitchen. "Silent Night" played on the radio and she smiled as she heard her mother begin to sing. The memory of all the other Christmases they'd spent here as a family warmed her the way the fire in the woodstove never could. Now all she had to worry about was this Christmas.

"Come on," her youngest niece cried. "Grandma just got through making fudge. She said we could have some as soon as you got here."

They all clambered toward the kitchen. "Maria, you cut each of the children one piece of fudge," she heard her mother say.

"One?" came the universal cry.

"One," Mary Margaret McCumber said sternly. "Behave while I see to your aunt Marni."

Marni felt her stomach roil, her nerves suddenly strung taut. The moment of truth. She felt as if she might throw up.

She looked at Chase. He stood inside the door, his hands at his side, his face set in stone. She recognized that expression, seen it enough times on his handsome face since yesterday. Stubborn determination. But there was something else about him that caused a fissure of concern to run through her as Mary Margaret McCumber came out of the kitchen. Worry. She read it in his eyes. Was he not as sure as he wanted her to believe? Or was something else bothering him?

Mary Margaret stopped in the middle of the room to dry

her hands on her apron, give Chase Calloway the once-over, and a disapproving nod, then turned her gaze on Marni. Her mother was tall with graying blond hair that she kept long and in a no-nonsense braid down her back.

"Your sister" was all her mother said with a wave of her hand down the hall toward the sewing room. With a shake of her head, she turned back to the kitchen. "I have to rescue the fudge. I made pot roast. I saved some for you, so of course you're eating."

Leave it to Mother to think her cooking could solve all their problems. Marni only wished it could as she led the way to the back of the house and the sewing room.

At the closed door, she hesitated, glancing over her shoulder at Chase to be sure he was still with her. Then she turned the knob and stepped in, leaving Chase in the hallway.

Elise sat in the middle of the bed in the makeshift bedroom, propped up with dozens of pillows, surrounded by books, magazines, videos, a laptop, fax machine and beauty supplies. She looked bored—and very pregnant.

When she spied Marni standing in the doorway, she smiled with an eagerness that made Marni's heart hurt. "You're back. I've been going crazy. Mother—" She waved a hand through the air with no need to continue along those lines; it was a McCumber form of communication all the women in the family understood. "What happened? Why didn't you call? Or at least E-mail or fax me."

Just like El, the E-mail junkie. Just because she spent hours on E-mail with friends, she assumed everyone did. She didn't realize some people didn't even have a computer, let alone a fax machine.

"Didn't Mother tell you the snowstorm knocked out the phone and the electricity?" Marni said.

"Well, yes, but surely there was *something* you could have done. Is Chase all right? You did see him, didn't you? What did he say—"

"I brought him with me," Marni interrupted.

"Here?" Elise cried, picking up the hand mirror from her pile of beauty supplies. "Oh no, I'm a disaster!"

Marni watched her sister primp and felt tears rush her eyes. Her twin had a special beauty that Marni knew was only partially due to the pregnancy. "You look great."

"Really?" El asked.

"Really. Are you ready?" Marni wished *she* were ready for this.

Elise nodded enthusiastically, a hundred-watt smile on her face. Marni moved aside to let Chase enter the room.

MARNI HEARD CHASE step into the doorway. She didn't turn around to look at him. Instead, she watched her sister's face. The smile faded. Elise frowned and seemed to be trying to see past Chase out into the empty hallway.

"What's going on?" El asked. "I thought you said you brought Chase?"

"I did." Marni spun around, thinking he must not be behind her. "This is Chase. Chase Calloway."

Elise shook her head. "Not the Chase Calloway I know."

Thank God, Marni thought as she faced her twin.

"This is not Chase," El repeated.

Marni turned to look at him again. He smiled, letting out a relieved sigh as he raked his fingers through his hair. Marni didn't even mind his I-told-you-so look. Her heart thundered in her ears. Chase hadn't fathered Elise's baby. Just as he'd said. Just as Marni had prayed. She felt such a wave of relief she had to sit down on the edge of Elise's bed.

"What's going on here?" Elise asked, looking confused.

"It's a long story," Marni said. "The good news is that you aren't carrying Chase Calloway's baby."

"Then whose baby am I carrying?" El cried. "Are you

sure you went to the Calloway Ranch in the Horseshoe Hills?''

''El, I went to the right ranch. I met the whole family. Believe me, this is Chase Calloway. You're sure he isn't the man who fathered your child?'' she asked again.

''Did he tell you he fathered my child?'' she asked, shooting him a look.

''Well, no, as a matter of fact he said— Never mind.'' Marni looked up at Chase. ''You're just sure this isn't the man you met last summer?''

''Positive,'' El said, giving her twin a questioning look. ''How many times do I have to say it?''

Marni laughed, and smiled at Chase. Elise and the baby were safe. ''El isn't carrying your baby.''

''I know,'' he said, sounding as relieved as she felt.

''But there is a resemblance,'' she heard El say behind her. Marni swung around to look at her sister.

''A resemblance?'' Chase asked, stepping closer.

''Oh yeah, there's definitely a resemblance,'' El said, taking a closer look. ''You look enough like him to be his brother.''

Marni felt her heart leap into her throat.

''Why don't you describe your Chase Calloway for us,'' he suggested as he pulled up a chair beside Elise's bed.

El leaned back against the pillows, her gaze on him. ''This is very strange.''

If only she knew how strange, Marni thought.

''Tell me about the guy,'' Chase encouraged. ''He definitely used the name Chase Calloway, right?'

El nodded. ''It isn't a name you're apt to forget.''

Chase smiled at that. ''What exactly did he look like?''

''Handsome,'' Elise said with a smile. ''Like you but different.'' She studied Chase for a moment. ''His eyes weren't quite as pale blue. His hair was neater.''

Marni suppressed a smile. Chase's hair was its usual rumpled mess. But she realized that she loved it that way. It made her want to run her fingers through it. She shook off such thoughts, suddenly picking up on El's last words.

"And his hair wasn't quite as dark," Elise said.

She had just described both Dayton and Hayes. "Did he have a mustache?" Marni asked.

Elise nodded and laughed. "A cute little one that curled over his lip like a caterpillar." Leave it to Elise to forget that highly significant little detail.

Dayton. Marni's gaze met Chase's.

He shook his head. "Both of my brothers had mustaches last summer."

"You think the man was one of your brothers?" Elise asked. "Why would he lie about his name?"

"Both brothers are...married," Marni said.

El let out a small cry and buried her face in her hands. "I can't believe this. We were so perfect together. He said he loved me. That he wanted a life with me. He wanted my baby."

"He probably does want your baby," Chase said.

"My God," Marni breathed as the full impact hit her. Elise was pregnant with either Dayton's or Hayes's baby. The first grandchild. And since Jabe didn't change his will— "Oh, Chase."

He nodded. "This definitely complicates things."

"Do you have photographs of your brothers?" El asked.

Chase shook his head. "But we can get them. Meanwhile, is there anything else you can tell us about the man?"

Heavy tears coursed down El's face. She shook her head, no.

MARY MARGARET knocked on the open door, took one look at Elise and narrowed a glare at Chase. "What's she crying about?" she demanded.

Marni jumped to Chase's defense, making her mother

raise an eyebrow. "Chase isn't *the* Chase who—" She waved a hand through the air.

Her mother, who'd perfected this form of communication, understood immediately. "Then who in all the saints is?"

"That's what we intend to find out," Chase said, getting to his feet.

"Not until after dinner," her mother announced. "I'll bring you a tray," she told Marni before she could protest. "You can eat with your sister. Chase— That really is your name, isn't it?"

"Yes, ma'am," he replied quickly.

"Chase will eat with me in the kitchen," she ordered. "We have some things to talk about."

THE KITCHEN SMELLED of pot roast and fresh homemade bread. Chase tried not to breathe too deeply. It was a smell he knew better than to become accustomed to. And yet he found himself breathing it in the way a drowning man fights for oxygen.

"You're in love with my daughter?" Mary Margaret asked, catching him completely off guard as she set a plate for him at the kitchen table.

"I've never seen Elise before today," he said quickly.

She gave him an impatient look. "I'm referring to my other daughter, Marni."

He opened his mouth to speak but nothing came out.

"What have you done to her?"

He almost choked. "Nothing. She—"

"She what?" the woman asked, eyeing him intently.

Marni had tried to make him fall for her, that's what. A confirmed bachelor. Worse than that, a man who had no desire to get involved, let alone married. And a man who'd never wanted children. Still didn't. He'd been quite happy. Damned happy. Well, happy enough. Until she came along. "She turned my life upside down," he said truthfully.

Mary Margaret made a disgusted face. "She's in love with you."

"What?"

"Surely you can see that?"

Chase glanced through the open kitchen door back toward the sewing room. It had never dawned on him that Marni might really be in love with him. Sure, she'd pretended she was, but that was when she was pretending to be Elise. And sure, there was some chemical attraction— "I'm not real sure she even likes me."

Mary Margaret shook her head as she began to fill his plate with pot roast, potatoes, carrots, onions and gravy. "These vegetables are from my garden."

He stared down at the food. The woman was mistaken about Marni's feelings. Not that he wanted even to think that it might be true; he was having a hard enough time trying to sort out his own feelings.

"You'd best tell me what kind of trouble my El is in," Mary Margaret said, changing the subject so fast she gave him whiplash.

He started to avoid the truth but she stopped him with a shake of her head. "Don't even bother," she said, then handed him a piece of warm homemade bread, which she'd already lathered with butter. "As I've always told my children, lying to me is a very bad idea."

He nodded, feeling like one of those children and wishing he didn't like the idea so much. He started with his father changing his will and ended with Elise's statement that the man she fell in love with could be his brother, the resemblance was that strong.

Mary Margaret crossed herself, then said, "You'll take care of Marni."

It wasn't a question, but he answered it anyway. "Yes. If she'll let me."

Marni's mother smiled at that. "There is nothing wrong with a headstrong woman."

"If you say so."

"One more thing. Promise me my daughter will be home for Christmas."

He started to tell her he couldn't promise that but she cut him off.

"You bring her home for Christmas," she ordered.

He considered straightening her out on a few things, but decided she'd find out soon enough. Even if her daughter was in love with him, which was ludicrous. He wasn't bringing her home for Christmas. This house, this McCumber lifestyle, was a trap, one he fought to resist. Just the way he fought the idea that he might be falling in love with Marni McCumber.

"Eat," Mary Margaret said. "You're going to need your strength."

"ARE YOU GOING to tell me?" Elise said.

Marni looked up at her twin. "Tell you what?"

"About Chase."

"Yours or mine?" *Mine?* Where had that come from. "The one I brought here?" she quickly amended.

Marni watched El nod and pick at her food, no doubt knowing Mother would eventually make her eat.

"It's complicated," Marni said, not sure what El was getting at.

El made an impatient noise. "Do you think Mother is settling for that line?"

Marni would bet Mary Margaret was forcing every detail out of Chase at this very moment.

She looked at her twin, knowing she had to be honest with her. "It's not good news, El." She told her about Jabe's will and the fortune he'd left the firstborn grandchild. "There's a very good chance you're carrying that child.

Because of the large amount of money involved, Chase is worried that—''

''You're saying I might be in danger?''

''I'm afraid so,'' Marni admitted. Reluctantly, she told her twin about her mishap in the attic, Hayes's accident in the barn and the fire that had destroyed her car. She finished with Jabe's death and Chase's suspicion that his father didn't kill himself.

Elise took it better than Marni had expected.

''But you don't have anything to worry about here at the farm,'' Marni reassured her. ''No one could get past Mother, let alone our brothers.''

Elise actually smiled at that, then sobered. ''You and Chase are going to try to find my baby's father, aren't you?''

''I don't know about Chase,'' Marni said, ''but I am.''

''That means you have to keep pretending to be me, huh?''

El was no fool. ''Yes.''

''Oh, Marni,'' she said, pulling her sister into a hug. ''I wish I'd never gotten you into this.''

El wiped at her tears and straightened, that McCumber determination back. ''I know he loves me. I wish he hadn't lied to me, but I can understand now why he did.''

Marni didn't want to believe love could be that blind. It scared her. ''You just worry about junior here.''

For the first time, Marni laid her hand on her twin's stomach, surprised at how hard it felt. The baby moved and Marni smiled, thrilled to feel the life inside her sister.

''I know it's silly to still make Christmas wishes,'' El said, placing her hand over Marni's.

Marni smiled, remembering the December nights as girls when they'd stared up at the stars, silently making Christmas wishes on the brightest star overhead. ''I don't think it's silly to wish. After all, Christmas is a time of miracles, right?''

El nodded, tears in her eyes.

And Marni promised herself that with or without Chase's help, she'd find the father of her twin's baby and try to give El the happy ending she so desperately wished for. Marni just worried it would take nothing short of a Christmas miracle to make it happen.

Chapter Thirteen

December 22

"Thank you," Marni said as they drove down the driveway the next morning. Chase could see the farmhouse in the rearview mirror and Mary Margaret standing on the porch, her hands knotted in her apron. He didn't have to see her face to know she was worried. So was he.

"For what?" he asked, wondering what Marni could possibly have to thank him for. He'd been cold and abrupt with her most of the morning, dreading going back to Bozeman, hating that she was determined to use herself as bait to draw out the killer, and worse yet, angry with himself because he wasn't about to let her do it alone. Not that he was being chivalrous. Even if she hadn't been in trouble, he wasn't ready to part company. Not yet.

"For taking time to bring me up here."

"I had to prove that I wasn't Elise's lover," he said. "This seemed the fastest way to do it."

Marni nodded. "I should have believed you. I wanted to."

He waved that away. "It should be easy to find out which of my half brothers is. Then hopefully by now the sheriff will have the autopsy back and know that Jabe didn't kill himself, there will be an investigation and—" And what?

Did he really believe one of his brothers was a murderer? Someone in that family was, he reminded himself. The same person who'd made attempts on Marni's life?

The only thing he was reasonably sure of was that Elise would be safe with her large family looking after her. He'd met her four brothers, all large and mild-mannered but very protective. Especially of their sisters. He'd come away knowing they wouldn't let any man hurt their sister. Either sister.

Not that he personally had anything to worry about. True, he seemed to have feelings for Marni, but these feelings had come on too quickly, too strongly. He didn't trust them. So he promised himself he was going to take some time to try to make sense out of them before he did anything…rash.

"As soon as they find the murderer, it will be over," he finished. "Meanwhile, your sister's safe."

"At least it's not a concern of yours anymore," Marni said.

He looked over at her. Did she really expect him to walk away now? What kind of man did the woman think he was, anyway? Certainly not the kind a woman like her would fall in love with. Not that he believed she had.

"You can just drop me off at my place."

"So you can wait for the killer to come for you?" he demanded. Did she really think he could distance himself from all this just because he wasn't the father of her twin's baby? True, distance was his specialty. And he had been a jackass all morning.

"This isn't your problem," she said, that chin of hers going airborne.

It was all he could do not to stop the pickup and kiss some sense into her. *Great idea.* "It's my family. It's my problem. And anyway, I can't let you do this alone." He felt her gaze on him. "We're in this together whether you like it or not. You're carrying my baby… At least the world thinks you are. So it only makes sense that you stay at my place.'' He groaned inwardly at the mere thought.

He'd lain in the narrow twin bed in one of the boys' rooms last night feeling more at home than he ever had anywhere before. Thinking about what Mary Margaret had said about Marni being in love with him. Thinking about the kisses they'd shared, the touches, the looks. Was it possible?

This morning Mary Margaret had taken one glance at him and laughed happily. ''You look like you slept with the angels.''

He couldn't remember a night when he'd slept more soundly. Nor a breakfast he'd enjoyed more. Noisy, disorganized, utter chaos. He'd sat listening to all the chatter, wishing he and Marni never had to leave the farm. Telling himself that it was because she was safe here and wouldn't be once they went back to Bozeman. But in his heart, he knew it was so much more, more than he wanted to admit. He'd liked the idea that Marni might be, if nothing more, attracted to him. And he'd liked feeling a part of this noisy, boisterous family temporarily.

That's why he had to get out of there. It made him forget how painful loving could be. And for a while he'd forgotten the promise he'd made himself beside his mother's deathbed. He'd seen what his mother's love for Jabe Calloway had brought her, and what his love for his mother had cost him. He'd promised himself he'd never know that kind of pain again because he'd never let himself love anyone that much.

And he'd looked down the table at Marni. Her smile had seized his heart in a death grip and his mood had gone sour. This woman had the ability to do more than just break his heart.

''We're going to do this together,'' he said. ''It's settled.

So don't even bother to argue.'' To his amazement, she didn't.

"You think it's Dayton?'' she asked later as they neared the first Bozeman exit.

"Sounds like Dayton. He's had his share of affairs.''

"I hate to think he's the man El fell in love with,'' she said.

"Women fall in love with the wrong man sometimes,'' he said, thinking of his mother, thinking of Marni, if she was indeed falling for him.

"If it is Dayton, then he has two women pregnant,'' she said. "Covering his bets, you think?''

He wished he knew. "What I don't understand is why when you showed up at the ranch, one of my brothers didn't react more…strongly. Why didn't one of them say something to you? The real father of the baby must have been shocked when he saw you there.''

"Both seemed surprised,'' Marni said. "But everyone in your family was surprised. You know,'' she said thoughtfully. "That night after dinner, Hayes was waiting in the alcove on the stairs for either his mother or me. If he hadn't been there—''

He glanced over at her. "What?''

"Oh, Vanessa dropped her scarf on the stairs and I stepped on it and—''

"You almost fell down the stairs?'' he demanded.

"I didn't, but I could have if Hayes hadn't been there. He seemed very upset with his mother and said something about it not happening again.''

"I wonder what that was about?'' Chase said, eyeing Marni. "Why didn't you mention that you'd had a close call on the stairs?''

"I guess it slipped my mind,'' she said.

He could see there was more. "Did anything else happen I don't know about?''

"Someone came by my room later that night and tried my door."

"You think it was Elise's lover?" Chase asked.

She shrugged. "Surely he would have made some attempt to talk to me while I was at the ranch. He had to know he would be exposed eventually. If he thought I was Elise, he'd have tried to reason with me, don't you think? And if he realized I was an impostor, he would have confronted me. He couldn't just think this would all blow over."

Unless he thought Elise would be dead before anyone found out the truth, Chase thought. What was the father of Elise's baby going to do next? he wondered as they drove into Bozeman.

"Bet he was confused when I didn't seem to recognize him and was claiming that you were the father of my child," Marni said.

Chase nodded. "Unless he thought you were trying to get even with him for lying to you. But still, it would seem like he would have come forward. After all, you were seemingly carrying Jabe's first heir and a bundle of money."

"Maybe he was protecting himself. He didn't want his wife to know, afraid she might leave him. Or—"

Chase looked over at her. "Or because he was afraid of what she'd do to you?"

"You're thinking of Lilly," she said.

He cut her off before she could defend Lilly. "I wouldn't want to meet either Lilly or Felicia in a dark alley. Especially if they thought I was trying to take something of theirs."

"Elise didn't even know he was married."

"Like that would make a big difference to Lilly or Felicia," Chase said more sarcastically than he'd meant to. Sometimes Marni was too naive and trusting. He reminded himself that she hadn't grown up the way he had. Nor did she have the Calloways as family.

''More than likely, the reason one of my brothers didn't come forward had nothing to do with his wife,'' Chase said. ''He was probably more concerned about Jabe's reaction. Jabe wouldn't have liked his first grandchild to be born to a son who already had a wife. Worse yet, a pregnant wife, if it turns out to be Dayton.''

''Do you think Jabe would have been so angry he could have changed back his will before the baby was born?'' Marni asked.

''It's a possibility, or cut that son out entirely.''

''The father of El's baby can't be the killer,'' Marni said firmly as they neared the Bozeman exit and he heard her putting on the maternity form again.

''I hope you're right,'' Chase said.

The Christmas lights glittered at the stoplights along Main Street—red, gold, blue, green. For a while, Chase had forgotten about Christmas. And the promise Mary Margaret had asked of him. He told himself he'd find the killer before Christmas Day. Not for Mary Margaret. Not for Elise. But for his own selfish reason. He wanted Marni out of this charade. He wanted her safe. He had three days.

Marni's house was what Chase had expected. A cute cottage with a white picket fence, a wide pillared porch with a swing and paned windows with pale green shutters. A dollhouse all decorated for Christmas with lights strung along the eaves and a snowman in the yard complete with carrot nose and an old slouch hat.

''Nice snowman,'' he said.

''The neighborhood kids and I built him,'' she said proudly. ''I'm surprised it weathered the storm.''

Chase held the storm door open while Marni dug out her key. The door swung in to reveal shiny hardwood floors, colorful throw rugs and pretty papered walls, trimmed in oak.

A collection of teddy bears huddled in a large overstuffed

chair, bright and cheerful in red and green ribbons and bows. Reindeer drew a sleigh across the mantel over the small fireplace, pulling a cheerful Santa and a bulging bag full of presents.

Everywhere in the room he felt Marni. The decor reflected her strong roots, her good taste, her secure sense of herself, from the handed-down Christmas decorations, the mementos on the shelves, the photographs on the walls, the hand-crocheted tablecloth on the dining-room table. Even the furniture itself.

The place had a homeyness that tugged at the part of him that had yearned for such a house in his youth. He found himself wishing for Marni's childhood, just as he had at breakfast the last two mornings.

He'd so desperately wanted a family, roots, a feeling of belonging somewhere. He and his mother had moved from town to town, living in dark, dingy basement apartments. He'd picked up odd jobs in the neighborhood to help support them, and later had to quit school and work full-time when his mother became so ill.

It wasn't until he was fourteen and his mother realized she was dying that she finally told him about his family. And he'd gotten his wish, he thought bitterly. The Calloway clan. Someone should have warned him to be careful what he wished for.

Well, it was too late to change his childhood, too late to change the man he was. Not even Marni McCumber could do that, he told himself.

Marni took a couple of steps into the room and stopped. "Someone's been here."

Chase glanced quickly around the room, seeing nothing that looked amiss. "Why do you say that?"

She pointed to one of the rugs on the floor. The corner of it had been kicked up.

That was her proof? "You have to be kidding."

She went to the rug and straightened it, then looked around, her gaze coming to a halt as she stared at one of the dining-room walls. "The photograph's missing."

"What photograph?" he asked, his heart suddenly in his throat.

"One of me and Elise."

He moved then, covering the rest of the house. The small neat kitchen and dinette with light pouring in from the many windows. The two upstairs bedrooms. The bathroom.

There were tracks in the backyard coming up the steps but the snow had blown them in, making them just hollows. When he checked the back door, he found the lock had been jimmied open.

Chapter Fourteen

"Let's get you packed and out of here as quickly as possible," Chase said. "Whoever has the photo must have suspected something before he broke in."

"He still doesn't know which of us is carrying a Calloway baby."

"Not yet. We're going to have to find him before he does. Pack what you'll need for a couple of days," he ordered, anxious to get out of this house.

This house, Marni and that stupid maternity form, her big warm family, everything about the woman made him feel vulnerable, he thought as he followed Marni upstairs.

He stood for a moment in the middle of her bedroom, watching her pull out a suitcase and start putting a few items into it, and realized this room was exactly as he'd thought it would be. What was he doing even thinking about her bedroom? He let out an annoyed growl and headed for the hallway to wait.

"I'm hurrying," she said, misinterpreting his growl.

She packed quickly and efficiently, something he doubted her twin could have done with a dozen people at her beck and call. Although the two sisters looked identical except for their hairstyles, he'd noticed the differences and found himself pleased by them.

There was a strength to Marni that he liked, he realized,

standing in the hallway, unable to keep his eyes off her. He was counting on that strength to get them through the next few days.

As they were leaving the house, a big gray-striped cat hopped down from the fence to snake around Marni's legs. She bent to give it a pat and scold it about staying out of the street.

"Your cat?" he asked, not surprised now that he thought about it. She was the type. Snowman in the yard. A loyal feline waiting at the door each evening after work.

But she shook her head. "My neighbor's. We share. Ivan spends the day with her then comes to wait for me on the porch each night when I get home from the boutique. It's nice. Do you have a pet?"

Chase shook his head. "It wouldn't be fair to an animal since I spend so much time at work." He was used to coming home to an empty house. He liked it fine that way. And the silly cat wasn't even hers. So why did she make him feel bad because he didn't have a pet?

She wasn't the one making him feel bad, he reminded himself. *Marni and her shared cat makes you remember that puppy you found as a kid.* He didn't want to think about the puppy or what had happened to it. He still felt sick, more than twenty-five years later, about the puppy he'd been forced to leave behind.

As he drove down South Willson Avenue, large historic houses glittered with fresh snow and Christmas lights under old-fashioned streetlights. He thought how different his own Bozeman neighborhood was and wondered what Marni would think of it. He knew it would be a test; he just hadn't realized how badly he wanted her to pass.

"I should stop by my boutique, just to be sure everything's all right," Marni said.

Did she really think she could go back to her old life as if nothing had happened? "You can't very well show up at the shop seven months pregnant in the middle of the day without having to do a lot of explaining.''

''You're right, I just keep forgetting who I am.''

He knew that feeling.

''Chase?''

He glanced over at her, surprised sometimes by the effect just looking at her had on him. ''Yes?''

''Do you really think this will be over by Christmas?''

''Yes.'' He hoped. ''Otherwise, Santa will have to find you at my place.''

''You're sure that won't be an imposition?'' she asked.

An imposition? He wanted to laugh. It would be pure hell to be trapped with her in his small apartment. But he had no choice. He feared for Marni's life as long as she was wearing that maternity form. And whoever wanted Elise out of the way would eventually come for her.

''I must warn you, though,'' he said. ''My place is pretty…basic.''

HER FIRST CHRISTMAS away from her family. The thought instantly depressed her. She'd never missed a Christmas at the farm with her family. This year especially she wanted to be at home on Christmas morning.

Chase reached over and took her hand, and she felt a rush of contrition. How could she be thinking about herself at a time like this. Chase had just lost his father. And El's life was in danger. There would be other Christmases.

Marni watched the familiar streets blur by, thinking how different Bozeman looked. But Bozeman hadn't changed; she had. Marni McCumber was a different woman from the one who'd gone to work two days ago with her only care in the world the holiday rush. The last forty-eight hours had changed that. Had changed her. She knew it was more than pretending to be pregnant. More than being in danger, or worrying about her sister.

She glanced at the man beside her. She knew it was Chase and the feelings she had for him. She'd lain in bed last night, looking out at the stars, thinking about Chase. Making her own Christmas wish, one she didn't dare acknowledge now in the daylight.

Marni was surprised when Chase pulled up in front of a small grocery store in a northside Bozeman neighborhood that had seen better days. The grocery was one of those old-fashioned kind before convenience stores. A green awning hung over the front. The neon sign read simply Burton's. Chase opened the pickup door to get out.

"Do we need groceries?" Marni asked.

"No, sweetheart, this is home." He sounded offended as he reached in the back for their suitcases. "I told you it was basic."

She said nothing as he led her up open wooden stairs to the second floor over the grocery store. He slipped a key into the lock, opened the door and reached in to turn on a light. Then he stood aside to let Marni enter, obviously waiting for her reaction.

She braced herself, fighting not to let her thoughts show as she stepped in. The spacious apartment ran the entire width and length of the store below. Before her was a sparsely furnished living room with an arched opening into a kitchen and breakfast nook, both of which were large and roomy. Through another open door, Marni saw an older bathroom and past it, what had to be the bedroom, large and empty except for the double bed sitting like an island in the middle of the room. As she glanced toward the other two rooms, she noticed that one seemed to be an office of sorts, the other empty except for a few boxes of what appeared to be used plumbing and electrical supplies.

What hit Marni was the total lack of anything that told her about the man who lived here. No mementos. No photographs. Nothing personal. It reminded her of the bedroom he'd used at the ranch. Except she suspected he didn't live out of an open suitcase in the bottom of his closet. But it was possible. And yet, the apartment told her so much about the man who lived there.

"It's—" She searched for the right word.

"Basic?" he asked.

It fit the picture Jabe had painted of his oldest son. A man who wouldn't let himself get attached to anything. Especially a woman. "It's you," she said, meeting Chase's gaze.

He looked as if he was almost positive that wasn't a compliment. "You can take the bedroom." He carried her suitcase in and put it on the bed.

The bedroom was no different from the rest of the apartment. Clean, but without any personal touches. If he thought his apartment would push her away, he was wrong. Marni felt herself wanting so desperately to reach out to this man. To nurture him. To love him.

She heard him in the living room rewinding his answering machine and couldn't help overhearing the messages from the calls he'd had. Most sounded like business, she thought as she changed clothes. Then the sheriff's voice came on, saying he had the autopsy results, followed by Vanessa with a short, to-the-point message to let Chase know that the funeral would be at 10:00 a.m. the next morning at Sunset Memorial.

The machine stopped. None of the messages had sounded personal or from a woman. Marni felt more relief than she should have. Then realized a woman was exactly what Chase needed in his life. He just didn't know it yet.

CHASE HURRIEDLY DIALED the sheriff at his home number.

"I've got the autopsy results." Silence.

Chase held his breath.

"You did know Jabe was dying?"

The sheriff could have told him Martians had landed in

the Gallatin Valley and he'd have been less surprised. "Dying?"

"The coroner found a large amount of prescription drugs in Jabe's system. Painkillers. He was dying of cancer."

Chase felt his head swim. Flashes of memory. Glimpses of weakness he thought he'd seen in Jabe. The feeling that his father was in trouble long before the first accident.

"That's why he wanted a grandchild so badly," Chase said, more to himself than the sheriff. It also explained Jabe's one last attempt to get Chase into the family business. Dying of cancer. Just like Chase's mother. The irony of it made him sick.

"Given that," Sheriff Danner continued, "and the other evidence, the powder burns on his right hand, his prints on the .38, no sign of a struggle, his death has been ruled a suicide."

Chase raked his hand through his hair. "You said he had a lot of painkillers in his system. Enough that he couldn't have put up much of a struggle?" he asked, still trying to deal with the fact that his father had been dying.

"Yes, but there's no evidence to support homicide. Maybe the pain of dying was just too much for him. I'm sorry."

Jabe Calloway would have hung on until his very last breath, Chase thought as he replaced the receiver and looked up to find Marni standing in the bedroom doorway—sans the maternity form. Looking…great.

"Do you think you should be without—" He waved his hand through the air but he obviously didn't have the McCumber women's knack for nonverbal communication.

"Without what?" she asked.

"The baby," he said without thinking.

She looked confused.

"The maternity form."

"I know what you're referring to," she said patiently.

"You didn't really expect me to wear it all the time, did you?"

He hadn't thought about it, but now that he did, yes, he expected her to wear it. Not that he needed that stupid maternity form between them to keep him away from her. "What if someone stops by?"

She was giving him a strange look that said she thought he was overreacting. "I could put it on before you open the door."

He could tell she thought he was making too big a deal out of this. "Fine." He told her what the sheriff had said.

She stumbled to a chair and sat down, looking shocked. "Chase, I saw your father take some pills."

"When?"

She frowned. "That first day. And again the next, the day he died."

Was it his imagination or was her hair getting blonder each time she washed it? He'd thought it was redder the first time he'd seen her standing in the foyer at Calloway Ranch. The color had struck him somehow as wrong for her. He shook his head, realizing his mind had wandered in a direction he hadn't wanted to go.

Fighting to keep his distance, he headed for the door. "I have to go down to the store. I'll be right downstairs, so don't worry. You'll be safe and I won't be long." He turned and left without looking at her, wondering how he could spend time in that apartment with that woman without— Without what? Going crazy, he assured himself. Nothing more than that.

MARNI WALKED to the front window and looked out into the neighborhood. The houses she could see from the window looked old and in need of repair. She thought of the man who'd rented this apartment and realized how little she knew about Chase. Just like Elise, she reminded herself. They both had fallen in love with mystery men.

What did Chase do for a living? She had no clue. Whatever it was, it had him living in an apartment over a grocery store on a rundown side of town. If he thought that would put her off, he was sadly mistaken. Her own father had been a farmer until his death. He'd taught her that work shaped a person and made them strong and independent as well as gave them a purpose in life.

She smiled as she thought of her father. He'd applauded her when she worked her way through college to get her business degree, then took out a small business loan to open her boutique. He'd lived long enough to see her make a success of the shop and she'd reveled in his pride in her.

Her boutique. Marni called her manager and gave her the number where she could be reached, explaining that something had come up and she wouldn't be in the shop for a few days.

"You had a call earlier. From—just a minute, it's right here—a woman who said her name was Lilly. That's all she left. No number."

"I have her number, thanks," Marni said. "Did she say what she wanted?"

"She sounded a little…strange."

Very diplomatic. "Like she might have finished off a bottle of wine before she called?" Marni asked.

"I'm afraid so."

Long after Marni hung up, she couldn't get Lilly off her mind. Finally she picked up the phone and dialed the ranch. Hilda answered on the second ring. "I'm calling for Lilly."

"She can't be disturbed."

Passed out probably. "Is Vanessa around?"

"Just a moment," Hilda said.

Vanessa came on the line and Marni hoped she hadn't made a mistake by asking for her.

"Yes?" She sounded irritable.

"It's Elise McCumber," she said quickly.

"Yes?" Vanessa's voice got chillier.

"I'm calling about Lilly."

Silence.

"I'm worried about her."

"Lilly is not your concern, Miss McCumber." She hung up, but not before Marni heard another sound on the line. A faint cry. One single word. "Elise."

Marni quickly dialed the ranch again.

"I'm sorry, Lilly isn't taking phone calls," Hilda said.

"Can't I at least leave my number so she can call me?" Marni pleaded.

"I'm sorry. Mrs. Calloway gave specific instructions."

Marni bet she did.

Hilda hung up.

CHASE WALKED IN in time to hear Marni swear and then chastise herself for doing so.

"Something wrong?" he asked.

She spun around, obviously embarrassed at having been caught. But was it for swearing or something to do with the phone call? She hesitated a little too long answering and he decided it was the phone call.

"Just the usual problems at the boutique," she said vaguely.

He nodded, admiring her obvious inability to lie well. Nor did she seem to like doing it, he thought. Just like swearing. "Is it something you have to see to?"

"No, they seem to have everything under control now. I just worry too much."

Yeah, she did. About other people. Not about her boutique. Who was it this time? Her twin? Or someone else?

"I thought I'd make us something to eat, unless you'd

like to go out," he said, heading for the kitchen with a bag of groceries under his arm.

"I could help you," she said.

He groaned. Exactly what he needed, the two of them in the kitchen. As large as it was, it wouldn't be large enough. "Sure," he said, telling himself he could be warm and charming and distant at the same time. Hell, who was he kidding? He didn't know how to be warm and charming. It wasn't his nature. And if he couldn't keep his thoughts off her—as well as his hands—he'd have to depend on his nature to keep them apart.

But as he started taking the groceries out of the bag and felt her beside him, he wasn't even sure he could be distant. Or nasty enough. It had worked on other women, but not Marni McCumber. He didn't like the feeling that he was in over his head. And worse yet, Marni knew it.

CHASE SUGGESTED they eat on TV trays in the living room instead of in the breakfast nook. "There's a Jazz basketball game I'd like to see. If you don't mind."

She didn't mind. Not that she didn't realize why they weren't eating in the breakfast nook. And why he wanted the TV on while they ate. Look how he'd been in the kitchen. A man who seemed to have nerves of steel suddenly dropping the can opener, rattling pans, spilling the soup.

Marni had watched as Chase heated a can of tomato soup. She'd offered to help but he'd assured her he was an old hand at soup-heating. She didn't doubt that.

But she'd leaned against the counter and watched him, something that for some reason had made him very nervous. Was it possible she had more effect on him than he wanted to admit?

As she ate her soup and pretended to watch the basketball game on television, she found her thoughts returning to

Lilly. Why wouldn't Vanessa let her talk to her? It only deepened Marni's concerns. At least she would get to see Lilly at the funeral tomorrow and make a point of talking to her. Feeling better, Marni turned her attention to her soup, Chase and the game.

Chase seemed relieved when the game ended, the Jazz winning, and the meal officially over.

Marni washed the dishes while Chase put clean sheets on the bed. When she came out of the kitchen, he was making up a bed on the couch.

"I can sleep there," Marni offered.

He shook his head. "It's only temporary."

Subtle, she thought as she thanked him for the bedroom.

"I called the hospital. I guess the whole family is there. I thought we'd go see Hayes during visiting hours. It would be a good time to let the family know you're staying with me." He was also concerned about his half brother, Marni knew. He cared more about that family than he wanted to admit.

He studied her a moment. "You realize what this means. You're making yourself a sitting duck as long as you wear that maternity form. It's not too late to change your mind."

She shook her head. Better she and Sam be the bait than Elise and the baby. "It will just take me a moment to get ready."

BOZEMAN DEACONESS HOSPITAL sat up on a hill overlooking the city. When Chase parked, Marni spotted a new car parked in the lot with the license plate CALOWAY, misspelled obviously to make it fit.

"Vanessa?" Marni asked.

Chase nodded.

"I expected she'd drive something a little more..."

"Pretentious?" he suggested. "She only drives her Mercedes in the summer." He pointed to one of the Calloway

Ranch pickups and a small red four-wheel drive with FE-LICIA plates. "Looks like the whole family's here."

Marni hoped that meant Lilly, as well. She couldn't throw off the bad feeling she had. Nor forget the way Lilly had cried that one single word. "Elise."

They found everyone, Felicia, Dayton, Lilly, Vanessa, Hilda and Cook in Hayes's room. Hayes lay in bed, his head bandaged, his face ashen. Lilly sat in a chair next to him. Marni tried to get her attention but realized it was futile. Lilly appeared to be either highly inebriated or sedated.

Vanessa motioned for Dayton to take them out into the hall. Felicia came along.

"How's Hayes?" Chase asked.

"He seems to be okay. They gave him something to help him sleep," Dayton said. He shot Marni an angry look as if he blamed her for Hayes's accident.

"No memory loss?" Marni asked, thinking of Chase's accident. Would Hayes remember what had happened? Would he remember that Marni wasn't pregnant? But more important, would he remember Elise, *if* he was her lover?

"The docs say he responded to all their questions just fine," Dayton said, eyeing Marni suspiciously. "Why?"

"One Calloway who can't remember is enough," Chase said in answer. "Elise is staying at my place."

Dayton stared at his brother. "You're buying that this is your kid?"

"Yeah, do you have a problem with that?" Chase asked.

Marni felt Dayton's gaze, hot with hate. Was there a chance he thought she *was* Elise? Thought she was only pretending Chase was the father of her baby to get back at him? Or was it just because he thought she carried Jabe Calloway's grandchild, a child who could take the money from his own?

"I can't believe how much this baby has grown," Felicia said, her hand going to her stomach almost on cue.

She did look as though she'd grown overnight, Marni noted. Or maybe it was only the new maternity top that made her look that way.

Felicia linked a hand through Dayton's arm with a possessiveness that surprised Marni. "The doctor is a little worried I might deliver early, all the excitement," Felicia said.

"I suppose Jabe's will hasn't turned up," Chase said pointedly to Dayton.

"I heard you're determined to prove that Father was murdered," Dayton said with no little disgust.

"Yes," Chase said. "I am. Let me know if there's any change with Hayes." He put his arm around Marni's shoulders, his touch warm and reassuring. She reminded herself he was just doing this for show.

They left Felicia and Dayton standing outside Hayes's hospital room door. When Marni looked back, she saw that they appeared to be arguing over something. She wondered what.

"She's hoping she has that baby before yours," Chase said, following her gaze.

Did that explain the way Felicia was acting? Marni felt a chill. Did Felicia suspect Elise might be carrying her husband's child?

Chase seemed lost in his own thoughts. And from the scowl on his face, they were dark.

"I've been thinking," Marni said as they walked to his pickup.

Chase opened her door for her and gave her a look that said he wasn't sure he wanted to hear what she'd been thinking.

"If Dayton's telling the truth, and he came into the library immediately after the gunshot and there was no one else in the room except Jabe, then the killer was either still in the room or found another way out."

Chase didn't comment as she climbed into the pickup. He closed the passenger door and went around to the other side.

"Everyone was accounted for moments after the shot, so the killer wasn't still in the room," Chase said as he slid in next to her and started the pickup. "And there isn't another way out. Which means Dayton was lying."

"Maybe not. I think I know how the killer got away so quickly," Marni said.

Chase started to drive away from the hospital but stopped to turn and look at her.

"I think that house is a maze of secret stairways and passages," she said, launching into her theory enthusiastically. "Jabe told me it was originally built by a horse thief turned politician. A man like that would need ways to get around the house—and out of the house—without being seen." She took a quick breath, afraid he would think her theory foolish. "I have a feeling there's a passageway into the library."

He studied her but said nothing.

"And that's how the murderer got away, possibly with the will." She waited, but still he said nothing, as if he anticipated what was coming next. "There's one way to find out."

"Go back to the ranch and search for secret passages," Chase said.

"Everyone's at the hospital. It would be the perfect time."

He looked as though he might argue, desperately wanted to argue. "How did I know that's what you were thinking?"

"You do have a key to the house, don't you? It wouldn't be like breaking and entering."

He groaned. "You're going to be the death of me."

She certainly hoped not.

THEY DROVE to the ranch, the sky a dark velvet dusted with starlight. Just as Marni had said, no one was home. Chase used his key and let them in and Marni went right to the spot behind the stairs. She inspected the paneling closely, thinking about the way it opened and trying to remember exactly where Lilly had been standing when she'd unlocked it.

After a few futile attempts, Marni pressed a spot and the door slid open. She turned to find Chase watching, his eyes wide with amazement as he glanced into the passageway.

"How many more of these are there, do you think?" he asked.

Marni shook her head. "I would imagine there's at least one on every level, but I suspect there's more. The house could be a honeycomb of secret passageways. Anyone who knew them could get around without being seen."

"The question is, how many people know about this," he said, glancing up the stairwell.

"Lilly and the person who pushed over the armoire that day in the attic. Maybe more."

"Or maybe just one person," Chase said as he stepped into the stairwell. "How do you close the door?"

"I don't know." Marni started up the stairs behind him, immediately aware of being in the confines of the passageway with Chase.

The door slid closed behind them and Chase stopped with a start.

"There must be a device in one of the stairs," Marni said.

"I hope you're right and there's one that reopens it," Chase said. He pulled a flashlight from his jacket and lit the way as they climbed the stairs, stopping at the first landing to search for other doors.

They found one that opened onto a long narrow tunnel and followed it. At the end of the tunnel was a short flight of stairs that dropped to the first floor and what appeared to be a dead end. But as they neared the wall at the bottom of the stairs, a panel door slid open.

"It's the library," Chase said, shining his flashlight into the room. "Just like you thought."

"That's how the killer got away so fast with the will before Dayton came in."

"Unless Dayton is the killer," Chase said. He looked down at her, his body so close she could feel his heat radiating toward her. For just a moment she thought he might kiss her. She touched her tongue to her upper lip, her heart pounding. He let out a curse. "Come on," he said gruffly. "We don't know how much time we have."

They followed the stairway up, discovering an intricate system of corridors that appeared to run throughout the house and to all the bedrooms.

"Well, we know how the killer could have gotten away," Chase said. "But we haven't narrowed our list of suspects much."

Marni nodded in agreement. "Anyone who knows about the secret passages could have killed Jabe."

"Lilly is still at the top of that list," Chase reminded her as they reached the bottom stairs and the door automatically opened. "As far as we know, she might be the only person in the house who knows about the passageways."

They drove out of the ranch and were past Maudlow, almost to Poison Hollow, when they spotted headlights coming up the road. "We got out just in time," Chase said, sounding relieved.

As they passed the Calloway Ranch truck and Dayton, Marni looked back to see him hit the brakes.

"I think he recognized your truck," she said. "He'll know we were at the house."

Chase nodded. "That might work to our advantage, now that I think about it. If he's our killer, it will make him more nervous. He'll do something stupid."

"And if he's not?" Marni asked, trying not to think about what stupid thing the killer might do.

"Then he'll surely mention it to Vanessa and everyone in the house will know. It's impossible to keep a secret in that house."

Marni wasn't so sure about that. Jabe's killer was still at large. So was the person who wanted her dead.

Chase drove through a fast-food burger joint, and bought them both meals. They ate in the semidarkness of a shopping center, listening to golden oldies on the radio.

Back at the apartment, Chase made a big production out of how tired he was. Marni took the hint and headed for the bedroom. She climbed into bed, wondering about him, wondering about herself. How could she have fallen in love so quickly and with a man who wanted nothing to do with her? More important, what was she going to do about it?

CHASE BALLED UP the pillow and dropped his head onto it, determined Marni McCumber wasn't going to keep him from getting a good night's sleep.

But the ghosts of his past weren't about to let him sleep. He kept thinking about his father dying of cancer and keeping it a secret. Someone knew though. The same person who had filled Jabe full of painkillers and then blown a hole in his head.

No matter what the sheriff said, Jabe Calloway had been murdered. More than two attempts had been made on Marni's life. And one on Jabe's before that. The question was, Who was behind them?

One of his brothers was the father of Elise's baby. With the will as it was, that baby stood to inherit a huge portion of the Calloway fortune. Not that there wasn't plenty left for the rest of the family. But they were a greedy lot and he had to assume the money was the murderer's motive.

The family knew now that Marni was staying with him.

And eventually, one of them would make his or her move. Chase hoped he could figure out which one before that happened. But he was ready nonetheless. Under the couch was his .357, loaded and ready. Meanwhile, he had to find out which brother was Elise's lover.

While down in the grocery store earlier, Chase had called a friend of his, a photographer at the *Bozeman Chronicle,* and asked him if he could dig up shots of Dayton and Hayes Calloway from the file. Both of his brothers had been in the news for one business profile or another.

His friend Doug hadn't asked why, just said he'd have them tomorrow and would be happy to make Chase copies.

Getting the photos was at least a place to start, Chase thought. Not that he thought either of his brothers had tried to kill Marni and his own baby, especially a baby worth a small fortune. Certainly not to keep their wives. Lilly didn't even pretend to care for Hayes. Chase knew Felicia had to be aware of Dayton's many indiscretions. It wasn't as if he tried to keep them secret. No, Chase couldn't see either brother attempting murder to save his marriage.

But he could see either brother killing Jabe. The Calloway boys, himself included, hated their father for a variety of good reasons, Chase thought.

He closed his eyes, searching for sleep, praying for sleep. He groaned as his thoughts went straight to Marni. As much as he'd tried not to, he'd caught a glimpse of her as she'd come out of the bathroom wearing, of all things, a chenille robe. Wrapped modestly around her, covering everything but about two inches of her nightgown, sticking out the bottom of the robe. Flannel.

God, a woman in a flannel nightgown and a grandmother kind of robe and he couldn't get the image off his mind. Nor could he forget the scent of her. Soapy clean. Her face shiny. Her hair brushed and floating around her shoulders. Her feet and ankles bare.

He groaned again, sitting up on the couch to beat his pillow into submission, before he lay back down. Once again he started to tell himself all the reasons why it would never work, the two of them, then he remembered the phone call.

He reached over, picked up the receiver and hit redial. The phone rang and rang. He thought he'd been wrong. Maybe she had called the boutique as she'd indicated earlier. Maybe it was only his suspicious mind that made him think she hadn't wanted him to know whom she'd called.

The phone kept ringing. The boutique would be closed now. No one would answer. He was ready to hang up, feeling bad about suspecting Marni, when the phone quit ringing.

"Hello." The voice of a woman. Awakened from sleep. "May I help you?" Hilda asked.

She'd already helped him, Chase thought, hanging up. Now all he wondered was why Marni had called the ranch and why she felt the need to lie about it.

Lilly. He shook his head and lay down again, with a curse. Why couldn't Marni see that befriending Lilly was a big mistake? Because it was Marni's nature. She saw Lilly as defenseless and in need of an advocate. But Chase wondered just how defenseless Lilly Calloway really was. And if Hayes turned out to be Elise's lover, who knew what Lilly was capable of?

When Marni came out of the bathroom a second time, she wished him a good-night, turned out the light and closed the bedroom door.

He groaned as he heard the springs on the bed squeak as she climbed between the sheets. It was going to be a long night.

Chapter Fifteen

December 23

The next morning, Chase insisted Marni go down to the store for coffee while he made a few phone calls.

She got the impression he hadn't slept well. Also that she made him uncomfortable. She could see that whenever she was around him. And more and more, she hoped it might be because he shared some of her feelings. It made her smile as she took the stairs to the store.

To Marni's surprise the small grocery was nothing as she'd expected. The moment she opened the door she smelled fresh coffee. And something else. Cookies baking. Chocolate chip. Marni stood for a moment, amazed how light and airy the store was. And immaculately clean.

Somewhere behind the neat aisles music played softly. But it was another sound, children giggling, that Marni followed to the back of the store, past rows of canned goods.

"Good morning," a robust woman said from behind the counter and smiled. "You look like a woman who could use a cup of coffee."

"You read my mind," Marni said as the woman handed her a pottery cup filled with a wonderful almondy aroma.

"The store's specialty. You must be new to the neighborhood." She held out her hand. "I'm Angie."

Marni took her hand, thinking how different this little store was from the chains she'd been in. "Marni Mc-Cumber." Then quickly added, "Just call me Elise. Everyone does."

Angie smiled broadly. "Welcome to Burton's." She motioned to several comfortable-looking chairs set around a small round oak table. Behind the chairs were two bookshelves full of used paperbacks. Sunlight streamed in the windows, making the little setting so inviting Marni was tempted, but she knew Chase would be down any minute and anxious to go. He seemed awfully impatient this morning.

She heard the giggles again. They had an impish quality that drew her deeper into the store. She peeked around a corner into a large open room filled with sunshine, soft couches and chairs and toys. Large colorful animals had been painted on the walls. This room was not only the source of the music but the giggles.

Marni peered over the back of one of the couches to find a half-dozen preschool-age children huddled together amidst a pile of toys, playing a game with a young college-age woman. Whatever the game was, it had the kids in hysterics.

Marni smiled, unable to resist.

"They're having a grand old time today," Angie said. "Here, you'd better try one of these."

She offered Marni a cookie, straight out of the oven. "You run a day care in the back of the grocery," Marni asked as she took a bite of the cookie. "Oh this cookie is…delicious."

Angie smiled. "My own recipe." She looked back at the children. "It's something the owner of the store started. A place where the neighborhood could come not just to buy groceries but to visit, let the kids play for a while and give their moms a break. Some of the mothers in this neighborhood are going back to school, trying to get jobs, trying to better themselves. Burton's just helps them with a little free baby-sitting.''

"That's incredible," Marni said, looking around the store.

"It's kind of a haven in an area of the city that's seen better days," Angie said. "Chase says the neighborhood will get better if there's hope. That's what Burton's is. Hope."

"Chase?" Marni asked in surprise. "Chase Calloway *owns* Burton's?"

Angie laughed. "I thought you knew."

She looked around the store, seeing it with different eyes. Chase Calloway never ceased to amaze her. But she wondered if she'd ever get to know the real him or would he always try to hide that from her? That's if he even gave her a chance to get to know him, she reminded herself.

Behind her, Marni heard the door of the store open with the faint tinkle of the bell. She turned, expecting to see Chase. Instead, a young woman came through the door. Two things instantly struck Marni about her. Her long dark hair and her enormous pregnant stomach.

"How are you doing, Raine, dear?" Angie inquired as the woman worked her way back through the rows of groceries.

"I can't wait until I have this baby," Raine said, sounding exhausted. She smiled at Marni, taking in Sam.

Marni was surprised how young the woman was.

"At least finals are over and next semester will be easier," Angie said, totaling up the small amount of groceries the young woman put on the counter.

When Raine reached into her purse to pay, Angie stopped her. "Chase says since you've been volunteering in the back it's his treat today."

The woman looked up, surprised and instantly relieved.

"Thank you, Angie. Please tell him when you see him how much I appreciate this."

"Not at all. You just take care of yourself and that baby. And if you need anything, anything at all, Chase says for you to let him know."

"Does Chase take that kind of interest in all his customers?" Marni asked after Raine left.

"That one he worries about. So young. Got herself in a bind. But she'll be fine once she has her baby."

Marni wanted to ask more about Raine, but the bell over the front door tinkled again and this time Chase's broad shoulders filled the doorway. He gave her a curt nod, then retreated outside.

"I'd better get going," Marni said, finishing the wonderful coffee and handing Angie the cup. "What do I owe you?"

Angie shook her head. "No charge for new people in the neighborhood. Just come back soon."

"I will," Marni said, hurrying out to find Chase waiting for her in the pickup. She climbed in, pleasantly surprised to find that he'd let it run and warm up for her.

"That's quite the store you live over," Marni said, glancing back. "Although I do wonder how the owner makes a living, giving away free child care and groceries."

If Chase heard her, he didn't take the bait. She doubted he'd ever volunteer any information about himself.

"I have to check on a couple of jobs," he said, shifting the pickup into gear.

"Jobs?" He had other jobs?

They had only gone a few blocks when Chase pulled up in front of a small rundown house that was in the process of being remodeled. "I'll only be a moment," he said and got out.

Marni watched him through the front window of the house, talking to an older man doing carpentry work inside.

A few minutes later, Chase came back to the pickup. He drove a block to another house, this one in even worse repair than the last.

"You're a carpenter?" she asked when she couldn't stand it any longer.

"Would that surprise you?" he asked.

Nothing about him would surprise her. And yet everything did. Especially Burton's. Why had he named it that? she wondered. "I've wondered what you did for a living ever since I found out you didn't work for Calloway Ranches," she said.

Not surprisingly, he didn't respond.

"Shouldn't you be working? I mean, will you lose your job?"

He smiled. "Are you worried that I'll go hungry?"

She laughed. "Not as long as you live over that grocery store. I'm sure the owner would see that you didn't starve until you got on your feet again."

Chase opened his door. "I can take a few days off without being evicted. I'll be right back."

They checked a couple more of Chase's jobs, all in the same neighborhood as his apartment, then Chase took her back to his place where he opened a can of bean with bacon soup and they ate an early lunch in front of the TV.

Marni realized he was using the TV to keep from having to talk to her. She suspected he was using the apartment and the soup to try to send her a message. Only he didn't know how many ball games she could watch, how many cans of soup she could eat. Nor did he know that by pushing her away he only made her more determined to find the Chase he was trying so hard to hide from her. She wasn't just a sucker for people in trouble; she had the patience of Job. She could wait out Chase Calloway, she told herself.

CHASE SAW MARNI gazing out the window wistfully. He glanced around the apartment, suddenly aware of how drab it looked. Certainly no sign that Christmas was only two days away.

He felt almost guilty for the way he'd been behaving. Almost. He was just being himself. Fighting for his life was more like it. *Whatever you say, Scrooge.* He groaned silently. Okay, so maybe he'd been laying it on pretty thick with the canned soup in front of the television, the fast-food burgers in the pickup cab.

He looked at Marni's slim back, her hair golden in the light, and felt a stab of contrition. Marni was trying to save her pregnant twin and what was Chase Calloway doing to help? Not much. He was too busy trying to shore up the walls around his heart.

"I have to run an errand. Just to be safe, would you mind staying with Angie in the store until I get back? I won't be long." He knew he sounded mysterious. "It's a quick job I have to do." He knew she'd understand work if nothing else.

When he came back, he found her in the day-care part of the store, playing a game with the kids. He stood watching her, overwhelmed with emotions that choked him up and made him angry with himself. He'd hoped these ridiculous feelings would go away but, if anything, they seemed to be getting stronger. If he didn't know better, he'd think he was falling in love with this woman.

"Come on," he said after she'd finished the game. "We have to get ready."

She looked up at him, surprised, it seemed, to find him standing there. He suspected she knew what he'd been feeling moments before. Sometimes he felt as if she could see into his heart. That was a frightening thought, when he didn't even know his own mind around her, let alone his heart.

"I got you something," he said as they climbed the stairs.

He felt suddenly foolish. What if she read more into the gift than he'd meant her to? He mentally kicked himself for feeling anxious as he opened the door to the apartment for her and watched her face to see her reaction.

MARNI STARED at the hopelessly lopsided Christmas tree standing by the front window.

"It was the only one left in town," Chase said quickly. "I know how you are about Christmas and all. . ."

Her eyes filled with tears. "It's the most beautiful Christmas tree I've ever seen," she said, turning to look at him.

He smiled, appearing relieved and at the same time embarrassed. "I picked up some lights and I thought—"

"The kids in the day care would make ornaments," she finished for him. "Maybe string some popcorn and cranberries and make a party out of it."

He laughed and nodded. "That's exactly what I thought you'd say."

She flew to him, wrapping her arms around his neck in a hug. "Thank you."

"It's nothing," he said softly as his arms came around her.

Marni stood in the circle of his arms, her arms around his neck, looking up into his gaze.

He drew her closer, his lips coming down on hers. Gentle, tentative, then demanding.

He drew back to look into her eyes. "We'd better get ready for the funeral." And pulled away.

SUNSET MEMORIAL CEMETERY sat on a wooded hillside overlooking Bozeman. Most days only pine trees and tombstones silhouetted the winter sky. Today hundreds of cars lined the narrow cemetery roads.

"Vanessa loves a spectacle," Chase said in disgust as he parked the pickup. "She's finally found a role she can excel at—Jabe Calloway's grieving widow." He motioned to the camera crews around Vanessa. The widow wore black and appeared to be sniffling into a hankie.

Chase led Marni up the freshly plowed road to stand at the back of the large crowd of mourners. Other camera crews had set up their equipment graveside, anxious to get thirty seconds of the rich, notorious and dead on the nightly news. Chase wondered how many of the mourners were there for the chance to see themselves on TV, how many had come out of morbid curiosity and how many wanted to be sure Jabe Calloway was dead and gone.

One thing Chase knew for sure, none had attended out of friendship. Jabe Calloway had no friends that Chase knew of. Only enemies. And family. And at least one of them was an enemy, too, he thought.

As the service started, Dayton took his place between his mother and wife. Chase watched Felicia and Vanessa scan the crowd furtively from behind their black veils.

"Do you see Lilly?" Marni whispered beside Chase.

Lilly was conspicuously absent. "Vanessa was probably afraid Lilly would embarrass her."

Vanessa had called earlier that morning at the apartment.

"The media will be at the funeral," she'd announced.

"So?" he'd said, still half-asleep and always easily annoyed with Vanessa and her idea of important life matters. He'd also had a long, sleepless night on the couch he didn't even want to think about.

"We must present a united front."

"What the hell does that mean?" Chase asked.

"We must look like a family."

"Well, for that, you're going to have to do a lot more than get everyone to show up at Jabe's funeral," Chase snapped.

"The point is, I want you there."

"That's a first, Vanessa."

A deep sigh. "Can I count on you, Chase, or not?" she asked with somewhat controlled anger.

"Vanessa, there is only one thing you can count on from me. I know someone in this big, happy family murdered my father and made several attempts on Elise McCumber's life. I plan to see that person behind bars."

"Have you lost your mind?" she hissed into the phone, obviously afraid the hired help might overhear. "The coroner ruled it a suicide and Elise— Really, Chase, she staged those accidents, any fool can see that. The only problem was, one of them went awry and now Hayes is in the hospital."

Chase swore. "That's ridiculous. Elise could have been killed that day in the barn if I hadn't gotten there when I did."

"But she wasn't and my Hayes was almost killed," Vanessa said, her voice pure ice. "I don't understand why you, of all people, believe anything that woman says. Unless you are the father of her baby."

He gritted his teeth. "You might as well hear it from me, Vanessa. Elise is carrying a Calloway baby."

"The family will demand a paternity test. Imagine the bad publicity if it gets out."

He wanted to laugh. "Vanessa, imagine the bad publicity when someone in the family goes down for murder. And it will happen. I'll see to that."

Chase could hear the anger as hard and brittle as Vanessa Calloway herself. "Keep throwing around that kind of talk and I'll have the family lawyer slap you with a suit so fast it will make your head swim."

"Truth is an absolute defense, Vanessa."

Vanessa had slammed down the phone.

"So much for that big, happy family," Chase had said and hung up.

A breeze whispered through the pines now, sending snow

showering down as the pastor began to speak, referring t
Jabe Calloway in glowing terms. Chase felt ill and wishe
he hadn't come. Vanessa would be furious that he hadn'
arrived on time anyway. And even more angry that h
hadn't stood with the "family." That made him feel a littl
better.

All Chase could think about was getting photographs o
his half brothers and sending them to Marni's twin. H
wanted the mystery of Elise McCumber's lover solved a
quickly as possible. Then he would find the person wh
killed Jabe and made attempts on Marni's life.

MARNI SEARCHED the crowd for Lilly, hoping Chase wa
wrong. Worry stole through her when she realized Lill
hadn't made the funeral. Something was terribly wrong
Marni felt it more strongly this morning. Lilly had looke
so out of it at the hospital last night.

A car came speeding up the road, sending snow flyin
into the air. A murmur moved through the crowd as the ca
came to an abrupt stop and the driver's door slammed open

"What the hell?" Chase said beside her.

Marni stared at the mourners, wondering what the com
motion was about but unable to see the car and who ha
arrived in it.

Then she heard Lilly's voice calling Vanessa's name a
she moved through the crowd. The reverend halted in mid
sentence and everyone turned as Lilly burst through th
mourners, almost falling onto the casket.

"Lilly." Vanessa's voice carried across the cold ceme
tery. So did her obvious shock and disbelief.

Lilly stood smiling at her mother-in-law. Two things in
stantly struck Marni as odd. One was Lilly's inebriated state
considering she'd obviously just driven in from the ranch
The second was the scarf she had on. She wore basic funera
black, except for the bright multicolored scarf around he

neck. Even from this distance, Marni recognized it as the scarf Vanessa had been wearing the first night she'd met her. It was the same scarf Marni had slipped on or the stairs.

Vanessa staggered. Dayton reached for her but she dropped too quickly.

"My God, she's fainted," Marni heard someone cry.

Suddenly the crowd obscured both Vanessa's fallen form and the rest of the family.

"I don't believe this," Chase said, shaking his head.

By the time Vanessa had been revived and the crowd moved back to let the funeral service continue, Lilly and her car were gone. And Marni wondered how a woman that drunk could get away that quickly. She remembered the look that she'd seen pass between Vanessa and Lilly.

"Something's wrong," she told Chase as the service broke up. He hurriedly ushered her to the pickup to avoid a pack of media bearing down on them.

"You're just starting to notice that?" Chase asked as he pulled away before a camera crew could reach them.

"There's something going on between Vanessa and Lilly," Marni said, recalling the scene they'd just witnessed. "How did Lilly disappear so fast?"

"Maybe Dayton got her out of there before she could cause any more trouble," Chase suggested.

"I still think Lilly is in some kind of trouble, more trouble than just her drinking."

Chase sighed as he pulled over a few blocks from the cemetery and turned to Marni. "Look, I know you see Lilly as the underdog here, but you could be wrong, Marni. Lilly looked like she could take care of herself at the funeral, whatever all that was about."

"Lilly tried to reach me at the boutique. She left a message, but when I called her back at the ranch, Hilda wouldn't let me talk to her. Chase, I heard her on the line a moment before I was cut off. She only said one word."

"Help?"

Marni gave him an impatient look. "Elise."

"Elise?" he asked skeptically.

"It was the way she said it."

"Lilly's been in trouble for years, Marni. When she'
drinking, she doesn't even know what she's doing."

"I just have this bad feeling."

"So do I. The only difference is, my bad feeling say
Lilly might be a murderer."

Marni chewed at her lower lip for a moment. "You reall
think I could be that wrong about her?"

"I don't want to take any chances." He raked a han
through his hair. "Look, Marni, I admire your compassion
I even admire you putting yourself on the line for your sis
ter. I don't mean to sound callous but Lilly isn't our prob
lem. Our problem is finding out which of my brothers is th
father of Elise's baby. And you seem to have forgotten tha
someone wants you dead."

"There haven't been any more attempts," Marni said.

"Right, and maybe there won't be." He didn't sound a
if he believed that any more than she did. "Look, I have
friend getting photos of Dayton and Hayes to show Elis
We should be able to pick them up."

"Elise has a fax machine at the farm," Marni said, anx
ious to get this over with. "And I have one at the boutique."

THEY DROVE to the boutique after picking up the picture
and parked in the alley. Marni had called her manager t
let her know they would be coming.

Marni noticed barricades going up downtown and sud
denly realized why. "I'd completely forgotten. The Christ
mas Stroll is tonight," she said, a little sad she wouldn't b
at the boutique. It was the busiest night of the year, but als
one of the most fun. She always baked Christmas cookie
and made hot apple cider to give away. It was the last bi

event before Christmas, one that brought the town together in the true spirit of the holiday.

"There's next Christmas," Chase said, reading her thoughts.

Next Christmas? "This one isn't over yet," Marni said, thinking of her Christmas wish.

"What do you want for Christmas?" Chase asked, surprising her.

She glanced over at him. "Why are you asking me that?"

He shrugged. "I just wondered."

"You're afraid we aren't going to get this thing solved by Christmas, aren't you?"

"Maybe I just wanted to get you something," he said softly. "It looks a little bare under the tree. If there's something you really want, I wish you'd tell me." When she didn't say anything, he got out.

Tears filled Marni's eyes and she felt so choked up she didn't dare speak as she followed him. Snowflakes began to lazily fall from the heavens and she breathed in the cold air, intensely aware of the man walking beside her. Oh yes, there was something she really wanted. She'd made her Christmas wish that night at the farm, staring up at the stars. Hastily she wiped her tears and looked over at Chase. "I'll think about it."

Marni unlocked the back door and stepped into the small, neat office. The door into the boutique was closed but Marni could hear the sound of shoppers in the next room.

She shrugged off her coat and mittens, then took the two photographs Chase handed her. She dialed the number at the farm and told Elise what she planned to do.

"One of them has to be my Chase, huh," Elise said.

"Yes," Marni agreed. "Call me here at the boutique on the private line and let me know which one." She hung up.

Putting the first photo facedown in the fax machine, Marni dialed the number at the farm again and hit start.

Slowly the photo of Dayton rolled through the machine. Then the one of Hayes.

Marni glanced at Chase. He looked as nervous as she felt. The phone rang, making her jump. She picked up the receiver on the first ring.

"That's him," El cried, sounding close to tears.

Marni shot a glance at Chase. "Which one? The first photo or the second?"

"The second," Elise cried. "Who is he?"

"Chase's half brother Hayes."

"He's the one in the hospital?"

"Yes, but he's doing fine."

Elise began to cry. "And he's married?"

"Yes."

"Oh, Marni, I don't understand. I just don't understand."

"Neither do I, but we'll find out. Meanwhile, listen to me, you have to think of the baby."

"He loves me," El cried. "He loves our baby. I know he does." She hung up.

Marni replaced the receiver and looked over at Chase again, stunned. "I'm so surprised. I thought it would be Dayton. Not Hayes." And yet, hadn't she found it impossible to believe her sister could ever fall for a man like Dayton? "How could Hayes do this to my sister?"

"I have to admit it surprises me," Chase said. "But there's history there you don't know about."

"What kind of history?" Marni asked.

"When he married Lilly it was because he thought she was pregnant with his child. When the baby was born, there were complications. That's when Hayes discovered he wasn't the father. It was no secret, not even to him, that Lilly had been in love with someone else and married Hayes on the rebound. Then when the baby died, Lilly had a breakdown of sorts."

"How horrible for Lilly. And Hayes."

"I don't think they ever had much of a marriage," Chase said.

"Then why did he stay with her?"

Chase shook his head. The noise in the shop grew louder. "I guess we'll have to ask him."

CHASE PUSHED OPEN the door to Hayes's hospital room for Marni. Hayes saw her, sat up in surprise and quickly lay back. "You're not Elise."

"No," Marni said. "I'm her twin, Marni McCumber."

"But Elise is why we're here," Chase said, closing the door behind him as he approached his brother's bed.

Hayes closed his eyes for a moment. "I can explain."

"There is only one thing I need to know," Marni said. "Do you love my sister?"

Hayes looked over at her for a moment, then smiled. "You look so much like her. When I saw you at the house— I guess I don't have to tell you what a shock that was. Especially to find out Elise was pregnant."

"You didn't know?" she asked in surprise.

"How could I? The last time we'd talked was August and I'd been so…foolish. I thought that's why you were pretending Chase was the father of your baby."

"Why did you use *my* name?" Chase demanded, trying to hold in the anger he felt. For all they knew, it had been Hayes who'd tried to kill Marni.

"I guess I wanted to be you," Hayes said. "Unencumbered. Elise was the first woman I'd met who—" He looked away, his face reddening. "I'm sorry I involved you in this, Chase. I never thought it would go past an innocent lunch."

"You never answered my question," Marni reminded him.

Hayes met her gaze. "Do I love Elise? Oh God yes. When I saw you at the ranch and thought you were Elise,

I knew you had to be carrying my baby. I was overjoyed. Just the thought of us having a baby together—''

"You came to my room that night," Marni said.

He nodded. "I had to see you. To try to explain. To tell you how happy I was about the baby. And to warn you about Lilly. She'd found out about us."

"Excuse me," Chase interrupted. "You're telling us Lilly knows about you and Elise?"

"She has for months. She was so angry—"

"I would imagine she was," Chase said. "What did you think was going to happen?"

"You don't understand," Hayes said. "I've wanted a divorce for years. But I couldn't."

"Because Jabe would have disapproved," Chase said with disgust. "And Vanessa would have thrown a fit that you might want to soil the family name with Lilly's dirty laundry, because I'll bet Lilly wouldn't have gone quietly."

"I didn't care. Not about any of that. Do you really think what Father and Mother thought would make me stay in a loveless marriage? Especially after I'd met Elise? Do you really think I'm that shallow?"

Chase looked at Hayes. Yeah, that's exactly what he'd thought. Shallow and spineless.

"Lilly told me if I ever left her, she'd kill herself. I believed her."

"Lilly needs help, professional help," Marni said.

"Don't you think I tried to get it for her?" Hayes cried. "Vanessa and Jabe wouldn't hear of it. I went behind their backs and set up an appointment for Lilly. She refused to go and told Vanessa. Now Lilly has made herself a prisoner in that house with Vanessa as warden."

"Surely there is some way to make Lilly see that she needs help," Marni said.

"Right now, I'm more worried about Elise," Hayes said. "Is she all right? And the baby?"

Marni nodded.

"Someone's trying to kill Marni because they think she's Elise and carrying a Calloway baby," Chase said. "Want to tell us what you know about that?"

"I was afraid of this," Hayes said, his expression pained. "I've never seen Lilly so…upset. That's why I sent that note for you to meet me in the barn," he said to Marni. "I wanted to warn you about Lilly. Then I realized you weren't Elise."

"Someone had fixed the latch on Wind Chaser's stall so it wouldn't lock," Chase said. "Marni says she smelled Lilly's perfume just before the accident. It wasn't the first accident, either."

Hayes looked sick. "I talked to Lilly this morning. She says she wants a divorce. I don't think she'll bother you or Elise again."

"If she's the one who tried to hurt me," Marni said. "I don't think she was."

"Marni is a little too trusting," Chase said, shaking his head.

"I'm not going back to the ranch," Hayes said. "I've been thinking about leaving the family business for some time. Now with Father gone, there's nothing stopping me." He addressed Marni. "When can I see Elise?"

"Not until the killer is behind bars," Chase said.

"You don't think I would harm Elise and my baby, do you?" he asked Chase angrily.

"We don't want to lead anyone to Elise," Chase said, realizing he did trust Hayes.

"Find this guy," Hayes said emotionally. "Don't let anything happen to Elise and my baby, please, Chase."

Chase took his brother's hand and squeezed it. Maybe there was more to Hayes Calloway than he'd thought all these years.

Chapter Sixteen

As Marni and Chase left the hospital it started to snow. They drove toward town and the Christmas Stroll. Christmas music played as musicians roamed through the crowds filling the barricaded streets. Marni rolled down her window as Chase drove slowly along one of the open streets, dodging shoppers, street performers and vendors.

The smell of roasted chestnuts, hot apple cider and peppermint sticks wafted through the air. A theatrical group from *The Nutcracker* danced on a street corner. A group of singing Santas moved through the crowds in a wave of bright red.

Shoppers roamed in and out of the stores, their arms filled with packages as overhead, Christmas lights glittered in the falling snow and bundled-up children waited in line to sit on a real Santa's broad lap and tell him their last-minute Christmas wishes.

"I'm sorry about your Christmas," Chase said.

"It's not so bad. Who knows, maybe by Christmas Eve there'll be a happy ending." She turned to see Chase's profile, his jaw set, his expression one of stubborn determination. "For Hayes and Elise and their baby," she added hastily.

He didn't comment, just wound his way back to Burton's parked in the dark shadows of the store, but didn't get out

Instead he sat, staring out into the darkness. There weren't a lot of Christmas decorations on the houses in this part of town. Nor many streetlights.

He raked a hand through his hair. "Maybe you should go to the farm until this is over."

"You think the killer will eventually come after me here, don't you?" Marni asked quietly.

He nodded and glanced out his side window. Snow had begun to pile up on the windshield, obscuring the darkness.

"I'm not leaving you," she said.

He shook his head. "Staying with me could be the biggest mistake of your life."

She doubted he was talking about the killer who was after her. "I'm willing to take my chances."

He turned to look at her. The tension in the pickup cab arced between them like an electrical short. She met his gaze, feeling the heat of it warm her skin. She knew if he ever let himself go—

"You don't understand," he said, his voice so filled with anguish it was all she could do not to pull him into her arms.

"My childhood wasn't like yours. You have no idea what it was like."

"Tell me," she whispered.

He leaned his forearms over the steering wheel, his gaze still directed into the darkness. "I didn't have a home, just a series of rented apartments, some little more than shacks." The words seemed to come with great difficulty. She knew how hard it must be for him to tell her and her heart broke for him.

"We kept on the move, my mother living in fear that Jabe would find out she hadn't had the abortion, that he'd come and steal me away from her, and all the time she was dying of a broken heart because he didn't come after her."

She didn't speak, just waited as the snow fell silently outside the pickup.

"I used to desperately want what other kids had," he went on. "A home. A family. Someone who loved me and took care of me. My mother was dying of a broken heart from the time I was born and finally from cancer. She wasn't there emotionally most of the time nor physically at the end."

The windows began to fog over, the cold to creep in around the doors. Marni hugged Sam as she watched Chase struggle with words to describe his childhood, his pain.

"My mother taught me not to get attached to anything or anyone. About the time I made friends, we moved. What was horrible was that she never stopped loving him, couldn't seem to stop no matter what he'd done to her. I watched her love him and saw that love kill her long before the cancer did and I promised myself I would never love like that, certainly never that stupidly, that blindly."

Marni stared at his profile, a dark silhouette in the pickup cab, finally understanding why Chase had fought his feelings for her so hard.

He turned to look at her. "For thirty-five years I've managed to keep that promise to myself."

She could see the pleading in his eyes. The last thing he wanted was to fall in love with her.

"The Christmas Stroll must be breaking up," he said, glancing past her.

Marni could still hear faint Christmas music in the distance. A group of people passed in front of the store, their laughter carrying on the night air. Just a few blocks away she knew the police would be removing barricades as street cleaners came in to sweep up the last of the Christmas Stroll.

The air suddenly felt colder in the pickup; the night darker as she felt Chase pull away from her and yet not move a muscle. Snow fell harder, covering the windshield.

"We better go in," he said, sounding as though that was the last thing he wanted to do.

Marni opened her door and stepped out, her hand going to Sam, a connection to Chase, although a tentative one. As she stepped from the pickup into the pool of darkness beside the grocery store, she heard a sound and turned. He came out of the blackness under the stairs to the apartment. At first he was only a movement. Then a flash of white beard against the red of his costume. Santa Claus. Under the stairs?

He rushed at her, knocking her off balance. She fell back into the side of the pickup as her purse was wrenched from her grasp. A cry escaped her lips. She heard Chase slam his door and take off running past her after the mugger.

Santa sprinted across the street to the alley, her purse under his arm, with Chase in hot pursuit.

Marni leaned against the truck, her legs trembling, her pulse a drum inside her head. The sound of them running died away into the night. Cold and darkness closed in. Snowflakes fell in a white sheet of silence, cocooning her. She suddenly felt incredibly alone.

Chase. She had only a moment to fear for him before she heard it. Movement. Followed by an unerring icy awareness that the sound had come from under the wooden stairs. In the black hole of blackness beneath them. The same place the Santa mugger had hidden.

She looked but could see nothing, falling snow and night cloaking whatever hid there, as she felt for the door handle behind her, thinking she might have a chance to get inside the pickup before—

Something emerged from under the stairs, furtive, menacing, seizing her as effectively as hands around her throat.

She froze for that split second. Unable to move. To speak. To breathe. Something too large, too odd-shaped to be human moved quickly through the snow and darkness. And she knew it was coming for her.

CHASE SPRINTED after the mugger, his leg aching with the slamming movement. It was an ache he ignored. Cold anger fueled his body. He closed the distance between himself and the Santa. A mugger in Bozeman. In his neighborhood. He'd only heard of such a thing here one other time.

Santa had almost reached the end of the alley. A little closer and Chase could grab the guy's red suit. The mugger turned and Chase saw the eyes looking out of the white fake beard.

The memory came back in a sharp fast burst. Chase felt a jolt. A clear shot of memory. The truck barreling down on him and his father. The sound of the engine wound up. Streetlights reflecting off the windshield. The feel of the air, cold. The smell of snow. And the face behind the truck's steering wheel. Chase let out an oath as he saw the driver's face—the same face as the Santa in front of him.

Just then the Santa mugger flung Marni's purse hard at Chase's head. Chase didn't see it coming, didn't even know what it was until it hit him in the face, momentarily blinding him. It slowed him just enough. The Santa rounded the corner, ducked between two parked cars and disappeared into a crowd of people returning from the Stroll.

Chase stopped, leaning over to catch his breath, the memory still sharp and clear. The face of the hit-and-run driver. The face of the Santa. A man who used to work for Calloway Ranches. Monte Decker.

MARNI FUMBLED for the door handle, found it and pulled. Too late. The huge object came out of the snowstorm at her. Marni looked up it in surprise and confusion, shocked by its size, by its face. *Good God, it was the Nutcracker*. The giant toy threw itself at her, slamming her against the pickup, knocking the breath from her lungs as it tried to pin her there.

She struggled against its superior strength and size. The pressure lessened for just a moment and she thought it would run off. Then she realized that wasn't what it had in mind.

A hysterical scream jammed in her throat as she saw what it pulled from inside its costume and now held in its gloved hand. The knife blade glittered silver in the snowfall as it lunged at her.

Marni screamed.

CHASE HAD JUST bent down to pick up Marni's purse from the snow when he heard her scream.

He ran, the pain in his leg, the fire in his lungs, forgotten. Through the falling snow he could make out a shape. Huge. Misshapen. It stood over something lying on the ground beside his pickup.

My God! Marni. He didn't realize until later that he yelled. A shriek filled with anguish and fear. A war cry.

The strange figure scurried away into the snow and darkness behind the store. Chase flung himself to his knees in the snow at Marni's side and pulled her to him, feeling her warm blood soak through his mittens.

"Marni," he cried, a silent prayer racing through his head. Please, God, don't let her die.

"Chase," she whispered.

He heard a door open across the street. "Get an ambulance," he yelled. "Hurry."

Chapter Seventeen

Chase paced the floor of the hospital waiting room, too anxious to sit. He couldn't believe he'd been so stupid as to let a mugger trick him and draw him away from Marni so the killer could get that close to her. He cursed his stupidity, paced and prayed. When the doctor finally stuck his head out from the emergency room, Chase nearly pounced on him.

"Is she all right?" he demanded. "Tell me she's all right."

"She's fine," the doctor said quickly. "The wound is superficial. The maternity form she was wearing saved her from serious injury. She was very lucky."

"Can I take her home?" Chase asked, forgetting that just hours ago he hadn't wanted to be in the apartment with her, hadn't trusted himself.

"She's as anxious as you are to get out of here," the doctor told him. "I assume you've already talked with the police."

Chase nodded. The police had an APB out for Monte Decker and his unknown accomplice. "They've questioned Marni?"

"I believe they want her to make a formal statement later," the doctor said and pushed open the emergency-room door.

Chase saw Marni sitting on one of the gurneys, a white bandage showing through the slash in her maternity top. In the trash was her maternity form. She saw him and got to her feet, a tentative smile on her face. He shrugged off his coat as he walked toward her.

"Just a flesh wound," she said, sounding as relieved as he felt.

He draped his coat over her shoulders. "Let's get out of here. I called us a cab."

The cab was waiting outside the hospital when they came out. Chase opened the door for her and slid in beside her. He put his arm around her, not surprised how natural it felt when she curled against him.

"Are you cold?" he asked, feeling her tremble as the cab pulled away.

She shook her head, but still he pulled her closer.

"No reason to be cold," he said, holding her, looking out into the darkness, still filled with rage at the person who'd done this to her. "Or afraid. I called the ranch and told them you lost your baby. You're safe now." He hoped.

MARNI SNUGGLED against him, needing the feel of his arm around her, his warmth soaking into her. She felt as if Sam had been real. Had been her child. And Chase's.

Chase carried her up the stairs, against her protests, and into the bedroom where he placed her on the bed with the greatest of care. He stood for a moment as if he didn't know what to do.

"Chase," she said quietly when he started to leave.

He turned to look at her, his gaze locking with hers. "It's late," he said, but didn't move, didn't stop staring into her eyes. "It wouldn't work."

Her heart began to pound in anticipation. "What wouldn't work?" she whispered, hoping they were talking about the same thing and that he was dead wrong.

"If we made love it wouldn't change anything."

She started to tell him that she didn't care, but he cut her off.

"Making love to you would be a huge mistake," he said, moving closer. "I'd regret it. But worse, you'd regret it."

"I'd never regret it."

He shook his head. "You know when you look at me like that, what it does to me?"

"No," she answered truthfully. She only knew what his look did to her.

"And those nightclothes of yours…"

"My nightclothes?" she asked in surprise. Surely he wasn't talking about her flannel nightgown and chenille robe?

"Do you have any idea how sexy you look in them?"

She laughed, having no idea what he was talking about.

"Oh, yeah," he said, brushing a lock of her hair back from her face as he sat down on the edge of the bed next to her. "And when you sit there like that, all innocent, wide-eyed and trusting—" He let out a sigh as he brushed his bare knuckles across the skin of her cheek. "You're asking too much, Marni."

"What am I asking, Chase?" she whispered, her heart pounding at the look in his eyes.

"You're asking me to surrender my heart. I can't do it. That's what I've been trying to tell you from the moment we met."

"Not surrender," Marni said, bringing his fingers to her lips. "Just open it a little."

He cupped her face in his hands. "When I'm around you, I want to open myself up to you." He drew her to him. "Your mouth makes me crazy to kiss you. And when I look into your eyes—" He kissed her, his lips, his tongue, seeking, searching, demanding.

She gave herself to him, opening her lips to let him inside

to explore, to lay claim to her. He took her mouth with an intimacy that both shocked and excited her.

She wrapped her arms around his neck and kissed him back, wanting to give as much as to receive. She hoped enthusiasm would make up for her lack of experience.

He pulled back to look into her face. "If we do this, it won't be making love," he said softly.

She smiled. "I want you, Chase. I've never wanted anyone like I want you."

She watched him unbutton her top and slide it off her shoulders to expose the jogging bra she wore underneath. She wished she were the kind of woman who wore skimpy, lacy underthings.

But to her surprise, he let out a sigh of pleasure. She followed his gaze to her breasts, and saw that her nipples strained against the stretchy material of the bra. He ran a thumb over one taut nipple, making her shudder.

He kissed her again, this time with a fever that sent her pulse skyrocketing. She felt his hands cup her bottom and she let out a sigh of pleasure of her own.

He pulled back to look at her, his blue eyes dark and serious. "I don't want to hurt you."

"You won't hurt me," she said, not sure if they were talking about her flesh wound or her heart. Then she did something totally out of character. She drew the bra over her head, exposing her bare breasts to his eyes, to his mouth, to his hands.

She felt a jolt, the tremor centering deep inside her as he tasted, touched and teased her nipples into hard, aching nubs. "Please, Chase," she pleaded, reaching for the buttons of his shirt, fumbling them open until she could lay her palms against the silken hardness of his chest. She could feel his heart hammering beneath her hands. She slid his shirt over his broad shoulders to let it drop behind him.

They sat like that for a long moment. Breathing, hearts

pounding, just looking at each other. "Stop me now, Marni."

She shook her head. "I can't do that."

He slid off the bed to pull her to her feet. She melted against the warm strength of him as he tugged off her jeans. He smiled as he watched her fumble with the buttons of his jeans, then reached down to help her. As he slid out of them, out of everything, she felt his maleness against her. For one moment, she felt a sudden panic. Then she looked into his eyes and her heart filled with such love for him, she told herself nothing mattered but this moment.

She drew him down for a kiss, surprised at herself and a little embarrassed. Amusement flickered in his blue gaze. He lifted her into his arms and took her to the bed.

"Marni," he whispered as he lowered her to the mattress and lay down beside her. He ran his fingers across her lips, down her throat, over her breast. His eyes followed his fingers, then flicked back to meet her gaze when she moaned softly. "I want you so much it hurts."

She nodded, feeling her shyness come back as he pulled off her panties. To her surprise, he bent down to kiss the aching spot between her thighs. She cried out with pleasure.

"Please, Chase," she pleaded again, needing to feel him deep within her.

He slid back up her body, now slick with a fine sheen of perspiration.

"Marni, you have done this before, haven't you?" he said, looking into her eyes.

She kissed him in answer. He touched her and she opened to him, feeling both pressure and pleasure. Then he was inside her and she thought she might explode with all the sensations.

He took her with such gentleness, with slow, loving concern. And the sensations soared as high as the mountain peaks that circled the valley, as high as her hopes. Breathlessly, she held tight to him, letting him take her with him, knowing no matter what he'd said, he was making love to her.

LONG AFTER he'd felt the tremors in her subside, he held her, the heat of their bodies still melding them together as he imprinted the sensation of her skin in his mind.

He moved away from her slowly. Pushing himself up on one elbow, he looked down into her face, shocked by the feelings inside him.

Tears ran down her cheeks. She licked at them as they touched her lips. And smiled up at him.

"Why didn't you tell me?" he demanded, more angry with himself than her. He should never had made love to her. He thought he'd known the risk he was taking with his heart. He'd been dead wrong.

"It doesn't matter."

"Like hell it doesn't. You know I would never have made love to you if I'd known."

She smiled as she looked up at him. "Yes. I know."

He swung off the bed and pulled on his jeans, feeling too naked, too vulnerable. What had made him think he could do this and not feel anything? Even if this hadn't been her first time....

"Chase," she said, touching his bare back. "I don't regret it. I'll never regret it."

He looked at her, all the anger running out of him at the sight of her. "Why me, Marni?"

She took his hand and pulled him down onto the bed. He felt himself lean toward her kiss, unable to resist. He let himself enjoy her lips against his, her bare breasts brushing against his bare chest.

When she pulled back, he looked into her eyes and quit lying to himself. Those feelings he had for this woman. He couldn't keep telling himself they weren't love. Love.

He swore softly under his breath as he let her coax him back into the bed. He lay with her, still wearing his jeans as if they were protective armor. She snuggled into the crook of his arm and he pulled her to him. He could feel her breath on his chest. His heart ached just beneath the spot.

"I love you, Chase," she whispered.

"Go to sleep," he said as he pulled her to him. "We have a big day tomorrow."

Chapter Eighteen

Christmas Eve

Marni woke to warmth—and pounding. She opened her eyes, her first sensation Chase's body spooned around hers, his arms still holding her. She snuggled against him, breathing in the scent of him, memorizing again the feel of him. Then the pounding broke through her pleasant haze.

"Chase," Marni said, sitting up a little.

He didn't open his eyes, just pulled her closer against him. "Mmm, Marni."

"Chase, there's someone at the door."

He sat up then, blinking away sleep. "Don't move." He jumped up to pull on his jeans and hurried to the door.

"Raine," she heard Chase say in surprise.

"It's the baby," Raine cried. "I have to get to the hospital but my car won't start...."

"Don't worry," Chase said. "We'll get you there. Sit down. Let me get dressed. It won't take a moment."

Marni flew out of bed, searching frantically for her clothing. She was half-dressed when Chase came back into the room.

"One of the neighbors, a college student, she's—"

"Having a baby. I heard. Give me your keys and I'll start the pickup."

Chase tossed her the keys. "She looks scared."

Marni smiled, realizing that he was hoping she'd help with Raine. "You know me," she said.

He smiled back. "Yeah, I do."

When she came out of the bedroom, Raine was perched on the edge of the couch, leaning back, holding her swollen stomach in obvious pain.

"Has your water broken yet?" Marni asked, going to the young woman.

Raine shook her head. Marni took her hand and smiled. "I'm Marni McCumber. Everything is going to be fine."

"I remember you from the store yesterday." She frowned. "Weren't you pregnant though?"

"It's a long story," Marni said. "How far apart are your contractions?"

"I don't know. I just woke up to all this pain and I knew it was the baby coming."

Marni waited until Raine got through her next contraction before she said, "I'm going to start the truck. I've watched my sisters-in-law do this a half-dozen times. There's nothing to it."

Raine smiled. "Right."

Marni had the pickup running and warming up as Chase brought Raine down the stairs. Marni slid over to the middle to let Raine into the passenger side. Chase got behind the wheel and drove through the deserted early-morning streets. He talked, telling stories about house building, of all things. Marni doubted Raine was listening but Marni loved Chase's attempt to distract the young woman from her contractions, which were steadily getting closer together.

Once at the hospital, Raine was rushed to a birthing room, while Chase filled out forms. When he finished, he asked if he could do anything to help with her bill.

"It's been paid by the adoptive parents," the woman said.

"She's giving her baby up for adoption?" Marni asked in surprise as they moved to a waiting area.

"She's unmarried, has just started college and only has a part-time job that barely supports her, let alone her and a baby," Chase said.

"What about the baby's father?"

"He's not much older than she is and not ready for this kind of responsibility, emotionally or financially," Chase said. "Raine knows she's too young to be a single mother. It wouldn't be fair to her or her baby."

"Tell me about Burton's," she said as they sat down to wait.

He shrugged. "There isn't much to tell."

"I doubt that. You own Burton's. You're a carpenter. Why do I think there's more to it than that?"

"I never lied to you, Marni," he said seriously. "I am a carpenter, although I don't do much of the work myself anymore. I own Burton's. Actually six."

"Six Burton's? Why did you name them Burton's?"

"It was my mother's name. Charlotte Burton. It was my name for fourteen years." He glanced away. "I started the stores because of her. I'd like to think our lives might have been different if there'd been a Burton's in the neighborhoods we lived in when I was a kid. If there'd been someplace my mother could have found hope."

Marni reached over and took his hand and squeezed it, tears in her eyes. "And you're a carpenter?"

"I buy old houses and fix them up and—"

"Give them away," she said, getting the picture.

Chase laughed as he met her gaze, seemingly pleased that she understood. "Jabe insisted I acknowledge him as my father. He forced his name on me and his money, dumping large sums into my account on my birthdays. I took his name. I refused to spend his money. I was working on a house for an elderly couple in the neighborhood, and I realized how many more houses I would be able to repair with Jabe's money. How many more Burton's I could open. When I told him what I was doing with his money, he almost had a coronary.''

''But he kept giving you money each birthday?''

''Yeah, he did. Maybe he had a heart, after all.'' Chase stopped talking and looked away.

''You loved him,'' she said. ''That's nothing to be ashamed of.''

''I hated him, too,'' Chase said.

A nurse came down the hall toward them. ''Excuse me,'' she said. ''Your friend asked if you both would mind coming to the birthing room. I think she could use some reassurance.''

They found Raine in pain, but more scared than anything else, Marni thought.

''The contractions, they're getting so close together,'' Raine cried as Marni took her hand.

''That's good,'' Marni said. ''That means it's almost over. I'll help you breathe through them.''

Chase had gone to the other side of the bed. He pressed a cool cloth to Raine's forehead and Marni was struck with a vision of him tending his sick mother. The man who came up with Burton's, a little hope for the neighborhood. Marni felt such a rush of love for him.

An hour later, Raine delivered a tiny baby girl. Marni saw the infant come into the world. It captured her heart with its bright eyes, head of dark straight hair and tiny button of a nose.

But it was Chase's reaction that touched her the most. He stared at the infant for a long moment, then looked up at Marni, eyes misty. A surprise, from a man who never wanted a baby of his own.

THEY WERE in Raine's room, when Chase heard his name called over the paging system. He picked up the phone, surprised to hear the sheriff's voice on the other end of the line. "I thought you might be at the hospital visiting your brother," the sheriff said without preamble. "We've picked up Monte Decker."

Chase let out a sigh of relief and smiled over at Marni. She looked questioningly at him. "The sheriff's got your Santa mugger," he mouthed to Marni. "Did he tell you who he's working for?" Chase asked the sheriff.

"No, he says he's not talking until he gets a lawyer. But after we arrested him, we got a warrant and searched his apartment in Willow Creek."

Chase felt his heart pick up a beat.

"We found a photograph, probably the one you told us about that was missing from Marni McCumber's residence. She's an identical twin, right?"

"Monte had the photo," Chase said, trying to figure out what that meant, other than the fact that Decker had been the one who broke into Marni's house. "What about his accomplice, the person who attacked Marni?"

"We don't have anything yet, but when Monte made his one phone call, he called Calloway Ranch."

BY THE TIME they left Raine in her private room, Marni was glad to see that the young woman seemed confident that her decision to give up the baby was the right one.

"I just want my little girl to have a good home with two loving parents," she said. "Thank you for being here with me."

Marni left, thinking about that adorable baby girl in the nursery. She wondered if Chase was also thinking about the birth. It had been the first she'd ever witnessed and recalling it still moved her to tears, the miracle of it.

"Excuse me," a woman called out as they passed the front desk. "Mr. Calloway?"

"Yes?" Chase said, stepping over to the desk.

"I thought I should let someone in the family know. Your brother, Hayes Calloway. I'm afraid he checked himself out of the hospital a little while ago. Against his doctor's orders."

"You'd better call the farm and warn your family," Chase said as they headed out of the hospital.

"You think that's where he's headed?" Marni asked in surprise. "But how—" She stopped, realizing that she'd foolishly told the whole family all about the farm at breakfast a few days ago. It would be fairly easy for any of them to find the McCumber farm. "Oh, Chase."

"Don't worry, your brothers can handle it, not that I think Hayes is a risk. I'm sure he just wants to make sure for himself that Elise and the baby are all right. I'd do the same thing if I were him."

She looked at Chase. He would, she thought, more drawn to this man as each day passed, more in love with him.

Chase was unlocking the pickup when Dayton drove up and rolled down his window.

"Did you hear?" he cried.

Was he referring to Hayes leaving the hospital or had something else happened? Marni wondered with dread. Something to do with Lilly.

"Felicia had her baby." Dayton pulled into the parking place next to theirs and got out with a bouquet of roses in one hand and cigars in the other.

"Is the baby all right?" Marni asked. She thought about what Chase had said about Felicia's determination to have the baby before Elise.

"Oh, yeah," Dayton said. "It's a baby girl. Small, but doing fine, the doctor says." He stared at Marni. "Don't tell me you delivered yours, too?"

"There was an accident," Chase said solemnly. "She lost it."

Marni watched Dayton's expression, saw the relief and wondered if he'd been the person in the Nutcracker costume.

"That's too bad," Dayton said as he shoved a cigar into Chase's pocket and started toward the hospital.

"Not exactly Mr. Sensitive, is he?" Chase commented.

"I guess you can't expect him to be brokenhearted under the circumstances," Marni whispered back.

"Hey," Dayton called to them. "You're coming up to see her, aren't you? Candy Cane Calloway. What do you think of that for a name?"

Marni doubted Dayton would want to know what she thought. "We should probably go see the baby," she said to Chase, although she could tell by his expression that he wasn't wild about the idea.

"Candy Cane Calloway," Dayton repeated as the three of them entered the hospital. "Great name for a kid who's going to be loaded with dough."

When they reached the nursery, they looked through the window and saw that the Calloway baby's bassinet was empty. "She must be with Felicia," Dayton said, sounding a little worried.

CHASE DIDN'T WANT to think about Felicia and Dayton as parents. It frightened him more than thinking of himself as one. And it was something he'd thought about since Marni McCumber had turned up on his doorstep claiming to be pregnant with his child. After witnessing Raine's daughter's birth, he couldn't get it out of his head.

When they walked into Felicia's room, the nurse was handing Felicia her baby.

"It isn't going to spit up on me again, is it?" Felicia asked, awkwardly taking the baby.

"Babies do that," the nurse said.

Chase watched Felicia accept the warm bottle from the

nurse and poke it at the baby's mouth. Any doubts he had
about what kind of mother Felicia would make were quickly
answered.

The baby began to cry. "Here," she said, calling after
the nurse. "Do something with her."

"It's your baby, Mrs. Calloway," the nurse said and
closed the door behind her.

"We're going to get a nanny," Dayton said to no one in
particular.

"Dayton!" Felicia cried, holding the blanket-wrapped
baby out to him.

"Don't look at me," he said in horror.

Marni stepped to Felicia's bedside and took the wriggling,
crying infant from her. She held the baby to her breast and
rocked it gently, cooing softly. The infant hushed after a
moment, something not lost on Chase.

Chase watched, mesmerized by the sight. He felt a strong
tug on his heartstrings; Marni looked so right with a baby
in her arms.

She smiled as she peeked into the blanket. Then let out
a cry. Chase rushed to her side to see what was wrong.

"Is something wrong with my baby?" Felicia demanded.

Marni stood staring down at the baby, her eyes wide.
"This baby—"

Chase looked down at the infant in her arms and swore.
Marni hadn't been the only person pretending to be pregnant. His gaze flicked up to settle on Dayton.

"What's wrong?" Dayton demanded.

"This isn't your baby," Chase said.

"Of course it is."

Chase shook his head. "You'd do anything for money,
wouldn't you, Dayton? Even buy a baby and try to pass it
off as your own."

"Get the hell out of here," Dayton cried, sounding
tougher than he looked. "You have no right to—"

"I have every right," Chase said, advancing on his half brother. "I was there when this baby came into the world."

"What's going on in here?" the nurse demanded from the doorway.

"Could you take the baby back to the nursery?" Chase asked.

"Oh, Dayton," Felicia wailed. "I told you this wasn't going to work."

The nurse took a moment to assess the situation, then lifted the baby from Marni's arms. Chase saw how hard it was for Marni to give her up and wanted to bury his fist in Dayton's face.

"You're a liar, Dayton," Chase said through gritted teeth the moment the nurse left with the baby. "You just proved that. I've thought from the beginning that you killed Jabe. I didn't understand why. But I do now."

"You're wrong," Dayton said, holding up his hands. "I didn't kill the old man. All I did was adopt a baby. There's no law against that."

"You don't think trying to pass off this baby as your own to collect the inheritance is illegal?" Chase asked. "You knew Raine would deliver before Elise, you knew she was small and so was her baby. You figured you could pass off the infant as premature because of that. And it might have worked, if we hadn't been at that particular baby's birth."

"All right, maybe I was wrong but—"

"You had motive and opportunity to kill Jabe. You couldn't let him change his will back because you already had this baby scam going." But because of that, Chase realized Dayton had no reason to want Marni dead. He knew Raine would give birth first.

"I tried to talk him out of leaving his money to the first kid," Dayton cried. "He wouldn't listen. He was so determined to have a grandchild, preferably yours. And then when this—" he waved a hand in Marni's direction

"—woman showed up seven months pregnant— What choice did I have? Let you get the money? But I didn't kill Father. I *couldn't* kill Father."

Dayton looked at Marni then Chase. "So what's the big deal? Neither of us wins. You don't have a baby and neither do I. That means half of the old man's riches gets divided equally among the three of us, right? With half to Mother."

Chase wasn't about to tell Dayton that a Calloway baby would be born soon. Let him be surprised when Elise and Hayes's baby inherited the money. By then, Chase had hoped Dayton would be behind bars for the murder of Jabe Calloway. Now he wasn't so sure.

"Oh, Chase," Marni cried the moment they left Felicia's room. She threw herself into his arms. He held her tightly.

"Don't worry, the baby will be fine," Chase said. "We'll find someone else to adopt her. The baby is a little jaundiced, so she has to stay in the nursery for a few days anyway. By the time she's ready to leave, we'll have adoptive parents for her."

Marni nodded into his shoulder. "Just the thought of Dayton and Felicia—"

"I know. Let's get out of here."

"Where are we going?" she asked once they were in the pickup and headed down Highland Boulevard toward town.

"To lunch," he said, smiling over at her, hoping food would make them both feel better. "A late lunch, or an early dinner," he said, surprised to find it was late afternoon. "My stomach's growling," he lied. He just wanted out of the hospital and to be alone with Marni. But not back at the apartment. Not yet, anyway. "The sheriff can wait. We'll stop on the way and call the farm and warn them about Hayes."

She looked worried. "Everything's going to be all right now," he assured her, praying that was true.

By now his family would have heard that Marni was no

onger pregnant, he told himself. That should make her safe. He shoved away that little voice in his head that argued the killer was still at large and as long as he was, neither Marni nor Elise were safe.

"Lunch," he said. They'd have lunch, then he'd figure out what to do about the news the sheriff had given him.

"Lunch, huh?" she said, smiling back at him. "Let me guess? A can of soup, crackers and another ball game?"

"All right, I admit I was trying to keep you at a distance."

She laughed. "Do you think I didn't know that? Too bad I like canned soup and ball games on TV, huh?"

His look caressed her face. "I admit it didn't work."

She shook her head, no it didn't. "Are you sorry?"

His gaze turned so serious it scared her. "Only if I end up hurting you."

She heard the pain in his voice. "You won't," she said, sliding over to snuggle against him. "About that lunch, what exactly did you have in mind?"

He watched her, often surprised by what he saw. A freshness, a wholesomeness and yet a passionate, interesting, compassionate woman. Marni McCumber saw the good in everybody. What did she see in him? he wondered. What if she was wrong about him?

"No soup, no ball game, no crackers," he said, heading out of town.

She laughed when he pulled up in front of Guadalupe's Mexican restaurant. And seemed pleased when he asked for a back booth with candlelight, and ordered them both chile rellenos and kissed her the moment the waiter left the table.

"Mmm," Marni said. "What did you have in mind for dessert?"

"We need to talk," Chase said seriously.

The waiter returned and put a bowl of salsa and chips in front of them and two tall beers. Marni took a sip of beer.

"Everything's happened so fast," he said, knowing how lame that sounded. "Marni, I don't know how I feel about some...things."

"About me, isn't that what you mean?" she asked quietly.

"No, I know how I feel about you, dammit. I'm just having a hard time seeing myself married."

"Who said anything about marriage?" she asked, a catch in her voice.

He wanted to laugh. "Marni, you're the marrying kind." She started to interrupt, probably to argue that she wasn't but he stopped her. "I'm not sure about marriage, let alone kids. And don't tell me you don't want babies. I saw how you were with Raine's baby girl."

Marni touched her cheek to brush away a tear. "Pretending to be pregnant with your baby made me realize that I do want a baby." She looked into his eyes. "I want your baby, Chase. But I'll wait as long as it takes."

"That's what I'm trying to tell you, Marni. I'm not sure I can give you that. Ever."

The waiter brought their food and Chase mentally kicked himself for killing both of their appetites. His timing was amazing but he'd felt he needed to be truthful with her. He cared too much about her not to be.

He changed the subject, telling her what the sheriff had told him about the photo and Monte Decker's phone call.

"Someone at that house hired him," Chase said. He added, "Monte and Lilly were friends when he worked for Calloway Ranch. Maybe even lovers. Lilly knew about Elise and Hayes. Hayes said himself she was furious. When you add in her drinking problem—"

"What if Lilly doesn't drink as much as everyone thinks she does?" Marni asked. "What if she's just pretending to be unstable?"

He found himself staring at her in disbelief. "Why would Lilly do that?"

"She said something to me about being safe as long as they didn't know she knew what was going on."

"That shows how stable she is," he said.

"Look how she was at the funeral."

"Exactly."

"Don't you think it's amazing," Marni said, "that she was capable of driving all the way from the ranch if she was as drunk as she seemed? I just feel like there's more going on with her than we know."

"There is," he said, trying to keep his voice down. "She knows about Elise and Hayes and she thinks you're Elise. Isn't that enough?"

"She knew about Elise and Hayes when I was at the ranch and she thought I was Elise," Marni said. "Remember the day she gave me the baby booties? She said then that she should hate me but that I wasn't the one to blame."

He raked his hand through his hair. "Marni, for all we know she had just tried to kill you in the attic. She came back to see if she'd succeeded and must have heard the two of us talking by the toppled armoire. So she snatched the booties and gave them to you to sucker you in."

Marni started to argue but he cut her off. "What if Lilly's dangerous as hell? What if she's behind all these accidents? After her baby died, she blamed everyone. She was convinced for a while that Vanessa had purposely killed it." He sighed. "I didn't tell you this, but Lilly had an accident during her pregnancy. She fell down the stairs. She blamed Vanessa. Said Vanessa somehow…tripped her. Then later, when the baby died—"

"No wonder there doesn't seem to be any love lost between Lilly and Vanessa," Marni said thoughtfully. "If Lilly really believes Vanessa purposely tripped her— That's what Hayes meant about it not happening again. I just wonder what that scene was about at the funeral. It seemed so...strange.''

''The point is,'' he continued, ''Lilly has a lot of bitterness in her. She hated Jabe. Not that I blame her. When it came out that her baby wasn't Hayes's, Jabe threatened to throw her out on the street.''

''You don't really think she killed Jabe?'' Marni asked in surprise.

''Jabe had so many enemies in that house, who knows. But Lilly was definitely one of them. And let's face it, Jabe's guard was already down because of the painkillers. Lilly would have seemed so harmless to Jabe. He might not have realized she put painkillers into his drink. A woman could have helped Jabe pull the trigger after the amount of painkillers he'd ingested.''

When Monte Decker confessed, would he link Lilly to his crimes? Dayton? Or someone Chase was overlooking?

They finished their meal and Chase ordered them both flan for dessert.

''Your father mentioned that you're a Jane Austen fan,'' Marni said out of the blue.

''I used to read Austen to my mother when she wasn't feeling well. She never got tired of hearing *Pride and Prejudice*.''

Marni reached across the table, smiling as she took his hand and squeezed it. ''You never cease to amaze me, Chase Calloway.''

He saw the love in her eyes, unconditional, and said the words that had filled his head and his heart for days. ''I love you, Marni.''

The words instantly brought tears to her eyes. Her smile widened. ''Do you believe in Christmas wishes?'' she asked.

His heart gave a leap and he realized with a start what

day it was. Christmas Eve. And he hadn't gotten Marni anything for Christmas.

"Surely you wished for more than that," he said. "I wanted to buy you something special."

"Chase," she said, meeting his loving gaze with one of her own. "Telling me that you love me is the best, most special Christmas present you could have given me."

As they left the restaurant, Chase found himself wanting to give her any and everything she wished for. But could he give her the one thing he knew she wanted more than anything on earth?

They started across the road to his pickup and Chase heard a sound that made his blood freeze solid.

A car, engine revved to the max. As it bore down on them, Chase felt that split second feeling of déjà vu.

Chase grabbed Marni and flung them both into the snow-filled barrow pit beside the road. The car sped past, the wheels so close Chase could hear them throwing up chunks of ice. The car rounded the corner and was gone.

"Are you all right?" Chase cried, getting to his feet.

She nodded as he helped her up. She looked shaken but unhurt. "What about you?"

He nodded, too, relief filling him that she was all right.

"Hold me?" she said, stepping into his arms.

He wrapped his arms around her and they stood that way for a long time.

"Don't you think we'd better call the sheriff?" she said, pulling back to look at him.

"Did you see the person driving the car?"

She shook her head.

All he'd seen was a dark car. He hadn't seen the driver this time. He glanced toward the restaurant. The road was empty, the curtains drawn behind the windows.

He'd wanted to believe that Marni was safe. Monte Decker was in jail. As far as the family knew, Elise Mc-

Cumber had lost her baby. So why had someone just tried to run them down?

Maybe it had nothing to do with Jabe Calloway's firstborn grandchild. Maybe it was much more personal. Lilly still had reason to hate Marni even if Marni was no longer pregnant. And Dayton had reason to hate them both. Or maybe the hit-and-run hadn't even been for Marni. Maybe it had been someone who didn't want him to find out who killed Jabe Calloway.

AFTER THEY'D GIVEN their statements to Sheriff Danner, Chase drove back to the apartment, trying to form a plan. Monte Decker wasn't talking yet, the sheriff said. And it was Christmas Eve. But more important, Marni was still in danger.

He heard her filling the tub, the sweet rich scent of the vanilla bubble bath he'd bought for her at the store filling the air.

He went to stand in the open doorway and watch her undress, reveling in the sight.

She smiled at him as she climbed into the tub. "Did you want to join me?"

Yes. He ached to join her. But he wanted her safe even more than he wanted to make love to her.

He could no longer stand the thought of her risking her life further. Every instinct in him fought to protect her, to rush her to safety, but he knew no place would be safe until the killer was caught.

He raked a hand through his hair and looked at her. "I want this over with."

"So do I."

He stepped to the tub and she pulled him down for a kiss. He smiled at her as he straightened, his love for her overpowering every emotion. "Give me a second and I'll join you."

He headed toward the kitchen for two glasses and a bottle of wine.

That's when he noticed for the first time the light flashing on the answering machine. For just an instant, he almost ignored it. But it might be the sheriff with good news. He hit play.

"Elise." A woman's voice, slurred with either booze or emotion. "I know who killed Jabe." Chase cursed silently. Lilly's voice. "I have proof. I also have Jabe's will, the one he wrote the day he died. But they're never going to let me leave here alive. They keep me doped up. If they knew I was calling you now—" A sound in the background. "Oh, I should have known it would be you—" A thud. Something heavy hit the floor. The phone bounced on the hardwood. Someone picked it up before it could bounce again. Silence. Then they hung up.

Chase locked up to see Marni standing in the bathroom doorway in only a towel. He took one look at her face and knew they were going back to the ranch.

Chapter Nineteen

They drove through the moonless night, the stars distant, the sky a black hood. Marni sat on the bench seat beside Chase, staring out the window at the ice-glazed highway, her heart a fierce thunder in her chest.

Not far out of Dry Creek, the pavement turned to snow-pack. Christmas lights disappeared with the farmhouses. Soon there was nothing but rolling snow-covered hills and sagebrush, rocky bluffs and creek bottom. And eventually, she thought, Calloway Ranch. And Lilly.

Marni felt Chase's trepidation. Someone in this family still wanted one or both of them dead. Tonight's near hit-and-run proved that. Was Lilly behind it as Chase thought? Or was she in just as much trouble—or more—than they were?

They'd tried to call the ranch but the phone was off the hook.

"You know this could be a fool's errand," Chase had said before they left the apartment.

"Even you're worried about Lilly," she said, looking over at him as she picked up her coat.

Now he drove the pickup, the headlights probing the darkness ahead, the tires busting through the occasional drift where the snow had blown across the country road.

As they followed the creek, the dark silhouette of the

mountains disappeared, snow filled the sky, obliterating everything, giving Marni the impression of driving into a bottomless pit.

They crossed the narrow bridge. Marni could feel Chase's tension, as strong as her own. Through the snowfall, she saw Calloway Ranch, a dark beast that seemed to hunker in the storm, waiting for something. Or someone.

"This house gives me the creeps," Marni said, more to herself than Chase as he parked the pickup in the yard. A single light shone in the house. Unless Marni missed her guess, it was coming from Jabe's library.

"I guess I don't need to tell you I don't like this," Chase said. "But I wasn't about to leave you at the apartment alone." He had insisted on calling the sheriff before they'd left; a deputy was supposed to meet them out here. But there was no sheriff's car parked with the other cars in front of the house.

"We should wait for the deputy," Chase said.

"It might be too late by the time he gets here." It might already be too late.

Chase let out a low curse as he opened the glove box and pulled out a flashlight. He shoved it into his jacket pocket next to his .357 in the holster under his arm, then reached across the seat to take Marni's hand in his. He gave it a quick squeeze before he opened his door.

They walked up the steps to the porch, their breaths white clouds in front of their faces. Chase knocked. Silence and snow enveloped them and the house. He tried the door. It opened to his touch and he looked over at Marni, and frowned.

"This feels too easy," he whispered.

"Lilly might have left it open for us," Marni said.

Chase didn't look relieved by that thought. Were they walking into a trap? Was this something Lilly had planned all along, sucking in Marni just as Chase suspected?

They stepped into the foyer. Light spilled out of the open door of the library. And the sound of voices, several raised in anger. Vanessa's and Dayton's voices. They were shouting, so it wasn't surprising they hadn't heard Chase knock.

The two stood facing each other in front of the fire. Felicia sat in a chair off to the side, a wineglass in her hand, a sour look on her face.

"What is this, a falling-out among thieves?" Chase said from the doorway.

The three turned in surprise.

"What are you doing here?" Dayton demanded.

"We came to see Lilly," Marni said.

"Whatever for?" Felicia laughed and took another drink.

"Haven't you caused enough trouble for one day?" Vanessa snapped. She swept across the room to the liquor cabinet, tossed in several ice cubes, then splashed bourbon into her glass.

"So you heard about Dayton's little baby scam," Chase said. "Or were you in on it from the beginning?"

Vanessa shot him a withering look. "I most certainly was not. But what choice did he have under the circumstances?" Her cheeks were flushed, her hair not quite as perfect as it usually was. She'd discarded her widow black for a jewel-tone dress that fit like an expensive glove.

"The choices we make are what life's all about, don't you think, Vanessa?" Chase said, settling his gaze on Dayton. Dayton squirmed.

"Chase is convinced that I killed Father," Dayton whined to his mother.

Vanessa looked shocked. Marni watched her, surprised at how nervous she seemed. "Why in God's name would Dayton do that?"

"To keep Jabe from changing his will back," Chase said calmly. "For the money."

"Where is Lilly?" Marni asked, growing more worried by the minute. Something felt wrong, horribly wrong.

The ice in Vanessa's drink rattled. "She should be down any moment. To open Christmas presents."

"I think we'd better go look for her," Chase said.

"Good luck," Felicia said. "Who knows where the little waif is hiding."

Marni knew Felicia was right. If Lilly didn't want to be found, they'd never find her in this house. But if she was in trouble somewhere—

"Lilly is fine," Vanessa said with obvious aggravation. "I don't know why you're so concerned with her, why you're so concerned with my family." Her gaze came to rest on Marni's flat stomach. "There seems to be no reason for it."

"Lilly's probably passed out somewhere," Dayton said with disgust as he plopped into a chair.

"We got a strange phone call from her," Chase said. "She said she knew who killed Jabe. She also said she has Jabe's will, the one he wrote just before he died. The call was interrupted and we think she might have met with an accident, Calloway style."

Vanessa put down her glass a little too hard. "That's ridiculous," she said, splashing more bourbon into the glass before moving back to the fire. "Lilly's fine. And all this talk of another will is just holding up probate. I'm sick of it. I need money to run this place, and Lilly—" Vanessa stopped, her face contorted in anger. "Jabe didn't write another will."

"Yes he did," came a voice.

Vanessa dropped the glass in her hand as Lilly's muffled voice echoed through the room. The glass hit the hardwood floor, shattering as the door to the secret passageway opened at the corner of the bookshelf by the fireplace and Lilly stumbled into the room.

At first Marni thought she was drunk, then she saw the blood. It had run down her face from a gash in her left temple, staining the pale pink dress she wore.

Marni and Chase both stepped toward her but Lilly motioned for them to stay back with a hand that held a gun. In her other hand was the scarf Lilly had worn to the funeral, Vanessa's scarf.

"You know there's a will because Jabe told you all about it," Lilly said to Vanessa. "I heard everything from in there." She pointed at the open doorway to the passageway.

"Lilly, you're hurt," Marni cried, staring into Lilly's dirt-smudged face. My God, where had the woman been?

Lilly waved the pistol to hold everyone back. "Vanessa tried to kill me. Then she hid my body in the wall when she heard Dayton and Felicia come home."

"She's drunk," Vanessa said, her voice unsteady. "She probably fell down."

"Yes," Lilly said, glaring at her mother-in-law. "Just like I fell down the stairs when I was pregnant. You knew it wasn't Hayes's baby, didn't you? You even tried to kill Elise McCumber."

"She's babbling," Vanessa said. "And bleeding all over the floor. Dayton, why don't you get Lilly something to calm her down."

Lilly swung the pistol around and aimed it at Dayton. "You aren't going to keep me drugged up anymore, you aren't going to make me think I'm crazy anymore, either. I know what you've been doing. You put my nursery furniture in that room. You put that doll in my baby's crib. And the tape recorder. You did that and then you made it look like I did. You tried to make me think I was losing my mind."

Marni felt sick at the hate she heard in Lilly's voice. And the fear. My God, Marni thought, Lilly still wasn't sure she hadn't done all those things.

"I don't know anything about a room or a tape recorder,"
Vanessa said, shaking her head at Lilly.

"Liar!" Lilly screamed, pointing the pistol at her. "I
know what you're capable of. I heard Jabe tell you he was
cutting your sons out of the will and leaving everything to
Chase, the only son he could trust."

Marni saw that Vanessa had gone as stone-cold white as
the snow outside; her look said she *could* kill Lilly.

"You got him a drink and tried to reason with him, but
he wouldn't listen," Lilly continued, hatred in her eyes. "I
saw you put the pills in the drink. I waited, just like you
did. Then I saw you put the gun to his head and pull the
trigger. And I have proof." She held out the scarf. "You
used your scarf to hold the gun. You got Jabe's blood on
it."

Marni stared at the scarf in Lilly's hand. Even from where
she stood, she could see the dark red stain on it.

"Probably her own blood," Dayton said, coming to his
mother's defense, but not sounding very convincing. He got
to his feet, looking as if he might bolt from the room at any
moment.

"Everyone saw your reaction at the funeral when I
showed up wearing this scarf," Lilly said to Vanessa. "You
hid the scarf after you killed Jabe, but I saw where."

Vanessa hadn't moved. She stood, visibly trembling, her
face ashen, a look of horror in her eyes. "A scarf with blood
on it. What does that prove? No one will believe anything
you say, Lilly. Not the word of a lush."

"I have the will, Vanessa," Lilly said, smiling at the
older woman. "You were afraid I had it and I was going to
tell someone, weren't you? That's why you tried to kill me
when you overhead me call Marni."

Marni? Marni shot Lilly a look. How did Lilly know her
real name? Had she figured it out when she'd seen the pho-

tograph of the two sisters? The photo Monte Decker had taken when he broke into Marni's house.

Marni felt sick. Maybe Chase had been right all along. Maybe Lilly had killed Jabe, had made those attempts on Marni's life, had staged this whole thing to get even with Vanessa for the accident on the stairs that she believed had caused her baby to die.

"You thought Jabe hadn't written the new will yet, but then you started to suspect that he had," Lilly said as she edged her way over to the bookshelf. "If I had the scarf, maybe I had the will, huh?"

"What does this new will say?" Felicia asked.

Lilly swayed slightly as if weak from her loss of blood. Marni felt Chase tense beside her. She placed a hand on his arm in warning. Lilly seemed a little unsteady on her feet, but she was still armed and still seemed capable of shooting anyone who moved toward her.

Lilly dropped the scarf on the couch and pulled out a book, one of the Jane Austen books that Marni suspected had belonged to Lottie Burton. Of course that would be where Jabe would hide the will. Lilly opened the book and removed a folded sheet of paper with writing on it.

Vanessa moved more quickly than Marni had thought possible. She leaped forward and snatched the paper from Lilly's hand and tossed it into the fireplace before anyone could react. The flames devoured the sheet instantly.

Lilly let the hand holding the pistol drop to her side. She looked tired, but sober, even sane. "You just implicated yourself, Vanessa. In front of witnesses. You didn't really think that was the actual will?"

Vanessa turned slowly to glare at Lilly, her face twisted in rage.

"Jabe lied to you, Vanessa," Lilly said calmly. "He didn't cut your sons out of his will. He was just angry and taking it out on you. Instead, he did what he'd promised

Chase he would, amended his will to leave half of his estate to you, and the rest equally divided among his three sons. Too bad you won't get your share now.''

Lilly must have anticipated Vanessa's next move. Just as Vanessa lunged at her, Lilly stepped into the secret passageway.

Chase grabbed for Vanessa, but not quickly enough. Dayton jumped between them, shoving Chase aside. Chase stumbled back into a chair, righting himself just as Vanessa disappeared after Lilly into the walls of the house. Dayton sprang after them; the panel door closed before Chase could reach it.

He swore and turned to race from the library toward the other entrance under the stairs with Marni at his heels. Felicia hadn't moved. She sat watching with a bored look on her face, her drink still in her hand.

Marni rushed to the paneling and quickly opened the door under the stairs. Chase pulled the flashlight from his pocket and started up the steps. Marni followed. They'd gone only a few steps when a gunshot thundered above them and a scream echoed through the inner walls of the house. Another gunshot boomed. Then silence.

Chase swore and pulled the .357 from his holster. "Stay right behind me.''

They followed the stairway up, in the direction of a faint sound overhead, until they reached the attic. Marni wasn't surprised to find the door open.

The smell of old furniture and dust mingled with Lilly's scent, gardenia. And Marni realized that Lilly hadn't been wearing perfume in the library. So why did the attic smell of it? She felt a chill as they stepped deeper into the walls of antique furniture.

The beam of Chase's flashlight skittered across the floor, across the massive furniture, then back to a tallboy a few feet away. The light lingered on a corner of an old oak buffet. A piece of clothing had caught on the rough edge. The torn cloth was pale pink.

Marni hung close to Chase as he stepped around the buffet and stopped abruptly. She heard him curse. Looking down, she saw Dayton Calloway lying sprawled on the floor in a pool of blood.

"Oh God, Chase," Marni cried.

He pulled her to him for a moment, holding her with his free arm. "Do you hear that?" he whispered.

Marni felt a chill as she listened. The tape recorder of the baby crying. Lilly's baby. And Vanessa's voice as she tried to soothe the child.

Cautiously they stepped around Dayton, around the toppled armoire and edged their way toward the nursery. Marni could hear the sound of the baby crying softly and Vanessa's voice growing more impatient. Then another sound. The squeak of a rocker, rocking back and forth, back and forth. It made her blood run cold.

The door to the nursery stood open. Marni could see Lilly sitting in the rocker by the window, holding something in her arms, crying softly. Where was the gun? And where was Vanessa?

"Oh God," Marni heard Chase say.

Off to their right, sitting on the floor, her back against the wall, was Vanessa. She stared straight ahead, a look of horror on her face, her hands clutching her chest, blood seeping out through her fingers. Chase looked back at Lilly, still rocking, her gaze at the window.

"She still has the gun," Marni cried.

"Stay here." Chase bent to enter the room. Marni watched as he carefully neared the rocker. "It's over, Lilly," he said in the same tone he talked to the horses. Gentle. Soft. Caring. It brought tears to Marni's eyes.

Lilly looked up at him and smiled. "I took the will from

the book and stitched it inside the doll,'' she said, unfolding the blanket to reveal the worn rag doll.

''Where is the gun, Lilly?'' Chase asked.

She glanced back past Chase, then raised her hand slowly to point at Marni. Marni frowned, momentarily confused. Then she felt two strong arms grab her from behind and felt the cold steel of the gun's barrel against her temple.

''You're right, Chase,'' Dayton said. ''It's over and you lose.''

Chapter Twenty

Chase turned slowly, feeling the weight of the gun in his hand, realization weighing down his heart. Dayton stood, the wound in his side still bleeding but a smile on his face and a pistol pointed at Marni's head. Behind Chase Lilly continued to rock as if oblivious to what was happening. Or maybe she just didn't care anymore. From in the crib came the sound of the baby again, whimpering softly.

"Nice trick, huh?" Dayton said. "Thought I was dead." He shook his head at his brother. "And Father thought you were the smart one, the special one."

"Is that what this is all about?" Chase demanded.

"I got so sick of hearing about Chase, how wonderful he was, how worthless Hayes and I were," Dayton said angrily.

"Jabe was a fool. But Marni doesn't have anything to do with this. Let her go. This is between you and me now."

Dayton laughed. "Marni has everything to do with it."

Chase had been so sure Lilly was the culprit. "You were the one who tried to kill her. You hired Monte Decker." The steady movement of the rocker almost drowned out the soft crying sound of a baby coming from the crib. "You tried to run Marni and me down earlier."

Dayton smiled. "That was foolish. This is so much better. Everyone will think it was Lilly, poor sick, drunk Lilly. Killed her whole family. Except for Dayton Calloway. Only wounded, he managed to get away and call for help. I'll be a hero. A very rich hero.''

Lord, Chase thought. The man had shot himself. Chase knew now exactly what he was dealing with. His fear level rocketed upward. He met Marni's gaze, silently promising her he'd do whatever he had to, even if it meant giving his own life.

She shook her head, tears flooding her eyes. ''I love you,'' she mouthed.

''Drop the gun, Chase,'' Dayton said angrily. ''You're just sappy enough to try something stupid.''

''What do I have to lose?'' Chase asked, holding tight to the .357 in his hand. ''You plan to kill us all anyway. Maybe I'll kill you before you kill me.''

''Maybe,'' Dayton said, looking a little worried. ''But then you'll have to see Marni's brains blown all over this attic. If you drop the gun, I'll kill you first and spare you that.''

Yeah, Chase just bet he would. But still, he had little choice. He lowered the pistol to the floor, praying that Dayton would slip up and give him just one small chance. That's all he'd need.

''Very good,'' Dayton said. ''Now kick the gun into the corner and come on out of there. You too Lilly.''

Behind him, Chase heard the rocking stop and Lilly rise slowly from the chair. ''You did this, didn't you?'' Lilly said, looking over at the crib. ''To make me look crazy.''

''You are crazy,'' Dayton said. ''You just didn't know how crazy you were until I helped you find out. Crying over that rag doll, listening all the time to that tape with your dead baby crying on it.''

Chase bent to come out of the room and Dayton stepped back, pulling Marni with him. Lilly followed, clutching the rag doll still wrapped in its blanket.

''You should listen to the tape,'' Lilly said to Marni.

"I'm not the one who's crazy. I wasn't the one who killed my baby."

Lilly advanced on Dayton and Marni, the doll in her arms.

"Get back, you stupid woman," Dayton cried.

Lilly didn't seem to hear him. "See, Dayton," she said as she pulled back the baby blanket. "See what you've done."

Chase watched Lilly, his pulse thundering in his ears. Lilly would either get them all killed or—

Lilly grabbed the doll from the blanket with one hand, thrusting it into Dayton's face at the same time she thrust with the other hand, the hand still hidden in the baby blanket.

Dayton recoiled at the sight of the worn rag doll. But not quickly enough because he couldn't drag Marni with him. Lilly went in from the side, driving the knitting needles into his side. Dayton screamed.

Chase sprung, throwing himself at the gun in Dayton's hand. Dayton got off only one shot. But it went wild as Chase knocked the gun away. The sound thundered through the attic.

Chase pushed Marni aside, driving his fist into Dayton's face. Dayton fell back, the knitting needles still stuck in his side, agony in his features as he hit the floor hard. He reached for the gun lying between him and Vanessa but she reached it first. She lifted the gun, pointing it at Dayton.

"You don't understand, Mother," Dayton cried. "If you went to prison for Father's murder— The bad publicity. But if you were killed by Lilly—"

The gun wavered in Vanessa's hand as she stared at her son, her favorite son, the spoiled one. She let her arm drop. Marni quickly picked up the pistol and handed it to Chase.

From inside the nursery, he could hear the baby crying loudly now on the tape. Then Vanessa's angry voice. "All we need is another bastard in the family." The baby's crying stopped abruptly. The tape ended.

Epilogue

Christmas Eve
One year later

Marni smiled as snow began to fall the moment they turned onto the road to the farm.

"You're going to get your white Christmas," Chase said as he reached across the seat to squeeze Marni's hand. "I know how you love Christmas."

Had it only been a year ago that she'd made a Christmas wish on a star in this same winter sky? She glanced at Chase, realizing she'd gotten more than she could have ever wished for.

"Oh, Chase, I can hardly wait." She took his hand and placed it on her swollen stomach. "Feel that?" she asked and saw his eyes widen. "That's your son."

He smiled at his wife, his gaze filled with love. "Our son." In the car seat behind them, their daughter let out a cry of delight as she spied the falling snow. "Jingle Bells" came on the radio and Chase began to sing along to Laramie Burton Calloway's delight. She clapped her hands, laughing at the faces her daddy made at her in the rearview mirror.

Ahead, the bright Christmas lights of the large old farmhouse glittered brightly. Marni felt her heart race with excitement and sheer happiness at the sight. So much had happened in the past year, but they were finally coming home for Christmas. It didn't seem possible that so much good could come out of so much pain.

Elise had given birth to a beautiful baby girl, Elizabeth Marni Calloway, in early February, just days after Hayes's divorce was final. By Valentine's Day, Elise and Hayes were married. Hayes doted on both mother and daughter.

Lilly had spent some time in a private hospital out of state, then had enrolled in business school. The last Marni heard from her, she was thinking of opening her own business. A knitting shop. She'd met a man in her weekly therapy group. Like her, he'd lost a child.

Monte Decker had confessed that Dayton hired him to run down Jabe Calloway and later to lure Chase away from Marni on the night of the Christmas Stroll. Dayton swore he'd only wanted Monte to frighten his father—not hurt him. As for Marni, Dayton finally admitted that he'd been behind Marni's accidents, including the knife attack outside Burton's. It hadn't been anything personal, he'd said. He just couldn't let her give birth to the first grandchild of Jabe Calloway.

From the beginning, he'd planned to implicate Lilly. He knew she often hid in the tiny room off the attic, mourning the loss of her baby. He'd made it into a nursery after Marni arrived at Calloway Ranch looking seven months pregnant and claiming to be carrying Chase's baby.

Dayton had bragged that the tape recorder in the crib had been a stroke of genius. He'd stumbled across the tapes in Lilly's room and realized that right after her baby was born she'd left a tape recorder going in the nursery at night, afraid for her child since the family had found out the baby wasn't a real Calloway.

Her paranoia had paid off for Dayton. Once he'd started playing the tapes, Lilly had gotten much worse, believing Vanessa had killed her baby. The truth was, the baby had died of sudden infant death syndrome. But Lilly had convinced herself Vanessa was to blame. That obsession only made Lilly look all the more guilty of Dayton's crimes.

Dayton had hired Monte Decker because he knew of Monte's relationship with Lilly. Monte hadn't known Dayton was planning to frame Lilly. It had been Monte who'd told Lilly that Elise had an identical twin named Marni McCumber. When Hayes left the hospital, Lilly had known he'd gone to meet Elise and that the woman she knew had to be Marni.

Shooting his mother that night in the attic had been an accident, Dayton claimed. Dayton still felt bad about it, he said.

After he'd pleaded guilty, the judge sentenced him to forty years without parole at Deer Lodge, the Montana state prison. The last Marni heard, he was making horsehair key chains and still blaming what had happened to him on bad luck.

Vanessa died the night of the shooting. The blood on her scarf turned out to be Jabe's just as Lilly had said. Lilly's testimony convinced the sheriff to change Jabe Calloway's death from suicide to murder.

Felicia Calloway fled the state and the scandal. The last Marni heard, she'd changed her name and was dating a computer business tycoon.

With Jabe's will from inside Lilly's rag doll, Hayes and Chase inherited the entire Calloway estate. Hayes moved back to the ranch and took over for his father. At one point he thought about tearing down the house, but when he and Elise got married, she talked him out of it.

"Wait until you see what I can do with this place," she'd told him. Hayes and Elise and their baby girl brought happiness to the old house, something it had never known. Elise replaced the darkness inside with light and brought all the original antiques down from the attic. And with her dramatic style, she threw parties that brought laughter into the house, chasing away the ghosts.

Last year, Chase and Marni arrived at the farm just as the sun came up on Christmas Day, just in time to watch the kids open their presents.

The happy clamor of the McCumber clan helped ease the horror they'd both just lived through.

Later that day, after the family had scattered, Marni had found Chase standing before the Christmas tree. She'd come up behind him and put her cheek against his back as she wrapped her arms around him.

"Are you all right?" she'd asked softly.

She felt him nod.

"There's two things I need to ask you," he said, turning around to face her.

She held her breath.

"I never thought I'd ever say these words but, Marni, you've made me realize how much was missing from my life," he said quietly. "I can't imagine life without you now. Nor do I want to." He took her hands in his, his blue-eyed gaze searched her face. "Will you marry me?"

"Oh, Chase," she cried, throwing herself into his arms. "I can't imagine my life without you, either."

He laughed and held her tightly to him. "I was hoping you'd say that. But does that mean yes?"

"Yes, oh yes," she cried, pulling back to look into his face. "But you said you had two questions to ask me."

He nodded. "I couldn't ask you to marry me unless I was ready to have a baby, Marni. You and babies, they just seem to go together. I can't wait to get you pregnant."

She laughed. "Chase, you've made my every Christmas wish come true."

"Except one," he said solemnly. "There's one more wish I'd like to grant you, Marni McCumber."

She'd looked into his handsome face, her heart pounding.

Could he mean what she thought he did? Her eyes filled with tears. "You don't mean—"

"What would you say to us adopting Raine's baby?"

Marni had burst into tears, amazing for a woman who seldom used to cry before. "Oh, Chase," was all she got out. Her Christmas wish had come true beyond her wildest dreams.

Now, as Chase pulled up in front of the farmhouse, Marni saw the Christmas-tree lights blinking at the front window. She got out of the car to the sound of Christmas carols as the front door burst open and her family spilled out onto the porch to welcome them.

Marni blamed her tears on hormones as she watched Chase lift their daughter from her car seat, and the three of them headed into the welcoming arms of the McCumber family.

Finally, Chase had found a home and a family. And Marni had found a happiness and contentment she'd never dreamed possible. She smiled as she thought of all the Christmases they would spend in this old farmhouse.

But just as she started up the walk, something caught her eye. She looked upward, catching the glitter of stars poking through the clouds and snowfall. Tears filled her eyes as she thought of her father. For years as a young girl her only Christmas wish was that her father could be with them for Christmas.

Now Marni gazed up at the stars shining through a break in the clouds. Snowflakes tumbled down, touching her face lightly. And she knew he'd always been there, every Christmas. Just as he was this one.

"Are you all right?" Chase asked from the porch, concern in his voice.

Marni shifted her gaze to her husband and daughter. Her hand went to the son she'd give birth to before the new year. "Oh, yes," she said, smiling as she walked up the steps to join them. "Oh, yes."

*Brittany Grayson survived a horrible ordeal at the hands
of a serial killer known as The Professional...
who's after her now?*

*Harlequin® Romantic Suspense presents a new installment
in Carla Cassidy's reader-favorite miniseries,*
LAWMEN OF BLACK ROCK.

*Enjoy a sneak peek of
TOOL BELT DEFENDER.*

*Available January 2012
from Harlequin® Romantic Suspense.*

"**B**rittany?" His voice was deep and pleasant and made
her realize she'd been staring at him openmouthed through
the screen door.

"Yes, I'm Brittany and you must be..." Her mind suddenly went blank.

"Alex. Alex Crawford, Chad's friend. You called him
about a deck?"

As she unlocked the screen, she realized she wasn't
quite ready yet to allow a stranger inside, especially a male
stranger.

"Yes, I did. It's nice to meet you, Alex. Let's walk around
back and I'll show you what I have in mind," she said. She
frowned as she realized there was no car in her driveway.
"Did you walk here?" she asked.

His eyes were a warm blue that stood out against his
tanned face and was complemented by his slightly shaggy
dark hair. "I live three doors up." He pointed up the street to
the Walker home that had been on the market for a while.

"How long have you lived there?"

"I moved in about six weeks ago," he replied as they

walked around the side of the house.

That explained why she didn't know the Walkers had moved out and Mr. Hard Body had moved in. Six weeks ago she'd still been living at her brother Benjamin's house trying to heal from the trauma she'd lived through.

As they reached the backyard she motioned toward the broken brick patio just outside the back door. "What I'd like is a wooden deck big enough to hold a barbecue pit and an umbrella table and, of course, lots of people."

He nodded and pulled a tape measure from his tool belt. "An outdoor entertainment area," he said.

"Exactly," she replied and watched as he began to walk the site. The last thing Brittany had wanted to think about over the past eight months of her life was men. But looking at Alex Crawford definitely gave her a slight flutter of pure feminine pleasure.

Will Brittany be able to heal in the arms of Alex, her hotter-than-sin handyman...or will a second psychopath silence her forever? Find out in
TOOL BELT DEFENDER
Available January 2012
from Harlequin® Romantic Suspense
wherever books are sold.

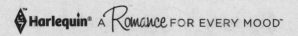